Popi

A Rising Tide

By

Innocent Karikoga

Published by

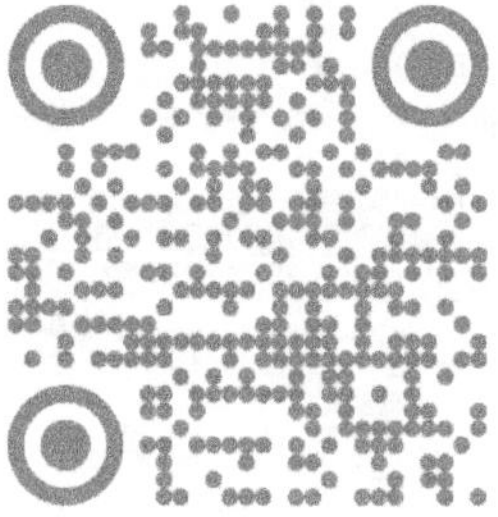

ISBN: 978-1-0689798-0-4

Popi: A Rising Tide

<u>Popi - A Rising Tide</u> is loosely based on the inspiring story of Pierre Poilievre, tracing his journey from his humble beginnings as an adopted infant to becoming one of Canada's most influential politicians. The narrative weaves anecdotes from his early life with significant milestones in his political career, highlighting his perseverance and dedication. At just 45 years old, Pierre's political journey already spans two decades, showcasing his rise from relative obscurity to the national stage. The story captures the essence of his leadership and his impact on the Canadian political landscape.

Meet the man

Affectionately known as Popi, Paul Peters was a beacon of resilience in his community. His journey, a testament to his unwavering determination, was like a sapling thriving in rocky soil. Adopted at birth by loving parents, his unwed teenage mother's brave decision set him on a path to a remarkable beginning, blossoming into a charismatic young man.

Popi's parents instilled in him a deep sense of optimism, a testament to the profound influence of his upbringing on his character. Their role in shaping his character and values was significant, as they taught him that it doesn't matter where you come from; just focus on where you are going. They emphasized, "You have power over your mind – not outside events. Realize this, and you will find strength."

Popi's heart was a wellspring of cheerfulness, a quality he carried with pride and conviction. He offered a helping hand to those in need, regardless of age or background. His spirit was like a refreshing breeze on a sweltering summer day, bringing relief to all who crossed his path. Popi embodied the saying, 'A kind heart is a fountain of gladness, making everything in its vicinity freshen into smiles.'

His sense of humour was like a silver lining on the sometimes dark cloud of life, making him a cherished figure in his community. Parents in the community held him up as an exemplar for their children because his actions embodied the

Popi: A Rising Tide

virtues of compassion, kindness, and community.

Though Popi often shied away from contentious discussions, preferring to seek common ground, he never forgot that his father once taught him that at some point, one must eventually take a stance and defend it. In the tapestry of life, neutrality can be a safe harbour, but it's not a place where you can achieve actual change and progress.

Popi's father's gift of 'Free to Choose' by Milton Friedman became his guiding star, shaping his political and economic beliefs. As Marcus Aurelius advised, 'Waste no more time arguing about what a good man should be. Be one.' Popi aimed to be a good man dedicated to conservative values, and in doing so, he enriched the lives of all those he touched, leaving an indelible mark on his community and the world.

As Popi embarked on his university journey, it was as though he had set sail on a ship with a favourable wind, his sails billowing with the promise of a bright future. The young man who had been a beacon of optimism in his community now found himself in the bustling halls of academia, ready to engage with the world in new and profound ways.

In the early years of his university journey, Popi's vibrant spirit found expression in various clubs and activities, notably in the chess and debate clubs. These clubs were like fertile grounds where his intellect and eloquence could flourish, much like a field that produces an abundant harvest after being lovingly tended. His journey of self-discovery was soon to be sculptured by his thoughts and actions, which propelled him forward, shaping his academic and personal pursuits.

Popi's presence in the chess club was akin to a knight on a chessboard, moving with purpose and strategy. He approached every game with a mind as sharp as a double-edged sword. Much like the sage advice, "The game of chess is not merely an idle amusement. Several precious qualities of the mind, useful in the course of human life, are to be acquired or strengthened by it," attributed to Benjamin Franklin.

In the debate club, Popi's voice was like a clarion call, resonating with the wisdom of ages. He formed his opinions not through the whims of emotion but through a thoughtful consideration of ideas and principles. Above all, he understood that having a sound mind was not enough; it must be applied. Popi applied his intellect to the art of debate, and his words were like arrows aimed at the heart of ignorance, seeking to illuminate the truth.

Popi's involvement in the chess and debate clubs was a testament to his unyielding spirit and a significant chapter in his personal growth. It was a journey that reminded him of the age-old saying, "The pen is mightier than the sword," for his words and ideas had the power to shape the world around him.

As Popi continued to forge his path to higher education, he was not only learning the art of chess and debate but also the transformative power of knowledge and open debate. His university years were about to be a testament to the potential of a determined and curious spirit. His journey through academia was an ode to the transformative power of knowledge and open debate, guided by the wisdom of the ages.

Popi's academic journey from high school to university was a tapestry of excellence. His insatiable thirst for knowledge and talents, shining most brilliantly in the social sciences and

Popi: A Rising Tide

humanities, were the hallmarks of his journey.

Popi was like an archaeologist in social sciences, delving deep into the past to uncover the secrets of human behaviour and society. His curiosity was boundless, much like a river that flows ceaselessly, carving its path through the landscape. His grasp of sociology, psychology, and economics was profound, and he possessed a keen awareness of the interconnectedness of the human experience.

Within the humanities, Popi was a literary aficionado, traversing the pages of classic works with the passion of a poet recounting epic tales. The classics were not just books to him but portals to different eras and minds. His understanding of literature and philosophy was akin to a gardener cultivating a garden of wisdom, tending to the delicate blooms of thought and contemplation.

Popi's academic achievements were a testament to his dedication and the support of his loving parents, who had instilled in him the values of optimism and the importance of nurturing one's intellect. As the old English saying goes, "The roots of education are bitter, but the fruit is sweet." Popi had tasted the fruit of his efforts, which was indeed sweet.

His journey through the social sciences and humanities was a testament to the enduring power of human inquiry and the pursuit of knowledge. Popi's mind was a treasure trove of wisdom. He excelled not merely in academics but in his ability to apply that knowledge to navigate the complexities of the human experience.

Popi's academic journey, like a well-crafted sonnet, was a harmonious blend of passion, intellect, and the unyielding pursuit of understanding. His love for the social sciences and humanities was a testament to these fields' timeless relevance in unravelling the human condition's intricacies. This love served as a beacon of inspiration for all who had the privilege of knowing him.

Popi's passion for conservative values was not just a flame but a blazing fire deeply rooted in the values instilled by his family and his love for his homeland. His family, with their strong sense of tradition, responsibility, and respect for the past, was the bedrock of his conservative beliefs. Just as a sturdy oak tree is anchored in the soil, his beliefs were firmly grounded in these principles, inspiring all who knew him.

His reverence for conservative values was a testament to his understanding of the importance of family. He saw the family as the cornerstone of society, a cherished institution that must be preserved and protected. Popi believed that a nation's strength rested upon its families' strength.

Popi's love for Canada was not just a fondness but a profound and abiding affection akin to the bond between a poet and his verses. He treasured the country's rich natural beauty, like a precious gem in the crown of the world. The grandeur of Canada's landscapes, from its majestic mountains to its pristine lakes, was not merely scenery to him; it was a source of inspiration and a reflection of the nation's character. In the beauty of nature, he found solace and inspiration. Canada's natural splendour provided a canvas for contemplation and reflection, evoking a deep sense of patriotism and appreciation in all who heard him speak.

Popi: A Rising Tide

Popi's love for Canada also extended to its people. He saw the nation as a tapestry woven from diverse threads, where different cultures and backgrounds merged to create a vibrant and harmonious whole. He believed Canadians' unity and shared values were the bedrock of national pride.

His deep appreciation for Canada's cultural diversity was not just a recognition but a commitment to freedom. This commitment reflected his conservative values, mainly guided by his cherished copy of Milton Friedman's 'Free to Choose.' Popi understood that the principles of limited government and personal responsibility were not just political ideals but the foundation of a prosperous and free society.

Just as a poet's verses can evoke profound emotions, his love for Canada and conservative values stirred a sense of loyalty, gratitude, and a commitment to preserving what was cherished.

In a world where values and national pride can sometimes be elusive, Popi's unwavering dedication to conservative principles and his love for Canada were a shining example of the power of one's convictions to shape one's identity and strengthen one's commitment to one's homeland. His heart was like a torch, lighting the way for others to appreciate Canada's enduring values and natural splendour and embrace the wisdom found in tradition and responsibility. His impact was not just felt but also a source of inspiration and motivation for those who shared his beliefs.

Popi's enthusiasm for educating others about national politics and economics from a conservative standpoint was like a lantern in the darkness, illuminating the path for those willing to listen and learn. His dedication to spreading his convictions was a testament to his deep-rooted beliefs and desire to contribute positively to his community.

Popi's efforts were akin to a gardener tending to the fertile soil of minds, sowing the seeds of conservative values with care and diligence. He knew that nurturing understanding required patience and a willingness to engage in open and respectful dialogue, even on complex and contentious topics. His approach made everyone he interacted with feel valued and respected, regardless of their views.

His passion for educating others was in harmony with the old English saying, "Give a man a fish, and you feed him for a day. Teach a man to fish, and you feed him for a lifetime." Popi believed that by imparting knowledge about conservative values and economic principles, he could help individuals make informed decisions that would benefit them and their society in the long term.

Popi's dedication to education encouraged continuous self-improvement and learning. He understood that it wasn't enough to hold conservative beliefs; one must also be able to articulate and share those beliefs with others. In doing so, he embodied the ancient proverb, 'Knowledge is like a garden: if it is not cultivated, it cannot be harvested.' His belief in the power of education made everyone he interacted with feel enlightened and empowered.

This passion for educating others about national politics and economics from a conservative standpoint was a beacon of hope in a world often filled with divisive discourse. He sought to bridge gaps and create understanding, like a bridge connecting two shores. His actions demonstrated that one

Popi: A Rising Tide

person's commitment to enlightening others can have a profound ripple effect, inspiring a community to think critically and make well-informed choices.

In an age where information is abundant but understanding is scarce, Popi's dedication to educating others was a reminder of the importance of actively engaging in exchanging ideas and knowledge. His commitment to sharing conservative values and economic principles reflected his belief that an informed citizenry is the bedrock of a healthy and prosperous society.

Popi's role as a mediator in heated disputes over controversial political and economic topics was a testament to his commitment to fostering understanding and unity. His ability to offer a balanced perspective and a listening ear, much like a wise mediator, earned him the trust of many.

Popi's ability to settle disagreements and bridge divides was a beacon of hope in a world often filled with passionate opinions. His composed and reasoned approach was a welcome respite, a reminder that even in the midst of a storm, there can be calm. He embodied the wisdom in the old English saying, "Where there is no counsel, the people fall, but in the multitude of counsellors, there is safety."

While his willingness to engage in discourse might have occasionally irked some, it also drew others who valued his insight and ability to find common ground. Popi recognized that in a diverse and complex world, the ability to find a middle ground and build bridges of understanding was a precious gift.

Popi's efforts to settle disagreements on controversial topics were a powerful demonstration of the potential of informed discourse. He believed in the power of dialogue, even when opinions clashed, to lead to greater unity and enlightenment.

Though some may have been annoyed by his dedication to facilitating discussions, Popi's commitment to constructive dialogue reflected his deep belief in the importance of reasoned discourse and the capacity of individuals to find commonality despite their differences. In a world where polarization often reigns, Popi's efforts to bridge gaps and settle disputes were a testament to the enduring power of open-minded conversation and the pursuit of understanding.

Popi's willingness to consider different political ideas and economic schools of thought was like that of a seasoned traveller, exploring various landscapes of thought and philosophy. Popi understood that the world of ideas is vast and diverse, and he embraced the opportunity to expand his horizons.

Popi's humility and eagerness to learn shone like a beacon of intellectual honesty when he could not defend his position. His attitude was reminiscent of the old proverb, "He who is not ashamed to ask shall be ashamed to learn." He saw every question as an opportunity for growth, a chance to refine his understanding and strengthen his convictions.

Popi's open-mindedness reflected his belief that the pursuit of knowledge is a lifelong journey and that one should remain open to new perspectives and ideas. As Milton Friedman wrote in "Free to Choose," "The power to do good is also the power to do harm. Free choice can be a blessing or a curse."

Popi's willingness to engage with different perspectives and his

Popi: A Rising Tide

readiness to learn from others were a breath of fresh air in an era marked by ideological rigidity. He served as a reminder that growth and enlightenment often come from a willingness to step outside one's comfort zone and embrace the unknown.

Popi's approach to argumentation was a skillful blend of Socratic questioning and the eloquence of a seasoned rhetorician. He wielded the power of rational inquiry as if it were a finely honed sword, always seeking to illuminate the flaws in his opponent's position before crafting a compelling argument grounded in his logic.

Popi's method frequently guided his interlocutors through a series of thought-provoking questions, much like a skilled navigator charting a course through uncharted waters. He aimed to help them see the inconsistencies or weaknesses in their arguments, understanding that genuine understanding often arises from self-discovery. Popi's approach was reminiscent of Socrates' famous words, "An unexamined life is not worth living."

Once carefully dissected an opponent's position through probing inquiry, Popi would construct his argument like a masterful architect designing a sturdy tower. His logic was sound, and his reasoning was clear, leaving little room for counterargument. He saw every debate as an opportunity to sharpen his understanding and to help others arrive at more coherent conclusions.

His approach was akin to a chess grandmaster who anticipates every move, setting the stage for a checkmate. Popi knew that solid arguments were like a fortress, and he constructed his positions with the strength of stone walls, making them impervious to hasty rebuttals.

Instead of resorting to hostility or seeking to overpower his opponents, he employed reason, empathy, and respectful discourse to guide them toward more sound and defensible positions.

Popi's technique reflected his commitment to the pursuit of truth and his dedication to the art of constructive debate. He approached argumentation not as a contest of egos but as a collaborative effort to uncover a more profound understanding. In doing so, he encouraged thoughtful and meaningful discussions, leaving a legacy of intellectual curiosity and the pursuit of truth for all who had the privilege of engaging with him.

Popi's willingness to acknowledge when his words may have offended while standing firmly by his opinions demonstrated a rare blend of humility and conviction. He understood the importance of fostering respectful dialogue and building bridges of understanding, even when discussing sensitive topics.

Like a wise person once said, "Apologizing doesn't always mean you're wrong; it means you value your relationships more than your ego." Popi's apologies were not admissions of being mistaken in his opinions but rather expressions of respect for the feelings and perspectives of others. His actions reflected that empathy and mutual respect should guide civil discourse.

Popi strived to be a good man, not by avoiding contentious topics but by approaching them with an open heart and a willingness to listen. He recognized that even when holding strong opinions, one should remain open to the possibility of

Popi: A Rising Tide

refinement.

Popi's ability to apologize for the offence without compromising his convictions was like a skilled tightrope walker, maintaining a balance between his own beliefs and the feelings of those around him. He understood that while others could fiercely hold their opinions, actual progress often came from building bridges rather than walls.

His approach was a testament to the power of humility in discourse. By apologizing for any offence caused, Popi created an environment where diverse opinions could coexist and dialogue could flourish. He encouraged open and respectful exchanges, demonstrating that differences need not be divisive and that, even in disagreement, mutual respect and understanding can be achieved.

Popi's unapologetic stance on his deeply held conservative opinions was a testament to his unwavering commitment to his principles. He understood that genuine conviction required a firm and resolute stand, even when faced with opposition or criticism.

It is often necessary to be unyielding in one's beliefs in politics and ideology, much like a sturdy tree standing against the storm. Popi believed in the good that conservative principles could bring to society and was unapologetic in his commitment to them.

His unwavering stance on his conservative opinions was not a sign of inflexibility but rather a recognition that his values were a part of his identity. He would not compromise on principles that he believed to be essential to improving his community and country.

In his spare time, Popi's love for Canada and its natural beauty was like a wellspring of inspiration, and he seized every opportunity to share that enthusiasm with his colleagues and the public. He understood that a deep appreciation for one's homeland is not merely a personal sentiment but a gift to be shared with others.

Popi's passion for his homeland and his commitment to educating others reflected his belief in the importance of connecting people with the land they call home. Just as the old English saying goes, "Home is where the heart is," Popi believed that by instilling a sense of pride and wonder in his country, he could help others connect more deeply with their surroundings.

In his dedication to educating others about the beauty of his country, Popi acted as a cultural steward, preserving and celebrating Canada's unique splendour. His enthusiasm for sharing his homeland's treasures was an invitation for all to partake in the wonder of nature and the awe-inspiring landscapes that graced the land.

In a world where the pace of life often distracts from the profound beauty of the natural world, Popi's commitment to educational outreach was a testament to the enduring power of connecting with the land and fostering a deep appreciation for one's roots. His actions served as an inspiration to all to become stewards of their environments and to find joy in the beauty that surrounds them.

Popi's skills and warm personality made him an exceptional fit

Popi: A Rising Tide

for various roles that allowed him to positively impact his community. His dedication to serving others was a testament to his caring and giving nature.

As a part-time tour guide, Popi brought his deep appreciation for Canada's natural beauty to life for visitors from near and far. His storytelling ability and passion for his homeland transformed tours into unforgettable journeys, like a bard guiding travellers through a magical realm. His work allowed him to share the treasures of Canada with those who sought to explore its wonders.

Volunteering at the senior centre reflected Popi's compassion and respect for the senior citizens. He understood the importance of connecting with and supporting older generations. His presence at the centre provided companionship and a sense of community for those with so much wisdom to share.

In his role at the office of his member of parliament, Popi served as a bridge between the community and the government, much like a skilled diplomat. His ability to listen, understand, and communicate effectively made him an invaluable asset. He channelled his passion for politics and his commitment to conservative values into practical service to the members of his constituency.

Popi's multifaceted roles reflected his dedication to making a positive impact at both the local and national levels. He chose to be a force for good in his community, the lives of the seniors he volunteered with, and the constituents he helped to serve.

In a world where selflessness and dedication to community

service are often undervalued, Popi's example was a reminder of the enduring power of kindness, compassion, and active engagement in one's community. His contributions left an indelible mark, enriching the lives of those he served and embodying the spirit of civic responsibility and care for one's fellow citizens.

A profound sense of responsibility marked Popi's transition into independent adulthood and love for his parents. Even as he embarked on his journey at university and moved out, he made a heartfelt promise to regularly visit his parents, particularly on long weekends and special holidays.

His bond with his parents was like an unbreakable thread, connecting their hearts no matter the physical distance that separated them. He recognized the sacrifices they had made to provide him with the opportunities he now enjoyed and understood the importance of maintaining a close relationship with them.

Popi's commitment to visiting his parents was a testament to the enduring values instilled in him since childhood. He knew that family was the cornerstone of his life, and like the saying, "Blood is thicker than water," he held the ties of family dear to his heart. He honoured and respected his parents, understanding the value of their guidance, love, and the sacrifices they had made for him.

Popi's dedication to maintaining a close connection with his parents, even as he ventured into the world as an independent adult, reflected his understanding that roots remain a source of strength and nourishment no matter how far they reach.

A Clash of Cultures

Amid the bustling diversity of the university campus, where students from around Canada and from every corner of the globe converged like the confluence of a hundred rivers, a vibrant scene unfolded. Like a grand tapestry woven from the threads of countless cultures, the campus buzzed with the collective energy of eager minds and open hearts. It was a place where the richness of human experience flourished, much like a garden filled with a riot of colourful blooms.

As the sun painted the sky with hues of red and gold, a group of students gathered in the central courtyard. They hailed from every corner of the globe, each with unique traditions and backgrounds. It was a microcosm of the world, and their camaraderie reflected the wisdom of an old English saying: "United we stand, divided we fall."

In this mosaic of diversity, they had chosen to share a moment of unity and understanding. Popi started this tradition as a joke and a way to have breakfast together every morning. Each student brought with them a small dish representing their home cuisine. The aroma of spices, the warmth of freshly baked bread, and the tang of exotic fruits wafted through the air like a symphony of flavours.

As the students shared their stories, their laughter rang out like the joyous notes of a traditional folk song. They spoke of their families, journeys, and dreams, each tale like a precious gem in a tapestry of life. In that moment, they embodied the teachings of Marcus Aurelius, "The happiness of your life depends upon the quality of your thoughts."

Their compassionate hearts and open minds reflected their understanding that diversity was not just about appearances but about exchanging ideas, cultures, and perspectives.

The scene on the campus was a testament to the enduring power of human connection and shared experiences. It was a living illustration of the wisdom in the saying, "A friend is a second self," reminding us that when we embrace one another's stories and cultures, we become more prosperous, more complete versions of ourselves.

The university campus stood as a beacon of hope and unity in a world often marked by divisions and misunderstandings. It was a place where students, like travellers on a shared path, could learn from one another, celebrate their differences, and, in the spirit of compassion and understanding, build bridges that spanned the boundaries of culture and race.

A challenging incident unfolded in the university campus's diverse and culturally rich environment. An international student, Ahmed, found himself facing accusations of using insensitive language about what some considered sexual assault during a campus discussion. The incident opened a window into the complexities of cross-cultural understanding and the importance of fostering respectful dialogue in the face of disagreement.

As the allegations against Ahmed emerged, the campus community buzzed with conversations. The situation was as delicate as a fragile porcelain vase teetering precariously on a shelf. Accusations were like cracks in the porcelain, threatening to shatter the peace and harmony that had defined the campus.

Students and faculty gathered to discuss the incident, with varying opinions and emotions swirling around like leaves in the wind. Some were deeply hurt by Ahmed's words, feeling that they had transgressed the boundaries of tolerance and respect. Others advocated for Ahmed's right to express his cultural beliefs and language, echoing Popi's principles of free speech.

Ahmed's intention became a central point of contention as the dialogue progressed. Some argued that everyone should consider and respect cultural differences. In contrast, others believed there were universal boundaries when it came to respecting the rights and dignity of others. It was a delicate balance, like a tightrope walker navigating the tension between free expression and cultural sensitivity.

Amid the discourse, the saying: "If it is not right, do not do it; if it is not true, do not say it." resonated. The School Administration recognized the need to address the situation with empathy and understanding while upholding the principles of respect for all.

A compassionate dialogue ensued. The Administration aimed to find common ground, to learn from one another, and to foster a deeper understanding of the complexities of cultural diversity and its interaction with freedom of expression.

Ahmed, recognizing the impact of his words, spoke with humility and willingness to learn. He understood that, as an international student, he had a responsibility to appreciate the values and beliefs of his new community, even while cherishing his cultural background.

Despite endless apologies and even a handwritten letter of regret, the calls to expel Ahmed only got louder. There was no way to calm the situation, and anyone with even the least information was calling for Ahmed's expulsion and immediate deportation from Canada.

As the Administration discussed Ahmed's alleged actions, emotions ran high, and opinions varied. Some, with the mind of Meghan, believed that harsh consequences, such as expulsion, were necessary to send a clear message about respecting others' rights and dignity. They echoed the idea that preserving harmony often required difficult decisions, like pruning a tree to ensure its growth.

Others, however, urged caution and a more nuanced approach. They highlighted the principles of fairness, empathy, and the need to educate individuals rather than simply punishing them.

The Administration recognized the delicate balance between accountability and understanding. They believed that education and dialogue were powerful tools to address such incidents and prevent them from escalating. Ahmed's accountability was not a matter of punishment alone but a chance for him to learn and grow as a responsible member of the community.

In this tense atmosphere, someone had to answer a fundamental question about the role of institutions in shaping individuals. It was basically about the importance of giving students the freedom to express themselves while holding them accountable for their actions. The campus community sought to strike a

Popi: A Rising Tide

balance that respected the principles of free expression and individual responsibility.

The discussions reflected the Administration's commitment to the safety and well-being of all while respecting the rights of students like Ahmed. They recognized that while accountability was crucial, it needed to be accompanied by a compassionate approach that allowed for growth and understanding, much like a gardener nurturing a young sapling into a thriving tree.

The Administration, led by the student union executive, tried to find a resolution that upheld the principles of respect, accountability, and freedom of expression. They argued to create an environment where individuals could learn from their mistakes and work toward harmonious coexistence while cherishing the wisdom of the old proverb: "An eye for an eye makes the whole world blind."

The accusation that insensitive language could be a precursor to untold violence on campus was a serious concern, one that resonated with the idea that words can shape actions. The accuser, in this case, Meghan, was passionate about the safety and well-being of the campus community. She was also a vocally loud feminist who deemed Ahmed's words to be the sexiest and most misogynistic statement she had ever heard in her life. She argued that the university, in its infinite wisdom, should not allow a person to expose and promote any ideology that can promote sexism and misogynism on the university campus and around the country.

Ahmed's situation had grown increasingly daunting as the spectre of expulsion and immediate deportation loomed over him. The weight of potential consequences bore down on his shoulders like a heavy burden, casting a dark cloud over his once-promising academic journey. As he contemplated the prospect of returning home, he couldn't help but feel the impending domino effect that would cascade through his life.

The fear of expulsion and immediate deportation was a chilling reminder that choices, actions, and even words could have far-reaching consequences. It starkly illustrated the old saying, "A single spark can start a prairie fire." Once filled with academic accomplishments, Ahmed's future now hung in the balance, like a delicate house of cards teetering on the brink of collapse.

The situation's impact extended beyond Ahmed's fears and cast a shadow over his family. They had once been proud of his academic achievements, much like a farmer who rejoices in the rich harvest of his fields. However, the thought of his potential expulsion and deportation was like a sudden frost threatening their pride and dreams.

Ahmed's family, who had invested so much hope in his education, now faced an uncertain and distressing future. They, too, were part of the domino effect. The potential disruption of his academic journey was like a stone tossed into a still pond, creating ripples that would touch their lives in ways they had not anticipated.

Ahmed, his family, and the Administration grappled with the quality of their thoughts as they navigated the turbulent waters of this predicament. Meghan was not relenting, and her campaign to expel and deport Ahmed was gaining steam.

The situation was a stark reminder that our words, actions, and choices could have profound and often unforeseen consequences for us and those who care about us. It emphasized the importance of empathy, understanding, and the pursuit of a balanced resolution considering all involved's well-being. The student union faced a difficult decision, and they recognized the need to approach it with compassion and wisdom, keeping in mind the adage, "Measure twice, cut once."

In a heartfelt attempt to defend himself, Ahmed pointed to the difference in culture and understanding that had led to using "insensitive language." He emphasized that in his culture and country of origin, what he had said to rile up Meghan might have been considered acceptable or innocuous. He said, "I didn't think much of it when it occurred. I'm truly sorry and beg everyone to forget about this incident."

Ahmed's plea was a testament to his genuine remorse and desire to bridge the cultural gap that had unwittingly caused offence. His perspective resonated with the idea that cultural diversity often gives rise to different interpretations and reactions to words and actions.

The Administration found itself at a crossroads, torn between the need to uphold the principles of respect, accountability, and free expression while acknowledging Ahmed's sincere apology and cultural context. They understood, "To err is human; to forgive, divine." Ahmed's plea for forgiveness was a call for compassion and understanding.

The Administration recognized that the incident had illuminated the complexities of cross-cultural communication and the potential for misunderstandings.

While the Administration couldn't simply forget the incident, they appreciated the opportunity to engage in dialogue and education as they sought to build bridges of understanding and prevent future incidents. They recognized the value of learning from one another's perspectives.

In this challenging situation, the Administration grappled with the delicate balance between accountability, forgiveness, and the power of cultural differences. They aimed to create an environment where individuals could learn from their mistakes, grow in their understanding, and foster respectful dialogue, recognizing that, in the process, students had learned a profound lesson in cultural sensitivity.

Meghan's formation of a growing coalition and others who shared the same sentiment added a layer of complexity to the situation. They were resolute in their demand for Ahmed's immediate expulsion, reflecting their deep sense of concern and commitment to what they believed was necessary for the well-being of the campus community.

The campus was now like a divided village, where two factions stood firmly on opposing sides of the river. The coalition's demand was a call for justice, as they believed that swift action was essential to uphold the principles of respect and safety for all, in line with the old proverb, "Justice delayed is justice denied."

The Administration faced a challenging dilemma. They recognized the importance of fostering an environment of respect and understanding. Yet, they also understood the need to address the concerns of those who felt deeply harmed. It was a reminder of the adage, "Two wrongs don't make a right," as they navigated the intricacies of the situation.

Popi: A Rising Tide

The coalition's stance posed a significant test for the Administration, forcing it to carefully consider the values it held dear and the principles it wished to uphold.

In response, the Administration emphasized the importance of dialogue and open communication. They recognized that fostering an understanding environment required a balanced approach that considered the perspectives and well-being of all individuals involved. Their goal was to find a resolution that upheld their commitment to respect and fairness while also considering the consequences of expulsion.

The campus now stood at a critical juncture, faced with the challenge of balancing the demands for expulsion with the principles of fairness, accountability, and cultural sensitivity. Amid the storm, they held fast to the belief that compassion, empathy, and open dialogue were essential to navigating the situation's complexities and finding a path forward.

As the Administration grappled with the demands for Ahmed's expulsion, his friends rallied to his side in an effort to appeal to the Administration's conscience. Recognizing the gravity of the situation, they began a petition, hoping to present a unified front and seek a lighter punishment if the Administration couldn't dismiss the issue entirely.

The petition was like a beacon of hope amid uncertainty, a tangible expression of their belief in Ahmed's potential for growth and their commitment to his well-being. Their actions echoed the old English saying, "A friend in need is a friend indeed."

In their petition, Ahmed's friends emphasized his sincere

apology and willingness to learn from his mistakes. They highlighted the importance of education and dialogue to bridge cultural gaps and prevent future misunderstandings.

The Administration now faced competing voices, each advocating for their perspective on the situation.

In response, the Administration recognized the importance of compassion, understanding, and fairness. They acknowledged that the situation had brought to light the need for a nuanced approach that would consider all individuals' well-being. Their goal was to find a resolution that upheld their commitment to respect while acknowledging the values of accountability and cultural sensitivity.

The petition served as a symbol of friendship, support, and the belief in second chances. It was a testament to the enduring power of empathy and the capacity for growth and change in individuals. Amid the challenging situation, the campus community continued to grapple with the delicate balance between accountability, cultural differences, and the pursuit of a fair and compassionate resolution.

When Popi was asked to sign the petition in support of Ahmed, the issue took on a deeply personal significance for him. It became a battle that resonated with his core beliefs and values—the fight for freedom of speech.

For Popi, the principles of free expression were like a guiding star, illuminating the path of individual liberty and the importance of upholding the right to speak one's mind. It was a cause he felt deeply connected to, much like a warrior who carries the banner of a noble quest.

Popi: A Rising Tide

Popi believed that open dialogue and the free exchange of ideas were the bedrock of a vibrant and diverse society. He saw in this situation not just a defence of Ahmed's right to speak but also a defence of the fundamental principles upon which a free and open society stood.

Popi saw the need to look things in the face and know them for what they are. The situation had become a stark reminder of the importance of understanding and defending the values underpinning a democratic and free society.

Popi's involvement in the petition was like a warrior donning armour to enter the fray, determined to protect the right to express diverse viewpoints, even if those viewpoints sometimes led to uncomfortable or sensitive conversations. It was a fight he felt born to wage, a battle for the principles he held dear.

The situation had transformed from a personal issue for Ahmed into a broader struggle to preserve free speech and nurture an environment where differing opinions could coexist. Amid this personal war, Popi stood as a champion of these ideals, ready to defend the principles he believed were the foundation of a just and open society.

With a sense of purpose and a deep commitment to defending freedom of speech, Popi began seeking more information about the incident. He knew that before taking a stand, he needed a thorough understanding of the situation, including the perspectives of all parties involved.

Popi's quest for information was like that of a diligent researcher uncovering the layers of a complex narrative. He engaged in conversations, gathered accounts from witnesses, and delved into the details of the incident, much like a detective sifting through evidence to uncover the truth.

Popi recognized the nuances and complexities at play as he learned more about the incident.

Popi was driven by a sense of responsibility to uphold the principles of free expression and individual rights in his quest for information. He understood the gravity of the situation and was willing to risk his academic life at the institution to defend what he believed was a fundamental and essential value.

Popi's determination was like a knight donning his armour and pledging to defend a just cause. His actions were a testament to his unwavering commitment to the fight for freedom of speech and the importance of open dialogue in a democratic society.

In the face of a complex and potentially contentious situation, Popi remained steadfast in his resolve to stand by Ahmed, even if it meant facing challenges and adversity. He understood that the principles he was defending were worth the risk, and he was prepared to champion the cause of free speech, even in the face of adversity.

Unapologetically passionate

After a dedicated day of research, Popi felt he had gathered a comprehensive understanding of the issue. Armed with knowledge and a heartfelt belief in freedom of speech, he approached Ahmed. Popi understood that this was not just a matter of defending an individual but also a fundamental principle at the heart of a democratic society.

In the shade of a grand oak tree on the campus, Popi found Ahmed and extended a hand in greeting. "Ahmed," he began, his voice brimming with conviction," I heard you've been causing problems on this campus, and I've spent some time researching the incident, and I'm deeply passionate about freedom of speech and expression."

Ahmed, still burdened by the situation, looked at Popi with a mixture of hope and apprehension. "I appreciate your support," he replied, "but I fear the consequences of my words."

Popi nodded empathetically. "I understand your concerns, Ahmed. The free exchange of ideas and respectful dialogue are the cornerstones of our society. In the words of Milton Friedman, 'We must protect and promote the freedom of individuals to pursue their values.' I am committed to defending your right to express your views, even if they differ from others."

The conversation continued, like two philosophers engaged in a debate, exchanging ideas and perspectives. Popi shared the insights he had gathered during his research, emphasizing the importance of cultural sensitivity, education, and open dialogue in fostering understanding and preventing misunderstandings.

Ahmed listened attentively, his apprehension slowly giving way to a sense of hope. "I never intended to cause harm," he confessed. "I would like to learn from this experience and ensure it doesn't happen again."

Popi smiled warmly, recognizing the genuine remorse in Ahmed's words and the potential for growth and learning.

"I'm here to support you in this journey," Popi assured him. "Our campus should be where diverse ideas and backgrounds are tolerated and celebrated. We'll work together to foster understanding and respect while defending the principles we hold dear."

The meeting between Popi and Ahmed was pivotal, an example of the power of compassionate dialogue and the pursuit of shared values. As they continued their conversation beneath the oak tree, they understood that their commitment to freedom of speech was a shared mission.

Underneath the shade of the grand oak tree, Popi embarked on a passionate lecture that lasted hours, weaving the narrative of Canada's rich history and its founding principles. He spoke of the country's beauty, not just in its landscapes but in the values that had shaped it. With unwavering dedication, he shared the story of a nation built on the bedrock of freedom of conscience, speech, and choice.

Popi: A Rising Tide

"Ahmed," he began, "Canada is not just a land of breathtaking natural wonders; it's a land of profound ideals. Our forefathers understood the importance of individual liberty. They envisioned a nation where people could express themselves without fear, where diverse voices could find a home."

As the hours passed, Popi's words were like a vivid tapestry, illustrating the struggles and triumphs of the country's journey. He recounted the battles for freedom, the sacrifices made by those who believed in the power of open discourse, and the importance of nurturing an environment where differing opinions were not just allowed but encouraged.

He continued, "In the spirit of Marcus Aurelius, we believe in looking at things for what they truly are. Freedom of speech is not just a right; it's the cornerstone of our democracy. It allows us to engage in discussions, learn from one another, and, when needed, stand up for what we believe in."

Ahmed, deeply moved by Popi's impassioned lecture, nodded in understanding. He realized that he had become part of a broader narrative—a story of a nation that celebrated the open exchange of ideas. While challenging, he saw that the incident was an opportunity to learn and become a steward of these foundational principles.

Popi concluded, "Our campus should reflect these values, where diverse perspectives are tolerated and embraced. I believe in your ability to grow from this experience and to be a part of the legacy of freedom and respect that defines Canada."

Popi and Ahmed were profoundly impacted by the hours spent under the grand oak tree. They shared a newfound sense of purpose, understanding, and commitment to fostering an environment where the principles of freedom of conscience, speech, and choice could thrive. The lecture had been more than words; it was a call to action, a reminder of the beauty of Canada's foundational principles and the importance of defending them for future generations.

In a moment of deep sincerity, Popi looked Ahmed in the eye and said, "Ahmed, while I may not agree with everything you said that led to this chaos or how you said it, I'm going to fight for your right to say it." His words reflected his unwavering commitment to the principles of free speech and individual liberty.

Ahmed, touched by Popi's unwavering support, nodded in appreciation. "Thank you, Popi. I never expected someone to stand by me after what happened."

Popi smiled warmly. "In Canada, we understand that freedom of speech is not just about the words we agree with; it's about defending the right to express different perspectives. Like Milton Friedman said, we must protect the freedom of individuals to pursue their values."

The conversation between the two new friends reaffirmed their shared mission—to protect and promote the principles underpinning their democratic society. Popi's dedication to defending the right to express differing opinions was like a torch illuminating the path ahead.

Grateful for Popi's support, Ahmed recognized that this was a personal battle and a collective effort to preserve the values they held dear. They understood that even in the face of

Popi: A Rising Tide

controversy and disagreement, the principles of free speech were worth defending, for they were the bedrock of a society that celebrated the beauty of diverse ideas and the power of open discourse.

Popi's commitment extended beyond being "Ahmed's lawyer;" he had vowed to become an agent of freedom of speech for everyone who called the school home. His dedication was not limited to one individual. Still, it encompassed a broader mission to protect and promote the principles they held dear.

As he embarked on this mission, Popi understood that the incident with Ahmed was an opportunity to embody the values of free speech, education, and open dialogue.

Popi became a beacon of hope, a voice for those who may have felt their right to free expression was at stake. He was determined to foster an environment where diverse perspectives could coexist, like the different threads of a tapestry weaving together to create a beautiful whole.

The School Administration began to see in Popi a champion of their shared principles, a reminder that freedom of speech was not just a right but a responsibility. Popi's actions were like a ripple effect, inspiring others to join the cause, much like the saying, "Where there is unity, there is always victory."

His vow to be an agent of freedom of speech was a testament to the enduring power of one individual's dedication to a just and noble cause. Like a guardian of liberty, Popi stood ready to defend these principles for the benefit of the entire campus community and for generations to come.

With Ahmed's permission and support, Popi embarked on his master plan to ensure that this challenging chapter was not the end for Ahmed at the school but only the beginning of a journey of growth and understanding. Popi was determined to leave no stone unturned and to go the whole nine yards in his mission to defend the principles of free speech and create a brighter future for Ahmed.

Popi's plan was meticulous, like a craftsman carefully shaping a work of art. He reached out to faculty, students, and administrators, engaging in conversations, open dialogue, and organizing educational events. He aimed to foster a campus environment where cultural sensitivity and freedom of expression could coexist.

Popi's actions were like a symphony, each note harmonizing with the other, as he strove to ensure that Ahmed could learn from his experiences and become a responsible member of the community.

As more students witnessed Popi's unwavering dedication, they were inspired to join the cause. They recognized the importance of upholding freedom of speech and creating an environment where diverse voices could flourish. They understood this was not just about one student but the values defining their educational institution.

Popi's master plan was a testament to the power of individual commitment to a just and noble cause. With Ahmed's support, he was determined to pave the way for a future where respectful dialogue and cultural sensitivity were not just ideals but a lived reality. Together, they set out to ensure that Ahmed's journey was not one of exclusion but of transformation and growth.

Popi: A Rising Tide

Popi's commitment to defending freedom of speech and freedom of conscience extended beyond the confines of the campus. He recognized the power of the written word in spreading his message, and he penned a passionate article that was published in a local newspaper. His words were like a beacon, shining light on the importance of these foundational principles.

His newspaper article eloquently conveyed the significance of freedom of speech and conscience in a democratic society. He emphasized that these principles were not just rights but responsibilities that required the collective effort of the entire community to uphold.

Popi's words were a call to action, a reminder that preserving these values required vigilance and a commitment to open dialogue and education. He urged readers to recognize that a diverse and vibrant society was one where differing opinions could coexist, and the beauty of such a society was in the exchange of ideas and the pursuit of understanding.

The article resonated with many, catalyzing further discussions on and off the campus. Popi's words were like seeds sown in the fertile soil of public discourse, hoping they would grow into a forest of enlightened perspectives and a deeper appreciation for freedom of speech and conscience.

As his article gained traction, Popi's efforts became a beacon of hope and a symbol of unwavering dedication to these cherished values. He knew the battle for freedom of speech and conscience was not won in a day but required a persistent and collective effort. His article was just one step in a journey to ensure that these principles continued to thrive, like the enduring flame of a torch carried through the generations.

Popi's determination to have his article published in the local newspaper with the highest circulation was a testament to his unwavering commitment to the cause of freedom of speech and conscience. The newspaper's initial hesitation was like an obstacle on his path, but he was not deterred. He knew that the message he carried was too important to be silenced.

He requested to speak with the editor-in-chief, determined to convey the significance of the article. In their discussion, Popi passionately articulated the importance of the principles of freedom of speech and conscience in a democratic society. He explained how these principles were abstract ideals and the essence of a free and open community.

Like a skilled negotiator, Popi used the power of persuasion and the weight of his conviction to sway the editor-in-chief. He emphasized that protecting and promoting individual freedom were fundamental to a just and prosperous society.

The editor-in-chief, influenced by Popi's dedication and the compelling message of the article, was convinced of its importance. They recognized that the article had the potential to ignite discussions and foster a deeper understanding of these critical values.

In the end, the article found its place in the newspaper, thanks to Popi's unwavering determination and ability to convey the significance of the cause. It was a testament to the power of a single individual's commitment to making a difference and ensuring that the principles of freedom of speech and conscience continued to be celebrated and protected.

Popi: A Rising Tide
The Priceless Treasure of Freedom: Nurturing Our Conscience and Speech

In the realm of democracy, a sacred duo of principles forms the bedrock of our free society - Freedom of Conscience and Freedom of Speech. These two pillars are rights bestowed upon us and a shared responsibility that binds us all in the tapestry of collective liberty.

Imagine a world without these freedoms, where individuals are constrained in their thoughts and silenced in their voices. Such a world would be bleak and desolate, devoid of the vibrant tapestry of ideas and the endless growth potential that freedom of conscience and speech offer. As we delve into the profound significance of these principles, we must understand that their preservation is not a given but rather a call to action that demands our unwavering commitment.

Freedom of conscience is the inner sanctum of our individuality. It is the foundation upon which we build our values, beliefs, and moral compass. In a democratic society, it allows us to explore, question, and refine our beliefs without fear of persecution. This freedom enables us to search for truth and meaning, allowing us to become better, more enlightened human beings.

Similarly, freedom of speech is the public manifestation of our inner conscience. It is our voice in the grand symphony of democracy, a tool to express our ideas, share our concerns, and question the status quo. It reflects the diversity of thought within our society, a mirror that, when polished and untarnished, is emblematic of a society's health and vitality.

These freedoms are not only a gift but a responsibility. They require collective effort, vigilance, and a commitment to open dialogue and education. In a world filled with diverse perspectives, it is essential to understand that the beauty of a society lies in the exchange of ideas and the pursuit of understanding.

We must recognize that our diverse and vibrant society is one where differing opinions can coexist. It is where we listen and engage with those whose ideas may differ from our own, not in a bid to silence them but to understand the world better and refine our own beliefs. In this exchange of ideas, we strengthen our collective conscience and enrich the landscape of freedom of speech.

To preserve these invaluable freedoms, we must take action. Education plays a pivotal role, as an informed citizenry is better equipped to safeguard its own liberties. We must encourage critical thinking, nurture the spirit of inquiry, and promote the responsible use of speech. Engaging in respectful discourse and listening with empathy will help bridge the gaps between differing opinions, fostering a society that thrives on collaboration rather than division.

In this information age, the responsibility to differentiate fact from falsehood and distinguish between constructive critique and harmful rhetoric is more significant than ever. As citizens, we must exercise our rights responsibly and be conscious of the impact of our words and actions on our community.

Above all, we must be vigilant. Preserving freedom of conscience and speech is not an isolated endeavour but a collective one. It requires us to stand together as guardians of these essential freedoms, defending them against those seeking to diminish or dismantle them.

In conclusion, the significance of freedom of conscience and speech cannot be overstated. They are the lifeblood of a democratic society, the nurturing ground for ideas, and the bridge between individuals of differing perspectives. Remember that these principles are not passive rights but active responsibilities, demanding collective effort and vigilance.

As we move forward in this ever-changing world, let us remain committed to open dialogue, education, and nurturing a society where differing opinions

Popi: A Rising Tide

coexist harmoniously. Through the exchange of ideas and the pursuit of understanding, we will continue to enrich the tapestry of our democracy and uphold individual liberty.

While Popi had worked tirelessly to have his article published in the local newspaper, he had also understood the importance of directly engaging with the School Administration. In a passionate letter to the Administration, he laid out compelling arguments for preserving and celebrating freedom of speech and conscience as fundamental pillars of democracy at a post-secondary institution.

His letter was not just a plea but a well-articulated thesis. Popi emphasized that an educational institution's role extended beyond transmitting knowledge; it was also a place where the exchange of diverse ideas and perspectives should be fostered.

He argued that protecting these principles was not just a matter of rights but a duty to ensure that the campus remained a place where students could express their thoughts, even if those thoughts were at odds with others.

In his letter, Popi highlighted the importance of cultural sensitivity, open dialogue, and education to prevent misunderstandings and promote respectful interactions among students from various backgrounds. He called upon the Administration to recognize that nurturing a community where differing opinions were not just tolerated but celebrated reflected the very values upon which their institution was founded.

Popi's letter was a passionate plea for a brighter future, where the principles of free speech and conscience were not just words on paper but a lived reality. He knew that the journey to safeguard these values required individual dedication and institutional commitment. His letter was a significant step in ensuring that these principles continued to thrive, not just in theory but in practice, within the hallowed halls of the institution.

Popi's dedication to the cause was unwavering, and he believed that having the support of his Member of Parliament (MP) would strengthen his message. He approached his MP, whom he also worked for, and requested that he sign the letter advocating for freedom of speech and conscience within the School's Administration.

His MP recognized Popi's passion and commitment and commended him on his work and the importance of the cause. "Popi," he said, "I admire your dedication to these fundamental principles and willingness to stand up for your beliefs. Your passion is truly commendable."

However, with the wisdom of experience, his MP also offered valuable advice. "It's important to choose your battles carefully," he continued. "Not every issue may be worth fighting for in the same way. While the cause you're advocating for is essential, it's also important to approach it strategically."

The advice was like a guiding star for Popi, a reminder that while his dedication was noble, there were moments when a nuanced approach was necessary. It echoed the old English saying, "Discretion is the better part of valour," encouraging him to consider the most effective ways to achieve his goals.

Popi appreciated the advice from his MP, recognizing that

Popi: A Rising Tide

sometimes, a more measured and strategic approach could lead to more significant changes. While his passion remained undiminished, he understood the importance of strategic advocacy and the need to navigate the complexities of the institution's administrative process. The wisdom he gained from his MP would serve as a valuable tool in his ongoing mission to protect and promote the principles of freedom of speech and conscience.

As Popi waited for a response from the School Administration, he recognized the need to keep the momentum of his cause alive and to galvanize support for freedom and democracy. With unwavering determination, he organized the "Rally for Freedom." He called on everyone who supported these fundamental principles to come together and show their support.

The rally was like a beacon of hope, drawing individuals from various backgrounds and walks of life, united by their shared belief in freedom and democracy. Popi's initiative emphasized the strength that came from a collective voice.

At the rally, Popi addressed the crowd, passionately advocating for freedom of speech and conscience, just as he had done in his article and letter. He urged those in attendance to recognize the importance of an open and diverse society and the need to defend these cherished values.

The rally powerfully demonstrated the community's support for freedom and democracy. Popi's efforts reminded the community that protecting these principles required the active engagement of the community as a whole.

Popi's rally for freedom kept the cause in the public eye. It showed the School Administration the depth of support behind the principles he was advocating for. It was a testament to the enduring power of an individual's dedication to a just and noble cause and the ability to mobilize others to pursue a common goal.

At the rally for freedom and democracy, Popi stood before the gathered students and called upon them to speak passionately about why freedom of speech and conscience were paramount to democracy. He recognized that the power of their voices could bring a deeper understanding and appreciation for these fundamental principles.

One by one, students stepped forward, their voices resounding like a symphony of conviction. They shared personal stories, experiences, and reflections that highlighted the importance of these principles in a democratic society.

One student eloquently spoke of their journey, highlighting how the ability to express their thoughts and beliefs freely had allowed her to grow and develop a deeper understanding of the world. She emphasized the need for open dialogue and exchanging ideas as essential for personal and societal growth.

Another student shared their family's history, recounting how freedom of speech had been instrumental in advocating for change and progress. She spoke of the importance of these principles in holding those in power accountable and ensuring that democracy continued to thrive.

The students' voices emphasized the value of individual freedom in promoting a just and prosperous society. They conveyed that freedom of speech and conscience were not just theoretical ideals, but also practical tools for creating a better world.

The rally became a platform for diverse perspectives and a reminder that protecting these principles required the active engagement and advocacy of the entire community. It was a powerful testament to the enduring power of passionate individuals who believed in upholding these values and their commitment to fostering a democratic society where diverse voices could coexist.

As the students shared their stories and convictions, the rally catalyzed greater understanding and a deeper appreciation for the principles of freedom of speech and freedom of conscience. The event was not just a demonstration but an educational experience. It reminded everyone that the battle for these principles was worth fighting for and that their preservation was vital for the community's well-being and the democratic society they cherished.

The "Rally for Freedom and Democracy" organized by Popi proved to be a monumental event that captured the attention of thousands of students, the local media and residents. It symbolized the enduring commitment to freedom of speech and conscience, drawing a diverse and passionate crowd.

The sea of attendees demonstrated the community's unity and shared belief in these principles' importance. The rally was like a magnet, attracting individuals from all walks of life who recognized that these values were not just theoretical ideals but the very foundation of a vibrant and democratic society.

The presence of the local media and residents further underscored the event's significance. It served as a reminder that the protection and promotion of these principles were not just a campus issue but a matter of broader importance to the entire community.

The rally became a focal point for conversations and discussions about the principles of freedom of speech and freedom of conscience. It served as an opportunity to educate and engage with those who may have yet to be directly involved in the campus community. Still, it recognized the universal importance of these values.

Popi's dedication and the collective efforts of the attendees transformed the rally into a momentous occasion, a celebration of freedom, democracy, and the power of a united community. The event was a demonstration and a call to action, inspiring others to join the cause and ensure that these cherished principles continued to thrive in their community and beyond.

The combined efforts of the rally, the published article in the local newspaper, and the passionate letter sent to the School Administration created a powerful wave of support for freedom of conscience and speech. Together, they drowned out any opposition, becoming a compelling force that could not be ignored.

The attention garnered by these initiatives served as a testament to the community's unwavering commitment to these principles. It reflected the wisdom of emphasizing the importance of protecting individual freedom for a just and prosperous society.

Popi: A Rising Tide

The arguments in the letter to the School Administration, the passionate article, and the heartfelt speeches at the rally resonated deeply with the community. They highlighted the significance of fostering an environment where differing opinions were tolerated and celebrated.

As a result, the School Administration recognized the depth of support behind the cause and the importance of preserving and promoting freedom of conscience and speech. The combined efforts demonstrated that these principles were ideals and lived values at the core of the institution's identity.

The community's collective voice had triumphed, and the resounding support for these fundamental principles overshadowed the opposition. The rally, the article, and the letter had not only created a sense of unity but also served as a reminder that the battle for these values was worth fighting for, as they were the bedrock of a just and democratic society.

In the face of such overwhelming support, the Administration was compelled to take action, reaffirming its commitment to freedom of conscience and speech. It was a victory for the community, a testament to the power of collective dedication, and a reminder that preserving these cherished values was paramount for a vibrant and democratic society.

In light of the overwhelming support for freedom of conscience and speech and to bring peace back to the school, the Administration made a prudent decision. They recognized that pursuing Ahmed's expulsion was not worth the negative publicity and the discord it would generate.

The decision to reconsider expulsion reminded individuals to choose their battles carefully and act with discernment. It also emphasized fostering a campus environment where diverse opinions could coexist.

By choosing a path that sought reconciliation and understanding, the Administration avoided negative publicity and upheld the principles of free speech and open dialogue. It served as a reminder that flexibility and empathy were sometimes vital in pursuing justice and harmony.

The campus community, including Popi and Ahmed, saw this decision as a victory for the values they had fought to protect. It reaffirmed the importance of engaging in respectful dialogue, education, and cultural sensitivity to prevent misunderstandings and promote an environment where diverse voices could thrive.

Ultimately, the decision not to pursue expulsion marked a turning point for the school. It reminded the campus of the enduring power of collective dedication and a commitment to the values that defined their community. The campus could now move forward with a deeper appreciation for the principles of freedom of conscience and speech and a more substantial commitment to nurturing an inclusive and democratic environment.

The decision not to pursue the expulsion of Ahmed and the overwhelming support for freedom of conscience and speech had a profound impact. The voices of those who sought to limit speech and constrain conscience quickly became a minority, and they recognized the futility of their position in the face of overwhelming opposition.

The collective dedication of the campus community, the rally for freedom, the passionate article, and the letter to the School Administration had shifted the discourse. It served as a reminder that the protection and promotion of these fundamental principles were paramount in a democratic society. The opposition, realizing that the majority of the community stood firmly for the values of free speech and open dialogue, wisely chose to reevaluate their position. This was a testament to the enduring power of collective dedication and the importance of defending principles that were not just rights but also responsibilities.

The school had become a place where the principles of freedom of conscience and speech were not just celebrated but also understood as essential to the growth and well-being of the community. The campus was a beacon of diversity, where differing opinions could coexist, and exchanging ideas was embraced as a tool for learning and understanding.

The voices of those who sought to limit speech had given up because they had witnessed the enduring strength of a united community committed to defending the principles they held dear and the overwhelming opposition. It was a victory for freedom, a triumph of collective dedication, and a reminder that these values were not just theoretical ideals but lived principles that defined their shared community.

After the dust had settled, Meghan approached Popi with the spoils of their debate. Though unhappy about the result, she wanted to congratulate Popi on his work, garnering support around the school and community by standing on his principles. Meghan was visibly displeased with the outcome because, while Popi strongly believed in promoting freedom of speech, Meghan held equally strong opinions about curtailing offensive speech.

Meghan's face betrayed her true feelings as she handed him the spoils. Popi, perceptive and empathetic, noticed the annoyance etched on her features. He knew that allowing this bitterness to fester could lead to future conflicts, and he decided to address the issue head-on, hoping to clear the air.

"Meghan," Popi began gently, his tone thoughtful, "I didn't want things to turn out this way. But you're too stubborn to listen or understand a different perspective, let alone admit that going to extremes was not the best way to handle the situation."

Meghan's eyes flashed with frustration. "Look, Popi," she retorted, "I don't take offensive language lightly. As a woman, I shouldn't take any language offensive to women lightly because I don't have to live in fear for my life every single day because of what a man can do to me."

Popi rose from his seat and approached Meghan, who was visibly upset. He wanted to bridge the gap between their views, knowing that unresolved tension could lead to more significant issues.

"The problem with you and others who think like you," Popi said, "is that you believe your way of seeing the world is the only way everyone should see it. That makes you a difficult person in my books."

Meghan stood her ground, responding firmly, "If a man, any man, makes fun of sexually assaulting women, I'll be damned if I don't put my own life on the line to bring that man to justice."

Popi: A Rising Tide

Popi sighed, trying to convey his point without further escalating the situation. "Again, your perspective wants to take things to the extremes, which is not how the conversation was intended. You were all having a friendly discussion about married life and marital infidelity. Ahmed, with a lighter tone, remarked that in his country, wives don't turn down their husbands for sex, so there's no reason for the husbands to cheat."

Meghan's anger grew, her clenched fists showing her rising frustration. In her mind, any man who trivialized violence against women was guilty, and now Popi seemed to be justifying it.

Seeing Meghan's clenched fists might have sent a message to many to flee, but Popi remained calm and composed. "What you did, Meghan, was despicable because you took Ahmed's words out of context to justify your anger."

Popi smiled as he looked into Meghan's eyes. "What if those women don't turn down their husbands because the sex is too good?"

Meghan laughed at herself but quickly suppressed it. "Yeah, very funny, but I'm sure that's not what he meant."

"Maybe that's not what he meant," Popi acknowledged, "but you also can't tell me that you knew exactly what he meant."

Meghan looked down, understanding the sense but feeling defeated simultaneously. Realizing this, Popi gently held her arm as he continued to explain, "In life, if you're not sure about something, the best thing to do is something very simple called asking. Your reaction could be justified if you sought clarification and understood exactly what he meant. However, your reaction was impatient and assumptive in this case. You cannot take anything you think is a negative sentiment, blow it out of proportion, and mount the biggest strike. Just now, we are talking, listening, and understanding. I'm currently holding your hand. Is this an assault on you?"

Meghan smiled and shook her head, indicating this was not an assault.

"I don't know," Popi joked, "maybe you're letting me hold your hand because you secretly like me because I'm just hard to hate."

Meghan chuckled, the tension easing slightly. "On a serious note, though," Popi continued, "it seems as if you have been through something or maybe someone you care about has, or perhaps you're just afraid of something like that happening to you. That might have made you blow things out of proportion. In either case, you should consider talking to somebody about it."

"Thanks for the talk," Meghan said as she turned to leave. "I better go and leave you to your work."

As Meghan walked away, Popi called out to her, "You are a very passionate individual, and I admire that passion. If you direct that passion to the right problems in the right way, I have no doubt you'll change the world someday. But if you misdirect that passion and go to extremes before even engaging in simple dialogue to see if there is an easier way to solve the problem, then you'll be a very dangerous person in this world. I think

Popi: A Rising Tide
you'll be good at identifying problems, like a fisherman being patient and using his fishing rod to catch one fish at a time. However, when you solve those identified problems, you are like a hungry man fishing with dynamite. Remember, going nuclear should only be the last resort because if you use that as your first resort, you take away any chance of solving the problem without causing more harm. Think about it."

Meghan nodded thoughtfully as she walked away, her mind turning over Popi's words.

The Local Hero

Since the news of the victory of Popi's tireless efforts to prevent the unjust expulsion of a fellow student had spread like wildfire, he had become a local hero both within the school and in his community. The transformative power of his commitment to defending the principles of freedom of conscience and speech had not only safeguarded one individual's rights but also illuminated the path toward a more inclusive and democratic society.

The atmosphere within the school had shifted. Popi was no longer just a charismatic and cheerful student but an embodiment of the principles they all held dear. His dedication was like a guiding star, showing that one individual's unwavering commitment could lead to significant change. It emphasized the importance of protecting individual freedom for the well-being of society.

In the community, Popi's actions had inspired admiration and respect. He had become a symbol of resilience and a testament to the power of standing up for what one believed in. The old English saying, "One man's courage is a majority," seemed to capture the essence of Popi's impact. He had shown that one person's dedication could rally others to defend shared values.

As Popi walked through the school halls and his community, he was met with nods of appreciation, pats on the back, and heartfelt expressions of gratitude. He had not only saved a fellow student from injustice but had also revived the spirit of

Popi: A Rising Tide

unity and understanding within their community.

Popi saw things for what they were and acted according to his principles. His efforts not only protected an individual's rights but also rekindled the flame of freedom of conscience and speech in the hearts of others.

The victory of Popi's mission had not only made him a local hero but had also served as a potent reminder that the battle for justice and freedom was worth fighting, and that one person's dedication could ignite a spark of change that could illuminate an entire community.

Popi's newfound status as a local hero didn't just resonate within the school and community but also had a significant impact on his positions at work and in his volunteering activities. His unwavering commitment to defending the principles of freedom of conscience and speech had elevated him to a position of influence and respect in all aspects of his life.

At work, his colleagues and superiors recognized his dedication and passion in advocating for freedom of speech and democracy. His commitment was a personal cause and a reflection of the principles they held dear. This ripple effect increased recognition and respect for Popi in his workplace.

His role as a volunteer at the senior centre and in his work with the Member of Parliament also saw a transformation. Popi's newfound status as a local hero inspired those he worked with. They saw him as a source of guidance and an individual who could inspire positive change. The saying, "A rising tide lifts all boats," captured how Popi's efforts positively impacted those around him.

Popi's influence extended beyond his academic pursuits. His work positions and volunteering activities became platforms for him to advocate for the values he held dear. His passion for freedom of speech and freedom of conscience was not just confined to one aspect of his life; it had become a driving force that shaped his interactions and actions in all areas.

His journey from a dedicated student to a local hero elevated his status. It showed the community the importance of standing up for what one believed in. Popi's influence was a testament to his character and a reminder that one individual's commitment to justice and democracy could inspire and elevate those around them like a beacon of light in a darkened room, illuminating the path for all to follow.

Popi's newfound recognition and influence were not limited to his academic and volunteer positions; they extended to a surprising new venture. Popi had become highly sought after as a tour guide, and his popularity was so immense that he decided to start his own small company, aptly named "Popi Tours."

His success as a tour guide was a testament to his charisma, knowledge, and ability to connect with people from all walks of life. Popi had a unique gift for bringing the beauty of his country to life, much like a skilled storyteller weaving tales of history and culture. His tours were not just about visiting landmarks; they were an immersive experience, a journey through the heart and soul of his homeland.

Popi's newfound venture also embodied the principles he had passionately defended. It was a testament to the importance of

Popi: A Rising Tide

open dialogue and the exchange of ideas, much like the values he had fought to protect in his academic and community activities. It was a living example of the role of individual freedom in a just and prosperous society.

Popi Tours quickly became known for providing an authentic educational experience. Tourists and locals alike were drawn to his tours to see the sights and understand the culture, history, and values that made Canada unique.

Popi's journey from a local hero to a successful entrepreneur was a testament to the transformative power of dedication and the ability to inspire positive change in one's community. It was a reminder that the principles of freedom of conscience and speech were not just ideals but could also be a driving force for personal and professional growth, like the branches of a sturdy tree reaching the sky.

Popi's visits to the senior centre became a cherished tradition, eagerly awaited by every senior in the community. Those two special days every week were a source of joy and inspiration, as they looked forward to listening to him talk about his passions and goals to make Canada a better place for everyone who called it home. His advocacy for freedom of speech, choice, and conscience resonated deeply with the seniors, who had seen the world transform and appreciated preserving these fundamental values.

His conversations with the seniors were like bridges connecting generations. They reminded him that these values were not just for the young but remained relevant and vital for all.

With their wealth of life experiences, the seniors shared stories and wisdom with Popi. It was a mutual exchange of ideas and perspectives, illustrating the power of open dialogue and knowledge exchange. It was a living example of the values Popi had passionately defended.

As Popi spoke about his dreams for a more inclusive and democratic society, the seniors became a source of encouragement and support. They understood the importance of passing on these values to the next generation and appreciated Popi's dedication to this cause.

The two days Popi spent at the senior centre were moments of conversation, a celebration of shared values, and a reminder that the principles he advocated for were not just theoretical ideals but practical tools for creating a better world. Popi's commitment influenced his peers and reached across generations, touching the hearts and minds of those who had witnessed the evolution of their community and country.

As Popi continued to visit the senior centre, something heartwarming and beautiful unfolded. Nearly every senior began to see him as their grandchild, a special connection that went beyond just conversations. They looked forward to personal time with him, whether for a quick chat or to express appreciation for his presence at the centre.

The seniors' affection for Popi was like a warm embrace, and he reciprocated their feelings with genuine care and respect. Their bond reflected their encouragement to cultivate solid and meaningful relationships with others.

With their years of life experience, the seniors wanted to share their wisdom and stories with Popi, much like passing the torch

Popi: A Rising Tide

of knowledge to the younger generation. They saw a bright future in him and were eager to impart their insights and guidance.

The small tokens of appreciation they offered, whether a heartfelt conversation, advice, or a simple box of chocolates, symbolized their deep gratitude for Popi's presence. It was a reminder that the impact one could have on others transcended age and generation.

Popi, in turn, treasured these moments with the seniors. Their conversations and gestures of appreciation touched his heart. They inspired his ongoing mission to make Canada a better place for everyone. Their connection was a testament to the power of building bridges across generations and the enduring influence that an individual's dedication and kindness could have in a community.

The bond between Popi and the seniors at the centre was a heartwarming example of the importance of intergenerational relationships, the passing down of knowledge and values, and the beauty of connecting with others on a deep and meaningful level. It was a reminder that the impact of one person's presence could have a ripple effect that touched the lives of many.

The special bond that Popi forged with Grace, one of the seniors at the centre, was a profound connection that transcended generations. Grace, a former teacher, saw in Popi a reflection of her late husband's passion and courage. These qualities had inspired her to become an educator. She shared with Popi that her husband's energy motivated her to teach, as she wanted to instill that energy in future generations.

Grace's words were a poignant reminder that a teacher's influence goes far beyond the classroom. Her mixed results with her students had not deterred her commitment to instilling the values of passion and courage in the young minds she had touched. She recognized in Popi, another teacher who had the potential to make a significant and positive impact on the future generation.

Her advice to Popi was both profound and practical. She encouraged him not only to learn from books but also from the people and experiences around him. It echoed the wisdom of emphasizing the value of continuous learning and self-improvement.

Grace's guidance didn't stop there. She also offered Popi some personal advice. Recognizing his controversial path in advocating for freedom of speech and conscience, she advised him to find a suitable partner, a woman who would stand by his side. She understood that a life committed to such principles could be challenging and that having a supportive and loving companion could make all the difference.

The bond between Popi and Grace became a source of mutual inspiration and wisdom. It reminded them of the importance of passing down not just knowledge but also life lessons and values. Grace's words resonated deeply with Popi and became a guiding light as he continued his journey to make Canada a better place for all, supported by the wisdom and encouragement of a cherished friend from another generation.

Popi's status as a local hero and his passionate advocacy for freedom of speech and conscience transformed him into a respected and influential figure at school. He had become the

Popi: A Rising Tide

go-to person for nearly every student with school administration issues. His rally for freedom highlighted the importance of these principles. It established a direct line of communication between the students, the school administration, and the community.

Students, recognizing his dedication and effectiveness, turned to Popi for guidance and assistance. His charisma and approachability made him a natural leader, someone they could trust to represent their concerns and advocate for their rights. Much like the saying, "When in doubt, go to the source," Popi had become the source of support and guidance for those in need.

His rally had created a lasting impact, fostering a sense of unity and purpose within the school community. The open dialogue and exchange of ideas championed at the Rally for Freedom had continued to thrive, and Popi had become a central figure in these conversations.

Popi's connection with the community also played a significant role. His presence at the senior centre, his work as a tour guide, and his involvement with the Member of Parliament further strengthened his network. It had become clear that his dedication extended beyond the school and encompassed the entire community's well-being.

The direct line of communication that Popi had established was a reminder of the power of a dedicated individual to create positive change and serve as a catalyst for open dialogue and understanding. Popi had become a local hero and a unifying force, bringing together different community segments to pursue shared values and a more inclusive and democratic society.

In the local community, Popi's presence had a remarkable and heartwarming effect. He had become a friend to just about everyone he encountered. His charisma, dedication, and passion for advocating freedom of speech and conscience had endeared him to the hearts of the community members.

Popi's ability to connect with people from all walks of life, whether during his tours, at the senior centre, or as a dedicated advocate, made him a trusted and respected figure in his community. His friendly and approachable demeanour allowed him to form connections quickly, and he embraced the opportunity to listen to the stories and perspectives of those he met.

The saying, "A friend in need is a friend indeed," seemed to capture the essence of Popi's role in the community. He was a local hero and a reliable and supportive friend to those who sought his guidance and friendship.

His commitment to making Canada a better place for all and his unwavering belief in the principles of freedom had become the common ground that connected him with others. Popi had demonstrated that pursuing justice and liberty was not just a personal journey but a shared mission that could bring people together.

In a world where divisions often prevail, Popi's ability to be a friend to just about everyone was a powerful reminder of the unifying force of dedication, compassion, and shared values. It was a testament to the enduring impact that an individual could have on a community and the depth of the connections that could be forged in pursuing a common goal.

Popi's demeanour, always wearing a warm and welcoming smile, enchanted everyone he encountered as he confidently walked around. It made the community fall in love with him even more. His presence radiated positivity and an open-hearted spirit that drew people towards him.

The old English saying, "A smile is a universal welcome," seemed tailor-made for Popi. His smile was like a beacon of light, spreading warmth and goodwill to all who crossed his path. It created an atmosphere of friendliness and approachability that resonated with everyone.

Popi's confidence was not just in his stride but also in the values he passionately defended. It was a reminder that standing up for what one believed in could be done with conviction and a kind heart. His charisma and openness became a reflection of the principles he held dear.

The combination of his confidence and smile was a powerful force that made people feel valued and appreciated. It invited conversations, fostered connections, and served as a reminder that one individual's actions could create a sense of unity and positivity.

Popi's ability to spread happiness and warmth through his presence was a living example of the values he held dear. It was a testament to the transformative power of kindness and the enduring impact of a smile. It was no wonder the community had fallen in love with him even more, as his spirit embodied the qualities that bound people together and created a sense of belonging and unity.

Popi's influence and impact at the university had reached a level that was impossible to ignore. When the university was seeking a representative to discuss social issues affecting university students at a regional gathering, it was no surprise that the university president personally reached out to him to represent the school.

This gesture was a clear testament to the trust and respect that Popi had garnered from both students and the administration. His dedication to defending freedom of speech and conscience made him a figurehead of positive change within the university community.

The old English saying, "Actions speak louder than words," was a fitting description of Popi's journey. He had not just talked about the importance of these principles but had lived and breathed them, inspiring others to do the same.

The invitation to represent the school recognized Popi's ability to inspire and lead, which reflected the values the university held dear. It also demonstrated the power of one individual to influence and shape the direction of a community.

Popi's journey from a dedicated student to a local hero and now a university representative was a remarkable testament to the transformative power of commitment and advocacy. It was a reminder that pursuing justice and freedom could lead to opportunities that allowed one to positively impact one's community on a broader scale. Popi's journey was proof that, indeed, one person could make a significant difference.

Popi's penchant for debates and his unwavering passion for freedom made him the ideal candidate to represent the school

Popi: A Rising Tide

at an event where arguments for and against freedom in a social context were expected. His ability to engage in respectful and insightful debates and his commitment to defending the principles of freedom of speech and conscience set him apart as the best student for this crucial role.

Popi's approach was like a breath of fresh air in a world where discussions surrounding freedom were often polarized. He was uniquely able to articulate his views and engage in constructive dialogues.

Popi brought his eloquence, knowledge, and deep conviction for the values he held dear to the table as a school representative. He was not just a debater but a champion of the principles he believed were essential for a just and democratic society.

Popi's presence at the event would serve as a reminder that advocating for freedom of speech and conscience was not just about defending one's perspective but also about fostering a culture of open dialogue and understanding. His participation would symbolize the school's commitment to engaging in meaningful conversations and finding common ground, even in the face of differing opinions.

The choice to have Popi represent the school was a testament to his ability to bridge divides and his commitment to creating a space where discussions about freedom could be conducted with respect and empathy. It was a recognition of his role as an advocate for the values that defined their community and his capacity to inspire positive change in a larger context.

A significant turnaround was observed when some of the students who had previously protested to have the university expel an international student for insensitive comments approached Popi. They sought his assistance in promoting their cause, which focused on fostering sensitive language around the school.

This change was a testament to Popi's ability to bridge divides and foster understanding. The students, who had once held opposing views, recognized his dedication to freedom of speech and his willingness to engage in open dialogue. They understood that Popi's commitment extended beyond a single issue and that he advocated for a more inclusive and democratic environment.

The turnaround also echoed the wisdom of encouraging individuals to approach situations with an open mind and a willingness to see things from different perspectives. Popi's desire to engage with those who held differing views demonstrated the value of empathy and open dialogue in finding common ground.

The students' decision to seek Popi's assistance in promoting sensitive language was a powerful symbol of their recognition that change could be achieved through constructive conversations and collaboration. It was a reminder that individuals could evolve and find a common purpose, even when they initially disagreed.

Popi's ability to build bridges and foster cooperation was a testament to the transformative power of open dialogue and the enduring impact of an individual committed to advocating for positive change. It demonstrated that his influence extended beyond his initial cause, reflecting his role as a unifying force within the school community.

Popi: A Rising Tide

When these students approached Popi, there was a sense of uncertainty. Given their history of differing opinions, they were curious if he would accept. However, Popi's response was both gracious and insightful.

He was flattered that they had asked for his help because he recognized that their request transcended their past disagreements. It indicated they understood the fundamental principles he had advocated – the right to express oneself and protect one's freedom of speech. Popi understood that their request was not about agreeing on every topic but about coming together to champion the more significant cause of open dialogue and the protection of individual liberties.

Popi saw their request as an opportunity to foster a culture of respectful and inclusive communication within the school, and he welcomed the chance to collaborate on this critical goal.

The willingness to put aside past differences and work together for a shared cause powerfully illustrated the potential for growth and change, even when individuals initially disagreed. It showed that the pursuit of shared values and principles could unite people who, at first glance, might seem opposed. Popi's response was a testament to his commitment to fostering understanding and positive change within the school community.

Popi embraced the philosophy that giving people skills to handle conflicts is more potent than merely guiding them through sensitive issues. He taught them fundamental principles:

"First, define your position clearly and understand the other side's perspective deeply. Second, assess how far apart your positions are and explore potential compromises. Be open to compromise yourself. Third, once you've identified areas for compromise, approach the other party to express your concerns and demonstrate genuine interest in understanding their viewpoint. Seek to understand before seeking to be understood. This approach ensures clarity about each other's positions and fosters a sense of mutual respect.

"If you still aim for a compromise, ask questions to deepen your understanding of their perspective, showing your willingness to engage with their ideas. Fourth, after understanding their viewpoint, it's time to present your arguments and position logically and respectfully. Remember, the goal isn't to force them to change their minds immediately but to encourage them to reflect on your perspective.

"Lastly, remember that Rome wasn't built in a day, and a journey of a thousand miles begins with a single step. Patience is vital to achieving lasting change. Ultimately, you're not trying to change their minds forcefully; you're presenting a different perspective in a way that allows them to reconsider their opinions voluntarily.

"I must note," Popi added, "this approach can be seen as manipulative, but it's far preferable to the alternatives, like conflict."

Popi concluded his lesson by emphasizing the importance of patience and respectful dialogue in fostering lasting change.

The events that had unfolded, from Popi's journey as a dedicated freshman to becoming a local hero and a unifying

Popi: A Rising Tide

force within the school and the community, were only the beginning. The end of his freshman year marked just the first chapter in a remarkable story of advocacy, unity, and the enduring impact of one individual's dedication to principles of freedom, open dialogue, and the pursuit of a better society.

As Popi entered his sophomore year and beyond, more challenges and opportunities were undoubtedly awaiting him. His journey was a testament to the transformative power of commitment and the potential for positive change when one takes a stand for what one believes in.

Popi had shown that even as a freshman, one could have a significant and lasting impact on their school and community. His story had been a reminder that the pursuit of justice, freedom, and the betterment of society was not limited by age or experience. Popi's commitment to these principles had already set a powerful example, and the chapters that awaited him in the years to come promised even more extraordinary achievements and contributions to the world around him.

Life Goes On

Popi's sophomore year marked a new chapter in his journey, filled with promise and uncertainty. As he continued to champion the principles of freedom of speech and conscience, he found himself at a crossroads, facing growing concerns from his parents about his activities and social circles. Their increasing worry reflected their love and concern for their son, but it also served as a source of tension between them.

His mother, deeply worried, saw Popi's path as potentially dangerous. She couldn't help but be concerned about his well-being and the risks associated with his audacious pursuit. To her, it felt like a treacherous journey into uncharted waters where the outcome was uncertain.

On the other hand, while maintaining skepticism about Popi's personal choices, his father was proud of his son's bold and audacious stance in life. He recognized Popi's unwavering commitment to his principles as a reflection of his strength and resilience. Rather than telling Popi to stop, his father chose a different approach.

Popi's father offered Popi words of encouragement and a strong caution. He reminded Popi of the need to be extremely careful while navigating the uncharted waters of his chosen path. It was a warning born out of love and wisdom, emphasizing the importance of determination tempered with a careful and considerate approach.

Popi: A Rising Tide

The situation within the family reflected the complexities that often arise when one chooses a path less travelled. It demonstrated the clash of parental concern and a young individual's unwavering commitment to their ideals. Popi's sophomore year was set to be a pivotal time in his journey, where he would need to balance his passion with the wisdom imparted by those who cared deeply for his well-being.

Popi's sophomore year saw him taking on even more responsibilities at school. His commitment to his advocacy and passion for creating positive change in the community led him to become an advisor to students involved in clubs focused on addressing social issues. This added role only made him busier, as he worked closely with these students to provide guidance and support in their endeavours.

As he embraced this new responsibility, it became evident that Popi's dedication was not limited to his advocacy. He was also deeply invested in mentoring and guiding the next generation of changemakers, reflecting the values he held dear.

His additional responsibilities were a testament to his belief in the importance of active engagement and the power of collective action. Popi's actions emphasized the role of individuals in shaping the world around them and the value of community efforts.

His sophomore year was a growth period for him and the students he advised. It was a time for them to learn from each other and work together to create a more inclusive and democratic school community. Popi's journey had also become about inspiring and nurturing the potential for positive change in those around him.

Popi's company, Popi Tours, which he had started the previous spring, was experiencing rapid growth. The demand from customers was surging, and even for someone who enjoyed working independently, it became clear that he needed to come to terms with the reality of his expanding business. The sheer volume of requests and customers made it necessary for him to seek help in the form of employees and a manager to assist in running the company.

The success of his tour company was not just a testament to his entrepreneurial spirit but also a reflection of his ability to meet the needs and desires of his customers. His dedication to showcasing the beauty of Canada had resonated with visitors, and it had translated into tangible success.

The financial gains from the company were substantial, and they held the potential to transform Popi's life. The prospect of graduating from university without a financial burden and with the means to lead a comfortable life during his academic years was a significant achievement.

As Popi navigated the challenges and opportunities of his growing business, he was shaping his future, contributing to the local economy, and providing job opportunities for others. His journey as a business owner was a reminder that individual success could positively impact the broader community and society.

His chosen path required adaptability, leadership, and a strong work ethic. Popi's sophomore year was marked by a significant shift in his role from sole proprietor to business owner as his company continued to flourish. His ability to manage this transition effectively was a testament to his resilience and

Popi: A Rising Tide

determination.

Popi's life in his sophomore year was a whirlwind of responsibilities and opportunities. Alongside the rapid growth of his tour company and his role as an advisor to student clubs, he also took on an increased course load with the ambitious goal of graduating early. While determined to achieve this goal, he put immense pressure on himself.

Pursuing an early graduation meant Popi had little time for a social life. His days were consumed by academic and entrepreneurial work, and his evenings were often dedicated to running his business and helping other students. The concept of free time had become a rarity; even the luxury of a whole night's sleep felt like a distant memory.

This period of his life reflected the demands that can come with pursuing one's goals with unwavering determination. Popi's pursuit of academic success and the growth of his business were commendable. Still, they came at a cost to his personal life and well-being. It emphasized the need to find a balance between ambition and self-care.

The stress and exhaustion that Popi experienced reminded him that the pursuit of excellence often requires sacrifices. However, it also highlighted the importance of self-awareness and the need to find moments of respite amid a busy life. Popi's journey was a testament to his resilience and determination. Still, it also served as a reminder that success should be accompanied by self-care and a sense of well-being.

Amidst the whirlwind of responsibilities and the relentless pursuit of his goals, Popi's life took an unexpected turn. He met Laura, a wonderful young woman who shared his passion for debate and upholding social values.

Their connection was a testament to the fate of life, where sometimes, amidst the chaos, one can find a sense of solace and understanding in the presence of another. The beauty of their shared interests and values brought them together, offering a reprieve from the demands of their busy lives.

Laura's presence in Popi's life was like a breath of fresh air, providing balance and companionship. Their shared commitment to debate and social values created a strong bond, reminding them that meaningful connections could be forged even amidst the most challenging times.

Laura's arrival brought a sense of joy and understanding to Popi's life, proving that love and connection could thrive amidst the demands of academic pursuits and business ventures.

Their relationship reminded them that as important as individual goals and achievements were, the support and companionship of a kindred spirit could be a source of strength and inspiration. It was a testament to the power of love and shared values to bring balance and fulfillment to one's life.

Popi and Laura's significant relationship faced its share of challenges. Their unwavering commitments to their studies and volunteer activities meant they often had to navigate a complex juggling act to find quality time for each other.

Their academic pursuits and volunteer work demanded much of their time and attention. They were both driven individuals who understood the importance of their commitments.

Popi: A Rising Tide

However, this shared understanding made their relationship all the more special. They recognized in each other kindred spirits equally passionate about positively impacting the world.

Despite their busy lives, Popi and Laura were determined to make their relationship thrive. Their love and shared values were like a compass guiding them through the busyness of their lives. They knew that their connection was worth the effort and sacrifices.

They mutually decided to reprioritize their schedules to create more time for each other. This meant carving out moments from their limited free time, even if it meant reducing their time with friends and loved ones. This choice underscored the depth of their commitment to each other and the significance of their relationship in their lives.

Their decision to reallocate their time reflected the age-old saying, "Where there's a will, there's a way." It emphasized that when something truly matters, people find a way to make it work, even in the face of challenges and constraints.

Popi and Laura's relationship symbolized their shared determination and mutual support. Their bond provided a source of comfort and joy and encouraged them to excel in their respective endeavours. It was a reminder that love and shared values could serve as powerful motivators to overcome obstacles and thrive amid demanding schedules.

Popi and Laura's relationship exemplified the transformative power of love and companionship as they navigated their busy lives. It was a story of two individuals who found strength, inspiration, and balance in each other's presence while pursuing their individual goals and collective growth.

In the first few months of their relationship, Popi and Laura managed to strike a balance in their busy lives, stabilizing their academics, work, and social interactions. Their love was a source of inspiration, enabling them to excel in their pursuits while nurturing their connection.

However, as time passed, a new challenge emerged in their relationship. Unapologetically passionate about her conservative beliefs, Laura started engaging in controversial conversations with a rhetoric that some found offensive. This shift in her approach became a concern for Popi, who believed in the importance of free speech but felt that Laura might have been taking it a little too far.

The clash between their values and approaches was challenging. Popi found himself in a position where he needed to step in and defend Laura or diffuse situations to prevent her from facing trouble with the school or the community. While he appreciated her passion and admired her for speaking her mind, it was becoming an increasingly annoying task for him.

Laura, to her credit, acknowledged that, at times, her strong beliefs got the better of her, causing her to use rhetoric that could be offensive. She recognized Popi's efforts to protect her and was grateful for his support. Popi, however, used the opportunity to remind her of an important lesson – that one should learn to tame their language if they can't tame their opinions.

This advice emphasized the importance of temperance and self-control. Popi's suggestion to Laura was a reminder that while

Popi: A Rising Tide

free speech was a cherished value, it was equally important to exercise it responsibly and consider others' feelings and sensitivities.

Their exchange highlighted the complexities of a relationship in which two individuals held strong beliefs and values. It was a reminder that love and understanding require shared values and the willingness to grow and learn from one another. Popi and Laura's relationship was evolving, and it was a testament to their mutual desire for personal and collective growth.

Popi's sophomore year, which had begun with a mix of challenges, took an unexpected turn as the year unfolded. While he had successfully navigated the demands of his academic pursuits, his thriving tour company, and his relationship with Laura, it became increasingly apparent that maintaining this delicate balance was taking a toll.

The strain on their relationship became palpable as the semester progressed. Popi, inadvertently caught up in the whirlwind of his commitments, became increasingly withdrawn. He didn't intend for it to happen. Still, the pressures from his various responsibilities had an unintended consequence on his connection with Laura.

On the other hand, Laura interpreted Popi's distance as a sign of indifference. Feeling disconnected and craving emotional intimacy, she was drawn to another guy with whom she believed she had a better connection. In a moment of emotional confusion, she decided to end her relationship with Popi, thinking it was the right choice for her at the time.

The breakup was a significant blow to Popi. This had been his first serious relationship, and the abrupt end of it left him feeling emotionally crushed. The pain of losing someone he had cared deeply for weighed heavily on his heart, and he was left grappling with a sense of loss and vulnerability.

After this emotional upheaval, Popi vowed not to enter another relationship. He chose to channel his focus entirely on his work and hobbies. This decision reflected a desire for self-discovery and healing. It was a period of introspection and growth, marked by a commitment to personal development and self-care.

This phase of his life was reminiscent of Marcus Aurelius's ancient wisdom, which encouraged individuals to self-reflect and seek resilience during adversity. Popi's choice to prioritize his aspirations and passions was a form of self-preservation, a way to regain balance and clarity.

While the ending of his relationship with Laura was a painful chapter in his life, it also marked the beginning of a new phase. It was a time for Popi to rediscover himself, to rebuild and renew his sense of purpose. The challenges and heartbreak he experienced became the crucible in which his resilience and determination were forged, setting the stage for personal growth and self-discovery in the chapters ahead.

Graduation Time

As the end of his junior year approached, Popi had a surprise in store for his parents, leaving them both delighted and amazed. With pride and accomplishment, he sat them down and announced that he would be graduating from university. Their initial astonishment was quickly replaced with a profound sense of joy, for they could see the unwavering determination and hard work that had led him to this moment.

Popi had not only met but exceeded his graduation requirements, having pursued a double major in economics and political science. It was a testament to his dedication and commitment to his studies. His academic journey, marked by countless hours of research, study sessions, and intellectual exploration, had reached a fulfilling conclusion.

But Popi's achievements extended far beyond his academic pursuits. At university, he embarked on the entrepreneurial journey of starting and running a successful tour company, Popi Tours. This endeavour provided financial stability and enriched his life with valuable experiences.

In addition to his business ventures, Popi had dedicated himself to improving the social dynamics of various social clubs within the university. He recognized the importance of fostering a sense of community and inclusivity, and his efforts profoundly impacted the clubs and the individuals involved.

Popi's influence didn't stop there. He actively shaped the

university's governance and administration, and his ideas and contributions left an indelible mark on the institution's operations. Popi's dedication to the university and the welfare of its students transformed him into a respected figure who embodied the spirit of leadership and positive change.

However, perhaps the most significant impact was Popi's role in society. He had become a beacon of hope, not just within the university but in the broader community. His commitment to his values, passion for freedom of speech and choice, and dedication to making Canada a better place for all its residents had made him a revered figure.

It was as if Popi had done it all. It was a remarkable journey that echoed the power of individual choice, responsibility, and hard work. Popi's journey was a testament to the idea that individuals could achieve extraordinary things with unwavering determination and a clear sense of purpose.

As he stood on the precipice of graduation, it was evident that this was just the beginning of his journey. Popi's life had been a testament to the power of resilience and a reminder that there were no limits to what one could achieve with dedication, commitment, and a deep-rooted sense of purpose. Like any wise parent, his parents could only look upon their son's accomplishments with pride, knowing he was destined for greatness.

Following the end of his first serious relationship, some onlookers might have assumed that Popi was experiencing loneliness. However, in his chosen solitude, he was thriving in his unique way. Popi's post-relationship journey was characterized by a dedicated focus on increasing his value and striving for accomplishments that would bolster his sense of pride.

Ironically, while he had become everybody's friend and a pillar of support for many, only a few truly reciprocated the same level of friendship. Popi's nature was such that he enjoyed keeping to himself, finding solace in solitude, and using the time to delve deeper into learning about the world.

He adopted an observer's perspective, closely scrutinizing the ever-changing landscape of events and ideas unfolding around him. This penchant for observing and learning made him a more informed and engaged citizen who understood the value of knowledge and its power in shaping a better world.

Popi's path was reminiscent of the age-old saying, "He who knows others is wise; he who knows himself is enlightened." In his solitude, he found the opportunity to know himself honestly, discovering his strengths, values, and the importance of continuous self-improvement. His journey was a testament to the belief that, at times, the most profound growth occurs when one steps back from the world's noise to reflect and refine one's character.

Despite lacking a close-knit circle of friends, Popi's life was far from void. He was surrounded by knowledge, immersed in self-improvement, and committed to becoming a more informed and engaged citizen. His journey was one of self-discovery, personal growth, and a profound sense of fulfillment that came from learning, observing, and understanding the complexities of the world around him.

Popi's graduation was a celebration that extended far beyond the walls of his family home. It was an occasion that resonated throughout his entire community. The achievements he had amassed during his university journey had not gone unnoticed, and his impact reached far and wide.

As he walked across the stage to receive his degree, the applause and cheers that filled the auditorium were a testament to his community's collective pride and admiration. They had witnessed his unwavering dedication, hard work, and positive influence on those around him.

Popi's journey had been one of personal growth and accomplishment and a shining example of the potential within each individual to make a meaningful impact in their community. His graduation was a moment of collective celebration, a reminder that one person's success could inspire and uplift a community.

The joy reverberating through his community that day was like a harmonious symphony, echoing the spirit of unity and shared pride. Popi's achievements had become a source of inspiration and a symbol of the possibilities that lay before them all.

In the words of Marcus Aurelius, "The happiness of your life depends upon the quality of your thoughts." Popi's accomplishments and graduation celebration were a testament to the quality of his thoughts, his commitment to personal growth, and his positive impact on those around him.

His community's celebration was not just a recognition of his achievements but a collective acknowledgment of the potential that resided within each of them. It served as a reminder that, with dedication, hard work, and a sense of purpose, individuals

Popi: A Rising Tide

could achieve great things and, in doing so, inspire and uplift their entire community. Popi's graduation was a testament to the power of individual accomplishment and its ripple effect on the world.

After his graduation and the community's celebration of his achievements, Popi made a significant and life-altering decision. He chose to sell his successful tour company and bid farewell to life in the small city that had been his home since birth. With a steadfast determination to pursue a new path, he set his sights on the capital, Ottawa, where he aimed to embark on a political career.

His decision to leave behind the business he had built and the familiar surroundings of his small city was not made lightly. It was a bold step that echoed the saying, "A ship is safe in the harbour, but that's not what ships are for." Popi was ready to venture into uncharted waters, eager to use his knowledge, passion, and dedication to make a difference on a larger scale.

Ottawa, the political heart of Canada, held the promise of opportunities to effect meaningful change and contribute to the betterment of his country. Popi's decision to enter the world of politics was rooted in a desire to apply the principles of freedom, choice, and conscience to the decision-making processes that shaped the nation.

Popi's choice to pursue a political career manifested his belief in these principles and his commitment to champion them.

Popi's journey was a testament to the idea that one person's dedication and commitment could resonate nationally, fostering a sense of hope and optimism for the future.

The decision to sell his company, leave behind the comforts of his small city, and venture into the world of politics was not the end of Popi's remarkable journey. It was, in fact, just the beginning of a new chapter filled with challenges, opportunities, and the potential to profoundly impact his nation's political landscape.

The decision to embark on a political career in Ottawa had been made, and Popi's determination was unwavering. However, this decision brought about a deep divide within his family, most notably with his mother, who was adamantly opposed to the idea.

The clash of wills reached an explosive point as strong convictions and differing visions for Popi's future collided. His mother, concerned about his well-being and safety, had vehemently expressed her fears and reservations. Still, Popi had already made up his mind.

Amid the heated exchange, it became evident that Popi's resolve was unshakeable. His father, observing the impassioned argument between his wife and son, recognized that there was nothing he could say or do to change Popi's mind. The die had been cast, and the path toward a political career had been chosen.

The conflict within the family mirrored the complexities of pursuing a personal calling that might involve significant risks and challenges. It was a reminder that there could be opposition and sacrifices in pursuing one's dreams and convictions, especially when the path chosen was unconventional.

Popi's journey to Ottawa would be a testament to his

Popi: A Rising Tide

unwavering commitment to his beliefs and the courage to follow his chosen path, even in the face of familial opposition. The clash of perspectives within his family served as a reminder that personal growth and change often required navigating uncomfortable and challenging moments, which, in the end, were catalysts for personal development and resilience.

As Popi prepared to embark on his journey to Ottawa and his father, Mr. Peters, attempted to support his son's decision, he felt compelled to share a deeply personal matter. Mr. Peters had been recently diagnosed with Parkinson's disease, a profound revelation that he hadn't disclosed to anyone, including his wife, Mrs. Peters.

In opening up about his health condition to Popi, Mr. Peters did not intend to burden his son with guilt or concern. Instead, he wished to underscore a poignant lesson about life's challenges and the need to summon the courage to move forward, even in the face of adversity.

This revelation was a reminder of the wisdom encapsulated in the saying, "Life is 10% what happens to us and 90% how we react to it." Mr. Peters' diagnosis powerfully illustrated life's unexpected obstacles and the importance of resilience and determination in overcoming them.

The shared moment between father and son allowed Mr. Peters to emphasize that challenges, although daunting, could be met with courage and a positive outlook. It was a lesson in facing adversity head-on and finding the strength to continue moving forward despite the hurdles life may place in one's path.

The heart-to-heart conversation between father and son

became a poignant reminder that life was a journey filled with ups and downs. The character and determination of individuals like Popi defined how they navigated those twists and turns. Mr. Peters' courage in the face of a challenging diagnosis mirrored the same courage he saw in his son as he embarked on his political journey.

This intimate and heartfelt exchange served as a bond between father and son, reinforcing the idea that challenges could be met with resilience and the unwavering belief that one could overcome them. It was a moment of shared strength and a reminder that there was always a path forward, no matter the obstacles life presented.

With the weight of his father's recent Parkinson's diagnosis on his mind, Popi grappled with the idea that perhaps his decision to move away to Ottawa was not as wise as he had initially thought. The sense of responsibility toward his family, especially his father, weighed heavily on him. He felt a strong urge to be there for his father, to navigate the challenges and uncertainties of the disease together.

However, amid these conflicted emotions, Mr. Peters displayed a remarkable depth of understanding and faith in his son. He insisted that Popi proceed with his plans and give his best shot at life. He recognized the intelligence and character he had instilled in Popi and had complete confidence in his son's ability to make wise decisions.

Mr. Peters' concern was not rooted in Popi's ability to make good choices but rather in the fear that his passionate and principled nature might lead him into confrontations that could potentially harm his personal and professional life. This

Popi: A Rising Tide

reflected a father's unwavering love and support, always ready to offer the best advice to help his son navigate life's challenges.

In this father-son dynamic, a profound lesson emerged—that the support and encouragement of loved ones could anchor one's life, providing the strength and confidence needed to pursue one's dreams. While Popi may have contemplated staying close to his family in a time of need, he realized that the best way to honour his father's trust and belief in him was to continue on his chosen path, striving to impact the world positively.

The conversation between father and son underscored the value of family bonds, trust, and the understanding that one's pursuit of personal dreams could coexist with the responsibilities and love shared within a family. It was a poignant reminder that, in the face of life's challenges, the support and wisdom of family could serve as a guiding light, helping individuals spread their wings and achieve their goals.

After several days of not seeing his mother following their heated argument, Popi noticed a change in her demeanour when she returned home. She had seemingly softened her stance and expressed a different sentiment. She wished him the best and, with a hint of concern, begged him to consider returning home if he ever felt the slightest adversity in the political arena.

In a heartfelt conversation, his mother opened up about her feelings, revealing her deep love and concern for her son. She conveyed her unwavering trust in him and immense pride in his accomplishments. Her support for his goals remained steadfast. Still, as any loving mother would, she couldn't help but worry about the potential challenges and adversities her son might face in politics.

Her plea for him to take good care of himself was a testament to the profound connection between a mother and her child. It echoed the saying, "A mother's love knows no bounds," highlighting the unconditional love and concern that a mother feels for her child, regardless of age or accomplishments.

The exchange between mother and son became a poignant reminder of the importance of familial bonds and parents' enduring love for their children. It was a heartfelt moment in which Popi's mother acknowledged her son's independence and strength while expressing her hope that he would always remain safe and well.

While his mother's concerns naturally expressed love and care, Popi's resolve remained resolute. He understood the complexities and challenges that lay ahead in his political career. Still, he was prepared to face them with determination and the lessons of wisdom and support imparted by his family.

The conversation with his mother reminded him of the importance of staying grounded, maintaining a solid connection with one's roots, and understanding that the support and love of family would always be a source of strength and encouragement, even in the most challenging times.

Settling in the Big City

Settling into Ottawa was proving to be a formidable challenge for Popi. The transition from his smaller, familiar hometown to the bustling metropolis of Ottawa was a significant adjustment. The city's size and activity level were entirely different, and it felt like stepping into a whole new world.

However, Popi's determination and adaptability shone through as he endeavoured to find footing in this new environment. He recognized that navigating the complex landscape of a bustling city like Ottawa required resilience and resourcefulness, qualities he had honed during his academic journey and community work.

A smooth sea never made a skilled sailor, and Popi was determined to face the challenges head-on. He knew the trials he encountered in Ottawa would ultimately contribute to his growth and development.

Despite the initial difficulties, Popi remained committed to doing his best. He understood that, like any new endeavour, there would be a period of adjustment and learning. His resolve to adapt and thrive in Ottawa reflected his unwavering dedication to his chosen path in politics and his commitment to positively impacting the world.

As he continued to navigate the city's bustling streets, the experiences he encountered would serve as valuable lessons, enriching his journey and helping him become a more informed and capable citizen. Ottawa's challenges were significant, but so was Popi's determination to rise to them, driven by his passion and the pursuit of his dreams.

In his efforts to adapt to life in the bustling city of Ottawa, Popi reached out to his former boss and the Member of Parliament (MP) from his hometown, hoping to establish a connection that would help him start his political career. However, he quickly realized that life in the city was markedly different from the close-knit community he had grown accustomed to.

The city presented a dynamic and fast-paced environment, starkly contrasting with the tight-knit and supportive community he had left behind. The complexities of urban living, the intricacies of city politics, and the diverse array of individuals he encountered were all new and challenging aspects of life in Ottawa.

The move to Ottawa introduced Popi to an entirely new set of circumstances, making it necessary to adapt and learn quickly to thrive in this dynamic urban setting.

Despite the initial differences, Popi remained steadfast in his commitment to making a meaningful political impact. He recognized that his challenges were part of the journey and that his ability to adapt and learn would be crucial to his success.

While life in the city differed from what he had known, Popi's unwavering determination and the wisdom he had gained from his upbringing and past experiences would continue to guide him on his path, even in this new and bustling environment.

Having sold his successful touring company, Popi was in a

Popi: A Rising Tide

fortunate financial position, and money was not an immediate concern. However, his primary goal in Ottawa was establishing himself in the political arena and making a meaningful impact. He recognized that securing a job on the political scene was crucial to achieving this.

Popi's financial stability allowed him to pursue his passion without the immediate pressure of financial burdens. This financial security was a testament to his dedication and hard work, allowing him to focus on his political aspirations.

However, he knew that making a mark in politics required more than financial resources; it demanded active involvement, dedication, and a strong presence within the political community. Securing a job in politics would enable him to gain the experience and connections needed to contribute effectively to the political landscape.

Popi's commitment to his chosen path in politics reflected his unwavering determination to be an agent of change and advocate for freedom of speech, choice, and conscience. His financial stability gave him the freedom to pursue this path. At the same time, his determination and passion drove him to make a lasting impact on the world of politics in Ottawa.

After several weeks of navigating Ottawa's intricate political landscape, Popi's determination and commitment to making a meaningful impact began to gain recognition. His reputation as an individual who stood up for justice and fairness, exemplified in his advocacy for the international student, had spread in some circles throughout the city.

During this time, Popi was approached by a man and a woman

who recognized his qualities as a moral and compassionate advocate. They offered him help as city natives in navigating the complexities of the city and the political atmosphere. In return, they pled for assistance in addressing a pressing matter: dealing with their former boss, who had allegedly fired the young man for his sexual orientation and the young woman for refusing to engage in inappropriate actions with him.

The request for Popi's assistance was a testament to his growing influence and reputation among a specific demographic. It reflected the ripple effect that his advocacy and commitment to justice had created within the community he served. People turned to him for his knowledge of Canada and economics, unwavering principles, and dedication to upholding what is right.

The situation also highlighted the interconnectedness of personal values and professional opportunities. Popi's commitment to fairness, justice, and advocacy not only made him a respected figure in his hometown but also led to opportunities for him to address critical issues and help those in need.

As he considered this new challenge, Popi realized that his journey in Ottawa was taking him down an unexpected but meaningful path. This path would allow him to continue making a positive impact in politics while advocating for justice and equality in his new community.

Popi found himself at a crossroads, facing a decision that carried significantly higher stakes than any he had encountered before. While daunting, the challenges of defending the international student were relatively contained within the academic sphere. However, the task before him now involved taking on a powerful politician in a new city, where he had limited familiarity with the political landscape and the intricacies of city politics.

The man and woman who sought his assistance recognized the gravity of the situation and understood Popi's hesitancy. They emphasized the magnitude of the risks involved, including the potential impact on his political career and personal life. They encouraged him to weigh the consequences carefully.

However, they also appealed to Popi's deeply held beliefs and principles, reminding him of the values he had consistently championed, such as freedom and justice. They emphasized that if he genuinely believed in these principles, the potential risks to his political career could not be compared to the greater good of standing up against injustice.

The decision was not taken lightly, as Popi deliberated on the implications and ramifications of getting involved in such a high-stakes situation. He knew this choice could define his political career and even impact his life beyond politics.

In this pivotal moment, Popi's inner moral compass and dedication to the principles he held dear would guide him in making a choice that aligned with his unwavering commitment to justice and the values he had always advocated for.

Popi's decision to get to know Donna and Kyle personally before committing to the challenging task they presented was a significant gesture of trust and empathy. It marked a turning point for them, as they had faced outright rejection and dismissal when seeking assistance from others.

The willingness to establish a personal connection with Donna and Kyle demonstrated Popi's genuine concern for their well-being and his commitment to understanding their story and motivations. It was a reminder of the proverb "Walk a mile in someone else's shoes," which encapsulates the importance of empathy and understanding when addressing complex and sensitive issues.

In a world where many people might pay no heed to the problems of others, Popi's approach was a beacon of compassion and solidarity. His desire to forge a personal connection before embarking on a challenging endeavour reflected his belief in the power of genuine relationships and the importance of working together to address injustice.

As they began sharing their stories and experiences, Popi, Donna, and Kyle developed a bond of trust and understanding. This connection would serve as a strong foundation for the arduous journey they were about to undertake, demonstrating the power of personal connections in the face of adversity and injustice.

Donna's multicultural upbringing had instilled in her a deep appreciation for the diverse fabric of Canadian society. Her family's journey from Italy to Montreal was a testament to the nation's identity as a land of immigrants. This experience allowed her to grow up with a keen awareness of different cultures and languages, giving her a unique perspective on the values of inclusivity and acceptance.

Her linguistic prowess reflected Canada's bilingual nature, with French and English being official languages. Donna's fluency in Italian added an additional layer to her cultural tapestry, and she

Popi: A Rising Tide

cherished the ability to communicate in multiple languages. Her family's heritage was an essential part of her identity, and she proudly carried forward the traditions and values of her Italian roots.

Donna's temperament was a study in contrasts. While she exuded cheerfulness and warmth in her everyday interactions, her passionate side emerged when she delved into debates and discussions close to her heart. It was in these moments that her assertiveness shone through. Still, she did so with a degree of tact, ensuring that her arguments were always balanced and respectful.

One of Donna's distinguishing qualities was her aversion to confrontation. She was acutely aware of the potential negative consequences of conflicts. She always tried to steer clear of situations that might lead to harm or misunderstandings. This demonstrated her prudence and a strong sense of self-preservation.

Donna's love for travel was an extension of her fascination with Canada. Exploring her vast and beautiful homeland had become a passion. She believed that the country's landscapes and natural wonders were a gift to be shared with the rest of the world. Her dream of establishing a travel and tour guide company aimed to do just that—introduce tourists to the breathtaking beauty of Canada, from its pristine forests and majestic mountains to its serene lakes and vibrant cities.

Despite being only a year younger than Popi, Donna's wisdom and balanced perspective often made her seem beyond her years. When discussing her passions or advocating for causes close to her heart, she demonstrated a remarkable understanding and an ability to articulate her views eloquently.

In Popi, she found a kindred spirit who shared her passion for promoting Canada's beauty and was willing to champion her vision. Their shared enthusiasm and purpose would become a driving force as they navigated the challenges ahead in their mission to bring change and justice to the City of Ottawa.

Kyle's journey to self-acceptance was a personal and profound one. While he had recently come out as gay to Donna, there had been long-standing rumours about his sexuality circulating within his social circles. Even in a liberal city like Ottawa, the stigma and discrimination associated with one's sexual orientation could still manifest in subtle and hurtful ways. The unverified reports suggested that when his boss learned of his sexuality, he reacted with disgust and promptly sought a pretext to terminate Kyle's employment.

Despite the challenges he faced, Kyle was a charismatic and warm-hearted individual. His upbeat and often humorous demeanour endeared him to others, making him a pleasure to be around. Underneath his cheerful exterior, he was a kind and considerate person who had always felt a sense of loneliness in his life. Meeting Donna had been a turning point, and their friendship had grown over five years, evolving into a deep and meaningful connection.

Kyle had recently taken a significant step by moving out of his parents' home. His reluctance to discuss his relationship with his parents hinted at personal struggles and a complex family dynamic. Being sensitive to his feelings, Donna chose not to probe further into this matter. She understood the importance of respecting Kyle's boundaries and allowing him the space to

Popi: A Rising Tide
open up when he was ready.

Kyle's eyes lit up enthusiastically when the conversation shifted to his hobbies and passions. He had an immense love for the arts in all its forms, from paintings and sculptures to the intricate world of architecture. His dream was to pursue a formal education in architecture, but the weight of his challenges made it seem like an insurmountable goal. However, he found fulfillment in his work in politics, striving to positively impact his community while nurturing a love for the arts that continued to inspire and uplift him.

Kyle's story was a testament to the strength and resilience of the human spirit. His friendship with Donna was a source of support and companionship that enriched both their lives. Together, they embarked on a journey that would demand courage and determination as they confronted the injustices and obstacles that awaited them in the city of Ottawa.

Popi's response to Donna and Kyle's stories demonstrated his genuine empathy and commitment to approaching their situation with maturity and responsibility. He recognized their challenges and appreciated their resilience in the face of adversity. Their limited budget and personal struggles didn't deter him from wanting to help but also made him aware of the need to find the best possible course of action.

Rather than making promises he couldn't guarantee, Popi chose to take a measured approach. He was determined to conduct thorough research and explore the most effective way forward, understanding that the stakes were higher in this case than in his previous endeavours. This decision reflected the wisdom of the proverb "Measure twice, cut once," emphasizing the importance of careful planning and consideration before taking action.

Popi's commitment to approaching conflict with maturity and thoughtful consideration indicated his growth and evolution as a responsible advocate for justice and fairness. It also underscored his dedication to making a positive impact in the city of Ottawa, even if it meant navigating complex and potentially challenging situations.

The decision to explore the city together allowed Popi to immerse himself in Ottawa, learn about its intricacies, and become familiar with its diverse community. Popi's curiosity knew no bounds, as he wanted to know every nook and cranny of the city, its people, and all the experiences it had to offer newcomers like him.

Their shared adventure through the city was marked by a remarkable openness and camaraderie, as if they had been friends for years. The connection they formed throughout that evening was a testament to the power of human connection and the ability to find joy and companionship even in the face of life's challenges.

The evening of exploration and enjoyment served as a welcome distraction from their struggles, allowing them to temporarily set aside their worries and savour the moment. It was a reminder of the importance of finding joy in life's simple pleasures and embracing the bonds of friendship as they navigated the complexities of their new lives in Ottawa.

As the night went on, Kyle couldn't help but notice that Donna and Popi were growing increasingly comfortable and close with each other. It was only their first night out together, yet their connection seemed to deepen rapidly. The bond they were forming was undeniably intense, leaving Kyle somewhat uneasy.

Despite their initial camaraderie, the dynamic between Donna and Popi was taking on a different hue. Their connection appeared to be evolving into something more profound, and this transformation didn't go unnoticed by Kyle. While he valued their friendship and Donna's presence in his life, he grappled with a sense of displacement as the interactions between Popi and Donna grew increasingly intimate.

The situation left Kyle in a state of uncertainty. He couldn't help but wonder how these changing dynamics might impact his relationship with Donna. He questioned whether this closeness between her and Popi would alter their friendship and what it might mean for their future interactions. For Kyle, this new dimension added an unexpected layer of complexity to their already intricate relationship.

Kyle found himself navigating uncharted waters, uncertain where this evolving connection between Donna and Popi might lead.

Getting Down to Business

Since his arrival in Ottawa, Popi had been diligently working from his modest apartment. One evening, he invited Donna and Kyle to brainstorm a strategy to address their case. Both had faced unjust dismissals—Donna for rejecting her boss's inappropriate advances and Kyle due to his sexual orientation. Popi knew this delicate situation required more than just legal maneuvering; it needed compassion, understanding, and a clear, strategic plan.

As Donna and Kyle entered his cozy apartment, the aroma of freshly brewed coffee greeted them. Popi gestured for them to sit at the round wooden table in the centre of the room, its surface cluttered with legal pads, pens, and a stack of relevant documents.

"Thank you both for coming," Popi began, offering each a cup of coffee. "I know this situation has been incredibly tough on you both, and I want to ensure we handle it with the care and precision it deserves."

Donna sighed, her frustration evident. "It's just so infuriating, Popi. I stood up for myself, and instead of being supported, I got punished."

Kyle nodded in agreement. "And for me, it's as if my identity is a crime. It's dehumanizing."

Popi leaned forward, his eyes filled with empathy. "I

understand, and your feelings are valid. The old saying goes, 'A smooth sea never made a skilled sailor.' We are navigating rough waters, but we can chart a course towards justice together."

He took a deep breath and began outlining their plan. "First, we need to gather all the evidence—every email, every message, every detail that can support your claims. Donna, your rejection of his advances needs to be documented clearly. Kyle, we need to highlight how your dismissal was a direct consequence of your sexual orientation. This documentation is the foundation of our case."

Donna nodded, her resolve strengthening. "I've kept all the messages. I knew something like this might happen."

"Good," Popi replied. "Next, we must define our position clearly and understand the Councillor's standpoint, no matter how unjust it seems. It's like the old proverb, 'Know thine enemy and know thyself.' We must anticipate his defences and be prepared."

Kyle frowned, still visibly upset. "How do we compromise with someone who sees us as less than human?"

Popi's tone was compassionate but firm. "Compromise doesn't mean surrender. It's about finding a middle ground where we can push our case forward. Suppose the Councillor sees that we understand his position, however flawed. In that case, it can disarm his aggression and open a door for negotiation. Remember, 'A gentle answer turns away wrath, but a harsh word stirs anger.' Our goal is to be strategic, not confrontational."

He paused, allowing his words to sink in. "Once we have our evidence and understand the other side, we approach the Councillor with our concerns, demonstrating our willingness to understand his position while presenting our case. This shows we are not just there to fight but to seek justice through dialogue. It's crucial to remember that 'Patience and perseverance have a magical effect before which difficulties disappear and obstacles vanish.'"

Kyle leaned back, a small smile forming. "It's a long road, but it's worth it."

Popi nodded. "Indeed, it is. 'The journey of a thousand miles begins with one step.' And this is our first step. Together, we will make a difference. We will hold him accountable, not just for you but for everyone who has faced such injustice."

The three spent the rest of the evening planning; their hearts united in their quest for justice. Though small and cluttered, Popi's apartment became a haven of hope and determination. They knew the road ahead was fraught with challenges, but with each other's support and a clear plan, they were ready to face whatever came their way.

There were disagreements, but Popi was convincing in his rationale. Donna and Kyle found themselves unable to keep fighting his logic.

Popi leaned back, his eyes reflecting the earnestness of his words. "I understand this is not easy to accept, but consider this: if we go in guns blazing, we risk escalating the conflict without achieving our goals. We need to be like the willow tree, which bends with the storm and survives, rather than the oak, which stands rigid and breaks."

Donna crossed her arms, her frustration still simmering beneath the surface. "It's just hard to compromise when we know we're in the right."

Popi nodded sympathetically. "I know, Donna. But remember, 'He who fights and runs away lives to fight another day.' We must choose our battles wisely. By approaching this with a cool head and a clear strategy, we stand a better chance of winning not just this battle, but the war."

Kyle leaned forward, his brow furrowed. "But what if they still refuse to listen, even after we present our case calmly and logically?"

"That's when we turn up the heat," Popi replied. "If he doesn't listen to reason, we escalate our efforts. We bring in the media, gather public support, and apply legal pressure. But we must first exhaust all peaceful avenues. 'In the confrontation between the stream and the rock, the stream always wins—not through strength, but by perseverance.'"

Donna sighed, but the fire in her eyes began to dim. "I guess it's just hard to swallow my pride and not lash out," she said.

Popi smiled gently. "Pride can be a formidable opponent, but humility often opens doors that pride would slam shut. 'Soft words butter no parsnips,' as the old saying goes, but in our case, soft words can open up conversations that rigid demands would close."

Kyle nodded slowly. "Alright, Popi. We'll follow your lead. But if this doesn't work, we won't back down."

Popi placed a reassuring hand on Kyle's shoulder. "Agreed. This is just the beginning. Our goal is justice, and we will pursue it with relentless determination. 'Rome wasn't built in a day,' and our journey for justice won't be won overnight. But together, we will see it through."

Donna uncrossed her arms, a reluctant but hopeful smile forming on her lips. "Okay, Popi. Let's do this your way."

Popi's eyes sparkled with gratitude. "Thank you, both of you. We are stronger together. Now, let's get to work and show them that our resolve is unbreakable."

As they delved back into their planning, the atmosphere in Popi's apartment shifted from one of tension to one of united purpose. Despite their initial disagreements, Donna and Kyle couldn't deny the sense in Popi's words. With renewed determination, they prepared to face the challenges ahead, ready to fight for justice with the wisdom of strategy and the power of perseverance.

Popi wanted to think long-term, particularly in dealing with such a complicated issue, as he feared confrontation might easily blow things out of proportion.

"Donna, Kyle," Popi began, his voice calm and measured, "I know the urge to confront this head-on is strong, but we must consider the bigger picture. A direct attack could escalate things beyond our control, like striking a hornet's nest."

Donna sighed, still visibly frustrated. "So, what do you suggest?

Popi: A Rising Tide

We just sit back and let them walk all over us?"

"Not at all," Popi reassured her. "We need to approach this strategically, like a game of chess. We need to think several moves ahead. 'Slow and steady wins the race,' remember? We need to build our case methodically and gather irrefutable evidence."

Kyle interjected, his tone skeptical. "But what if he continues to abuse his power while we're playing the long game?"

Popi leaned forward, his gaze intent. "That's where our strength lies. We document everything meticulously—every inappropriate remark, every unjust action. We gather witnesses and build alliances. We become the stream that carves through rock, not by brute force but by persistent effort."

Donna's expression softened slightly. "And what if we still don't see results?"

Popi gave a small, encouraging smile. "Then we escalate, but not in anger. We escalate with purpose. We use the media to shine a light on the injustice. We rally public support. 'The pen is mightier than the sword,' and we must wield it wisely."

Kyle nodded, starting to see the wisdom in Popi's approach. "So, we bide our time, build our case, and strike when the moment is right?"

"Exactly," Popi confirmed. "Think of it as planting seeds. We nurture them patiently, and they will grow into a formidable force in time. Our goal is to create lasting change, which requires patience and strategy. 'Good things come to those who wait,' and our perseverance will pay off."

Donna took a deep breath, her shoulders relaxing. "Alright, Popi. We'll follow your lead. But we won't lose sight of the end goal."

Popi's smile widened with a hint of relief in his eyes. "Thank you, both of you. Together, we will navigate this storm and emerge stronger on the other side. Let's now take the first step of our thousand-mile journey."

With renewed determination, they turned their focus back to their plans, ready to tackle the injustice they faced with a combination of patience, strategy, and unwavering resolve.

Popi planned to make the city of Ottawa's Councillor aware of their motives as a courtesy call and to test the waters by seeking a collaborative way to address the issue.

"Here's what we're going to do," Popi began, leaning over the table where Donna and Kyle sat. "We'll start by reaching out to the Councillor's office. We'll present our concerns as a courtesy call, showing that we're open to collaboration rather than confrontation."

Donna raised an eyebrow. "Do you really think he'll listen to us?"

Popi nodded thoughtfully. "It's worth a shot. Sometimes, extending an olive branch can disarm an adversary. We'll express our commitment to resolving this matter amicably and see how they respond. 'A gentle word opens an iron gate.'"

Popi: A Rising Tide

Kyle looked skeptical but intrigued. "And if he doesn't respond positively?"

Popi's eyes twinkled with determination. "Then we'll have a clearer understanding of his stance, and we can adjust our strategy accordingly. It's like testing the waters before diving in. We gauge their willingness to cooperate and plan our next steps from there."

Donna leaned in, her curiosity piqued. "So, what's our first move?"

Popi pulled out a notebook and began jotting down points. "We draft a letter outlining our concerns and request a meeting with the Councillor. We'll emphasize our desire to find a collaborative solution in the letter. We highlight the broader implications of the issues at hand, making it clear that we're not just fighting for ourselves but for the principles of fairness and justice."

Kyle nodded slowly. "And during the meeting?"

Popi smiled. "During the meeting, we maintain a composed and respectful demeanour. We listen as much as we speak, showing we're open to dialogue. We express our concerns clearly, backed by the evidence we've gathered. We seek his input on how to address these issues constructively. 'Seek first to understand before you seek to be understood.'"

Donna's eyes lit up with a newfound determination. "And if he stonewalls us?"

Popi's expression grew serious. "If he stonewalls us, we regroup and prepare for the next phase. We document his lack of cooperation and use it to bolster our case when we escalate the matter. But we always start with the path of least resistance, giving them a chance to do the right thing."

Kyle cracked a small smile. "Alright, Popi. Let's see how they respond to a courtesy call. It's worth a shot."

Popi nodded, his eyes gleaming with hope. "Exactly. 'He who sows courtesy reaps friendship,' and perhaps this approach will pave the way for a more amicable resolution. Let's draft that letter and take our first step."

They all knew the road ahead wouldn't be easy, but they were ready to navigate it with patience, strategy, and a commitment to justice.

Donna and Kyle wanted blood, but Popi advised against that, knowing it would likely do more harm than good for everyone involved. He emphasized that accountability doesn't have to be about public humiliation; making the person genuinely sorry through other means could achieve the same result.

"Popi, this guy deserves to be dragged through the mud," Donna said, her voice shaking with anger. "He can't get away with this."

Kyle nodded in agreement. "Yeah, he needs to pay for what he did. People like him should be exposed."

Popi listened intently, then took a deep breath. "I understand your anger, and it's justified. But going after him and intending to destroy him will only escalate the situation and could backfire on us. 'An eye for an eye leaves the whole world blind.' We need to think long-term."

Donna folded her arms, her brow furrowed. "So, what do you suggest we do? Just let him off the hook?"

"Not at all," Popi replied calmly. "Accountability doesn't have to be about public humiliation. There are other ways to make someone truly sorry and to prevent them from repeating their mistakes. It's about transforming them, not destroying them."

Kyle looked puzzled. "How do we do that without making it public?"

Popi leaned forward, his eyes serious. "We aim for a resolution that forces him to confront his actions and their impact. We push for mandatory sensitivity training, community service, and a formal apology. I have a feeling that he won't go for any of that, but he would be willing to make amends another way without inviting the public. We make him see the error of his ways and take steps to change. 'A soft answer turns away wrath, but a harsh word stirs anger.' After all, he's a politician and definitely cares about his public image."

Donna sighed, her frustration still evident. "But what if he doesn't change? What if he just goes back to his old ways?"

Popi nodded. "It's possible, but at least we would have tried to resolve this constructively. If he refuses to change, then we have documented evidence of our attempts to work with him, which will strengthen our case if we need to escalate it. And remember, the goal is to create a safer, more respectful environment, not just to seek revenge."

Kyle glanced at Donna, then back at Popi. "So, we try this first, and if it doesn't work, we take stronger actions?"

Popi smiled. "Exactly. Remember that patience and perseverance have a magical effect before which difficulties disappear and obstacles vanish. We start with a measured approach, showing that we're reasonable and fair. It puts us in a stronger position morally and legally."

Donna nodded slowly, starting to see the wisdom in Popi's words. "Alright, Popi. We'll try it your way. But if he crosses the line again..."

Popi raised a hand, signalling his understanding. "If he crosses the line again, we'll be ready to take the next steps. But let's give him the chance to do the right thing first. Sometimes, the most effective change comes from within, not external pressure."

Kyle sighed, the tension easing slightly. "Alright. Let's draft that letter and make our case. We'll give him a chance to make amends, but we won't back down if he doesn't."

Popi nodded, a sense of resolve settling over the group. "Agreed. Let's move forward with a clear plan and a commitment to justice. 'For every action, there is an equal and opposite reaction.' Let's ensure our actions lead to positive, lasting change."

Together, they began to outline their approach, determined to seek accountability and transformation, not just retribution. The path ahead was uncertain, but with Popi's guidance, they felt a renewed sense of purpose and hope.

Popi: A Rising Tide

The plan became clear: gather all the information about the Councillor and collect testimonies from other support staff, both current and former. Once they had a solid case, they would present the evidence to the Councillor and ask him to make amends.

Popi explained, "First, we must gather every piece of information we can. Talk to current and former staff members and get their stories. We need to build a solid case."

Donna nodded. "We'll get statements and document everything. People need to know they're not alone in this."

Kyle added, "We'll ensure every piece of evidence is irrefutable. He won't be able to deny it."

Popi continued, "Once we have everything, we'll present it to him and give him a chance to make amends."

"If he refuses, we'll threaten to start a rumour worse than his known actions. With our evidence, it'll be easy for his voters to believe the fabricated rumours." Popi joked, adding an evil laugh.

Kyle laughed out loud, but Donna's eyes widened. "But what if he still refuses?"

"Then," Popi said firmly, "we take it to the next level. We attack his donors and inner circle, including the mayor, as enablers of homophobia and misogyny. We'll use the same strategy one girl unsuccessfully used against me to try to keep me from defending Ahmed, the international student, amid his impending expulsion and deportation. We'll make it clear that if they protect him, they're just as guilty."

Kyle looked skeptical. "And you think this will work?"

Popi nodded confidently. "I've done this before. When the university wanted to expel Ahmed, I gathered evidence, rallied support, and showed them that their actions would have severe consequences. They backed down. We can do the same here. With a proven track record, I'm sure the Councillor will throw in the towel long before we have to use this 'scorched earth' approach."

Donna smiled, a newfound hope in her eyes. "Alright, Popi. Let's do this. Let's make sure he knows we mean business."

Kyle agreed. "We'll follow your lead, Popi. Let's bring him down, but in a way that shows we're better than him."

Popi looked at both of them, feeling a sense of unity and determination. "Remember, our goal is to create a safer environment for everyone. We'll hold him accountable and show that justice can be served without resorting to the same tactics he uses. 'The pen is mightier than the sword,' and we'll prove it."

With that, they set to work, knowing that their plan was just and their cause righteous. The road ahead was daunting, but with careful planning and steadfast resolve, they were ready to face whatever came their way.

As the evening wore on, Popi's apartment became a hive of activity. The three friends were seated around the table, surrounded by papers, laptops, and empty coffee cups. The dim light cast shadows on their faces, highlighting the seriousness of their mission.

Popi took a deep breath and looked at Donna and Kyle. "We've got a solid plan. Now, we just need to execute it. Are you both ready?"

Donna nodded with determination in her eyes. "More than ready. This isn't just for us, but for everyone he's wronged. We have to make sure he can't hurt anyone else."

Kyle added, "Over the next week, we'll get the statements, gather the evidence, and present a united front. He won't know what hit him."

Popi smiled, feeling a deep sense of camaraderie. "Remember, it's not just about taking him down. It's about making sure justice is served in the right way. Accountability doesn't have to mean public humiliation. Sometimes, making someone truly understand their wrongs can be a more powerful form of justice."

Donna reached across the table and placed her hand on Popi's. "Thank you, Popi. For everything. You've given us hope."

Kyle mirrored the gesture, placing his hand on top of Donna's. "Yeah, thanks, Popi. We couldn't do this without you."

Feeling a swell of gratitude and responsibility, Popi placed his other hand on top of theirs. "We're in this together. We'll see it through, no matter what."

With their plan set and resolve firm, they began assigning tasks.

Donna would reach out to former staff members, using her network to gather testimonies. Kyle would compile and document all the evidence, ensuring everything was meticulously recorded. Popi would strategize the presentation and prepare for the meeting with the Councillor.

As they worked late into the night, the sound of typing, quiet discussions, and the occasional laugh filled the apartment. The weight of their mission was balanced by the solidarity they felt in working together. Popi's apartment, once a place of solitary work, had become a war room for justice.

By the time they wrapped up, midnight was calling. They were exhausted but resolute.

Popi stood up and stretched, looking at his friends with a tired but proud smile. "We've done good work tonight. Let's get some rest and pick this up tomorrow. We're on the right path."

Donna and Kyle nodded, gathering their things. As they left, there was a sense of unspoken understanding and commitment between them. They knew the road ahead would be challenging but were ready to face it together.

Popi took a moment to reflect as he closed the door behind them. This was more than a fight for justice—it was a testament to the power of unity, determination, and the belief that doing the right thing was always worth it. He knew that with Donna and Kyle by his side, they could achieve anything.

With a sense of calm and purpose, Popi finally allowed himself to rest, knowing that the next day was another step towards making things right. And as he drifted to sleep, he felt a

Popi: A Rising Tide
profound sense of hope for the future.

Making Amends

The next day dawned crisply, the sun casting golden rays through the window of Popi's modest apartment. He sat at his small wooden desk, the morning light illuminating his thoughtful expression. The room was quiet, save for the soft hum of the city waking up outside. Popi knew this day would mark the beginning of a critical mission.

Popi took a deep breath and muttered, "Today's the day. We set sail on this journey for justice." He liked to think of his tasks in nautical terms as if each endeavour was a voyage across uncertain seas. It grounded him, reminding him of the old wisdom that "smooth seas do not make skillful sailors."

His thoughts drifted to Donna. Her fierce determination and unwavering spirit had captivated him from the start. He couldn't help but hope that he might also win her heart by bringing justice to her. As he packed his bag with the necessary documents and his laptop, he allowed himself a moment of daydreaming. "If I do this right," he mused, "maybe I'll have the courage to ask her out. Perhaps a stroll by the Rideau Canal or a quiet dinner at that little Italian place she likes."

With resolve, Popi headed out. The city of Ottawa bustled around him, but his mind was sharp and focused. He had a plan, and today was the first step. He arrived at the City Hall, a stately building that seemed to loom over him, a reminder of the power structures he was about to challenge.

Popi: A Rising Tide

It was a bustling day at City Hall, the corridors teeming with staff and citizens, each absorbed in their own matters. Popi knew that seeing the Councillor without an appointment would be no small feat, but he was never one to shy away from a challenge. He approached the reception desk, a confident smile playing on his lips.

"Good morning," Popi greeted the receptionist warmly. "I'm here to deliver urgent legal documents to Councillor Whitmore."

The receptionist glanced up, her eyes skeptical. "Do you have an appointment?"

Popi shook his head, maintaining his composed demeanour. "No, but these documents are time-sensitive. They need to be addressed immediately."

She frowned slightly, clearly unconvinced. "We have a strict policy about appointments. Can you leave the documents with me, and I'll make sure they get to him?"

Popi leaned in slightly, lowering his voice to convey a sense of urgency. "I'm afraid that's not an option. These papers require the Councillor's immediate attention, and I was instructed to hand them over personally. It's a matter of legal importance."

He wasn't exactly lying; he was presenting himself as someone more entrenched in the legal community than he actually was. The receptionist hesitated, her gaze flicking to the busy office behind her.

"Alright," she said finally. "Wait here. I'll see if I can get you in.”

After several delays and much anticipation, Popi finally found himself seated across from Councillor Whitmore. The Councillor's office, lined with shelves of books and awards, exuded authority, but Popi remained undaunted. He introduced himself with a calm, yet firm demeanour.

"Good afternoon, Councillor Whitmore. My name is Paul Peters, and I'm here representing two former employees who are seriously considering legal action against you."

Whitmore's eyes widened in shock, his composed exterior momentarily cracking. Popi seized the opportunity to continue, knowing he had only a brief window to make his case. He had an elevator pitch meticulously planned, ready to deliver the essential points before he was potentially thrown out.

"I understand this may come as a surprise, Councillor," Popi began, maintaining steady eye contact. "But the actions taken against Donna Greco and Kyle McKenzie were unjust and seriously violated their rights. Donna was fired after refusing inappropriate advances from you, and Kyle was dismissed solely based on his sexual orientation. We have gathered substantial evidence supporting these claims."

To his surprise, Whitmore did not interrupt or dismiss him. Instead, the Councillor leaned forward, curiosity and concern etched on his face. "Go on," he urged, clearly wanting to hear more.

Popi took a deep breath and continued, his voice unwavering. "We're not here to seek revenge or public humiliation. What we want is accountability and a genuine effort to make amends. We believe in resolving this matter internally without escalating it to a legal battleground."

Whitmore's expression hardened slightly, a defensive wall beginning to form. "I should probably consult with my legal team about this."

Popi shook his head gently, his tone now tinged with caution. "Councillor, once the toothpaste is out of the tube, it's impossible to put it back inside. Seeking legal advice might only complicate things further and escalate the situation. Instead, I'm proposing a more collaborative approach."

Whitmore's gaze locked onto Popi's, a battle of wills playing out in the silent room. After a tense moment, he sighed and nodded. "Alright, I'm listening. What exactly are you proposing?"

Popi emphasized that he wasn't looking to embarrass the Councillor but wanted to secure some form of justice for Donna and Kyle, to soothe their hearts and let the matter rest. With the meticulously prepared documents in hand and the deal he offered on a ticking clock, the Councillor quickly described the negotiation as a shakedown. Popi resented the term but agreed to a financial settlement, ensuring that Donna and Kyle's grievances were acknowledged and compensated.

"You must understand," Popi said, his tone steady and compassionate, "we're not here to destroy you. We seek justice, not vengeance. Donna and Kyle deserve recognition for the wrongs they've endured. This settlement is a step towards healing."

The Councillor, beads of sweat forming on his forehead, reluctantly nodded. "I see your point, Mr. Peters. But what guarantees do I have that this matter won't resurface?"

Popi leaned in, his gaze unwavering. "If you ever engage in such behaviour again, Donna and Kyle will not hesitate to bring charges against you. This is your one chance to amend your ways and ensure no one else suffers the same fate."

The Councillor sighed deeply, the weight of the situation pressing down on him. "Alright, I'll agree to your terms. But I expect this matter to remain confidential."

Popi nodded. "Confidentiality is assured, provided you uphold your end of the bargain. Remember, accountability doesn't have to mean public humiliation. True justice is about learning from our mistakes and making genuine changes."

As an associate attempted to usher Popi out of the Councillor's office, the Councillor intervened firmly, stating it was a critical business meeting. Ignoring the awkwardness, the Councillor scribbled a number on a napkin and slid it across the desk to Popi. But Popi's expression hardened as he glanced at the figure; it was far too low.

"I'm sorry, but this won't suffice," Popi said evenly, his voice carrying a hint of steel. "Considering the implications if this were to go public, especially in today's political climate."

The Councillor's face paled slightly as he realized the seriousness of the situation. "I... I can offer more," he stammered nervously, reaching for another napkin to jot down a higher figure.

Popi: A Rising Tide

Popi nodded, his demeanour calm yet resolute. "Good. Let's resolve this properly to everyone's satisfaction."

After the financial matter was settled more appropriately, Popi leaned forward, his tone now advisory. "Additionally, I suggest you consider writing strong recommendation letters for Donna and Kyle in the future. It would go a long way in helping them secure more lucrative employment opportunities."

The Councillor, visibly shaken by the day's events, nodded in agreement. "Yes, of course. I'll make sure they have my support."

"And regarding your staff," Popi continued, his voice gentle but firm, "it would be wise to mend any bridges you may have burned. Your actions are under scrutiny now, and reconciliation could prevent further issues."

The Councillor exhaled heavily, the weight of Popi's words sinking in. "I understand. I'll take your advice seriously."

The Councillor, visibly shaken, reached for his chequebook and, with trembling hands, wrote out a substantial check. He handed it to Popi, his eyes pleading. "Please, keep your word. I can't afford this to get out."

Popi took the check, nodding solemnly. "You have my word. This matter stays between us as long as there are no further incidents."

Relief washed over the Councillor's face. "Thank you, Mr. Peters. Truly."

As Popi stood to leave, the Councillor, still shaken but now more composed, offered a rare smile. "You know, you have a real talent for this. You'd make a great politician someday."

Popi smiled back, a hint of warmth in his eyes. "Maybe. But for now, I'm just here to make things right."

With that, Popi exited the office, leaving behind a Councillor who had learned a valuable lesson in humility and accountability. Popi knew he had managed to achieve justice without resorting to extremes, upholding his principles and ensuring Donna and Kyle's grievances were addressed.

Popi felt a deep sense of accomplishment as he walked from city hall. He protected his friends and demonstrated that actual change could be achieved through integrity and resolve.

After leaving the Councillor's office, Popi met with Donna and Kyle at their favourite café. The sun was setting, casting a warm, golden glow over the city as they settled into a quiet corner booth.

Popi took a deep breath, feeling a mix of anticipation and nervousness. "It's done," he began, looking at both of them. "The Councillor agreed to settle. He wrote a check and promised to make amends with his staff."

Donna's eyes lit up with a brief flicker of hope. "So, justice is served?" she asked, her voice tinged with relief and uncertainty.

Popi nodded. "In a way, yes. He knows he's being watched now and promised to keep things clean. I also made sure he'd write you both strong recommendation letters for future jobs."

Popi: A Rising Tide

Kyle frowned, his brows knitting together. "But what about real justice, Popi? A check and a promise? That's it?"

Donna's initial hope quickly turned into frustration. "You mean to tell me he just pays us off, and everything's swept under the rug? That's not justice, Popi. That's a bribe. We wanted him held accountable, publicly."

Popi sighed, understanding their anger. "I get it. Believe me, I do. But this was the best way to ensure he actually changes his behaviour without dragging everyone through a long, painful legal process that might not even give us a better result."

Donna's eyes narrowed, her voice rising. "No, Popi. This is not what we wanted. This feels like a betrayal. We trusted you to get real justice, not a payoff. You're no better than he is. You've sold out."

Kyle nodded in agreement, his face flushed with anger. "Yeah, Popi. We wanted him exposed, not just slapped on the wrist. How could you do this?"

Popi felt a pang of hurt and frustration. "I did what I thought was best for everyone involved. If we went public, it could have backfired and made things even worse for you both."

Donna stood up, her face flushed with rage. "You don't get it, Popi. This wasn't just about money or jobs. This was about standing up to someone who abused their power. And you let him off easy."

Kyle shook his head, looking disappointed. "We thought you were different, Popi. But you're just like the rest of them. A sellout."

Popi watched as they fumed, his heart heavy with regret. He had hoped they would understand his rationale, but their anger and disappointment were palpable. Sitting there, he couldn't shake the feeling that he had somehow failed them despite his best intentions.

Reflecting on his thinking over the last 24 hours, he thought he could figure out a better way to explain things to them without further inflaming the situation. The path to change, he also realized, was fraught with complexities and difficult choices. And sometimes, even the best intentions could lead to unintended consequences.

Popi watched as Donna and Kyle's anger bubbled over, and he knew he needed to make them understand his reasoning. He held up a hand to signal them to stay and listen, his voice calm and steady.

"Please, hear me out," Popi began, his eyes earnest. "In life, it's rarely a good idea to burn bridges. If we ruin this man's family and life when he's willing to make amends, it reflects worse on us than it does on him."

Donna's eyes flashed with anger. "So we just let him get away with it? Sweep it under the rug and move on?"

"No," Popi replied firmly. "We don't let him get away with it. He's been put on notice and made to realize the consequences of his actions. Trying to go for blood will likely end badly for everyone involved. No politician will ever want to work with you if you become known as someone who seeks vengeance rather than justice."

Kyle folded his arms, still skeptical. "But what about accountability, Popi? He needs to pay for what he did."

"The justice system is slow and unpredictable," Popi explained. "It could take years before a verdict is reached, and in the meantime, you both could be labelled as liars who were fired for being incompetent. That's a risk you have to consider. Justice doesn't always mean making the other person suffer. Sometimes, it's about getting them to admit they were wrong and ensuring they don't repeat their mistakes."

Donna sighed, her anger beginning to cool. "I just wanted him to pay for what he did. He hurt us, Popi."

"I know," Popi said softly. "But think about the bigger picture. By handling it this way, we ensure he's watched, warned, and knows he can't get away with this behaviour again. We also maintain our integrity and keep the door open for future opportunities. It's about balancing justice with pragmatism."

Kyle nodded slowly, seeing the sense in Popi's words. "So, this isn't the end?"

"No," Popi assured him. "This is just the beginning. If he steps out of line again, we'll have all the more reason to take stronger action. But for now, we've given him a chance to make amends. It's up to him to take it."

After minutes of arguing, Kyle saw Popi's reason. He took a deep breath, trying to calm his emotions, and nodded. "Alright, Popi. I see where you're coming from. And honestly, given our financial predicament, the money will go a long way for both of us."

Popi gave him a small, grateful smile. "I'm glad you understand, Kyle. It's about making the best of a difficult situation."

Donna, however, was still fuming. She paced back and forth, her fists clenched. "I can't believe we're letting him off so easily. He deserves to pay for what he did!"

Popi approached her gently. "Donna, I know how you feel. Believe me, I do. But sometimes, we have to think strategically. This isn't about letting him off; it's about ensuring we come out of this stronger and not as collateral damage in a prolonged fight."

Kyle chimed in, his voice steadying. "Think about it, Donna. This money can help us rebuild, maybe even fund a campaign to raise awareness about workplace harassment and discrimination. We can turn this into something positive."

Donna stopped pacing, her eyes brimming with frustration and pain. "I just... I wanted him to suffer like we did."

Popi placed a hand on her shoulder. "I know. And he will suffer in his own way, knowing he's being watched and on thin ice. But we can't let our need for vengeance overshadow our need for justice and progress."

Donna sighed heavily, her shoulders slumping. She still struggled to see the glass as half full rather than half empty. "It's just hard to let go of the anger."

Popi: A Rising Tide

Popi nodded in understanding. "I get it, Donna. But holding onto that anger will only hurt you more. Use it as fuel to make a difference, to ensure that what happened to you and Kyle doesn't happen to anyone else."

Eventually, Donna began to come around, though the longing for more justice lingered in her heart. "Fine. We'll do it your way. But if he ever steps out of line again, I won't be so forgiving."

Popi smiled, his eyes a mix of relief and determination. "Agreed. We'll be watching him closely."

Kyle thanked Popi for everything but excused himself as he had a few errands he needed to run, leaving Donna and Popi alone. Popi watched Kyle leave, bracing himself for Donna's reaction. He expected an outburst, especially with Kyle, who seemed to be holding Donna back, no longer there.

Instead, Donna looked at Popi with tears in her eyes. The anger that had been so evident earlier had given way to a raw, vulnerable emotion. "You're an amazing person, Popi," she said softly. "I hope you know that and never lose this part of you."

Surprised by her words, Popi's heart swelled with relief and empathy. Before he could respond, Donna moved closer and wrapped her arms around him in a passionate hug. He felt the intensity of her emotions in the embrace, and he gently held her, offering silent comfort.

"I know it's been tough," he murmured, his voice soothing. "But we'll get through this. Together."

Donna pulled back slightly, enough to look into his eyes. "I was so angry, Popi. I still am. But I see now what you were trying to do. You're not just thinking about today but about tomorrow and the days after. And that's something I needed to understand."

Popi smiled, wiping away a tear from her cheek. "We all have our moments, Donna. It's okay to feel what you feel. Remember that we're stronger when we think things through and work together."

She nodded, taking a deep breath. "Thank you for standing by us and showing me another way to fight."

"Anytime," Popi replied, his tone gentle yet firm. "We'll keep pushing forward, one step at a time."

In the quiet aftermath of their emotional storm, Donna felt a sense of peace she hadn't felt in a long time as they stood there. And Popi, knowing they had taken another step towards healing, felt more determined than ever to help his friends find justice and build a better future.

After holding each other for a while, Popi whispered to Donna, "You're so amazing, too, and I'm glad I met you."

Neither of them seemed ready to let go. Feeling excitement and nervousness, Popi said, "I'm not sure what's going on here, but if it is what I think is going on, I'd like that very much."

Donna smiled warmly. "Yes, I would like it too."

Popi's heart raced as he asked, "How about dinner tomorrow

evening? I'll find something fun and nice."

Donna's eyes sparkled with spontaneity. "How about right now? This is my city, and I know everything and everywhere. I'll show you the most exciting night in Ottawa because there's more than just politics here."

With that, she released the hug and held Popi's hand, leading him outside. Popi followed with a huge smile, his heart light and hopeful. He was about to embark on an unexpected, exhilarating evening with a girl he had only known for a few days but was already head over heels for.

Donna pointed out her favourite spots as they walked through the bustling streets, sharing stories and laughter. They explored hidden gems, quaint cafes, and vibrant nightlife. With each step, Popi found himself more captivated by Donna's energy and charm.

At one point, they stopped by a street musician playing a soulful tune. With a twinkle in her eye, Donna pulled Popi into a spontaneous dance. They moved to the rhythm, surrounded by the city's magic and the warmth of each other's company.

The night stretched on, filled with shared dreams and newfound connections. Popi realized that this evening was not just about discovering Ottawa but also about finding a deeper bond with Donna. As they finally made their way back, hand in hand, he knew that this was the beginning of something extraordinary.

Popi Makes a Big Move

After dating for several months, Donna started nudging Popi to run for office. They often discussed their dreams and ambitions over coffee, and it was during one of these moments that Donna first broached the subject.

"Popi," Donna said one evening, her voice soft but firm, "I think you should run for office."

Popi looked up from his cup of coffee, his brows furrowing. "Federal office? Donna, that's a huge step. Maybe I should start small like work for an established MP for a few years or try a municipal election first."

Donna's eyes sparkled with determination. "Popi, you're always so quick to stand up for others, but you hesitate when it comes to yourself. Why is that? If you saw an opportunity to get someone else elected, you'd jump on it without a second thought."

Popi sighed, the weight of her words settling on his shoulders. "It's not that simple. Politics is a big game, and I'm just a small player. I need more experience."

Donna leaned forward, her expression earnest. "Experience isn't everything. You've got empathy, intelligence, and integrity. These are qualities that make a great representative of the people. The man I fell in love with would take the bull by the horns."

Popi: A Rising Tide

The mention of love hung in the air like a soft melody, making Popi's heart race. It was the first time the word had been spoken between them, and it carried a weight of expectation and commitment.

Popi looked into Donna's eyes, seeing her faith in him. "Donna, I... I didn't realize you felt that way."

Donna smiled, reaching out to take his hand. "I do. And I believe in you, Popi. I believe you can make a difference. You always say, 'Nothing ventured, nothing gained.' This is your venture."

Popi was silent about the suggestion for a while, staring out the window at the city lights twinkling in the distance. Donna's words hung in the air like a challenging yet enticing proposition. She could see the wheels turning in his mind, the contemplation etched on his face. She knew pushing him too hard might backfire, so she waited patiently, giving him the space to process her suggestion.

Finally, Popi turned to her, his expression a mix of uncertainty and curiosity. "I'll think about it," he said softly, his voice carrying the weight of his inner turmoil.

Donna's face lit up with a smile, her eyes sparkling with excitement. "That's all I ask, Popi. Just think about it. And if you decide to go for it, know I'm with you every step of the way. It's not about winning but fighting for people and restoring faith in politics. You have that fire in you. I've seen it."

She paused, her gaze unwavering. "Remember how you fought for Ahmed? The passion and conviction you showed? That's what people need to see. That's what can make a difference. And I want to be there beside you in your corner until the fat lady sings."

Popi couldn't help but smile at her determination and unwavering support. He felt a warmth spread through him, a mix of gratitude and hope. Donna's belief in him was like a beacon, guiding him through the fog of his doubts.

Donna leaned in and kissed him gently, tenderly conveying her faith and love. "Goodnight, Popi. Get some rest. Tomorrow is a big day, and I hope you'll be on board with this idea."

As Donna left for the night, Popi sat in his quiet apartment, her words echoing in his mind. He realized that this decision was about more than just him—it was about the people he could help and the change he could inspire. With Donna by his side, he felt a newfound strength and determination.

He knew the road ahead wouldn't be easy, but as he prepared for bed, he made a silent promise to himself. He would give it his all, not just for himself but for Donna and the people who believed in him. He would face the future with renewed purpose tomorrow, ready to take on the challenge.

Popi thought about this long and hard. The federal seat Donna had urged him to fight for had been held by the Liberal Party of Canada in the previous two elections. Being a staunch conservative, he found it hard to see a path to victory as someone new to the political scene, let alone federal politics. The landscape seemed daunting, like navigating a dense forest with only the stars as a guide.

Popi: A Rising Tide

He didn't have many connections within the Conservative Party of Canada except for a weakening link with his former boss from his hometown, who was on the brink of retiring from politics. The uncertainty gnawed at him. Popi was keenly aware that entering the fray without a strong network could lead to an uphill battle like a knight charging into combat without a shield.

The only thing he knew he had for sure was Donna's support, but he struggled to find a way to capitalize on that. Donna's faith in him was a lighthouse in the storm, but he questioned whether that alone could steer his ship to safety. He knew that in politics, as in life, it was not enough to merely want something; one had to have the means to achieve it.

Popi decided to take the night and sleep on it. He hoped that the clarity of a new day might illuminate a path forward. As he lay in bed, his mind raced with possibilities and doubts, the weight of the decision pressing on him like a heavy blanket.

In the quiet darkness, he reminded himself of an old saying his father used to repeat: "Fortune favours the bold." But as the minutes ticked by, he couldn't help but wonder if boldness alone would be enough.

When Donna came at the crack of dawn with coffee and muffins to start their day, she expected to find Popi still asleep, groggy and unprepared. She was ready to gently nudge him into action, knowing that mornings were not his favourite. However, as she stepped into the apartment, she saw Popi sitting in a corner by his computer, a weary but determined look on his face. He looked like he hadn't slept much, and the dark circles under his eyes testified to a restless night.

"Popi," she said softly, setting down the coffee and muffins, "I didn't expect you to be up so early. Have you been up all night?"

Popi looked up, a tired smile spreading across his face. "Couldn't sleep much. I only managed a few hours before I had to get up to use the washroom. After that, I couldn't get back to sleep, so I started working."

Donna walked over and handed him a coffee. "So, what's on your mind?"

He took a sip, savouring the warmth and aroma. "I've been thinking about what you said. At first, I was overwhelmed by the thought of jumping straight into federal politics, especially in a riding that's been held by the opposition. But then I realized you were right. This isn't just about winning—it's about showing people what I stand for, about fighting for what I believe in."

Donna's eyes lit up with pride and excitement. "So, does that mean...?"

"Yes," Popi interrupted, smiling. "I've decided your idea is a great one. I'm not going to look at this as a must-win battle. Instead, I'll treat it as an introduction, a chance to show the people what I can do. It's the perfect way to get started in politics."

Donna couldn't contain her excitement. She threw her arms around him, hugging him tightly. "Popi, this is fantastic! You're going to be amazing. The people will see your heart, your passion. They'll see what I see every day."

Popi: A Rising Tide

Popi laughed softly, touched by her enthusiasm. "I hope so, Donna. I really do. But we have a lot of work to do. This is just the beginning."

"Don't worry," Donna said, her voice brimming with determination. "We'll take it one step at a time. And remember, you're not alone in this. We're in this together."

Popi nodded, feeling a renewed sense of purpose. "Together," he echoed. "Now, let's get to work."

As they sat down to map out their strategy, the first rays of sunlight streaming through the window seemed to symbolize a new beginning. With Donna by his side and a newfound resolve in his heart, Popi felt ready to face whatever challenges lay ahead.

The research Popi had stayed up all night doing ranged from studying the incumbent party's strategies and weaknesses to understanding the intricacies of the Conservative Party he hoped to represent in the upcoming by-election, which was only a couple of months away.

Campaigning for the election itself was not his primary concern at the moment. The first hurdle he had to overcome was getting the nomination to represent the Conservative Party of Canada in this riding. This nomination contest was a complex and often murky process, heavily influenced by favouritism and nepotism, where merit alone was seldom enough to secure a position.

Popi knew he couldn't count on favours or personal connections, as he had no friends or family within the Conservative Party. His only asset was his merit, but he was well aware that selling merit in politics could be extremely tricky. The world of politics was a battlefield, and he was stepping into it armed with nothing but his principles and Donna's support.

As Popi and Donna sat together, planning their next steps, he shared his findings. "Donna, this nomination process is going to be an uphill battle. There's so much favouritism and nepotism. It seems like merit alone won't get me very far."

Donna listened intently, her brow furrowing in concern. "I know it's not going to be easy, Popi. But you have something many of these other candidates don't—genuine passion and a track record of standing up for what's right. That's got to count for something."

Popi sighed, rubbing his temples. "I hope so. But how do I sell that in a political landscape that's more about who you know than what you stand for?"

Donna placed a comforting hand on his shoulder. "We start by showing people who you are. We highlight your past achievements, your integrity, and your vision for the future. We need to connect with the people on a personal level, make them see that you're not just another politician."

Popi nodded slowly. "You're right. We need to build a grassroots campaign that reaches out directly to the community. We need to engage with them, listen to their concerns, and show them that I'm here to represent them, not any special interests."

"Exactly," Donna agreed. "And remember, we're in this

together. We'll reach out to every person we can, leverage social media, hold community meetings—whatever it takes to get your message out there."

Popi felt a surge of determination. "Alright, let's do this. Let's start by organizing a series of community events. We need to get out there and meet the people face-to-face, show them who I am and what I stand for."

Donna smiled, her eyes shining with pride. "That's the spirit, Popi. We'll make them see the fire that you have, the same fire that made you stand up for Ahmed and confront that creepy councillor. We'll make them believe in you, just like I do."

Popi felt a warmth in his chest at her words. With Donna by his side and a clear plan in mind, he felt ready to take on the daunting challenge ahead. The road to the nomination would be tough, but he knew he could make a difference with determination and a steadfast commitment to his values.

As Donna sat down, they began eating and casually talking about how their night was and how much they had missed each other. The conversation naturally shifted toward the pressing issue of Popi's potential nomination. They explored various ideas, seeking ways to leverage Popi's strengths to his advantage in the nomination process.

"Popi," Donna began, sipping her coffee, "the only way things work in politics here in Ottawa is through quid pro quo. You need to determine what you can offer the Conservative Party, the Party leadership, or the people you hope to represent."

Popi nodded thoughtfully. "I know. But what can I offer them?

I'm new to this scene and don't have the connections or influence others might have."

Donna leaned forward, her eyes intent. "Think about what you do have. The Conservative Party might not expect to win this seat, but if you can show them a clear path to victory, they'll start seeing you differently. You need to present them with a concrete strategy that demonstrates you can win this riding."

Popi considered her words. "Alright, but what kind of strategy? What do I have that can convince them?"

"You have your story, Popi. You have integrity, ability to connect with people, and commitment to fighting for what's right. You must show them you can bring something fresh and genuine to the table."

"Okay, so how do we package that? How do we make it appealing to the party leadership?" Popi asked, biting into his muffin.

"We start by highlighting your past achievements," Donna suggested. "For example, the time you stood up for Ahmed shows you have the courage to fight for justice, even when it's not easy. We also emphasize your grassroots connections and how you've already positively impacted the community."

Popi's face lit up with a new idea. "What if we create a proposal that outlines a community-focused campaign? We could focus on local issues that matter to the people in this riding and show how my approach can resonate with them. We can present this as a blueprint for success."

Popi: A Rising Tide

"That's a great idea," Donna agreed. "We can also reach out to local organizations and community leaders to build a coalition of support. If we can show the party that you already have backing from key community figures, that will strengthen your case."

Popi's mind raced with possibilities. "We should organize town hall meetings, too. Let people come and share their concerns, and I can address them directly. It will show that I'm accessible and genuinely interested in their issues."

"Exactly," Donna said, smiling. "And we can document these interactions and create a social media campaign highlighting your connection with the community. People need to see that you're not just another politician, but someone who truly cares about making a difference."

Popi felt a surge of optimism. "This can work. We need to craft a compelling narrative that sets me apart from others. If I can demonstrate a real chance of winning this seat, it might just be enough to get the party's attention."

Donna reached across the table and squeezed his hand. "I believe in you, Popi. You've got the passion and heart for this. Now we just need to show everyone else."

"Popi, seriously, you have to think about this strategically," Donna said, sipping her coffee. "The Conservative Party isn't expecting to win this seat. Only if you can show them a path to victory will they listen. You need to offer something they can't refuse."

Donna leaned forward, her eyes sparkling with determination.

"Since I know the city and many people, we need to start some fundraising charity to help a marginalized group. If we can show that we have the community's support, it'll go a long way."

"That's a great idea," Popi replied, his interest piqued. "But how do we get the word out and make it impactful?"

"I can talk to some friends to help spread the word about the event online. We could aim to get some media attention, too. While you're no longer new to the city, you don't know it quite as well as I do. I'll handle finding a cause and target audience as well as a way to market the event. You can focus on crafting a message that resonates with people and shows your leadership qualities."

Popi smiled, feeling a sense of relief and excitement. "Alright, Donna. Let's do it. What cause do you think we should support?"

Donna thought momentarily, then said, "We need something that strikes a chord with the people here. Maybe something related to housing or education—issues that affect a lot of people directly. What do you think?"

"Housing sounds like a strong issue. While education is also a strong cause, that's provincial jurisdiction. If I focus on that, I may give my opponents armour to make fun of me that I think I'm running for a provincial seat." Popi responded. "Affordable housing is a major concern for many in this city. If we can tie our campaign to improving housing conditions, it will show that we're addressing real, pressing needs."

Popi: A Rising Tide

Donna nodded. "Exactly. We can organize a charity event to raise funds for a local shelter or a housing initiative. We'll involve the community and local businesses, creating a sense of unity and purpose."

Popi felt a spark of hope. "I like it. This way, we're not just talking about change—we're actively making a difference. And it will show the Conservative Party that I can mobilize support and address important issues."

"We'll need to act fast," Donna said, already mentally planning. "The nomination is only a few weeks away. We need to make a big impression quickly."

"I'll start drafting a message highlighting our commitment to the community and our plan to improve housing," Popi said. "We need to make sure it's heartfelt and genuine. People must see that we're in this for the right reasons."

"And I'll start reaching out to my contacts to get the ball rolling on the event," Donna added. "We'll need volunteers, donations, and media coverage. I'll also look into securing a venue and setting a date."

Popi took a deep breath, feeling the weight of the task ahead and a growing sense of purpose. "Thank you, Donna. I couldn't do this without you."

Donna smiled warmly. "We're in this together, Popi. And I believe in you. This is just the beginning."

With their plan set, they felt a renewed sense of determination. They knew the road ahead would be challenging. Still, with their combined efforts and unwavering support for each other, they were ready to take the first step toward making a real difference.

"What about organizing the largest car wash in Ottawa's history?" Donna proposed, excitement lighting up her eyes. We could raise money to help marginalized people living on the streets get a leg up and improve their lives. This would align perfectly with your values about self-sufficiency and independence."

Popi's eyes lit up in return. "That's a brilliant idea! People will notice if we can show we're making a tangible difference. And it's a great way to demonstrate our commitment to helping people help themselves."

Donna smiled, encouraged by Popi's enthusiasm. "We can involve local businesses to sponsor the event, get volunteers from the community, and use social media to spread the word. We could even make it a fun event with music, food trucks, and games for kids."

Popi nodded, already envisioning the event. "Yes, and we can use the opportunity to talk to people about our campaign and our vision for the community. It's a way to connect personally, show that we care and are willing to roll up our sleeves and work alongside them."

"I'll start reaching out to potential sponsors and volunteers today," Donna said, her mind racing with ideas. "We need to secure a venue and a date as soon as possible."

"And I'll start drafting a speech that outlines our goals and the importance of community support," Popi added. "We need to ensure our message is clear and resonates with everyone who comes."

Donna looked at Popi, admiration in her eyes. "This is going to be amazing, Popi. You're going to make such a big difference."

Popi smiled back at her, feeling a surge of gratitude. "I couldn't do this without you, Donna. Your support means everything to me."

"We're a team," Donna replied, taking his hand. "And together, we're going to show everyone what true leadership looks like."

They spent the rest of the morning brainstorming and planning, their excitement growing with each new idea. As they sipped their coffee and munched on muffins, they discussed logistics, potential partnerships, and marketing strategies. Popi felt more determined than ever, his initial doubts slowly dissipating in the face of Donna's unwavering belief in him and their shared vision for the future.

Popi admitted that the plan was a little complicated, but this was the kind of challenge he enjoyed. The more complex the situation seemed, the more excited he got. "Donna, I thrive on challenges like this. The more intricate, the better," he said with a glint in his eye.

Donna, sipping her coffee, leaned in, eager to know more. "Alright, spill the beans. What's the plan?"

Popi shook his head, a playful smile on his lips. "It's still brewing, Donna. I don't want to share a half-baked idea. Trust me, you'll be the first to know once it's fully formed."

Donna pouted slightly, feeling a bit left out. "You know, I was hoping for a front-row seat to this whole process. A backstage pass, if you will."

Popi reached across the table and took her hand. "I promise, you'll get all the details soon. For now, I need you to work your magic with your graphic design skills. Start designing some flyers and posters to promote the event. We need something eye-catching and inspiring."

Donna's eyes lit up, her initial disappointment in Popi's secrecy beginning to fade. "Alright, you got it. I'll make sure these flyers are impossible to ignore." She paused, looking at him with a mixture of admiration and curiosity. "Just don't keep me in the dark too long, okay?"

Popi smiled, squeezing her hand. "I won't. We're a team, remember? I just need to refine a few things first."

As Donna got to work, Popi's mind buzzed with the possibilities. He loved the thrill of creating something from scratch, the intricate dance of planning and execution. He knew that the car wash's success could be a game-changer for his campaign, a way to show the community and the party his potential.

Later, as Donna sketched out designs and brainstormed taglines, she couldn't help but glance over at Popi, who was deep in thought, scribbling notes and working on his laptop. Despite her initial frustration, she was reassured by his focus and determination. He was in his element, and that was a sight to behold.

Popi: A Rising Tide

As the day progressed, they continued to bounce ideas off each other, refining their plans and getting more excited about the event. Despite the initial hiccup of Donna feeling a bit sidelined, they found their rhythm, each bringing their unique strengths to the table. They were, as always, a formidable team.

Popi left the living room, heading to the washroom to clean himself up. As he moved through the apartment, his heart was beating with an excited rhythm as though it could sense the anticipation of something fabulous just around the corner. It was a feeling he hadn't experienced in a long time—a sense of purpose and possibility that stirred a profound, invigorating energy within him.

In the washroom, he took his time, methodically preparing himself. He washed up and refreshed his appearance, trying to clear his mind and organize his thoughts about the flyer ideas he had been mulling over. He spent about half an hour on his grooming, his thoughts racing with ideas for the campaign. He envisioned bold, vibrant flyers that could capture the spirit of their initiative, aiming to reflect the heart and passion behind their cause.

Popi felt a renewed surge of enthusiasm as he finished and returned to the living room. He was eager to share his thoughts with Donna to see how his ideas might mesh with her design skills. But when he entered the room, he was taken aback. Donna was hunched over her laptop, intently focused on her work.

A rough draft of a flyer lay on the coffee table. Its design was striking, with vibrant colours and compelling messaging that immediately grabbed Popi's attention. The tagline, **"Wash**

Away Worries: Support Our Community Car Wash," was prominent, surrounded by images that depicted a sense of community and hope. Donna had clearly poured her heart into it, and the result was impressive.

Popi's eyes widened in amazement. "Wow, Donna. This is incredible. How did you manage to get this done so quickly?"

Donna looked up from her work, her face lighting up with pride and satisfaction. "I've been working on it in my mind pretty much since you accepted the idea. I wanted to get a rough draft ready so we could start discussing the details. I know this is important, and I don't want to waste time."

Her determination and commitment struck Popi. It was evident that Donna wasn't just involved for the sake of it; she was fully invested in the project and in supporting him. Her quick work and draft quality spoke volumes about her dedication and enthusiasm.

"I can see that," Popi said, his voice filled with genuine admiration. "This draft is fantastic. You've really captured the essence of what we're trying to achieve. I'm impressed by how much effort you've put in already."

Donna smiled warmly. "I'm glad you think so. I just want to get things moving as quickly as possible. This is important to me, and I'm committed to seeing it through."

At that moment, Popi realized the depth of Donna's commitment. She wasn't just an ally in his campaign but an integral part of his journey, sharing the challenges and excitement. Her dedication reminded him of why he was taking this leap into politics in the first place—because he wanted to make a real difference, and he wasn't doing it alone.

"You're the real deal, Donna," Popi said, his voice full of gratitude. "I appreciate everything you're doing. It means a lot to me, and I'm grateful to have you by my side."

Donna's eyes softened, touched by his words. "I'm here for you, Popi. We're in this together, and I believe in what we're trying to accomplish. Let's make it happen."

Popi took a deep breath and sat across from Donna, still admiring the flyer. His expression was earnest, reflecting the gravity of his thoughts.

"Donna," he began, his voice softening, "I owe you an apology for brushing you off earlier. I didn't mean to seem dismissive. I was just trying to finalize the plan and wanted to make sure it was well thought out before sharing it."

Donna looked up, her curiosity piqued. "No worries, Popi. I understand. I was just eager to be involved and contribute. What's your idea?"

Popi nodded, appreciating her understanding. "I'm going to campaign on the idea of freedom, but not just in the usual sense. To me, it's about true freedom—the freedom to live your life on your own terms, without being dependent on government assistance."

Donna listened intently, her eyes fixed on him. Popi continued, "I believe that self-sufficiency is a cornerstone of a prosperous society. When people rely too heavily on social assistance, it can create a cycle of dependency. While some may make the most of the assistance, others may not have the incentive to work harder and improve their situation. And if we don't break that cycle, their children could end up in an even worse position."

He paused, letting his words sink in. Donna nodded slowly, absorbing his perspective. "That makes sense. What's your take on how this fits into the current political landscape?"

Popi leaned forward, his hands clasped together as he spoke passionately. "With the rising government debt, it's becoming more crucial to rethink our approach. If people become too dependent on government aid, the government will likely start cutting expenses when the debt becomes unmanageable. Unfortunately, social assistance is often one of the first areas to face cuts."

Donna's eyes widened. "So, you're saying that advocating for self-sufficiency is not just a philosophical stance but also a practical one, given the financial pressures on the government?"

"Exactly," Popi affirmed. "I want to make the case that we need to focus on creating pathways to self-sufficiency. It's about empowering people to take control of their lives and contribute to society rather than depend on a system that might not always be there for them. It's a matter of building a more resilient and independent community."

Donna nodded thoughtfully. "I see where you're coming from. It's a compelling argument, and it aligns well with your values. But how do you plan to communicate this effectively to the voters?"

Popi: A Rising Tide

Popi smiled, appreciating her insight. "That's where the car wash idea comes in. We'll use the event to showcase our commitment to helping marginalized individuals get back on their feet. We'll create a tangible example of what we stand for by demonstrating our dedication to self-sufficiency and independence. And by tying it into our broader message of freedom, we'll clarify that we're not just talking about ideals but actively working to make them a reality."

Donna's eyes sparkled with excitement. "I love it. This plan highlights your values and provides a concrete way to engage with the community and make a difference. It's a powerful combination."

Popi nodded in agreement, feeling a renewed sense of purpose. "I'm glad you think so. I'm excited to see how this unfolds. Your support and input are invaluable, Donna."

Popi leaned back, his eyes glinting with a spark of determination. "Donna, I envision a society where every individual is eager to contribute in ways that benefit themselves and the broader community. But I also believe that it's not the government's role to take care of everyone. The government shouldn't be seen as a caretaker; its primary responsibility is to create an environment where every citizen has the opportunity to thrive."

Donna tilted her head, intrigued. "So, you're saying that the government should act more like a referee than a coach?"

"Exactly," Popi affirmed. "The government's job is to ensure the rules are fair and everyone has a level playing field. It's not about hand-holding citizens or pushing them to succeed. Instead, it's about setting the right conditions so that people can stand on their feet and pursue their own success."

He paused, gathering his thoughts. "This perspective is rooted in the ideas I've absorbed from the lectures and writings of Nobel laureates like Milton Friedman. Friedman argued that economic freedom and individual responsibility are essential for a prosperous society. He believed that people should be free to make their own choices and that government intervention should be minimal."

Donna nodded thoughtfully. "So, you're drawing on these economic principles to advocate for a government that empowers rather than directs?"

"Precisely," Popi said, his voice steady with conviction. "The government should not be a coach or an assistant player in the game of life. It should be the referee, ensuring fairness and equal opportunity while letting people play the game on their own terms. By promoting self-sufficiency and independence, we align with these principles and create a more resilient society."

Donna's face brightened with understanding. "I see. You're aiming to foster an environment where people are motivated to contribute and thrive independently without excessive reliance on government support."

Popi smiled, encouraged by her grasp of his vision. "Yes, and by demonstrating this through concrete actions, like our planned car wash, we can show voters that this approach works. It's about making our values tangible and proving that a society based on self-sufficiency and opportunity can lead to real, positive change."

Popi: A Rising Tide

Popi's eyes gleamed with an enthusiasm that matched the intensity of his convictions. As he spoke, his passion for the principles of freedom of speech and conscience became palpable. "Donna, if you control the amount of assistance someone receives and the conditions under which they receive it, you inherently control their voice and thoughts."

Donna listened intently, her expression reflecting deep contemplation. "Are you suggesting that dependence on government aid can lead to a kind of coercion or control?"

Popi nodded vigorously. "Exactly. When people rely heavily on government assistance, they're not just dependent on financial support—they're often subject to the whims and biases of those in power. Imagine a scenario where a politician cuts off aid to individuals or groups who dissent or don't align with their political views. It's a dangerous precedent that can stifle free expression and limit personal freedoms."

He leaned forward, emphasizing his point with a palpable urgency. "It only takes one corrupt politician with the power to distribute aid to turn it into a tool of control. This could result in people being silenced, their voices quashed, and their ability to freely express dissent severely restricted. They might feel pressured to conform to the political ideologies of those in power, simply to secure the assistance they need to survive."

Donna's brow furrowed, her understanding deepening. "So, you argue that fostering independence and reducing reliance on government assistance not only empowers individuals but also protects their freedom of thought and speech?"

"Yes," Popi confirmed, his tone earnest. "By promoting self-sufficiency, we reduce the risk of individuals being manipulated or controlled through their dependence on aid. The more independent people are, the less susceptible they become to political coercion. A prosperous society is one where individuals are free to think, speak, and act according to their values and beliefs, without fear of losing their support or resources."

Donna's eyes sparkled with admiration. "That's a powerful argument, Popi. It aligns perfectly with your vision of an empowering and resilient society. If people can thrive independently, they're economically self-sufficient and free to express their true selves and contribute meaningfully to their communities."

Popi's face softened with a mixture of determination and hope. "That's right. When people are free from the constraints of dependency, they can fully engage in the democratic process, voice their opinions, and work towards their goals without undue influence. It's about creating an environment where freedom and prosperity go hand in hand."

Donna reached out and took Popi's hand, her support unwavering. "Your commitment to these principles inspires me. Let's make sure that our campaign not only reflects these values but also demonstrates them in action. We can show people that independence and freedom are not just ideals, but achievable realities that lead to a better society for everyone."

Popi's heart swelled with gratitude and resolve. "Thank you, Donna. With your help, we can turn this vision into reality and demonstrate the power of freedom and self-sufficiency. Together, we'll make a difference."

Popi: A Rising Tide

As they continued their discussion, the air was charged with purpose and possibility. Popi's commitment to fostering independence and protecting freedoms was clear. With Donna's unwavering support, they were ready to embark on their campaign with a shared goal of creating a more empowered and prosperous society.

By the time Popi had finished laying out his vision, Donna's enthusiasm was palpable. Her perspective had shifted dramatically, and she was now more aligned with the idea than ever.

Donna's eyes were wide with newfound clarity. "Popi, I have to admit, your perspective is eye-opening. I've always considered the government a necessary safety net, a way to help those struggling. It's been ingrained in me that this is the best way to address poverty and inequality."

Popi nodded, acknowledging her previous beliefs with respect. "I understand, Donna. It's a common view. Many people believe that government assistance is the primary solution to poverty. But my concern is that such dependence can unintentionally create a system where people are controlled by those who hold the purse strings."

Donna leaned forward, absorbing his argument. "So you're saying that while government aid can offer immediate relief, it might not be the best long-term solution for empowering people. Instead, creating opportunities for self-sufficiency could lead to more sustainable change?"

"Exactly," Popi replied. "When people are given the tools to help themselves, they're not just surviving—they're thriving.

They gain confidence, independence, and the ability to shape their futures. It's about creating a society where everyone has the chance to succeed on their own terms, without being beholden to government aid."

Donna's eyes sparkled with a blend of excitement and admiration. "I see what you mean now. By focusing on self-sufficiency, we're not just helping people get by; we're helping them build a foundation for a better life. It's about giving them the means to stand on their own two feet, and that's incredibly empowering."

Popi smiled, appreciating her shift in perspective. "That's right. It's about fostering an environment where people can flourish independently and free from the constraints of dependence. This approach not only benefits individuals but strengthens communities as a whole."

Donna took a deep breath, her resolve solidifying. "I'm all in, Popi. Your vision for a society that values freedom and self-sufficiency resonates deeply with me now. I want to help you make this vision a reality. I see the potential for real change and believe in the principles you're advocating."

Popi's face lit up with gratitude. "Thank you, Donna. Your support means the world to me. Together, we can show that it's possible to create a society where everyone has the opportunity to thrive, not just survive. We'll demonstrate that true empowerment comes from within and that freedom and self-sufficiency are the keys to a prosperous future."

Donna's heart swelled with a sense of purpose. "Let's get to work then. We have a lot to do, and I'm excited to be part of this journey with you. We'll make sure that your campaign reflects these values and inspires others to believe in the power of self-reliance and freedom."

Popi believed that the most effective way to help people was to provide them with the tools to help themselves rather than offering them handouts. He felt that true empowerment came from giving individuals the means and opportunities to stand independently, fostering independence rather than relying on government support.

Donna, on the other hand, had grown up with parents who championed the idea of a big government. For her, the notion of reducing government aid in favour of fostering self-sufficiency was a new and intriguing concept. She had always seen the government as a safety net designed to catch those who fell through the cracks, but Popi's perspective challenged her understanding.

As Popi articulated his vision, Donna's excitement grew. The idea of self-sufficiency resonated deeply with her. She began to see how much more fulfilling it could be for individuals to shape their own destinies rather than depend on external aid. The thought of a society where people enjoyed greater autonomy and independence sparked a genuine enthusiasm in her.

Donna's eyes lit up as she embraced this new perspective. "I'm excited about the potential of this approach. It's about giving people the freedom to make their own choices and the chance to build their futures. It's empowering in a way that handouts just can't be."

Popi smiled, seeing how Donna's understanding was evolving. "Yes, it's about fostering an environment that encourages growth and independence. And if we can show that this approach works, it could change how people think about government support and self-reliance."

Donna nodded enthusiastically. "I'm fully on board with this. I want to help make this vision a reality and demonstrate how much more fulfilling and effective it can be compared to traditional forms of assistance. It will be a challenging journey, but I'm excited about what we can achieve together."

Popi felt a surge of optimism. With Donna's newfound enthusiasm and understanding, they were both ready to embark on this challenging but promising journey. Together, they would advocate for a vision of self-sufficiency that promised to transform individuals' lives and reshape their community's approach to empowerment and freedom.

"Popi, I never thought about it this way before," Donna said, her eyes widening with realization. "It makes so much sense. Giving people the tools to help themselves is empowering. It's about giving them dignity and respect, not just a handout."

Popi's face lit up with gratitude. "Exactly, Donna. We need to shift the conversation about government assistance. It's not just about providing temporary relief—it's about creating opportunities that allow people to thrive independently and with pride."

Donna nodded, the enthusiasm in her voice unmistakable. "I can now see how much more fulfilling it is to support self-sufficiency than just offering aid. It's not just about addressing

Popi: A Rising Tide

immediate needs; it's about building a foundation for long-term success and personal growth."

Popi leaned in, his passion evident. "That's right. By focusing on self-sufficiency, we're helping individuals stand on their own two feet and encouraging a mindset where everyone can contribute meaningfully to society. It's about fostering a culture of empowerment rather than dependency."

Donna's eyes sparkled with determination. "I'm really excited about this. It feels like we're working towards something transformative. Not just for the people we want to help, but for the community as a whole."

Popi nodded, his confidence growing. "I believe in this vision, Donna. And with your support, I know we can make a real difference. Together, we can show people that there's a better way to approach government support—one that values independence and personal achievement."

Donna smiled warmly. "I'm all in, Popi. Let's make this vision a reality and prove that self-sufficiency can be a powerful tool for change. We're on the brink of something important, and I'm excited to be a part of it with you."

Popi felt a surge of optimism. With Donna's unwavering support and shared vision, they were ready to take on the challenge ahead. Their commitment to fostering self-sufficiency and empowering individuals was not just a campaign platform— it was a transformative idea poised to make a meaningful impact on their community and beyond.

After about an hour of animated discussion about Popi's vision,

Donna reluctantly glanced at the clock. "I hate to cut this short, Popi, but I really need to get some rest," she said, her fatigue evident despite her enthusiasm. "I've got a lot of work ahead of me, and I haven't slept much. I need to recharge if I'm going to be able to give this my all."

Popi nodded in understanding. "Of course, Donna. I'll take a break, too and get some rest before we dive back into our car wash project. We've got a busy road ahead, but we're both ready for it."

Donna gave him a reassuring smile. "I'm excited about this, Popi. This car wash isn't just an event; it's a launchpad for us. It's a chance for you to introduce yourself to the people and the party and for me to show you that I can support you in a big way. It's the first step towards something significant."

Popi's eyes reflected his determination. "Absolutely. It will be challenging, but I believe it's worth it. We're both in this together, and we'll make it work."

Donna gathered her things, her mind already buzzing with ideas and plans. "I'll see you later then. Rest up, and let's reconvene with fresh energy. This project is going to be the start of something great."

Popi watched her leave, feeling a sense of anticipation and resolve. The coming weeks would be demanding, but the prospect of making a real impact kept him motivated. He knew that this car wash, while seemingly simple, was a pivotal moment in their journey—a chance to build a foundation for their future endeavours and to prove their commitment to their shared goals.

Popi: A Rising Tide

With Donna's support and the clarity of their mission, Popi felt a renewed sense of purpose. He understood this was just the beginning, and the path ahead would be challenging and rewarding. For now, though, a brief respite was in order before they plunged back into their ambitious plans.

As Popi and Donna embarked on their ambitious journey together, they quickly found themselves navigating a labyrinth of challenges and setbacks. The nomination process for the Conservative Party was anything but straightforward. It was fraught with complexities, often overshadowed by favouritism and nepotism that tainted the otherwise merit-based system. Popi, a relative newcomer with limited connections, faced a formidable task. The playing field seemed rigged to favour those with established relationships and entrenched political alliances.

Undeterred, Popi and Donna leaned heavily on their strengths and the resources at their disposal. Donna's extensive network of contacts and her knack for rallying people became invaluable assets. She dove into her rolodex, reaching out to friends, local activists, and community leaders to drum up support for their cause. Donna's skillful use of social media also played a crucial role in amplifying their message. She created eye-catching flyers and posters designed to capture attention and convey Popi's core values of self-sufficiency and personal empowerment.

Despite these efforts, the road was often bumpy. They encountered skepticism from some quarters, with critics questioning Popi's lack of experience and connections. Political manoeuvring and party politics created roadblocks, making it clear that merit alone was rarely the sole factor in the nomination process.

Popi, however, remained resolute. His passion for his message and his belief in the power of individual freedom and self-reliance fuelled his determination. He worked tirelessly, speaking at local events, meeting with community members, and engaging in heartfelt conversations about his vision. Popi's approach was about winning over voters and demonstrating his commitment to creating a better society through genuine action.

One particularly challenging moment came when Popi was invited to speak at a town hall meeting organized by a local community group. The event was intended to introduce potential candidates to the electorate, but it quickly became apparent that many attendees were skeptical of Popi's intentions. The room was filled with seasoned political veterans who had seen countless candidates come and go, and they were not easily impressed.

Popi could feel the weight of the room's scrutiny as he took the stage. He took a deep breath and began his speech, his voice steady despite the nervousness that churned within him.

"Good evening, everyone," he started. "Thank you for allowing me to speak with you tonight. I understand many of you may be skeptical, and I don't blame you. I'm young, new and a different breed of politician, and I genuinely care about the issues facing our community."

He spoke passionately about his vision for a society where individuals had the tools and opportunities to succeed on their own merits rather than relying on government handouts. He talked about the importance of creating a supportive environment where everyone could thrive, emphasizing that true empowerment came from self-reliance and personal responsibility.

As Popi continued, he noticed a gradual shift in the room. Some of the skeptical faces softened, and a few heads nodded in agreement. By the end of his speech, he received a warm round of applause. It wasn't a resounding endorsement but a step in the right direction. Popi and Donna knew that every small victory mattered, and they took this as a sign that their efforts were beginning to bear fruit.

Throughout this period, Donna remained a steadfast ally. She worked late into the night designing promotional materials and organizing events, her dedication unwavering. One evening, as they reviewed the latest campaign materials, Donna looked up from her computer and said, "Popi, I know this isn't easy. I know we've hit some bumps along the way. But I believe in what we're doing. Your message is resonating with people. It might not be obvious, but we're making progress."

Popi smiled, feeling a surge of gratitude for Donna's unwavering support. "Thank you, Donna. Your hard work and belief in this cause mean more to me than you know. It's not just about winning the nomination; it's about making a difference. And with you by my side, I know we can do it."

Despite the obstacles, Popi and Donna's persistence began to pay off. They garnered more support from local activists and community leaders, and their message started to gain traction.

Popi and Donna faced new challenges as the nomination process continued, but their determination remained unshaken. They knew the path to victory was far from guaranteed, but they were driven by a shared vision and a deep commitment to their cause. For Popi, this journey was about more than just politics; it was about standing up for his beliefs and fighting for a better future. And with Donna's unwavering support, he was ready to face whatever challenges lay ahead.

One evening, after a gruelling day of organizing and strategizing, Donna looked at Popi with resolute determination. "We need to make this car wash unforgettable," she said, her voice steady and purposeful. "It has to be more than just a fundraiser. We need to show people that we can make a real difference."

Popi met her gaze, his own eyes mirroring her unwavering resolve. "We will, Donna. We just need to keep pushing forward and believe in our cause. If we let our passion and dedication shine through, people will take notice."

Donna's eyes softened as she replied, "It's not just about making a splash; it's about showing that we're committed to something greater. That we're here to fight for a better future, not just for ourselves but for everyone who believes in the same vision."

Popi nodded, feeling the weight of their mission but also a surge of excitement. "Exactly. This event is our chance to demonstrate that we're not just talking the talk. We're walking the walk. Let's make sure it reflects everything we stand for."

They continued their preparations with renewed energy, fuelled by a shared vision and a deep commitment to their cause. They knew their hard work and dedication would be tested as the event approached, but they were ready to face the challenge head-on. The car wash was more than just a fundraiser; it was

Popi: A Rising Tide

the first step towards realizing their dream of a better society.

The car wash was nothing short of a triumph. From the moment the first car rolled in, it was clear that Popi and Donna had struck a chord with the community. The buzz around the event was palpable, and as cars lined up down the street, the atmosphere was filled with a sense of purpose and excitement.

As the day wore on, it became evident that the event was more than just a fundraiser. It had become a celebration of Popi's message of self-sufficiency and independence. People from all walks of life came out to support the cause, their enthusiasm and generosity turning the car wash into a vibrant, bustling hub of activity. The sounds of laughter and conversation mingled with the rhythmic splash of water and the hum of vacuum cleaners, creating an infectious energy that carried through the day.

Local media outlets noticed the event's success and its compelling message. News reporters flocked to the scene, eager to capture the essence of Popi's campaign and the palpable sense of community spirit. Interviews with Popi and Donna highlighted their commitment to helping marginalized individuals and their innovative approach to fostering self-sufficiency.

Popi's speech about the importance of creating opportunities for people to thrive on their own terms resonated deeply with the public. His words about providing tools rather than handouts, about empowering individuals rather than merely assisting them, struck a chord with many. The media coverage painted a vivid picture of Popi's vision and the positive impact of his work, further amplifying his message.

As the event drew to a close, the financial success was matched by the emotional and ideological victories. The funds raised exceeded expectations, providing crucial support for the marginalized community. But perhaps more importantly, the event had established Popi as a rising star within the Conservative Party. His message of independence and self-sufficiency had not only won over the community but had also caught the attention of influential figures within the party.

In the following weeks, Popi began receiving invitations to meet with key party members and political leaders. His name was now being discussed in circles that had previously seemed out of reach. The car wash's success had put him on the map, demonstrating that he was more than just a newcomer—he was a force to be reckoned with.

For Donna and Popi, the event was a testament to their hard work and shared vision. It was a pivotal moment that marked the beginning of a new chapter in their journey. As they looked back on the car wash's success, they knew that it was a reflection of their efforts and a glimpse into the potential of what lay ahead.

Their partnership had proven to be a powerful combination of passion, determination, and strategic thinking. The car wash had set the stage for future endeavours. Donna and Popi were eager to build on their success, ready to face the challenges and opportunities ahead with the same zeal and dedication that had brought them this far.

Despite the initial hurdles, Popi was breaking barriers within the Conservative Party of Canada. His campaign, grounded in

Popi: A Rising Tide

the principles of freedom, self-sufficiency, and limited government intervention, resonated deeply with many voters.

Popi's message—emphasizing empowering individuals rather than offering mere handouts and advocating for a government that facilitates opportunities rather than micromanaging lives—struck a powerful chord with the electorate. His speeches were imbued with the conviction that actual progress comes from within rather than from reliance on external assistance. The grassroots enthusiasm and media attention garnered from the car wash had built a solid foundation for his campaign, helping to establish his credibility and visibility.

While the nomination outcome remained uncertain, Popi's journey had already made a substantial impact. His ability to articulate a vision for a more self-reliant society and his demonstrated commitment to improving the lives of marginalized individuals had earned him respect and admiration. Through his efforts, Popi showed his leadership qualities and sparked meaningful conversations about the role of government and the power of individual initiative.

The path ahead was still fraught with challenges, but Popi faced them with newfound confidence and a clear sense of purpose. His campaign was not merely about winning a nomination for an election but setting a precedent for a new kind of political engagement that valued empowerment over dependency and opportunity over entitlement.

For Popi, the nomination was just the beginning. His journey had laid a strong foundation for his future in politics, proving that with determination, clarity of vision, and the support of those who shared his values, he could turn even the most daunting challenges into opportunities for change.

Throughout this journey, Donna remained steadfastly by Popi's side, providing unwavering support and contributing her skills and insights to the campaign. Their relationship, initially sparked by a shared vision, deepened as they faced the complexities of politics together. Their bond was fortified by late-night strategy sessions, passionate debates about policy, and the shared exhilaration of their successes and setbacks.

Donna's role in the campaign was indispensable. Her graphic design skills brought Popi's ideas to life, transforming abstract concepts into compelling visuals that resonated with the public. Her connections and organizational acumen ensured every event, including the landmark car wash, ran smoothly and garnered the attention it deserved. Donna was not just a partner in the campaign but a true collaborator, using her expertise to amplify Popi's message and build momentum for their cause.

As they navigated the demanding world of politics, Popi and Donna learned to balance their personal and professional lives. Their shared mission became a cornerstone of their relationship, blending their strengths into a cohesive force. They found joy in their work and each other's company, discovering that their partnership extended beyond their professional endeavours. Each victory, no matter how small, was celebrated together, and each challenge was met with mutual support and understanding.

Their journey was not without its trials. The pressures of the campaign, the long hours, and the constant scrutiny tested their resolve. Yet, through it all, they leaned on each other for

Popi: A Rising Tide

support. They learned their relationship was as much about teamwork and resilience as it was about love. Their mutual respect and admiration grew as they faced each obstacle, and their ability to find solace and strength in one another provided a source of comfort amidst the chaos.

Popi admired Donna's unwavering dedication and ability to keep their vision focused amidst the campaign's turbulence. Donna, in turn, was inspired by Popi's passion and commitment to his principles, finding in him a partner who not only shared her goals but also challenged her to grow. Their journey together was a testament to the power of collaboration and the strength of a shared purpose.

As the campaign progressed, their bond continued to strengthen. They became partners in politics and life, finding that their shared experiences and mutual goals enriched their relationship. The balance they struck between their personal and professional lives became a source of strength, allowing them to enjoy their successes and navigate their challenges with a united front.

Ultimately, their journey was about more than just a political campaign. It was a journey of growth, finding strength in each other, and discovering the true meaning of partnership. Together, Popi and Donna faced the complexities of the political world and emerged more robust, connected, and committed to their shared vision of a better future.

One evening, after a particularly gruelling day on the campaign trail, Popi looked at Donna with a grateful smile, his exhaustion momentarily overshadowed by his deep appreciation. "I couldn't have done this without you, Donna. You've been my rock through all of this."

Donna returned his smile, her eyes gleaming with pride and affection. "And I wouldn't want to be anywhere else, Popi. We're in this together, every step of the way."

They shared a moment of quiet understanding, their bond strengthened by the campaign's shared trials and triumphs. Amid the chaos and endless demands of the political world, their partnership had become a source of solace and strength.

Popi's foray into politics was just the beginning of a new chapter in his life. Whether he won or lost the election, he had already achieved something profound. He had proven to himself and Donna that he could stand up for his beliefs and make a meaningful impact.

With Donna by his side, Popi faced the future with a newfound confidence and resolve. Their shared experiences had forged a partnership grounded in mutual respect and unwavering support. They had navigated the complexities of the political world together. Through their trials and triumphs, they had built a solid foundation for whatever challenges lay ahead.

As they looked toward the horizon, Popi and Donna knew their journey was far from over. Their commitment to their cause and each other had strengthened their resolve, and they were ready to face whatever came their way. With their combined strength, passion, and determination, they were prepared to continue their work and strive for positive change, confident in their ability to overcome any obstacle that might come their way.

The Campaign

After a few weeks of immersing himself in the capital of Canada and networking following his monumental car wash, Popi received a call from Hon. Hillcrest, an esteemed figure within the Conservative Party. The invitation was significant: Popi was asked to leverage his newfound platform and influence to help the party gain support in the very riding where he had held his successful event.

As Popi pondered the request, he felt a surge of apprehension. The thought of taking on such a responsibility, especially in the realm of federal politics where he was still a novice, filled him with self-doubt. He worried that his inexperience might hinder rather than help the party's efforts. Popi made his decision with a deep respect for the party and Hon. Hillcrest.

"I appreciate the trust you're placing in me, Hon. Hillcrest," Popi began with sincerity. "However, I'm still quite new to federal politics. I fear that my lack of experience might lead to more harm than good for the party's efforts. I wouldn't want to jeopardize the party's reputation."

Hon. Hillcrest, understanding the gravity of Popi's concerns, took a moment to respond with a blend of firmness and reassurance. "Popi, I understand your reservations. But this is a crucial moment for us, and your unique connection to the community and the enthusiasm you've generated are invaluable. Think of this as a stepping stone. I'm asking you as a personal favour. The party will look out for you in the future, and this could be a great opportunity for you to build your experience."

Popi considered the weight of Hillcrest's words. The promise of future support from the party, combined with the recognition of his unique position, began to shift his perspective. Despite his initial reluctance, he realized this was not just a challenge but an opportunity to grow and contribute meaningfully.

After some time of earnest persuasion from Hon. Hillcrest, Popi reluctantly agreed to take on the responsibility of reviving the Conservative Party of Canada's reputation in the riding, albeit with a caveat. "I'll do my best, but don't expect miracles," he said, his voice tinged with apprehension. "I'm still learning and don't want anyone to have high expectations based on my inexperience."

The situation was complex. The riding had been lost to the Liberal Party of Canada in the previous two elections, and there were members within the party who secretly hoped that Popi would falter. They planned to use his effort as a stepping stone to their own eventual success, positioning themselves for victory in the general election two years after the upcoming by-election, just a few months away.

Popi was aware of the underlying currents, sensing that some viewed his endeavour more as a calculated risk than a genuine chance for victory. Nevertheless, he resolved to approach the task with integrity and determination.

"Understood," Hillcrest acknowledged, recognizing the gravity of Popi's decision. "We appreciate your willingness to step up. Remember, this is about more than just the immediate results. It's about building a foundation for the future."

Popi nodded, bracing himself for the challenge ahead. The road

Popi: A Rising Tide

was uncertain, and the realities of party politics tempered the expectations. Yet, he was determined to give it his all, focusing on what he could control: his effort, message, and commitment to the people.

As Popi hung up the call, he couldn't shake the mix of anxiety and indifference that clung to him. The weight of the responsibility pressed heavily on his shoulders, and he felt a surge of nerves about the task ahead. Yet, his emotions were best captured in a simple text to Donna:

"The greedy fish took the bait. We need to start working on the campaign ASAP."

He called his father next, his voice tinged with both resolve and worry. "Dad, I've agreed to take on the campaign. But please, don't mention it to Mom. I don't want to add any more stress to her plate right now."

Understanding the gravity of the situation, Popi's father assured him he would keep the news under wraps. Popi then hung up, feeling a mix of determination and trepidation. He knew the path ahead would be fraught with challenges, but he was ready to face them head-on, starting with rallying Donna and setting their plans into motion.

Donna and Popi met soon after to celebrate the unexpected twist in their political journey. They were both brimming with excitement, and the evening quickly turned into a brainstorming session filled with zeal and creativity.

Their conversation naturally drifted into campaign strategy as they clinked glasses and savoured their celebratory meal. Donna suggested, "We should contact the team that helped with the car wash. They were amazing and could add value to the campaign. Plus, we should contact everyone we connected with at the event. They might still be enthusiastic about supporting our cause."

Popi nodded, his eyes gleaming with enthusiasm. "Great idea. And what if we do another car wash? It could raise more awareness and boost our visibility even further. It's a chance to reinforce our message and show our commitment to the community."

Donna's face lit up with excitement. "Yes! We can use this next car wash to support our cause and build your image as a social engineer. It'll be a powerful way to showcase our dedication and the practical steps we're taking to make a difference."

With plans set in motion, Donna and Popi spent the evening in a whirlwind of ideas, laughter, and strategic discussion. Their celebration was not just about the progress they had made but also about the journey ahead. They were determined to make their mark and elevate Popi's campaign with the same passion and commitment they had shown from the start.

Popi and Donna worked through the night, their enthusiasm fuelling their tireless efforts. Their minds buzzed with a flurry of ideas to make the campaign a resounding success. The quiet of the early morning hours was filled with the sound of clicking keyboards and animated conversations about strategy and outreach.

Popi, deep in thought, expressed his concerns. "Donna, I keep thinking that the party might be using me as a stepping stone.

Popi: A Rising Tide

They could be planning to insert one of their loyalists after I've repaired their image. If that's the case, we must exceed their expectations and ensure that even if I don't win this time, the people will demand that I be their candidate in future elections."

Donna looked up from her notes, her eyes meeting his with determination. "We'll make sure that doesn't happen. If we can make a real impact and connect with the community, they'll see the value in what we're doing and support you. It's not just about winning this election; it's about showing the people you're genuinely invested in their well-being and future."

Popi nodded, feeling a renewed sense of purpose. "Exactly. My goal now is to leave a mark so profound that the people will only want me to be their representative in the next election. It all starts with a heartfelt plea to the community, demonstrating my commitment to social engineering and self-sufficiency. I want to help underprivileged individuals achieve respectable independence while championing the principles of freedom of speech and conscience."

As dawn approached, their plan began to take shape. They decided to start with a series of community-focused events, building on the momentum of the car wash. Popi would speak directly to the people, sharing his vision for a society where everyone had the tools and opportunities to succeed on their own terms. With her graphic design skills, Donna would create compelling materials to spread their message and rally support.

By the time the sun began rising, Donna and Popi were exhausted but exhilarated. They knew the road ahead would be challenging, but they were more determined than ever to make a lasting impact. Their shared vision and dedication drove their campaign, setting the stage for what they hoped would be a transformative journey for Popi and the community he aimed to serve.

A few days after their intense brainstorming sessions, Popi's phone rang with a call that felt like a turning point in his journey. The party official on the other end of the line confirmed his official candidacy for the Ottawa riding for the by-election. Popi could hardly contain his excitement as he shared the news with Donna, who had been by his side throughout the process.

"Donna, it's official!" Popi said, his voice brimming with anticipation. "We're officially in the running for the Ottawa riding."

Donna's face lit up with a triumphant smile. "That's fantastic news, Popi! We've worked so hard for this moment. Now, it's time to put all our plans into action."

With their candidacy now confirmed, Team Popi was ready to hit the ground running. Their strategy was set: building on the success of the car wash, they would launch a series of community engagement events designed to showcase Popi's commitment to self-sufficiency and individual freedom.

Popi and Donna wasted no time in mobilizing their network. They reached out to the volunteers who had helped with the car wash and began organizing the next big event, leveraging the enthusiasm they had generated to build momentum. The upcoming car wash would raise more funds and serve as a platform to further amplify Popi's message and strengthen his connection with the community.

Popi: A Rising Tide

The days ahead promised to be filled with action and opportunity. Popi was determined to make every effort count, knowing their hard work and dedication would be crucial in shaping the campaign's success. With Donna's unwavering support and their shared vision, they were ready to embark on this new chapter with optimism and resolve.

While Popi and Donna's dedication to their campaign might have seemed unconventional for a couple navigating a new relationship, it was the very essence of their partnership. Their bond was forged in the fires of shared ambition and mutual support, and they were riding this wave of enthusiasm and purpose with unwavering commitment.

Though still officially residing with her parents, Donna had essentially moved into Popi's apartment. His place had become their command centre, a bustling hub of campaign activity and strategic planning. The apartment, once just a living space, had transformed into a beacon of their aspirations. Popi didn't merely tolerate Donna's presence; he welcomed and embraced it. Her influence had turned his home into a vibrant epicentre of hope and determination.

"Popi, it feels like we're creating something bigger than ourselves here," Donna remarked one evening, her eyes reflecting the glow of the desk lamp they had set up in the corner of the living room. "It's like we're building our own little kingdom, brick by brick."

Popi smiled, nodding in agreement. "It does feel that way, doesn't it? We're crafting something that's not just for us but for the people we're aiming to serve."

Their relationship deepened in the heart of their campaign amidst the hustle and late-night brainstorming sessions. They were not just partners in love but allies in a shared quest, and the walls of Popi's apartment echoed with the promise of their joint venture. Just as an oak grows strong through intertwining roots, their connection also strengthened through their common goal.

After several days of intense planning and strategizing, Popi and Donna were ready to hit the ground running. The party had provided a modest sum of money to kickstart their efforts. Still, it was clear that the financial support was more a token of gesture than a genuine commitment. Popi hadn't anticipated much, so he took the scant funds in stride, treating them as a mere stepping stone rather than a substantial asset.

However, tensions rose when the Conservative Party of Canada attempted to assign a rookie caucus member to assist with Popi's campaign. Popi saw this move as a potential disruption rather than a support. The rookie, though well-intentioned, lacked the experience and understanding of Popi's vision and approach. To Popi, this was not just a matter of principle but of practicality. He had a clear vision for his campaign and was determined to see it through on his own terms.

"No, I appreciate the offer, but I've got this," Popi said firmly during a call with party officials. "This is my campaign, and I need to build my team in a way that aligns with my vision. I'll be managing this my way."

Donna, ever by Popi's side, nodded in agreement. "We need to ensure everything is done with the same passion and dedication we've put into this. Bringing someone who isn't on the same

Popi: A Rising Tide

page might create more obstacles than solutions."

The party officials, recognizing Popi's resolve and understanding that they needed him more than he needed them, reluctantly conceded. They knew that Popi's ability to attract and rally support could turn the tide in their favour, so they allowed him to proceed as he saw fit.

This moment was a testament to Popi's resolve and the strength of his partnership with Donna. They were not just participants in the campaign but its driving force. Popi ultimately said, "We're building this from the ground up, and we're going to do it on our own terms. It's our vision and our effort that will make the difference."

Donna found an excellent workspace for their campaign—a place that felt practical and inspiring. It was a venue that could accommodate their growing team and ambitious plans. Although not everyone from the car wash could join them, they managed to gather a solid group of enthusiastic individuals who had previously rallied behind Popi and Donna's cause.

As Donna took charge, her authority was immediately apparent. She had developed a commanding presence, a skill she had honed by observing Popi's leadership style. With clear direction and a confident demeanour, she could delegate tasks efficiently without alienating anyone. Her ability to lead reflected the trust and respect she had earned from the team.

Though not present at the initial meeting, Popi had already established a foundation of trust and respect with the crew. They understood that Donna spoke on his behalf and that her directives aligned with his vision. This mutual respect was a testament to Popi and Donna's strong bond and shared commitment.

"I know we didn't all get together as planned," Donna said as she addressed the team, "but we've got a fantastic group here, and I'm confident we can make this work. Popi and I have put a lot of thought into this, and your involvement is key to our success."

The team responded with enthusiasm. Their previous experience with the duo had left them eager to contribute to the new project. The camaraderie and excitement were palpable, with everyone motivated by the prospect of making a significant impact.

Donna continued, "We've got a clear plan, and each of you will play a crucial role. Let's approach this with the same energy and dedication we had during the car wash. Together, we can turn this campaign into something truly remarkable."

The air was filled with a sense of purpose and anticipation. With Donna's capable leadership and Popi's vision guiding them, the campaign was poised to take flight. The team was ready to bring their shared goals to life, fully invested in the journey ahead.

Popi and Donna divided their roles with a clear sense of purpose. While Popi immersed himself in high-level meetings and strategic discussions with influential figures, Donna and Kyle dove headfirst into the grassroots efforts that would fuel their campaign.

Donna was a natural leader, adept at multitasking and thinking on her feet. Her background as a councillor's Chief of Staff had equipped her with the skills needed to navigate the campaign's complexities efficiently. The experience she had garnered in her previous roles now served her well as she took charge of the ground-level operations.

In her previous job, Donna had often faced constraints and limitations, working within the boundaries set by others. But now, with the reins of the campaign firmly in her hands, she found herself in a position where she could steer the project according to her vision. This newfound autonomy was exhilarating.

Her ability to juggle multiple tasks precisely and her keen strategic mind suited her exceptionally for this role. Donna approached each challenge with a combination of intelligence and determination. She orchestrated meetings, managed logistics, and motivated the team with a contagious fervour. Her leadership was about directing others and inspiring them to work towards a common goal with unwavering dedication.

Donna's confidence grew as she navigated the campaign's demands. For someone as smart and driven as she was, the responsibility of managing this campaign felt like a perfect fit. Her commitment to the cause and her knack for effective problem-solving ensured that every detail was attended to and every challenge was met with resolve.

As Popi worked to build connections and secure support from influential figures, Donna's hands-on approach grounded their efforts and ensured their campaign was dynamic and efficient. Together, they made a formidable team—Popi's strategic vision complemented by Donna's practical execution. The synergy in their roles was a testament to their shared passion and ability to turn their ambitions into action.

Popi and Donna were determined to build on their initial success with another car wash, this time with an added twist. At the end of the event, they planned to unveil Popi's candidacy for office, using it as a platform to announce his official run. Despite their modest budget, they were resolute in believing they could achieve remarkable results with their resources.

Popi's primary focus was not on raising money but on forging valuable connections and aligning himself with respected figures within the riding. He declined any offers of financial support, choosing instead to ask for assistance in promoting his upcoming events. His strategy was clear: rather than investing heavily in advertisements, he aimed to attract people through engaging, community-centred events. He aimed to bring people together in one place where he could connect with them personally, even briefly.

Popi's approach was reminiscent of the old saying, "You catch more flies with honey than with vinegar." By fostering personal interactions and engaging directly with the community, he hoped to build trust and support. Each car wash would serve as a fundraiser and an opportunity for Popi to showcase his commitment to the cause and make a lasting impression on the electorate.

Donna was instrumental in organizing these events, ensuring they ran smoothly and effectively communicated Popi's message. Her knack for logistics and her understanding of their strategic goals made her an invaluable asset. She worked tirelessly to maximize their impact as they planned the next car wash, from coordinating volunteers to handling promotional efforts.

Together, Popi and Donna envisioned a campaign built on genuine connections rather than flashy advertisements. They believed that by focusing on grassroots engagement and personal interactions, they could inspire and mobilize their community in a meaningful and memorable way. Their strategy was to create an environment where people felt connected and invested in Popi's vision, turning each event into a stepping stone toward greater recognition and support.

Popi and Donna's excitement was palpable as the day of the car wash approached. They knew that while their resources were limited, their creativity and dedication had the power to make a significant difference. Their unwavering commitment to their cause and innovative campaigning approach promised to turn challenges into opportunities and build a foundation for Popi's future in politics.

After weeks of meticulous planning, the second car wash was a resounding success. The turnout exceeded expectations, and the community's support was palpable. Popi and Donna managed to create an engaging and memorable event that raised awareness for their cause and further established Popi's candidacy.

However, just as things seemed to be going well, Popi received unexpected and distressing news. His mother, Mrs. Peters, had caught wind of Popi's political ambitions through the news. The reaction was nothing short of explosive.

Mr. Peters called Popi, his voice a mix of pride and concern.

"Congratulations, son! I heard the event went well," he said warmly. But in the background, Popi could hear his mother's furious outburst.

"Why are you so calm?" Mrs. Peters' voice thundered through the phone. "This is madness! Our son is throwing his life away! What on earth is he thinking?"

Popi could sense the tension and fear in his father's voice as he tried to soothe his mother. "Mom, please," Mr. Peters said, his voice strained. "Let's talk about this calmly."

But Mrs. Peters' distress was palpable, her words a cascade of fear and anger. "How can you be so indifferent? He's about to make a huge mistake, and you're just standing by? I'm about to lose my son to this reckless endeavour!"

Popi's heart sank as he listened. He knew how much his parents' opinions mattered to him. Still, he also understood that his choice was a significant departure from the path they had envisioned for him. The clash between his aspirations and his mother's fears was like a storm tearing through calm seas, and Popi felt the turbulence deeply.

"Dad, I appreciate your support," Popi said, trying to keep his voice steady. "But please, let Mom know I've thought about this deeply. I'm committed to this cause and believe it's the right path for me."

"Your mother just needs some time," Mr. Peters replied, his voice trying to bridge the growing chasm. "She's worried about you, Popi. We both are."

Popi: A Rising Tide

As the call ended, Popi grappled with his conflicting emotions. The enthusiasm and momentum from the car wash now felt overshadowed by his mother's vehement reaction. Despite the success of their efforts, Popi knew that navigating his decision's personal and emotional landscape was just as challenging as the political campaign itself.

Sensing Popi's distress, Donna reached out to him with a comforting presence. "Hey, I'm here for you," she said gently. "We knew this wouldn't be easy, but we're in this together. We'll find a way to address your mother's concerns while moving forward with our plans."

Popi nodded, finding solace in Donna's unwavering support. "Thanks, Donna. I just need to find a way to balance my commitment to this campaign with my mom's worries. It won't be simple, but I'm ready to face it all."

The rift between Popi's parents had been simmering for some time, but his decision to enter the political arena seemed to exacerbate their differences. His mother, Mrs. Peters, was adamant that her son should return home where she believed he would be safe from the tumult of politics. She saw the world as a place fraught with risks, and Popi's ambitions felt like an insurmountable danger to her.

On the other hand, Mr. Peters was a figure of quiet pride. Having spent decades as a manager in a factory, he had experienced the frustrations of dealing with unyielding senior management and the difficulty of enacting meaningful change from within a restrictive system. Despite his own lack of success in transforming his work environment, he admired Popi's courage to seize the reins and make a difference. To Mr.

Peters, his son's determination to tackle the challenges of politics was akin to taking the bull by the horns—something he had always dreamed of but never achieved himself.

In their respective ways, both parents were reacting to Popi's ambition through the lens of their own experiences. His mother's fears were rooted in a protective instinct, while his father's pride stemmed from a deep-seated desire for his son to achieve what he had only dreamed of.

Amid this family tension, Popi found himself caught between two worlds—one of maternal concern and another of paternal pride. His mother's wishes to see him return home felt like an attempt to pull him back from the precipice of his ambitions, while his father's support was a beacon of encouragement.

Popi reflected on his parents' contrasting responses with a heavy heart. He understood their perspectives and recognized the importance of pursuing his path. The struggle was about navigating the political landscape and reconciling his family's emotional responses with his aspirations.

Amid the swirling conflict between his parents and the mounting pressures of his political journey, Popi found himself grappling with profound self-doubt. It was as though he stood at the edge of a precipice, peering into the abyss of his own fears and uncertainties. For the first time, he questioned whether his pursuit was an act of bravery or selfishness, and the weight of his decisions seemed to grow heavier with each passing day.

The emotional clash between his mother's protective instincts and his father's proud aspirations created a storm within him.

Popi: A Rising Tide

While his mother's pleas echoed with heartfelt concern, urging him to abandon the perilous path he had chosen, his father's pride illuminated a different path, one of potential fulfillment and unfulfilled dreams. The conflicting messages left Popi at a crossroads, caught between his parents' divergent expectations and his own yearning for purpose.

As the minutes turned into hours, the strain of balancing familial expectations with personal ambition began to take its toll. Popi, who had always been stoic and self-reliant, felt an unprecedented loneliness. The isolation was not just physical but deeply emotional. After a successful car wash campaign, he was surrounded by supporters, strategists, and allies. Yet, the weight of his internal struggle made him feel like the loneliest person in the world.

In his moments of solitude, Popi wrestled with these questions: Was he pursuing a noble cause, or was he merely driven by a desire to prove himself, regardless of the personal cost? Was his commitment to politics a testament to his courage, or was it a reckless endeavour that could lead to disillusionment and failure?

He had never been one to share his vulnerabilities openly. His nature was to face challenges head-on and solve problems on his own. Yet, in these trying times, he longed for solace, someone who could offer a listening ear without judgment. He felt as though he was navigating a labyrinth of doubt with no clear exit in sight.

As he sat with Donna in his car, Popi reached out to Donna. The car's silence starkly contrasted with their campaign's bustling activity. The calm before the storm finally allowed him to unload his troubled conscience.

"Donna," he said quietly, his voice laden with exhaustion, "I don't know if I'm doing the right thing. I've never felt so conflicted. My mom is afraid for me, my dad is proud but regrets his own missed opportunities, and I'm stuck in the middle. Am I being brave, or am I just being selfish?"

Donna, his steadfast partner through the tumultuous journey, listened with empathy. She thought about this question momentarily, her presence a comforting anchor in the sea of his uncertainties.

"Popi," she began gently, "it's okay to have doubts. It doesn't make you weak; it makes you human. You're standing up for something you believe in, which takes immense courage. Your parents' feelings come from a place of love, but they can't dictate your path. You must listen to your heart and trust that you're doing what you believe is right."

She continued, her voice soothing, "No matter how hard it gets, remember why you started this journey. You wanted to make a difference, to fight for something greater than yourself. That's not selfish; it's noble. But it's also okay to feel overwhelmed. Lean on those who care about you and take it one step at a time."

Popi absorbed her words, feeling a sense of relief. Donna's reassurance and understanding were a balm to his troubled soul. At that moment, he realized that while the path ahead was fraught with uncertainty, he did not have to walk it alone. With Donna's support and the strength of his convictions, he could face the challenges with renewed resolve.

Popi: A Rising Tide

Ultimately, it was not the absence of doubt but the courage to confront it that would define his journey. Popi understood that he was embarking on a path of peril and promise. From an early age, his father always reminded him that courage is not the absence of fear but acting in spite of it.

As Popi ended his conversation with Donna, still absorbed in the wave of emotions from their conversation, there was a knock at the window of his car. It was a local businesswoman, Ms. Tina. Popi got out of his car, and she greeted him and introduced herself.

Ms. Tina was a well-known figure in the Greater Ottawa Area, having successfully run a couple of popular shawarma restaurants. Her presence was warm and unassuming, but her demeanour carried an air of sincere respect and admiration.

"Popi," Ms. Tina greeted him, her voice infused with genuine appreciation. "I couldn't help but be moved by your commitment to help the underprivileged and your bold step into federal politics. Your dedication truly resonates with me."

Still processing the recent conversation with Donna, Popi looked up with surprise and curiosity. "Thank you, Ms. Tina. Hearing that from someone as esteemed as you means a lot."

Ms. Tina extended a hand, her gesture both formal and heartfelt. "I wanted to offer my support and personally donate to your cause. But more than that, I'd like to extend a hand of friendship to you in your future endeavours. I also want to contribute tangibly—I'd like to arrange for my restaurants to donate leftover food every night and anything else that might be excess. It's my small way of supporting your mission."

The handshake they shared was firm, solidifying their agreement. Popi felt a sense of gratitude and hope swell within him. "That's incredibly generous of you, Ms. Tina. Your support means more than you can imagine."

Ms. Tina continued, her enthusiasm undiminished. "I also want to host an event for you and your campaign. It'll allow you to network with some influential women in Ottawa and perhaps gain more support."

Popi's eyes brightened with interest. "That sounds like a fantastic idea. I'd love to be part of it."

Just as Popi thought the conversation was wrapping up, Ms. Tina took a deep breath, revealing another layer to her offer. "There's one more thing I'd like to ask. My teenage son is in middle school, and I'd like him to gain real-life experience. If you could give him some work to do, I think it would be invaluable for him. He's disciplined and respectful, and if he causes any trouble, you can let him go without hesitation. I promise I won't take it personally."

Popi chuckled, appreciating the humour and sincerity in her request. "I'll certainly consider it. It sounds like a great opportunity for him to learn about responsibility."

They laughed together, the tension of the past few weeks easing momentarily. Their shared experiences of adjusting to new environments, especially coming from small towns, provided a common ground for connection. As they talked, they discovered more parallels in their journeys, which added a layer of camaraderie to their budding partnership.

Popi: A Rising Tide

Ms. Tina's offer and support breathed new energy into Popi's campaign. Her willingness to contribute financially and through community engagement was a testament to the power of grassroots support. Clearly, their collaboration would be a cornerstone in Popi's efforts to make a meaningful impact in the riding.

Popi felt a renewed sense of purpose and optimism as they parted ways. The challenges ahead were still formidable, but with allies like Ms. Tina and Donna's unwavering support, he was ready to face them head-on, fortified by the belief that he was on the right path.

As the evening unfolded, more business people came forward to meet Popi, each spending only a few minutes introducing themselves and leaving behind their business cards. Within a few hours, around his car was abuzz with congratulations for his successful event and good wishes for the upcoming by-election. Popi was struck by the sheer number of people eager to connect, and the brief encounters left him with a stack of business cards and a sense of mounting importance.

Among the crowd, Popi also encountered representatives from several local charity organizations. These individuals, who led initiatives supporting various causes in the Ottawa area, expressed their admiration for his efforts and impact. Their words of encouragement added another layer of validation to his work, reinforcing the significance of his mission.

Despite the growing popularity and support, a flicker of doubt crept into Popi's mind. The tension with his parents had weighed heavily on him, and he briefly considered stepping away from politics to restore family harmony. However, as he absorbed the respect and enthusiasm from those around him, he felt a renewed sense of purpose. The support he had garnered made him reconsider. Perhaps the sacrifices were worth it if they could lead to real, positive change.

In that moment, he reflected on his journey—was it an act of audacity or selfishness? Only time would reveal the answer. For now, the momentum and respect he had accumulated were powerful motivators. With a resolve that was as firm as it was uncertain, Popi decided to forge ahead. The path was fraught with challenges, but the opportunity to make a tangible difference provided the clarity he needed. He was ready to embrace the risks, knowing that the possibility of creating meaningful change outweighed the personal cost.

As the event drew to a close, the group began packing up and cleaning the venue. Popi and Donna, despite their exhaustion, were there from start to finish, working alongside their team. Their hands, stained with the remnants of the day's efforts, moved with a sense of camaraderie that spoke volumes about their dedication.

Eager to show his appreciation, Popi offered to buy all volunteers drinks as a gesture of thanks. However, the long day had taken its toll, and most of the team, worn out and ready for rest, declined the offer. They expressed their gratitude with warm smiles and hearty handshakes, their eyes reflecting the satisfaction of a job well done.

During the clean-up, it was decided to schedule a proper meetup for another day. The idea was to have a relaxed gathering where everyone could unwind and enjoy each other's company without the rush of responsibilities hanging over them. It would be a chance to celebrate their collective achievements and strengthen the bonds formed through their hard work.

Donna and Popi shared a quiet moment as they tidied up, reflecting on the day's success. Despite the fatigue, they felt a profound sense of accomplishment. The event had propelled Popi's campaign and forged connections with people who genuinely cared about the cause.

As the last of the equipment was packed away and the venue returned to its former state, Popi and Donna exchanged a look of mutual understanding. They knew the road ahead would be challenging, but moments like these—full of shared effort and collective pride—made the journey worthwhile. They were ready to face whatever came next, buoyed by the support they had garnered and the strength of their partnership.

Popi's phone rang, and he glanced at the screen to see the name of the Conservative Party leader, Mr. Church. His pulse quickened with a mix of excitement and apprehension. The leader of the official opposition had requested a meeting to discuss the recent car wash that had garnered so much attention. While Popi was pleased by the acknowledgment, he couldn't shake the feeling that there was more to this call than just a congratulatory message.

"Hello, Mr. Church," Popi answered, trying to keep his voice steady.

"Popi, it's good to speak with you," Mr. Church's voice came through the line, warm and authoritative. "I've been following the news and the impressive turnout at your car wash. Clearly, you've made quite an impact, and I'd like to discuss your efforts and plans."

Popi's mind raced. The leader of the opposition reaching out was a significant development, but the timing and circumstances hinted at a deeper agenda. "Thank you, Mr. Church. I appreciate your kind words. When would you like to meet?"

"Whenever you're available. I understand you've been quite busy, so let me know a time that works for you."

Popi agreed to meet the following week. After ending the call, he sat on the hood of his car, contemplative. The request for a meeting was flattering, but it also raised several questions. Was this a simple gesture of goodwill, or was Mr. Church considering a more strategic partnership or offer?

He shared his thoughts with Donna immediately. "I have a meeting scheduled with Mr. Church next week. He mentioned he was impressed by the car wash turnout. Part of me wonders if there's more to this than just congratulations."

Donna, ever perceptive, raised an eyebrow. "It's possible. Politicians don't usually make such overtures without a reason. This could be a chance to form alliances or gain additional support. It might be worth preparing for different scenarios—both the opportunities and the challenges."

Popi nodded, appreciating Donna's insight. "That's a good idea. I'll prepare thoroughly and keep our options open. Whatever happens, I want to ensure our goals and values remain front and centre."

Popi: A Rising Tide

They spent the evening brainstorming and strategizing, knowing the upcoming meeting with Mr. Church could be pivotal in Popi's political journey. The preparation was more than just about making a good impression; it was about aligning their mission with the broader political landscape and ensuring that their message of self-sufficiency and freedom continued to resonate with those in power.

As the sun set on what had been an extraordinary day, Popi found himself grappling with a profound internal conflict. The whirlwind of endorsement and support he had received had propelled him into the limelight much faster than he had ever anticipated. Yet, beneath the surface of triumph and excitement, a deep sense of unease lingered.

The day's events had unfolded seamlessly—meetings with influential figures, a surge of media attention, and a genuine outpouring of public support. Popi had become something of a political sensation, a phenomenon that seemed to capture the collective imagination of the riding and beyond. But the accolades and endorsements, while gratifying, did little to ease the turmoil brewing within him.

His parents' recent clash had left an indelible mark on his soul. His mother's fierce objections and his father's conflicted pride had created a rift that seemed to grow wider with each passing day. It was as though a weight had been fastened around his neck, a constant reminder of the familial discord that shadowed his political aspirations. Despite the external successes and the swelling support, Popi couldn't shake the feeling of being trapped between competing loyalties and emotions.

The juxtaposition of his growing prominence and the fracturing relationship with his parents felt like walking a tightrope. Every congratulatory message, every new connection, and every strategic meeting only seemed to heighten his internal struggle. The more he excelled in his campaign, the more pronounced the friction with his family became, casting a shadow over his achievements.

Ever perceptive to Popi's emotional state, Donna noticed the strain on his face as they reviewed their upcoming schedules. "You've had an incredible day, Popi," she said gently, "but it's clear that something is weighing heavily on you."

Popi sighed, his gaze distant. "It's this constant tug-of-war with my parents. On one hand, I'm getting all this support and recognition, which is fantastic. On the other hand, the rift within my family is like a constant anchor, dragging me down. It's hard to fully enjoy any of this when I'm torn in two directions."

Donna nodded sympathetically. "It's understandable. You're amidst a significant life transition, and it's natural to feel conflicted. But remember, you don't have to go through this alone. We can face these challenges together."

Popi appreciated Donna's support more than he could express. She had been his rock, a steady presence amidst the turbulence. "Thank you, Donna. Your support means everything to me. I'm just trying to find a balance to reconcile my personal life with my ambitions. It's not easy."

Donna reached out and took his hand. "We'll navigate this together. Let's focus on the positive impact we can make and remember why you started this journey in the first place. Your

Popi: A Rising Tide

family may be struggling to understand, but that doesn't diminish the good you're doing."

Popi took a deep breath, finding some solace in Donna's words. The road ahead was uncertain, but he knew that with Donna by his side, he could face the challenges ahead head-on. He resolved to address the personal issues with his family, even if it meant temporarily stepping away from the campaign. Finding a way to bridge the gap with his parents was crucial—not only for his peace of mind but also for the integrity of his journey.

Popi and Donna continued to plan as the night deepened, their conversations punctuated by moments of reflection and determination. Despite the trials and tribulations, they remained steadfast in their commitment to making a difference. For Popi, the path was fraught with obstacles. Still, with unwavering support and a clear sense of purpose, he was ready to face whatever came next, hopeful that time and effort would eventually mend the fractures in his personal life while he pursued his political dreams.

Popi was still riding high from the day's successes as he arrived home, basking in the glow of newfound opportunities and endorsements. The sense of triumph was palpable, almost tangible, and he felt as if he had already secured a victory in the upcoming by-election. But as he walked through his front door, the weight of reality came crashing down.

Donna's text arrived, marked by an unsettling urgency. Popi opened the video she had sent him with trepidation and curiosity. The footage was a viral sensation, racing across social media with alarming speed. It was a vicious attack on his character and campaign, accusing him of being a sympathizer to rapists and labelling his speech about freedom as a thinly veiled promotion of anarchy. The video twisted his actions, including the story of the international student he had once helped, into a grotesque narrative that painted him entirely contrary to his values.

Popi watched in stunned silence as the video's inflammatory rhetoric played out. The arguments were distorted and taken out of context to incite outrage and undermine his credibility. It was as if he had gone from the pinnacle of political promise to the depths of scandal in a single breath. His heart raced, and a cold sweat broke out on his forehead as the gravity of the situation sank in.

The phone began to ring incessantly. Calls from campaign staff, concerned friends, and a barrage of messages from every corner of his network flooded in, each carrying a mix of panic and confusion. Popi felt overwhelmed, as if he were caught in a vortex of scrutiny and suspicion. He knew he needed to address the situation, but the sheer magnitude of the storm made it difficult to think clearly.

With a deep breath, Popi took a moment to compose himself. He decided to leave an outgoing message for his callers, trying to convey calm and control amidst the chaos. He recorded a brief but measured outgoing voice message:

"Hello, everyone. I'm aware of the video circulating online and the serious accusations it contains. I want you to know that I understand the concerns and the gravity of the situation. Right now, I need some time to process these grotesque allegations and gather my thoughts. I assure you that I will address the video and the allegations as soon as possible. For now, please

Popi: A Rising Tide
give me some time to digest this. Thank you all for your understanding."

After setting the message, Popi switched off his phone, plunging himself into a disorienting silence. The cacophony of ringing and buzzing ceased, but the silence only amplified the weight of his thoughts. He sank onto his couch, feeling the crushing pressure of the political reality he had just stepped into.

The world outside had turned against him instantly, and the idealism that had fuelled his campaign now felt distant and fragile. Though unfounded and exaggerated, the accusations had shaken the foundation of his campaign and his sense of self. Popi felt as if he were in the eye of a storm, surrounded by a tempest of confusion and despair.

Popi struggled to find solace in the quiet of his home as the night stretched on. The peace he had once felt now seemed elusive, replaced by the stark reality of the political arena—a place where every action and word could be twisted and weaponized. Amid his turmoil, he resolved to confront the challenge head-on, to clear his name and reclaim his narrative. The path forward was uncertain, but Popi knew that he had to rise to the occasion, no matter how daunting it seemed.

The Final Stretch

With the viral video attacking his character and distorting his principles, Popi knew he had to act swiftly. Despite the advice to let the controversy simmer and hope it would eventually fade, Popi felt that waiting was risky. The viral nature of the video meant it could do irreparable damage if not addressed immediately. He resolved to confront the issue head-on, believing that a proactive response was the best way to manage the situation and regain control of his narrative.

Determined to take charge and steer the situation in his favour, Popi set up a video recording in his apartment. The room was dimly lit, casting a sombre but sincere tone. He took a deep breath and began speaking directly to the camera, his voice steady but imbued with the seriousness of the situation.

"Hello, everyone. I'm Paul Peters, but most of you know me as Popi. I want to address the recently viral video and the grave accusations it has brought against me.

Firstly, I want to acknowledge the concern and outrage generated by the video. I understand why it has stirred strong emotions, and I want to clarify my position as unequivocally as possible. The claims made in that video are misleading and fundamentally misrepresent the values I stand for and the principles guiding my campaign.

The video suggests that my advocacy for freedom and self-

Popi: A Rising Tide

sufficiency translates to indifference toward the safety and well-being of women. Let me be clear: this is not the case. I have always believed—and will continue to believe—that ensuring safety and promoting respect for all individuals are paramount. My commitment to freedom and self-sufficiency is not a shield from harmful behaviour or neglect of responsibility.

The specific story cited in the video regarding the international student I helped has been distorted. My involvement in that case was driven by a sense of justice and a desire to provide support where needed, not condoning or protecting any form of misconduct. I take these accusations seriously and am committed to addressing them with the utmost transparency.

I understand the gravity of the situation, and I want to assure you that my campaign's focus remains on promoting positive change and addressing the real issues facing our community. I've always advocated for a society where individuals are empowered to thrive independently. Still, that empowerment includes ensuring everyone's safety and dignity.

I sincerely apologize to those who have been hurt or offended by the video's misrepresentations. My goal has always been to uplift and support, not to diminish the importance of safety and respect.

I appreciate your understanding as we work through this challenge. I'm committed to continuing this journey with integrity and respect for all. Thank you for your patience and support as we address this matter."

Popi uploaded the video and shared it across his social media channels, taking a calculated step to control the damage and clarify his stance. He knew that while this video might not wholly quell the controversy, it was a necessary measure to address the allegations head-on and maintain his credibility.

As he finished and sat back, the weight of the situation was still heavy on his shoulders. He hoped his direct response would help neutralize the problem and restore faith in his intentions. The path forward would be challenging, but Popi was determined to navigate it with honesty and resolve.

As Popi watched the video he had just released, the immediate aftermath was sobering. Despite his best efforts to clarify and defend his position, the damage had already been done. The support he had garnered was wavering, and the fallout from the controversy was palpable.

In the twelve hours the video had been live on the internet, approximately one-third of his supporters had already turned away, disheartened by the controversy and the negative publicity. Among these were some dedicated volunteers who had been crucial to the campaign's early successes. Their departure left a significant void in both human resources and morale.

A third of his supporters remained neutral about the allegations in the viral video. The controversy had not swayed them, but they were also not entirely convinced by Popi's response. Their stance was delicate, meaning keeping them would be crucial. He had them for now, but it was not for certain.

The remaining third of his base was on the fence. They were undecided, torn between the allegations and Popi's defence.

Popi: A Rising Tide

This group held the key to shifting the momentum in his favour.

Popi knew that to turn the tide in his favour, he needed a multi-faceted approach. He reached out personally to former volunteers and supporters who had stepped back. He met with some of them individually or in small groups to address their concerns, offer apologies where necessary, and explain his commitment to transparency and integrity. He aimed to rebuild trust and show that he was still the candidate they had initially believed in.

Popi organized public forums and Q&A sessions to engage neutral supporters. These events allowed him to address concerns directly, clarify his positions, and demonstrate his dedication to his principles. By engaging directly with the public, he aimed to humanize his campaign and show that he was open to dialogue.

Popi and Donna then refocused the campaign's messaging on the core values that initially resonated with voters: freedom, self-sufficiency, and community support. They highlighted the positive impacts of the campaign's initiatives and the genuine efforts to help the underprivileged.

They also shared success stories and testimonials from individuals and organizations that had benefited from their efforts. By showcasing tangible results, they aimed to reinforce the campaign's credibility and effectiveness.

Recognizing the need for fresh energy and support, Popi's campaign actively recruited new volunteers and supporters. They reached out to community organizations, local businesses, and grassroots groups to expand their network and bolster the campaign's strength.

Leveraging the support of influential figures like Ms. Tina, Popi sought to forge alliances that could lend credibility and visibility to his campaign. These partnerships aimed to reinforce his commitment to positive change and counter the negative narrative.

Popi continued to address any further allegations or controversies with transparency. He maintained open lines of communication with the media and the public, ensuring that his responses were honest and forthcoming.

Popi and Donna focused on targeted campaigning in crucial areas to maximize their impact with the election approaching. They tailored their outreach efforts to address the concerns of undecided voters and emphasized the positive aspects of Popi's platform.

As Popi navigated this tumultuous period, he understood regaining lost support and winning over the undecided voters would require resilience, strategic planning, and unwavering commitment. The challenges were significant, but the opportunity to make a meaningful difference in the election and the lives of those he aimed to serve remained his guiding motivation.

Mr. Church's reaction was both surprising and encouraging for Popi. Despite the storm of controversy swirling around him, Mr. Church had taken a genuine interest in his potential. He recognized the value of his fresh perspective and relentless energy.

Popi: A Rising Tide

When Popi met with Mr. Church, the atmosphere was charged with a mix of tension and hope. The leader of the Conservative Party, a seasoned politician with decades of experience, addressed Popi with a level of sincerity that revealed his growing admiration.

"Popi," Mr. Church began, leaning forward slightly, "I'll be honest. When I first heard of you, I didn't have much faith. Your lack of experience in federal politics was a concern, and your methods seemed unconventional. But after witnessing your impact in your riding, I've had a change of heart. Your enthusiasm, your dedication—it's clear you've sparked something real."

Still grappling with the recent controversies and his wavering confidence, Popi listened intently. He could feel the weight of the moment, the potential for a turning point in his tumultuous journey.

"I see what you're doing," Mr. Church continued, his tone firm but appreciative. "You've faced immense challenges yet galvanized a community and pushed through adversity. Your energy is infectious, and we need that kind of vigour in a party that's been on the sidelines for over a decade. We need someone like you to help us navigate the general election."

Popi's heart raced as he absorbed the gravity of Mr. Church's words. Though tempered with the reality of political manoeuvring, the leader's endorsement felt like a lifeline amidst the turbulence. Mr. Church wasn't just offering words of encouragement; he was signalling an opportunity to be an integral part of a larger vision for the party's future.

"Whichever way things end up in this by-election," Mr. Church said, "I'm committed to finding a place for you within the party. Your passion and drive are qualities we need. I believe you have the potential to make a significant impact, and I want to ensure that talent doesn't go to waste."

Popi felt a mix of relief and renewed determination. Mr. Church's support was a beacon of hope, suggesting that despite the current setbacks, there was a future worth fighting for. It was a reminder that his efforts were being recognized and that there was a path forward, even in the face of adversity.

Mr. Church's endorsement encouraged Popi to reaffirm his commitment to the campaign. He knew that despite the recent setbacks, he needed to continue pushing forward with the same vigour that had initially sparked his candidacy.

Popi and Donna, buoyed by Mr. Church's support, recalibrated their strategy. They focused on re-engaging the neutral and undecided supporters, using Mr. Church's endorsement as a testament to Popi's potential and a sign of more incredible things to come.

With the support of influential figures like Mr. Church and Ms. Tina, Popi sought to rebuild momentum. They planned to leverage upcoming events and strategic outreach to showcase Popi's commitment and positive impact, aiming to counterbalance the negative publicity.

The campaign redoubled its efforts to communicate Popi's core message of self-sufficiency, freedom, and community support. By highlighting his achievements and the tangible benefits of his initiatives, they aimed to reaffirm his credibility and vision.

Popi: A Rising Tide

Amidst the whirlwind of political manoeuvring and public scrutiny, Popi took time for personal reflection. He pondered the reasons behind his journey and the values driving his ambitions, seeking to ground himself amidst the chaos.

The road ahead remained challenging, but with the backing of key figures and a clear vision, Popi was ready to face the hurdles. His journey, marked by trials and triumphs, was a testament to his resilience and a reflection of his unwavering commitment to effecting positive change.

Popi's resolve to push forward despite the setbacks reflected his determination to turn the tide. While Mr. Church's endorsement was uplifting, it was not a panacea for his challenges. For Popi, the stakes were higher than just winning an election; it was about validating his commitment and efforts through tangible success in the federal arena.

He doubled down on his campaign efforts, revisiting his strategies and focusing on regaining the trust of the neutral third and winning back some of the support he had lost. Popi's approach was to seize every moment and opportunity with renewed vigour, treating each interaction and event as a crucial step toward his ultimate goal. He believed that he could only validate his decision to pursue this demanding path in politics by securing a victory.

The mounting pressure from his mother was like a relentless storm battering against Popi's resolve. Her insistence that he abandon his political ambitions and return home weighed heavily on him, fuelled by her fears and concerns for his safety. Popi felt torn between his mother's emotional pleas and his commitment to himself and those who depended on him.

Yet, this pressure paradoxically became a source of motivation for Popi. The more his mother implored him to quit, the more he felt driven to succeed, not just for himself, but to prove that his efforts were worthwhile and that he was making a difference. He saw the stakes as more than just personal ambitions; they were about fulfilling a promise to those who had placed their trust in him.

Meanwhile, Mr. Peters remained a silent pillar of support behind the scenes. Although he managed to keep his support for Popi discreet from his wife, his quiet encouragement was a steady force for Popi. Mr. Peters, who had always been a steadfast worker and a figure of integrity in his own right, found a renewed sense of purpose in supporting his son. To him, Popi's drive and courage to challenge the status quo were qualities he deeply admired, and he wanted to ensure Popi knew he was not alone in this struggle.

To Mrs. Peters, however, Mr. Peters' seemingly indifferent stance on Popi's political aspirations only fuelled her frustration. She saw his lack of visible concern as a sign of apathy and selfishness. The more she saw Mr. Peters as detached from the situation, the more she believed he was failing to step up and help their son avoid what she saw as a potentially disastrous path. Her growing resentment toward Mr. Peters compounded her anxiety about Popi, further straining their relationship.

As Popi navigated these personal and familial tensions, he was driven by a dual purpose: to prove to himself and his supporters that he was on the right path and to demonstrate to his mother that his efforts were meaningful and not in vain. The pressure from his mother only heightened his sense of urgency and commitment as he channelled his energy into every campaign event and strategy, determined to show that his pursuit of a federal seat was more than just a personal dream—it was a vital endeavour that mattered to many.

Popi's campaign faced a daunting challenge: With only days left before the election and trailing in the polls, the viral video had done significant damage, and his base was beginning to waver. Doubt hung in the air like an unwelcome fog, threatening to cloud their progress. Donna knew they needed something extraordinary to counteract the negative narrative and reenergize their supporters.

She and Popi decided to create a compelling video documentary to address the three critical issues weighing heavily on their campaign.

Many supporters were puzzled by Popi's decision to refrain from attacking his opponents. The video aimed to clarify Popi's strategy, explaining that attacking others did not align with his principles of promoting constructive dialogue and positive change. By focusing on his vision rather than engaging in mudslinging, Popi hoped to maintain a higher ground and project a message of integrity and respect.

The viral video distorted the facts surrounding an incident in which Popi intervened to help an international student facing expulsion. The documentary would reveal the whole story, providing context and correcting the misleading information that had been circulated. Popi wanted to demonstrate that his actions were rooted in compassion and fairness, not the callous disregard implied by his critics.

The heart of the video was to reaffirm Popi's commitment to

his core values. He wanted to inspire hope and confidence in Canadians by showcasing his vision for a society where self-sufficiency and freedom of speech and conscience were paramount. The documentary aimed to reconnect with the electorate on a personal level, showing them why his message was more relevant and vital than ever.

Donna poured her creativity and expertise into the project, using captivating visual effects and engaging storytelling to make the documentary informative and emotionally resonant. Despite being 30 minutes long, the video felt like a brief, impactful experience to most viewers, thanks to Donna's masterful editing and presentation.

As the documentary neared its conclusion, Popi's voice took on a tone of resolute determination. The screen transitioned from a powerful montage of everyday Canadians and their stories to a focused shot of Popi standing in a well-lit room, his demeanour calm but confident. The message was clear: he was not just fighting for a position but for the principles he sincerely believed in.

"With just a week left before the election," Popi began, his gaze steady and earnest, "it is crucial that we address the real issues affecting the lives of everyday Canadians. Our country faces numerous challenges, from economic hardships to concerns about personal freedoms. Yet, instead of discussing these vital issues, we find ourselves mired in hyperbolic attacks and distractions."

He paused, allowing his words to sink in. The screen showed clips of people struggling with various issues—unemployment, affordable housing, and food insecurity—reinforcing the gravity

Popi: A Rising Tide
of the matters at hand.

"This election," Popi continued, "should not be a battleground for personal attacks but a forum for genuine debate on how we can improve the lives of Canadians. Therefore, I am challenging my opponent to a live debate. Let's remove the theatrics and focus on what truly matters: the concerns and hopes of the people we seek to represent."

Popi's confidence was palpable as he spoke. Debate was always his strongest asset, a skill honed through years of passionate advocacy and intellectual engagement. He was not merely defending his candidacy; he was standing firm on the principles that had driven him into politics in the first place.

"A debate," he asserted, "is not just an opportunity to present our ideas but a chance to show the people that we are committed to addressing their real concerns. I am prepared to discuss and defend my beliefs and urge my opponent to do the same. Let's have a debate that reflects the issues and offers constructive solutions."

As Popi's challenge was issued, the video cut to a call-to-action screen with information about where and when the debate would take place if his opponent accepted. The final frames were a testament to Popi's unwavering dedication and readiness to confront the issues head-on, no matter the cost.

The bold move was a calculated risk that Popi was willing to take. A defeat in the debate would not just signify a loss in the election but a setback to the very principles he championed. Yet, he was undeterred, knowing that his strengths lay in his ability to articulate his vision and engage in meaningful discourse. The debate was a strategic manoeuvre and a reflection of his commitment to transparency, integrity, and genuine representation.

With the documentary's release, Popi responded to the viral attacks and set the stage for a final, pivotal moment in the campaign. The outcome remained uncertain, but Popi's courage and conviction had given his supporters a renewed sense of purpose and a clear focus on the path ahead.

As the video began to circulate, it sparked renewed interest and engagement. Many viewers disheartened by the viral attacks found clarity and reassurance in Popi's explanations. The video effectively addressed the misinformation and highlighted Popi's unwavering commitment to his principles.

The documentary was a turning point for the campaign. It managed to win back a significant portion of the supporters who had been on the fence and reinvigorated the base. Popi's message resonated once more, and the final push toward election day became an opportunity to demonstrate his vision's strength and resolve. With the support of Donna and the newly galvanized base, Popi entered the last week of the campaign with renewed hope and determination, ready to face whatever challenges lay ahead.

As the debate was confirmed, Ms. George, Popi's opponent, doubled down on her attacks. She labelled Popi as just another misogynistic man attempting to impose his views on the "nice people" of Ottawa. Her rhetoric was unyielding, portraying him as a threat to the values she claimed to champion. Her relentless attacks seemed to fuel her campaign, casting Popi in a negative light with every utterance.

Popi: A Rising Tide

Despite the escalating vitriol, Popi adopted a strategy of deliberate silence and restraint. He chose not to engage directly with the accusations, letting Ms. George's attacks wash over him like a storm that he had no intention of feeding with his responses. His silence was not merely a reaction to exhaustion or annoyance; it was a calculated decision to maintain composure and focus on the issues at hand.

Popi's approach had a curious effect. Journalists, drawn to the spectacle of the heated exchanges between Ms. George and Popi, began to question him about the accusations and his strategy. When asked about Ms. George's relentless attacks, Popi responded with calm assurance, "My focus remains on addressing the real issues facing our community. While I acknowledge the criticism, I believe the people of Ottawa deserve a debate that centres on constructive solutions, not personal attacks."

In interviews, he continued to emphasize the importance of the debate rather than the attacks against him. "This election," Popi said with conviction, "is about the future we envision for Ottawa, not tearing down individuals. I aim to present my vision clearly and engage in a meaningful discussion about collectively addressing our community's needs."

The unintended consequence of Ms. George's attacks was the surge in Popi's visibility. The constant media coverage and the ensuing drama provided him with unprecedented exposure. The more Ms. George's accusations were broadcast, the more Popi's name and message were being discussed. It was as if the negative publicity had inadvertently become a vehicle for spreading his campaign's core message.

Now more eagerly anticipated than ever, the debate was shaping to be a pivotal moment in the election. Popi's calm demeanour and strategic focus helped him maintain his composure and gradually shifted the narrative. The more Ms. George attacked, the more Popi appeared as the principled figure standing above the fray, dedicated to tackling the real issues.

With just days remaining before the election, Popi and his team worked tirelessly to capitalize on the momentum generated by the media frenzy. The campaign was in full swing, and the message of self-sufficiency, freedom of speech, and genuine concern for the community resonated more than ever. Popi knew that the upcoming debate was a chance to solidify his position and address the concerns of the electorate directly. He prepared for the event with the same determination that had fuelled his entire campaign, understanding that this debate could very well be the turning point he needed to secure a victory.

The night of the debate came, and as the discussion began, the tension was palpable. The hall was filled with a mix of anticipation and skepticism. Popi took the stage calmly, ready to showcase his platform and challenge Ms. George's claims.

When Popi was ready to address Ms. George, he shifted the focus from personal attacks to substantive policy discussions. "Ms. George," he began, his voice steady. "Throughout this campaign, we've seen a lot of rhetoric about personal character. However, I believe the voters deserve to know more about your policies and plans. Can you provide specific details about your platform and how you intend to address the pressing issues our community faces?"

Popi: A Rising Tide

Ms. George, visibly taken aback, attempted to sidestep the question. "Popi, this election isn't just about policies. It's about ensuring leadership that respects and values everyone in our community."

Popi pressed on, his tone unwavering. "Respect and values are crucial, but they are not substitutes for clear policy proposals. I'm asking for specifics—how do you plan to address the issues of economic inequality, rising unemployment, and unaffordable housing in our riding? Instead of focusing on personal attacks, let's discuss what you intend to do to improve the lives of our constituents."

Ms. George's response was evasive. "My focus is on creating a safe and inclusive environment for everyone. I believe that's more important than any single policy detail."

Popi's frustration was evident, but he maintained his composure. "Ms. George, with all due respect, the people of Ottawa need more than just assurances of safety and inclusivity. They need concrete plans and actionable strategies. Simply stating that you are better than being accused of supporting harmful ideologies does not address the real concerns of our community. What are your specific proposals for fostering economic growth, improving public services, and ensuring that our communities and hospitals are equipped to meet the needs of every citizen?"

As the debate continued, it became clear that Ms. George struggled to articulate her policies beyond personal attacks and broad statements. The lack of detail and repeated emphasis on character rather than substance became apparent to the audience.

Popi's insistence on focusing the discussion on policy rather than personal attacks helped shift the narrative. His approach was about defending his platform and demanding clarity and accountability from his opponent. A shouting match ensured with Ms. George reiterating her personal attacks and calling Popi a rapist sympathizer and misogynist.

As the debate continued under the intense scrutiny of the audience and the crosstalk between Popi and Ms. George, an unexpected disturbance arose. A visibly distressed woman stood up in the crowd and began to shout, demanding to be allowed to speak. Her insistence was forceful enough to disrupt the debate, and the tension in the room heightened.

The moderator, initially hesitant, tried to calm the situation, but the woman was unwavering. "I'm not leaving until I'm given a chance to speak," she declared, her voice carrying a mix of frustration and urgency. "If you don't let me speak, I'll cause enough commotion to ensure this debate can't continue."

The audience murmured, and Popi and Ms. George looked on with curiosity and concern. Popi's heart raced as he tried to process the situation. The recent attacks on his campaign and his internal doubts about his decisions left him vulnerable. He began to mentally review every interaction he had had with women, fearing that this moment might devastate his campaign.

Ms. George seized the moment. "Since part of my platform is to encourage women to speak out and be heard," she said to the moderator, "I believe we should allow her to voice her concerns. If Popi truly supports freedom of speech, he should have no issue with this."

Popi: A Rising Tide

The moderator, faced with the audience's insistence and Ms. George's argument, agreed to grant the woman one minute to speak. She handed her the microphone, her face a mask of determination and anxiety.

After being handed the microphone to say her piece, the woman introduced herself as Meghan Dobbs, a former colleague of Popi. Ms. George, recognizing the gravity of the moment, began to smile—a gesture that seemed to reveal her anticipation of a potential blow to Popi's campaign.

Meghan took a deep breath and began her statement. "Thank you for allowing me to speak," she said, her voice trembling but firm. "There has been a lot of talk about Popi being a misogynist and a sympathizer of rapists. I'm here to set the record straight because I am the person who initiated the movement to have the student in question expelled from the university."

She paused for a moment, gathering her thoughts. "The student's name is Ahmed, and during a class discussion, he made a statement about women in his home country not refusing sexual advances from their husbands. I reacted poorly to this statement, allowing my insecurities and the complaints from other women on this topic to cloud my judgment. Instead of engaging with Ahmed respectfully to understand his cultural context, I overreacted and called him a rapist. That's how this whole mess started."

Meghan's eyes welled up as she continued. "Popi, who was in a position to help, stepped in to ensure that Ahmed wasn't unfairly punished or deported. I'm deeply grateful for what Popi did because I wouldn't have been able to live with myself if my actions had ruined Ahmed's life. The narrative being spread online is a gross distortion of what truly happened."

She looked directly at Popi, her voice breaking with emotion. "Popi, you're not a bad man. You've inspired me to be a leader through your work and dedication. I run a small travel agency inspired by your tour guide company, and I direct a charity helping young girls choose careers and become leaders, all of which were inspired by your example. I'm sorry that my past mistakes are now threatening your career. If people choose not to vote for you, let it be for the right reasons, not a false narrative that tarnishes a good man who often puts others before himself."

With her voice choking on the final words, Meghan turned and hurriedly exited the stage, unable to hold back her tears. Overwhelmed by the unexpected turn of events, Popi looked at the moderator, signalling his intent to follow her. The moderator, recognizing the emotional weight of the situation and the need for a pause, decided to take a break from the debate.

Sensing a potential shift in the debate's dynamics, Ms. George tried to protest. She questioned the validity of Meghan's words. Still, the moderator decided it was best to allow a moment for reflection despite the debate being streamed live.

Popi quickly moved towards the exit, his mind racing as he sought out Meghan. The moment was a whirlwind of emotions for him—hope, gratitude, and a deep sense of responsibility. He found Meghan in a quiet corner, sitting with her head in her hands, her shoulders shaking with the weight of her tears.

"Meghan," Popi said gently, approaching her. "Thank you for

speaking out. I know it took a lot of courage to come forward like that."

Meghan looked up, her face streaked with tears. "I just wanted to make things right, Popi. I didn't want my mistakes to destroy your chance to make a difference. I hope people can see the truth now."

Popi nodded, his own eyes misting over. "Your words made a huge impact tonight. I can't thank you enough for standing up and setting the record straight. It means more than you know."

After talking for a few minutes, Popi told Meghan that he had to go back inside but would like to have drinks with Meghan to catch up. She quickly composed herself and used Popi's hand to help herself up. They walked back into the auditorium together.

As Popi re-entered the debate stage, the atmosphere had shifted. Having taken a moment to verify Meghan Dobbs's identity and the accuracy of her statements, the moderator reassured the audience that Meghan was indeed who she claimed to be. Her revelations had confirmed Popi's innocence regarding the allegations, and this development had begun to turn the tide.

Ms. George, now on the defensive, attempted to steer the discussion back towards attacking Popi. She tried to frame the situation as Popi manipulating a woman for his benefit, hoping to recapture the narrative. But the tide of public opinion was moving against her as the debate's focus shifted.

The moderator interjected, recognizing the need to redirect the conversation to more substantive issues. "We've heard about the recent personal attacks and clarifications from both candidates. Let's now focus on the core issues at hand. We need to understand each candidate's plan for revitalizing the riding and addressing the real concerns of the constituents."

With this shift, Popi seized the opportunity to lay out his vision. "Thank you," Popi began, his tone steady and resolute. "My focus has always been on the people of this riding and how we can work together to improve our community. It's not just about promises but tangible actions and real results."

He continued, "I believe in promoting self-sufficiency and creating opportunities for everyone. My plan involves investing in local businesses, supporting educational initiatives, and providing resources for those who need them most. We must create a thriving environment where individuals can succeed based on their talents and efforts, not just their circumstances. For example, the money we have been raising with car washes is used to help those in need find a footing by helping them with a few months' rent and find stable employment or learn a skill they can use to make a living. The idea is to end the cycle of dependence by giving them a boost, whether it's the first and last months' rent or groceries, to ease food insecurity."

Ms. George, who had been trying to regain her footing, struggled to respond effectively. Her attempts to counter Popi's plans were overshadowed by the newfound focus on actionable policies rather than personal attacks. The debate had moved from sensationalism to substance, and Popi's clear, well-articulated plans began to resonate more with the audience.

Popi's confidence grew as he elaborated on other specific

policies, such as plans for infrastructure improvements, increased support for small businesses, and initiatives to engage with the community directly. His answers were direct and pragmatic, showcasing his commitment to meaningful change rather than mere rhetoric.

With the shift in focus, the audience began to engage more deeply with Popi's proposals. Once fraught with tension and personal attacks, the debate now centred around the real issues facing the riding and how each candidate planned to address them.

Popi felt a renewed sense of purpose as the debate drew to a close. The personal attacks had not only been refuted but had also refocused the conversation on what truly mattered: the future of the community and the plans to make a tangible difference.

Ms. George's attempts to pivot back to personal criticisms seemed increasingly desperate. Still, Popi remained composed, sticking to his message and commitment to the people.

As the debate concluded, it was evident that Popi had regained his footing. The conversation had shifted back to the real issues, and his clear, actionable plans for the riding starkly contrasted with Ms. George's repeated attacks and evasive answers. The debate had showcased Popi's strengths in discussing policy and his resilience in the face of adversity, solidifying his lead.

Yet, despite this significant victory, not all was settled. Some women in the audience remained skeptical about Popi's handling of the Ahmed incident. The viral video and subsequent revelations had cast a long shadow, and while Popi had convincingly defended himself, lingering doubts persisted.

Popi was met with a mix of congratulations and lingering concerns as he walked off the stage. Donna, who had been by his side throughout the ordeal, approached him with a look of both relief and determination. "You did great out there, Popi," she said, "but we still need to address the remaining concerns directly."

Popi nodded, his expression thoughtful. "I know. Some people are still uneasy about how I handled the situation with Ahmed. We must show them that I've learned from the experience and that my actions were rooted in genuine concern and integrity."

Donna told Popi that in the recorded history of Canadian elections, no election had ever had a voter turnout above 70%. "In fact, by-elections hardly ever go above 50%; current expectations for this riding is around a 40% turnout for this by-election." She added.

Popi's eyes widened as he absorbed Donna's words. The significance of the data sank in, and he felt a surge of hope. "So you're saying there's an opportunity here if we can drive up the voter turnout?"

Donna nodded, her face a mixture of determination and excitement. "Exactly. If we can engage more voters, we could tip the scales in our favour. We need to get people excited about this election and make them feel like their vote truly matters. It's not just about convincing them to vote for you, but about getting them to the polls in the first place."

Popi: A Rising Tide

Popi's face lit up with admiration and gratitude as he looked at Donna. "Donna, I love you because you are amazing!" His voice carried a note of exhilaration and determination. He jumped up from his seat, starting to pace back and forth. "So, while the polls are neck and neck right now, whoever brings out the most people to vote has a better chance of winning."

Donna, caught up in the excitement, rose from her chair and wrapped her arms around Popi. "I love you too," she said warmly, her voice filled with genuine affection. "I'm only amazing because of you. Together, we're unstoppable."

Their shared energy and commitment created a powerful synergy. With their hearts aligned and their goals clear, they knew their next steps would be crucial. As they embraced, both felt a renewed sense of purpose and optimism. They were ready to push forward, motivated by the election's stakes and their unwavering support for one another.

With their plan to boost voter turnout taking shape, they began to outline their next moves. They knew rallying the community and engaging new voters would be vital in turning the tide. As they set their plans into motion, they carried with them the strength of their partnership and the hope of making a meaningful impact on their campaign.

The next day, Donna and Popi threw themselves into strategizing ways to maximize voter turnout. They identified key initiatives to address barriers and educate the public. Popi's focus was on making sure everyone had the opportunity to participate in the election, especially those who might face challenges in getting to the polls.

They set up a system for providing free transportation for individuals with mobility issues, ensuring everyone could easily reach the polling stations. Additionally, they launched an educational campaign via social media to inform people about the voting process, emphasizing that citizens could register to vote on Election Day. The idea was to eliminate any confusion or hesitation that might prevent potential voters from casting their ballots.

During these preparations, Popi recorded a final, heartfelt video message. With a sincere and determined expression, he spoke directly to the camera. "I'm not here to tell you who to vote for," he said, his voice steady and compelling. "What matters most is that you exercise your right to vote. Whether you choose me or someone else, making your voice heard is important. This is your right, your chance to shape our future. Just go out and vote. It's your right."

The video ended with Popi's new slogan flashing across the screen: **"Just go and vote for anyone; it's your right."**

Popi and Donna hoped this message would resonate widely, encouraging as many people as possible to participate in the election. Their efforts were driven by a belief in the power of every individual's vote and a commitment to ensuring everyone had the chance to be part of the democratic process.

Popi was out and about on election day, doing everything he could to ensure a high voter turnout. He was busy driving around the city, coordinating with his team, and providing transportation for those who needed it. Every moment was spent engaging with voters, sharing his excitement about participating in the democratic process, and offering a helping

Popi: A Rising Tide

hand wherever possible.

As the day wore on and polling stations neared closing, Popi noticed an elderly woman working diligently in her garden. The sun was setting, casting a warm golden hue over her flower beds. Popi couldn't help but admire her dedication, so he pulled over and approached her with a friendly wave.

"Good afternoon! I couldn't help but notice you're doing a great job out here," he said with a warm smile, stepping onto the grass to join her. The lady looked up, her eyes crinkling into a smile as Popi knelt beside her and started picking weeds.

They chatted about the garden, and Popi shared a few tips on how to keep weeds at bay. "You know, adding a layer of mulch around your plants helps prevent these pesky weeds from coming back," he suggested. The lady was clearly delighted by his energy and enthusiasm, and Popi was reminded of his time volunteering at the senior centre back in his hometown.

After a few minutes of pleasant conversation, Popi gently steered the topic towards the election. "By the way, have you had a chance to vote today?" he asked, hoping to encourage her participation.

The lady shook her head, her expression a mix of indifference and resignation. "Oh, dear, I'm too old to care much about politics. It's not something I worry about anymore."

Popi, ever the optimist, responded with a thoughtful tone. "I understand where you're coming from. But you've got kids and grandkids, right? Voting isn't just about us; it's about ensuring a good future for the younger generation you care about."

She pondered his words for a moment, then nodded slowly. Popi took the opportunity to offer his assistance. "If you'd like, I can give you a ride to the polling station. It's not too late, and it might be worth it for your kids and grandkids."

The lady looked at him with a mixture of surprise and gratitude. "Well, I suppose that would be very kind of you." She smiled as Popi held her hand to help her out of the garden.

Energized by his day's efforts, Popi carefully loaded the elderly lady's walker into his car and helped her into the passenger seat. As they drove to the polling station, he chatted with her about her garden and the community, making the ride as pleasant as possible. The sun began to set, casting a warm glow on the city streets, and Popi felt a renewed sense of purpose.

When they arrived at the polling station, Popi assisted her out of the car and onto the sidewalk. She went inside the polling station and came out after a few minutes. Popi smiled as she walked out, and he helped her back into his car. While sitting in the car, The lady looked up at him with a curious expression. "Aren't you going to ask who I voted for?" she inquired, her eyes twinkling with mischief.

Popi shook his head with a smile. "No, I just wanted to make sure you had the chance to exercise your right to vote. That's what matters most to me."

She leaned in closer, her voice dropping to a conspiratorial whisper. "I voted for that young man everyone's talking about. Popi, I think he's going to win."

Popi's heart swelled with gratitude. "I hope so, too. I'm sure he appreciates your support more than you know."

After helping her inside her home, Popi promised to return for tea another time when he wasn't in such a rush. As he turned to leave, the lady stopped him, her curiosity piqued. "By the way, who are you? What's your name?"

Popi smiled warmly and asked her for her phone. He took a moment to find one of Donna's most recent viral videos and played it for her. The video showcased his commitment to community service and his vision for the future, and it was clear that she recognized the person in it.

As the video ended, Popi leaned in and gave her a gentle peck on the cheek. He then left her a business card with his personal number. "Thank you for your vote," he said sincerely before heading back to his car.

As he drove away, Popi felt a deep sense of fulfillment. The day had been a whirlwind of challenges and victories, but moments like these reminded him why he was fighting so hard. He hoped the positive energy and genuine interactions would resonate with voters and make a difference in the election.

As the night unfolded, the air was thick with tension and anticipation. Popi and his core team gathered around the television in the campaign office, their eyes glued to the live election results. The early returns brought a wave of anxiety as Ms. George led by a narrow margin. The initial numbers felt like a punch to the gut, a stark reminder of their precarious situation.

Popi, though visibly anxious, kept his composure. He knew that early results could be misleading and that the final outcome often depended on voter turnout, which they had worked tirelessly to boost. He held onto the hope that their efforts would pay off. His phone buzzed continuously with messages of support and anxious inquiries from friends, family, and supporters. He read them silently, trying to stay focused on the task at hand.

Hours passed, each moment stretching longer than the last. The results began to trickle in, showing Popi gaining ground. With every update, the mood in the room shifted from nervous tension to cautious optimism.

As the night wore on, Popi's lead grew more substantial. The initial discouragement faded as the numbers clearly showed a shift in momentum. The supporters, who had been waiting with bated breath, began to buzz with excitement. Cheers and applause filled the campaign office as Popi's numbers continued to climb, outpacing Ms. George by a significant margin.

The final result was announced with resounding cheers from the crowd: Popi had won the by-election with a commanding 20-point lead. This decisive victory marked not only his personal triumph but also a testament to his team and supporters' dedication and hard work.

Popi's celebration at his headquarters was a whirlwind of joy and excitement, yet something was amiss. As the night wore on, Popi noticed Donna's absence, and the cheers faded into the hum of congratulatory conversations. She had been a cornerstone of his campaign, and not having her by his side during this momentous occasion felt odd.

Popi: A Rising Tide

He tried calling her, but his calls went straight to voicemail. Concerned, he decided to drive over to her parent's house. The streets were quiet, and the victory celebrations had yet to reach this part of town. His mind was joyful from the win and anxious about Donna's whereabouts.

He pulled up to the house and saw an unfamiliar car parked outside. Donna emerged from the house before he could get out of his vehicle, her face illuminated by the soft streetlights. She was smiling, her eyes reflecting a happiness that seemed out of place for someone who had just been absent from the celebration.

Donna walked towards the parked car, where a man awaited her. Popi's heart skipped a beat as he saw Donna hug the man and kiss him on the cheek. The guy also handed her something that looked like a present before Donna laughed flirtatiously as she returned home.

Popi's mind raced as he processed what he had just witnessed. A wave of confusion and unease overshadowed the exhilaration of the victory. He felt a pang of betrayal, wondering why Donna had done this, especially after the close bond they had developed.

He sat in his car momentarily, trying to gather his thoughts. The joyous occasion of the victory now seemed bittersweet.

The celebratory buzz of the campaign victory felt hollow as Popi drove home, the once-sweet taste of triumph now tinged with bitterness. The night sky was a dark canvas, reflecting the turmoil churning within him. He felt like he was navigating through a fog of confusion and hurt, the weight of his victory now burdened by personal betrayal.

When he arrived at his apartment, he turned off his phone, not wanting to deal with the deluge of congratulatory messages or, more importantly, the barrage of calls from Donna. He needed space to think, to process the dissonance between his public success and his private anguish.

As he sat in the quiet of his apartment, the euphoria of his election win felt like a distant memory. The moment's reality seemed to erode his sense of achievement, leaving him feeling isolated and disconnected. Popi's mind raced through the evening's events—the thrill of his victory, the silent presence of Donna's absence, and the poignant image of sharing her with another man.

The victory celebration, which should have been a night of joy and camaraderie, now felt like a cruel irony. Popi was grappling with his emotions, the excitement of the campaign overshadowed by personal doubts and hurt. He couldn't understand why Donna hadn't been there to share in the moment, and the sight of her with someone else left him questioning their relationship and the future of his campaign.

Sitting alone in the darkened room, Popi found himself at a crossroads, not just in his political journey but also in his personal life. The victory he had fought so hard for now seemed clouded by the uncertainty of what lay ahead.

He knew he would need to address both the campaign's aftermath and his feelings for Donna. Still, for tonight, all he could do was sit in the silence of his apartment, trying to make sense of it all. The election's sweet victory had indeed ended

Popi: A Rising Tide

sourly, and Popi was left with the daunting task of reconciling his heartbreak with his professional success.

Turning Over a New Leaf

Popi stayed true to his word in the community, working tirelessly to regain the faith he had lost from some voters when he was labelled a rapist sympathizer. For weeks, he threw himself into his work, using every waking moment to rebuild the trust that had been shaken. He made it a point to be present in the community, listening to people's concerns and addressing them with genuine care and commitment. His days were a whirlwind of activity—attending local events, meeting with constituents, and ensuring that his actions spoke louder than the words of his detractors.

Despite his public efforts, Popi's personal life was in turmoil. Despite her desperate attempts, he had refused to talk to Donna. Her calls and messages went unanswered, leaving her in a state of anxious uncertainty. Popi's silence was as deafening as the accusations that had once threatened his campaign, and the memory of seeing Donna with another man on his biggest night gnawed at him constantly. That moment had turned his sweet victory into a bitter experience, casting a long shadow over his accomplishments.

Popi had confided in Kyle about what he had seen, seeking the blunt truth about Donna's loyalty. Kyle, ever the loyal friend, had tried to downplay the incident, suggesting there might be more to the story than what Popi had witnessed. However, Popi's heart was heavy, and he couldn't easily dispel the doubts that clouded his mind. The sight of Donna with another man had been a blow to his already fragile trust. Through Kyle,

Popi: A Rising Tide

Donna realized Popi had likely seen her or heard about the incident on election night.

Popi communicated through Kyle, but Donna was growing desperate to hear from Popi directly. The roundabout way of relaying messages was a far cry from the direct, heartfelt conversations they used to share. Each day of Popi's silence weighed heavily on her heart, amplifying her worry and longing for reconciliation.

Popi, meanwhile, was struggling with his emotions. Laura had once shattered his heart, leaving deep scars that made him wary of opening up to anyone again. He had sworn off relationships for fear of experiencing that kind of pain once more. When he met Donna, he dared to hope that she was different, that she was the one who could help him rebuild his trust and heal his wounds.

But the events of that fateful night had rekindled his old fears. Seeing Donna with another man had felt like a knife twisting in an old wound, bringing back all the heartache he had worked so hard to overcome. The emotional storm it unleashed was overwhelming, and Popi reverted to his old coping mechanism: focusing on the things he could control.

He threw himself into his work, dedicating every moment to his community and campaign promises. The routine provided a semblance of stability amidst the chaos of his emotions. Each interaction with the community, every handshake and conversation, was a way to regain his footing and distract himself from the turmoil inside.

Kyle, ever the mediator, found himself in the middle of Popi and Donna's strained relationship. He delivered messages with a heavy heart, knowing his friends were hurting. "Popi's just trying to process everything," Kyle would tell Donna. "He's not ready to talk yet, but give him time."

Donna's desperation was evident in her replies. "I just need to hear from him, Kyle. I need to explain to make things right. Please tell him I love him and am here, waiting."

Popi couldn't ignore Donna's messages entirely. Through Kyle, he heard her pleas and declarations of love. They tugged at his heart, reminding him of the deep connection they once shared. Yet, the fear of being hurt again made him hesitate to reach out.

"She says she loves you, Popi," Kyle would relay. "She's waiting for you to come around."

Popi would listen, his expression sombre. "I know, Kyle. I just... I need more time."

In the quiet moments alone, Popi would reflect on his past heartbreak. Laura's betrayal had taught him to build walls around his heart, but meeting Donna had been like a ray of sunshine breaking through those walls. Now, that light was dimmed, and he grappled with the fear of letting it in again.

Despite his resolve to focus on work, Donna's words haunted him. He remembered the joy and support she brought into his life, the way she believed in him even when he doubted himself. Shutting her out was not just punishing her but also denying himself the chance to heal and move forward.

While he was now busier with his work as an MP, Popi still

found time to focus on the social projects he had started during the campaign. Popi was determined to stay true to his word, unlike many politicians who let campaign promises fade into oblivion after an election. He didn't want to be just another politician who forgot about the people once in office. Instead, he vowed to continue working tirelessly to make his society a better place for all.

He juggled his parliamentary duties with community engagement, attending local events, and checking on the progress of various initiatives. Popi's schedule was hectic, but he thrived on the challenge, driven by his passion for positive change. Whether it was advocating for better social services, supporting local businesses, or addressing constituents' concerns, he remained dedicated to his mission.

His commitment to these causes was not lost on the community. People saw that Popi was not just another politician making empty promises. His actions spoke louder than words, and his genuine efforts to improve the lives of those around him earned him respect and admiration. Popi's unwavering dedication to his work and community became a hallmark of his tenure as an MP, reinforcing his reputation as a leader who truly cared about the people he served.

Within the Conservative Party of Canada, Popi struggled to gain the respect he deserved. Many party members considered him too young and idealistic to be a serious politician. His innovative ideas and fresh perspective were often dismissed as naive. However, Hon. Church saw Popi differently. To him, Popi was precisely what the party needed to connect with a younger demographic and breathe new life into their platform.

Hon. Church valued Popi's honest and unique perspective, which provided insights that others in the party missed. Unlike many of his colleagues, who were reluctant to oppose or criticize Hon. Church, Popi spoke his mind. This honesty was refreshing to Hon. Church, who was often surrounded by yes-men who were more concerned with securing better positions within the party or, should the party form a government, within the country.

Many saw Popi's youth and idealism as a liability, but in Hon. Church's eyes, they were his greatest strengths. They allowed him to see things differently and identify issues that more experienced politicians might overlook. This made Popi an invaluable asset to Hon. Church, who recognized the need for a more diverse range of voices within the party to address the evolving concerns of their constituents.

Despite the skepticism from his peers, Popi continued to work diligently, proving that his idealism was grounded in a genuine desire to create positive change. His commitment and hard work slowly began to shift perceptions, showing that being young and idealistic did not preclude one from being a serious and influential politician.

Popi never changed who he was, but the issue with Donna made him callous. He continued to work diligently with his team, holding weekly meetings to discuss future projects and community initiatives. These meetings were a testament to his unwavering commitment to his ideals and promises, even as personal turmoil threatened to overshadow his professional life.

Donna, however, avoided these meetings. She wanted to speak with Popi first, fearing the embarrassment of facing him in

Popi: A Rising Tide

front of their friends. The thought of being publicly confronted about what had transpired was too much for her to bear. Only Kyle knew the full extent of what had happened, and he remained a steadfast presence at the meetings, providing a semblance of normalcy amid the tension.

A noticeable shift marked Popi's interactions with the team. His once warm and approachable demeanour was now tinged with a growing hardness. He focused intensely on the tasks at hand, pouring himself into work to cope with the emotional pain. This callousness was a shield, protecting him from the vulnerability that came with heartbreak.

Despite this, he remained a dedicated leader, driving his projects forward with determination. Unaware of his personal struggle, the team admired his resilience and commitment. They saw a leader who, despite the challenges, never wavered in his mission to make a difference.

Donna's absence at the meetings did not go unnoticed, but the reasons behind it remained a mystery to the others. Kyle, carrying the burden of knowing the truth, watched his friends struggle in their own ways. He supported Popi as best as he could, understanding the importance of their work while also feeling Donna's pain and desperation to make things right.

Through it all, Popi's resolve never faltered. He continued to be the person he had always been—driven, compassionate, and unwavering in his commitment to his community. Yet, the issue with Donna left a mark on him, hardening his heart and making him more guarded. In his mind, focusing on what he could control—his work and his mission—was the only way to navigate the storm of emotions swirling within him.

One night, after a meeting where Popi had announced their last charity car wash of the year before winter set in, he was met by Donna as he walked to his car. Surprised but not shaken, Popi greeted Donna like a friendly acquaintance. Nothing in his tone suggested that the two ever knew each other beyond simple casual conversations. Donna greeted him back with a smile that matched his tone. After exchanging a few pleasantries, there was a moment of silence, and Popi excused himself to walk to his car. Donna stopped him, her voice trembling slightly.

"Popi, I know you probably don't want to hear this, but I just need to say it," Donna began, her eyes searching his for any sign of understanding. "I don't expect you to understand or forgive me. I only want you to hear me out."

Popi, apprehensive and conflicted, paused. His first instinct was to leave, to avoid reopening old wounds, but there was no way of leaving her without making a scene. He glanced around the nearly empty parking lot, then sighed and nodded, indicating she should continue.

"I messed up," Donna admitted, her voice barely above a whisper. "I didn't mean to hurt you. That night, what you saw wasn't what it looked like. In retrospect, it was a moment of terrible judgment, and I regret it every day. You mean so much to me, Popi, and I hate that I've caused you pain."

Popi remained silent, his expression inscrutable. Donna took a deep breath and continued, "I've tried to reach out, to explain, but I understand why you've been avoiding me. You have every right to be angry. But please, know that I never meant for this to happen. I made a mistake and am terribly sorry for hurting and betraying your trust. You deserve to know that I still care about you deeply."

"I don't know what you saw or heard, but I hope you can trust that I will only tell you the truth because in all the time I've known you, you've been nothing but kind to me, and you deserve nothing less," Donna added, her voice trembling.

Popi interjected, "Look, I really don't have much time, so can we please hurry this up?"

Donna composed herself and began, "I dated this guy in high school, and things were mostly fine, but he was selfish and rude to everyone. I was not too fond of that about him, but I thought he might change someday. He never did."

Popi rolled his eyes with a sarcastic cough, "Typical."

"Please, I'm trying to open up. You can mock me later," Donna pleaded.

Popi nodded and mimed, zipping his mouth.

"I couldn't handle the emotional abuse anymore, so I decided to break up with him. He tried to apologize and promised he'd change, but I refused his apology. When high school finished, we went our separate ways, and I never heard from him again until he called me on the day of the by-election. He said he was in town for the day and wanted to meet to say hi."

Popi smirked, "That wasn't just a 'hi' that I saw."

"Paul Peters, please!" Donna exclaimed.

Popi nodded in affirmation, biting his lips. He added, "You're so cute when trying to be serious and take charge."

After a sarcastic smirk, Donna continued, "He was nice, and every time I tried to excuse myself to leave, he would beg me to stay for a few more minutes. I admit I got a little too comfortable and neglected to show some decency. From the moment I agreed to meet up with him to missing your big night, I was betraying you, and the betrayal was only getting worse with each passing second away from you. Paul, I love you and never want to love or be loved by someone else. I need you in my life because you brought joy and excitement I never knew was possible when sharing your life with someone special. You're mad at me, and I understand. I know it's selfish." She paused, looked up, and smiled before continuing, "Well, I am selfish, so yeah."

"Well, that's not funny," Popi responded but couldn't contain his smile. He continued, "Well, Donna, you mean a lot to me, too, and I'm not going to stand here and pretend that you had no effect on me. You know my upbringing. I love my parents, but the dozens of times I was introduced as the adopted child were like a dagger to my heart. It was a constant reminder that someone had rejected me. Don't get me wrong, my parents never did anything to make me feel less than a child they truly loved, but it was those moments when I'd overhear some relatives or family friends mentioning the adoption directly or indirectly. While they all thought it was amazing what my parents did, a part of me still felt like I was only there because someone didn't want me."

"I'm sorry I made you feel like I didn't want you because that couldn't be any further from the truth," Donna said softly.

Popi: A Rising Tide

"I don't know, Donna. They say a burnt child dreads fire, and aside from feeling like I was dumped on the side of the highway, I was dumped by a girl who told me I meant the world to her. When that happened, I vowed never to enter another relationship. But then I met you and thought you were everything I wanted and needed in my life. You made me want to be in love again; every moment with you was amazing. And then you and your ex happened," Popi explained, his voice heavy with emotion.

"Paul, I'm truly down-to-earth sorry, and I will kneel and beg for your forgiveness if I have to. The last thing I want to do in my life is to ever hurt you again. I understand things may never return to how they were, but at least let me work with you because I enjoy doing these community projects with you and our team," Donna pleaded.

"Look, I don't hate you, and you're welcome to come and work with the team because they still look at you as their leader. I may sound callous, but I try to be pragmatic whenever possible, and I don't think I can ever trust you again. Fool me once, shame on you; fool me twice, shame on me. I won't allow you to make a fool of me," Popi responded firmly.

These words saddened Donna as Popi moved past her to go on with his evening. She was left there in tears, filled with anger and regret.

"See you at next week's meeting for our last charity car wash of the year. Don't forget to bring doughnuts for the team because they miss that about you the most," Popi said as he walked away. "Good night!"

Donna was crushed but relieved to have finally confronted what had been causing her sleepless nights. However, the thought that lingered in her mind was whether she was a bad person for hurting someone like Popi. She admired Popi for being selfless and always looking to find ways to spread smiles and cheer everywhere he went. Now, she had seen a selfish side of him, and she was the reason for it.

As Donna walked away from the encounter, her mind was a whirlwind of emotions. She felt disappointed in herself, questioning her actions and decisions. Was she indeed a bad person? Had her moment of weakness caused irreparable damage to someone who had only shown her kindness and love? She admired Popi for his unwavering dedication to others and his ability to brighten any room with his presence. Yet, she had brought out a side of him that was foreign, understandably guarded, and hurt.

Her admiration for Popi's selflessness clashed with the realization that she had been the catalyst for his pain. She knew Popi to be a man who always sought to make others happy and put others before himself. And now, because of her, he had shown a different, more guarded aspect of himself. It was a side born out of betrayal, and she couldn't help but feel responsible.

Disappointment in herself was the most fitting description of her state of mind. She had let down someone she deeply cared about, who had believed in and trusted her. Donna's thoughts were consumed with regret and self-reflection. She knew she had to live with the consequences of her actions, but the journey to self-forgiveness would be a long and arduous one.

A week later, Donna arrived at the meeting, greeted warmly by

Popi: A Rising Tide

everyone glad to see her back in action. The atmosphere was initially celebratory, with team members expressing relief and joy at her return. However, the mood was short-lived as Popi arrived with a palpable sense of urgency.

"Alright, everyone," Popi began, his tone serious and focused. "We've got a lot to do and need to start immediately."

Donna noticed the shift in energy as Popi outlined his concerns. "We've been raising funds and generating a lot of goodwill through our charity car washes. But if we don't start delivering more tangible results, our efforts and our fundraising will risk becoming irrelevant. People support us because they believe in what we're doing, and if we don't follow through, we will lose that trust."

Popi's words were a wake-up call for everyone. He continued, "We need to prioritize settling those we've been helping with meals using the money we've raised. If we don't act now, the momentum we've built could easily slip away. The community is watching us, and we must show that their contributions are making a real difference."

While processing her earlier conversation with Popi, Donna felt a mix of gratitude and guilt. The urgency in his voice reminded her of the responsibility they all shared. She understood now more than ever that the true measure of their success wasn't in the funds they raised but in the lives they could change.

Popi's insistence on focusing on tangible outcomes wasn't just about efficiency; it was about maintaining the integrity of their mission. Donna nodded in agreement, determined to channel her energy into ensuring their efforts paid off.

The team shifted their focus, rallying around Popi's directive. There was a renewed sense of purpose in the room. They set aside their previous distractions and began strategizing to allocate the funds and provide the promised support. The meeting started with a sense of celebration and now centred on action and commitment.

Donna watched as Popi's determination reignited their collective drive. Despite the personal challenges she faced, she knew that the work they were doing was vital. It was a chance to make amends and contribute meaningfully to their cause. As they worked together, Donna hoped that their shared goals would heal their community and bridge the gaps that had emerged in their relationships.

Despite his youth, Popi had cultivated a remarkable leadership style that focused on planting seeds of potential in those around him and inspiring them to rise to their best. His unique approach involved motivating others to follow and lead in their own right.

"Donna," Popi said with an authoritative and encouraging tone, "I need you to set up a meeting with Ms. Tina. We have to discuss collaborations to get basics like food, water, and shelter to as many people as possible before winter sets in. This is crucial, and we can't afford to delay."

While deeply invested in seeing the last car wash through to its conclusion—an endeavour she had poured her heart into—Donna understood the gravity of Popi's request. The urgency in his voice made it clear that this was not the time to argue. Their relationship had shifted significantly; what was once a partnership now felt more like a professional hierarchy, with

Popi: A Rising Tide

Popi assuming a more commanding role and Donna adapting to it.

Popi continued, "Also, please arrange a fundraising dinner with those who promised support even after the election. We need to keep their commitment alive and ensure they contribute as planned. We need to follow through on our promises."

Donna acknowledged the tasks, feeling the weight of the new dynamic between them. There was a clear distinction now between the personal and the professional. The camaraderie and warmth they once shared had transformed into a more formal interaction, marked by professional respect and clear boundaries.

As Donna moved forward with the arrangements, she did so with a mix of determination and resignation. While significant to her, the car wash project had to be momentarily set aside to focus on Popi's new directives. The shift in their relationship was palpable, yet she recognized the necessity of their roles in this new phase.

In arranging the meeting with Ms. Tina and the fundraising dinner, Donna approached her tasks with the same dedication she had shown in all their previous projects. Her commitment to making a difference remained unwavering, even as she navigated the evolving nature of her professional relationship with Popi.

As Donna walked away, carrying the weight of her new responsibilities, Popi turned to Kyle, who was still processing the dynamic shift.

"Kyle," Popi said with a determined edge, "I need you to take the lead on this charity car wash. Donna's been instrumental in this project, and we need to keep the momentum going."

Kyle hesitated, his expression a mix of reluctance and concern. "Are you sure, Popi? This is Donna's project. I don't want to step on any toes, especially hers."

Popi's urgency was palpable. "I know that, but we're on a tight schedule. We need to act fast. You'll need to coordinate the logistics and oversee the event. I need you to ask Donna to create some promotional material with a sense of urgency—this is the last charity car wash of the year. We only have a few days to get everything in place."

Kyle nodded reluctantly, feeling the weight of the task. The implications of taking over Donna's project were not lost on him, and he was uneasy about how Donna would react when she found out.

"Understood," Kyle said quietly, though his unease was evident.

As Kyle began to plan the transition, the rest of the team observed the shift with a growing sense of confusion. Popi's impersonal demeanour and the abrupt changes in their tasks created an atmosphere of discomfort. A more detached and formal dynamic replaced the camaraderie that had once defined their teamwork.

As Popi left the meeting, the room was filled with a palpable sense of confusion and unease. The abrupt shift in leadership and the sudden urgency left everyone wondering how to proceed. Eyes met across the room, a silent exchange of uncertainty about the new direction they were expected to take.

Kyle, sensing the collective hesitation, stepped forward with a renewed sense of determination. "Alright, everyone, let's get to work," he said, trying to infuse some enthusiasm into the group. "We will follow the template we used for the previous car wash. We know what works, so let's stick to it. Start contacting everyone you know, and let's involve as many people as possible."

Despite the tension, Kyle's energy was infectious. He quickly began to outline the plan, rallying the team to move with purpose. "Donna wanted to add something new this time," he continued. "Instead of just washing cars, she envisioned turning this event into an experience. We're not only washing cars, but we'll also be offering some additional services."

There was a murmur of curiosity among the team members. Kyle explained, "We'll include detailing services and check and swap tires for the season. Here in Ottawa, many drivers keep two sets of tires—one for summer and one for winter. With the change of season, tire swapping is in high demand. This will make our car wash more impactful and provide added value to everyone who comes out."

The team began to buzz with a mixture of excitement and apprehension. Expanding the car wash into a more comprehensive service had potential, but it also meant additional work. Kyle's leadership provided a new sense of direction. As the team started to execute the plan, the initial discomfort began to wane.

The inclusion of tire services and detailing turned the car wash into a unique offering in the community. The team worked diligently, embracing the challenge and focusing on the new tasks. Though Donna's absence was felt, her vision for a more memorable and impactful event was carried out with determination and a shared purpose.

While Kyle was initially apprehensive about taking over Donna's responsibilities, he was deeply aware of the weight of the task ahead. He knew all of Donna's plans for the charity car washes, and with that knowledge, he was executing her vision. Despite his nervousness, Kyle felt a surge of responsibility and was determined to uphold Donna's high standards. The thought of letting Popi down was unacceptable, and he was committed to working twice as hard to ensure the project's success.

Kyle's commitment was fuelled by his respect for Popi and their unique relationship. When Donna and Popi's relationship became strained, Kyle feared that the change might sour his relationship with Popi. However, the dynamic between them remained strong. During the tumultuous period of Popi and Donna's separation, Kyle became Popi's primary source of information about Donna. Popi would often inquire about Donna's well-being and any updates related to her, and Kyle, despite his conflicted feelings, provided Popi with the answers he sought. This made Kyle feel like an essential bridge between Popi and Donna during their estrangement.

Thanks to Kyle's updates, Popi already knew nearly everything Donna had shared about the by-election night. Kyle respected Popi deeply, especially after Popi's intervention secured compensation for their wrongful dismissal by the city councillor from their previous jobs. Popi's support and fairness had

Popi: A Rising Tide
earned Kyle's admiration and loyalty.

As Kyle settled into his new role, his regard for Popi grew stronger. He began to view Popi not just as a mentor or a superior but as an older brother figure—someone whose respect and approval he deeply valued. The responsibility entrusted to him was both an honour and a challenge. Kyle relentlessly worked to live up to Popi's expectations and maintain the trust and respect built over time.

The next evening, Donna decided to visit Popi's apartment in person. Having repeatedly failed to reach him by phone, she felt this was her only option to discuss something urgent. Popi was preparing for bed as she approached his door and appeared visibly annoyed by the unexpected visit.

Donna quickly apologized for her unannounced arrival. She acknowledged that she knew Popi was not fond of surprise visitors and that her timing was less than ideal. However, she emphasized that the matter she needed to discuss was pressing. Though initially frustrated, Popi assured her he was not intentionally trying to keep her away. He explained that he was focused on moving things forward and broadening the group's reach to accomplish more effectively.

Donna listened without arguing and began to explain the reason for her visit. Still standing by the door, she was about to delve into the details when Popi invited her in. He offered her the comfort of his home, suggesting she make herself tea or grab something to eat, but Donna declined, not wanting to overstay her welcome.

Once inside, Donna updated Popi on her recent visit to see Ms.

Tina. Although the meeting went relatively well, she had concerns about future projects. Donna felt that Ms. Tina might perceive it as rude or presumptuous if Donna was not properly introduced and her role explained. She worried that this could affect their collaboration and the overall perception of their efforts.

Popi listened attentively, nodding in understanding. He admitted that he should have handled the situation more thoughtfully. Acknowledging that he needed to introduce Donna properly or explain her role in future projects, he recognized that this oversight might lead to unintended consequences. Popi expressed his regret for not addressing the matter more delicately. He assured Donna that he would try to correct this mistake and improve their coordination going forward.

Donna also had another suggestion to share with Popi. She had evaluated their resources and determined that they could feasibly provide food and shelter for an appreciable number of people before winter set in. Her research had led her to several local community centres and churches willing to support this initiative. She recommended that, although she had made the initial contact, it would be more effective and respectful if Popi, as the sitting Member of Parliament, approached the leaders of these institutions to establish formal agreements. Donna emphasized that Popi's endorsement would carry significant weight and influence beyond what a community volunteer could offer.

Popi listened intently, appreciating Donna's thorough research and proactive approach. He acknowledged that having a formal agreement from these centres and churches would lend considerable authority and legitimacy to their efforts. Despite his packed schedule, Popi assured Donna that he would make a concerted effort to reach out to the leaders of the organizations she had identified. He understood the importance of this step and was committed to leveraging his position to maximize the impact of their project.

Donna, eager not to overstay her welcome, wished Popi a good night and made her way toward the door. As she walked, Popi stopped her and asked, "How are you doing?"

Donna said simply, "I'm fine," but Popi pressed further, "No, really—how are you doing?"

Donna paused, her eyes reflecting a mix of resignation and vulnerability. She sighed and replied, "I could be better, but life happens." She offered a small, wistful smile before opening the door and stepping out into the night.

After about five minutes, there was another knock at the door. Popi opened it to find Donna standing there once again. She looked both anxious and hopeful.

"Popi, I'm sorry to bother you again," Donna began, her voice tinged with urgency. "I wanted to ask you for a favour, and it's okay if you say no."

Popi invited her back inside, gesturing for her to sit. "What's on your mind?"

Donna took a deep breath before continuing. "Since Kyle lost his job, he hasn't been himself. He puts on a brave face around others, but he's struggling. He's passionate about working in politics and helping out, and I was wondering if there's any chance you could help him find some opportunities within the federal government."

Popi's expression softened, though he looked thoughtful. "I can't promise anything right now, but I'll do my best. I won't compromise my responsibilities or violate ethical boundaries, but I'll see what I can do."

Donna's eyes lit up with gratitude. "Thank you so much. Kyle's been through a lot—he's been lonely since coming out, and losing his job just made everything worse. Working with you on these charity projects has been a lifeline for him, even if he doesn't always show it."

Popi nodded, his respect for Kyle evident. "I've grown to like and respect Kyle a lot. I'm not doing this as a favour for you but for a friend who's shown himself to be dedicated and hardworking. I appreciate you bringing this to my attention."

Donna smiled, her relief palpable. "I appreciate everything you're doing for him. It means a lot, and it's helping him build his confidence."

Popi warmly smiled as he responded, "I'm glad I can help. I'll keep you updated on any progress."

Donna reached out and gave Popi a small peck on the cheek. "Thank you again, Popi. I really appreciate it."

With that, she gave him a grateful smile before turning to leave. Popi watched her go, feeling a mix of satisfaction and contemplation as he closed the door behind her.

Popi: A Rising Tide

After Donna left, Popi closed the door and walked toward his bedroom. As he moved through the dimly lit hallway, he found himself lost in thought, reflecting on the complexities of his recent interactions with Donna. He wondered if the way he was treating her was genuinely fair. Was he protecting himself from further hurt, or was he simply trying to make Donna suffer for the pain she had caused him?

He wrestled with these questions, feeling the weight of uncertainty pressing down on him. Without clear answers, he decided to soothe his mind with a simple, comforting routine. He poured himself a glass of milk and settled into his bed, hoping the quiet act would offer solace.

Despite his efforts, sleep took work. He tossed and turned, his mind a turbulent sea of thoughts and emotions. The challenges of his life seemed to converge into a single, overwhelming storm. The transition into federal politics, the strain of relationship turmoil, and the constant stress from his parents' ongoing arguments since he moved to Ottawa all combined to create a pressure cooker of worry and doubt.

Eventually, after hours of restless thought, he managed to quiet his mind enough to drift into a fitful sleep. As he lay there, he couldn't help but think about how everything happening in his life—unexpected career shifts, personal heartaches, and familial strife—was far beyond anything he had ever envisioned for himself. The weight of these new and uncharted responsibilities seemed to hang heavy on his shoulders, leaving him to navigate a path he had never anticipated.

The night stretched on, filled with fragmented dreams and uneasy thoughts, but eventually, he surrendered to the embrace of sleep, hoping for clarity with the dawn of a new day.

When Popi awoke the following day, he felt the weight of his responsibilities pressing down on him. Determined to address some of the pressing issues, he called Ms. Tina as soon as possible.

"Good morning, Ms. Tina," Popi began, his voice reflecting the gravity of the conversation he was about to have. "I wanted to personally apologize for missing the meeting with Donna. Things have been a bit chaotic at the office lately, but I assure you, I'm committed to making time for a face-to-face meeting soon."

Ms. Tina's voice was warm and understanding. "I appreciate the call, Popi. It's good to hear from you."

Popi continued, "Given my current schedule, Donna will be your primary contact for now. She's well-informed and will handle our discussions moving forward. However, if there comes a point where you feel it's necessary to speak with me directly, please let Donna know, and she'll arrange that as soon as possible."

Ms. Tina responded positively, "I understand, Popi. We need to establish clear expectations and formalize our partnership. Could we arrange an informal meeting soon to discuss what we can expect from each other as we move forward?"

"Absolutely," Popi agreed. "I'll coordinate with Donna to schedule a time that works for both of us. Thank you for your understanding and patience."

Popi: A Rising Tide

With that, they exchanged polite goodbyes and ended the call. Popi hung up the phone, feeling a sense of relief and determination. He knew navigating his responsibilities required a delicate balance. Still, he was committed to making it work for his new role and the community projects that mattered so much to him.

Throughout the day, Popi wrestled with a storm of conflicting emotions. The idea of reaching out to Donna and trying to mend their relationship tugged at him. Yet, the fear of facing heartbreak again loomed. He recalled the pain from his past relationship with Laura, the woman he had believed was "the one," only to be left shattered when she departed for another man. Donna had come into his life as a beacon of hope, someone who seemed to offer healing and a fresh start, but her betrayal had reopened old wounds and left him feeling even more uncertain.

Popi found himself caught between the desire to salvage what remained of his connection with Donna and the instinct to protect himself from further emotional pain. The thought of potentially being heartbroken a second time was almost unbearable. He grappled with whether reopening communication with Donna would serve as a lesson learned or merely a painful reminder of his vulnerabilities.

Despite the turmoil, Popi couldn't deny the value Donna had brought into his life. He admired her dedication and tenacity, qualities she displayed in every task, big or small. Her unwavering commitment to their shared projects had left a significant mark on him.

A small smile crept across his face as he tried to push these thoughts aside and focus on his responsibilities. The thought of Donna and her past connection was a bittersweet reminder of the highs and lows he had experienced. It was a reflection on the complexities of human relationships. While he acknowledged it as an interesting thought, he also recognized the need to move forward, to continue focusing on his work and the impact he could make.

In the end, Popi resolved to focus on his current responsibilities and the community projects that lay ahead. While the emotional weight of his past relationship with Donna remained, he decided it was best to channel his energy into his work and trust that time would bring clarity and healing.

Later in the afternoon, Donna called Popi, her voice carrying a tone of both urgency and calm. "Popi, Ms. Tina is ready to meet next week, and she's looking for a time that works for you. She's also invited some local business owners interested in what we're calling the 'Project of Hope.' They're all waiting for your availability to set up the meeting," Donna explained.

Popi nodded as he listened, the details already beginning to form a plan in his mind. Donna continued, "The church and community centre leaders are also prepared and just need to know when you're free. Additionally, I've been helping Kyle get the car wash ready. We've used our funds to buy all the necessary equipment and materials."

There was a pause as Donna took a breath before adding, "I understand you're incredibly busy. If you can't attend the meeting, I can take charge. I want to be clear that I'm not trying to usurp Kyle's role; I think keeping things moving is important. I know it's easy to spread yourself too thin with everything you're managing. These projects were my idea, and I want to see them succeed as much as you do."

Popi felt a swell of gratitude. "Donna, you're amazing. Thank you for everything you're doing. I really appreciate it."

Donna's voice softened, "I'm not doing this to get back into a relationship or anything. I'm just happy to contribute something meaningful to our community. Working with you is always a pleasure, and I truly care about both you and the projects we started. If any of these efforts fail, it wouldn't just be a failure of the project or yours—it would also be mine."

She wished him a wonderful day and a good night before hanging up. Popi sat for a moment, the weight of her words sinking in. Her commitment and genuine concern resonated with him, even amidst the complexities of their past. As he moved forward with his day, Popi felt a renewed sense of clarity and purpose, knowing that despite their differences, they were united in their mission to positively impact their community.

After hanging up the phone with Donna, Popi got a surprise visit from Mr. church. He asked if they could sit down and talk. Popi suggested they take a walk to discuss things privately. As they stepped out, the crisp air and the rhythmic crunch of leaves underfoot provided a welcome distraction from the tensions inside the office. Mr. Church's casual demeanour gave way to a more serious tone as they walked.

"Popi, I wanted to talk to you about something important," Mr. Church began, his voice taking on a gravity that hinted at the significance of his words.

Popi, sensing the shift in mood, nodded. "Go ahead. What's on your mind?"

"I've been hearing some chatter about your approach to the community projects," Mr. Church said. "I know you've been trying to keep things moving, and I respect that. But there are some concerns about the optics. Some folks think you're spreading yourself too thin and might be losing focus on the core responsibilities."

Popi frowned, "I've heard a few comments here and there, but nothing concrete. What exactly are they worried about?"

Mr. Church continued, "There's a sentiment that you're trying to do too much at once. Some people believe that while your community initiatives are commendable, they might detract from your effectiveness as an MP. It's not just about managing the projects but also about how your role as a representative is perceived. They're worried it might dilute your political focus."

Popi sighed, taking in the feedback. "I appreciate you bringing this up. I'm aware of the delicate balance I need to maintain. The community work is close to my heart, but I also understand the need to prioritize my responsibilities as an MP."

Mr. Church nodded, "Exactly. And I know you're passionate about these projects. But maybe it's worth considering delegating more day-to-day tasks and focusing on the strategic aspects. It could help you effectively manage your role as an MP and your community commitments."

Popi paused, reflecting on Mr. Church's advice. "That makes sense. I'll have to think about how best to adjust my approach.

Popi: A Rising Tide

I want to ensure I make the most impact without overextending myself."

Mr. Church smiled, "That's all anyone can ask. And remember, if you ever need help navigating these concerns, don't hesitate to reach out. We're here to support you."

They continued their walk in contemplative silence, the conversation leaving Popi with much to ponder. As they returned to the office, Popi felt a renewed sense of purpose and clarity about the path forward.

As they strolled back to Mr. Church's office, Mr. Church asked casually, "So, Popi, how's everything going in the office? Is it what you expected? Any surprises?"

Popi, ever the optimist, responded with a smile, "Well, it's not all roses, but I'm making it work. Coming into this, I knew there would be challenges, and there certainly are. But I've always believed in facing obstacles head-on. I'm committed to making it work."

Mr. Church raised an eyebrow, impressed by Popi's demeanour. "It's good to hear you're staying positive. The by-election win was a big step, but the general election will be a whole different ballgame. Are you feeling prepared for the challenge?"

Popi's smile widened, a hint of excitement in his eyes. "Absolutely. The general election will be tougher, no doubt about it. But I'm looking forward to it. It will be a battle, and I'm ready for it. The stakes are high, and we have a strong platform to stand on. I'm not letting the pressure get to me— I'm using it as motivation."

Mr. Church nodded appreciatively. "That's the spirit. The enthusiasm and resilience you're showing are exactly what the Party needs. Keep that energy up; you'll navigate these challenges just fine."

As they reached Mr. Church's office, Popi felt a renewed sense of determination. Despite the hurdles and complexities of his new role, he was ready to tackle whatever came his way with the same vigour and optimism that had brought him this far.

The atmosphere grew more serious as they settled into Mr. Church's office. Leaning back in his chair, Mr. Church began with a candid assessment of Popi.

"I have to admit," Mr. Church started, "when you first came into the party, I wasn't thrilled about it. You were a newcomer, and there were a lot of long-standing members who had been working tirelessly for years—sometimes decades. Seeing someone come in so quickly ahead of them didn't sit well with me initially."

Popi listened attentively, nodding as Mr. Church continued.

"But," Mr. Church said, "after getting to know you and seeing what you've done, my opinion has changed. I think you might be one of the best assets we have. Your ability to communicate effectively and handle tasks and responsibilities has impressed me."

Mr. Church's tone turned more serious as he added, "You should be cautious, though. Trusting people in politics is tricky. Most are in it for themselves, and if they get the chance to bring you down to get ahead, they might take it. I don't want you mixed up in the wrong projects, deals, or groups."

He leaned forward slightly, a thoughtful look on his face. "I've been in politics longer than you've been alive. Seeing your energy reminds me of myself when I was starting. It took me a long time to get where I am, but I've accomplished quite a bit, from passing numerous bills to holding my seat for over 30 years. While it may be a hard sell to give you major files right now, I want you close. Your unique perspective is valuable."

Mr. Church paused momentarily before adding, "One thing I respect about you is your honesty. You've stuck to your guns from the moment you were asked to represent the Conservative Party of Canada. If you were going to try to impress anyone, it would have been then, but you stayed true to yourself. That's a solid trait, and it means you're likely to stay true to your principles even after winning the election."

Popi felt a mix of gratitude and relief. Mr. Church's words were both reassuring and a reminder of the high expectations he was now facing.

Mr. Church's serious tone conveyed the gravity of the upcoming challenges. "Popi, I need to level with you," he began. "We're facing a tough battle with the next general election, although still over a year away. Our main concerns are reaching younger demographics and new Canadians and dealing with the bleeding support to the left-leaning parties. After two consecutive losses, the party is growing impatient. They're ready to replace me if we don't turn things around, and I know this is my last shot at winning."

Mr. Church leaned forward, his expression intense. "I've

watched you, and your ability to mobilize people is impressive. From the international students' fight to your rapid rise to win the by-election, you might be the Party's best hope for the general election. If you succeed, it could mean a comeback for the party after over a decade of sitting on the sidelines."

Popi nodded, absorbing the weight of Mr. Church's words. "I understand the stakes," he replied. "I'll take some time to think about it. Developing a comprehensive plan might take a couple of weeks to a few months, but I assure you, my word is my bond."

He continued, "I truly appreciate your honesty and the trust you've placed in me. I wouldn't want to work under anyone else but you for now. This upcoming election feels like a make-or-break situation for both of us."

Mr. Church smiled, acknowledging Popi's commitment. "I'm glad to hear that. Your dedication and honesty are what we need. We're in this together, and your success will be a significant part of our future."

With that, Mr. Church and Popi concluded their conversation, both fully aware of the high stakes and the pivotal role they would play in the coming months.

Popi's reflections were filled with the complexity of his new reality in federal politics. As he navigated the treacherous waters of party dynamics, he realized just how cutthroat and precarious his position was. The growing animosity from other MPs and the heightened scrutiny were signs of a battle that was not just political but deeply personal.

Popi: A Rising Tide

Realizing that the Conservative Party of Canada was rife with internal conflicts and not as united as he had assumed was a sobering insight. The apparent unity he had expected was a façade, concealing the deep-seated rivalries and power struggles that could either propel him forward or spell his downfall. This new understanding made him acutely aware of the dangers and challenges he faced.

Despite Mr. Church's support and the strategic advantage Popi might have due to his proximity to the Party leader, he couldn't ignore the hostility brewing around him. The fact that his presence and success were causing discomfort among his colleagues underscored the precariousness of his position. The growing number of enemies who could directly impact his career added another layer of urgency to his need for a solid strategy.

With Mr. Church's leadership at stake, Popi understood that any success he achieved was directly linked to Mr. Church's ability to secure the Party's position in the next election. If the Conservative Party of Canada failed to form a government, it wouldn't just mean a loss for Mr. Church; it would also jeopardize Popi's future and trust in politics. The stakes were indeed high.

In this environment, Popi knew he had to make every move count. Crafting a winning strategy for the upcoming election would influence the party's fate and ensure his survival and success. He had to balance his actions carefully, leveraging the support he had while mitigating the risks posed by his growing list of adversaries.

As Popi walked away from these thoughts, he knew that staying focused and strategic was crucial. He needed to channel his energy into creating effective campaign strategies, building alliances, and preparing for a fiercely competitive electoral battle. His ability to navigate this challenging landscape would ultimately determine his future and the success of the Conservative Party of Canada.

The Defining Period

Popi knew hiring Kyle would be resisted, especially given the political climate and internal party dynamics. Despite this, he was determined to bring Kyle on board, not just as an act of loyalty but because he genuinely believed in Kyle's abilities.

When the news of Kyle's hiring spread through the office, it was met with skepticism and whispers of favouritism. Some questioned whether this was a move to fill a diversity quota or an act of affirmative action. Popi, anticipating this backlash, was prepared to address it head-on.

During a team meeting, one of the more vocal staff members bluntly asked Popi if Kyle's hiring was purely for affirmative action. Maintaining his composure, Popi responded confidently, "Kyle wasn't hired to meet any quota. He was hired because he's better at this job than most people in this office. Give him a chance, and you'll see what I mean."

To prove his point, Kyle was given a challenging task that required excellent typing skills and impeccable file management. Within less than a day, Kyle completed the task with such efficiency and precision that it left no room for doubt about his capabilities. His typing speed was remarkable, and his organizational skills were top-notch. Files that had been messy for weeks were sorted, categorized, and filed correctly.

Seeing Kyle's prowess firsthand silenced many of the skeptics. The office, which had been buzzing with dissent, now hummed with a grudging respect. Kyle's performance was undeniable, and his presence shifted the office dynamics positively.

Observing this change, Popi felt relieved and vindicated. He had taken a calculated risk by hiring Kyle. By proving Kyle's worth through his skills and work ethic, Popi demonstrated that his decision was based on merit, not favouritism. This move not only strengthened Kyle's position in the office but also subtly reinforced Popi's authority and judgment as a leader who could make tough, unpopular decisions for the right reasons.

With Kyle's success, the office began to operate more smoothly, and the initial uproar subsided, replaced by a more cohesive and efficient team dynamic. Popi's gamble had paid off, underscoring the importance of recognizing and leveraging true talent, regardless of initial perceptions or biases.

Despite Kyle's successful integration into the office and the respect he had earned from his colleagues, Popi decided to trade Kyle with an office worker from Mr. Church's office after a week. This move was strategic and not taken lightly. Popi knew it would disappoint his team, but he believed it was necessary for the larger goals they were aiming to achieve.

As the news of Kyle's departure spread, the office buzzed with disappointment and confusion. The team had just started to appreciate Kyle's efficiency and had grown fond of his presence. The sudden change felt like a loss, and morale took a hit.

During a team meeting, Popi addressed the elephant in the room. He stood in front of his team, sensing their frustration and sadness. "I know you're all disappointed about Kyle leaving," he began, his tone firm but empathetic. "But sometimes, we must make tough decisions for the greater good. Kyle's skills are needed elsewhere right now, and this trade will benefit both our team and Mr. Church's office."

One of the team members couldn't help but voice their frustration, "But we just got used to him, Popi. Why now?" Popi nodded, understanding their sentiment. "I get it. Change is hard, especially when we lose someone valuable. But I need you all to suck it up and get on with your lives. We have important work to do, and I need everyone focused and performing at their best."

The team fell silent, processing his words. They respected Popi's judgment, even if they didn't fully understand his reasoning. Slowly, they shifted their focus back to their tasks, determined to prove their resilience and dedication.

Meanwhile, Kyle's arrival in Mr. Church's office was met with curiosity. Mr. Church had been briefed about Kyle's capabilities and was eager to see how he would adapt to the new environment. Though initially surprised by the trade, Kyle approached his new role with the same diligence and efficiency he had shown in Popi's office.

As the days went by, Kyle's presence began to positively impact Mr. Church's team, much like it had in Popi's office. His organizational skills and work ethic quickly won over his new colleagues. Mr. Church, observing Kyle's integration, felt reassured about the trade.

Back in Popi's office, the initial disappointment gradually faded. The team, driven by Popi's encouragement, adapted to the new dynamics. The office worker from Mr. Church's team who replaced Kyle brought fresh perspectives and new energy, helping to fill the void Kyle left.

Popi monitored both offices closely and was pleased that his strategic decision yielded positive results on both fronts. He understood that leadership often required making difficult choices and that his team's ability to adapt and thrive under these circumstances would ultimately strengthen them.

By the end of the month, both teams had adjusted well to the changes. Popi's office continued to operate efficiently, and the trade with Mr. Church's office reinforced the collaborative spirit between the two leaders.

Kyle's newfound confidence propelled him to excel in Mr. Church's office. He was determined to prove to Popi that his trust had not been misplaced. The transformation from being fired as an administrative assistant in the municipal government to working alongside the potential next Prime Minister of Canada was surreal for Kyle, and he was willing to go above and beyond to solidify his place in this new environment.

His energy and enthusiasm were infectious. Kyle took on every task with a level of dedication and precision that impressed not only his new colleagues but also Mr. Church himself. He meticulously managed files, coordinated schedules, and streamlined office procedures, making the office more efficient than it had ever been.

Kyle's evenings were often spent thinking of improving processes and contributing more effectively. He voluntarily stayed late, ensuring every detail was perfect. His willingness to help extended beyond his job description. He assisted colleagues with tasks, provided valuable insights during meetings, and even took on additional responsibilities without complaint.

One day, Mr. Church called Kyle into his office. "Kyle, I've been observing your work, and I must say, you've exceeded all expectations. Your dedication and efficiency are exactly what we need, especially with the upcoming general election."

Kyle beamed with pride. "Thank you, Mr. Church. I'm just grateful for the opportunity and want to do my best."

Mr. Church nodded, a smile playing on his lips. "I'm confident you will. Keep up the good work."

Meanwhile, Popi kept a close eye on Kyle's progress. He received regular updates from Mr. Church and was pleased to hear about Kyle's exceptional performance. Popi knew placing Kyle in Mr. Church's office was the right decision. Not only was Kyle thriving, but his presence also bolstered the collaboration between their offices.

Popi also felt a sense of responsibility towards Kyle. He remembered the difficult period Kyle had gone through after losing his job and the subsequent struggles. Seeing Kyle flourish brought Popi a sense of satisfaction and reaffirmed his belief in giving people second chances.

Kyle's success didn't go unnoticed by his former colleagues in Popi's office either. They were initially disappointed by his departure, but news of his achievements in Mr. Church's office made them proud. It also motivated them to step up their game, creating a ripple effect of increased productivity and dedication.

As weeks turned into months, Kyle's confidence continued to soar. He developed a keen understanding of the political landscape, provided valuable input during strategic discussions, and became an integral part of Mr. Church's team. His journey from a low point to working alongside a potential Prime Minister was nothing short of inspiring.

Kyle remained grateful to Popi for the opportunity and silently vowed to always have his back. The bond between the two grew more robust, built on mutual respect and trust. Kyle knew that wherever his political career took him, he owed a great deal to Popi's faith in his abilities.

With the general election approaching, the stakes were higher than ever. But Kyle, buoyed by his confidence and the support of his mentors, was ready to face any challenge that came his way. He was determined to prove his worth and contribute meaningfully to the success of the party and the community projects that had brought him and Popi together in the first place.

Back at the constituency office, things were bustling with activity. An unexpected number of people sought Popi's help with various issues, ranging from community problems to personal grievances. The office was filled with the hum of conversations, the ringing of phones, and the constant shuffle of papers.

Popi had managed to maintain a strong presence in his constituency despite his busy schedule on Parliament Hill. The one-hour drive between the two locations allowed him to be on-call and accessible to his constituents. He had always believed that staying connected with the people who had

Popi: A Rising Tide

elected him was crucial to his role as their representative.

On this particular day, the volume of requests was overwhelming. Popi's small team was doing their best to manage the influx, but they were clearly stretched thin. Popi quickly took charge, directing his staff with calm authority.

"All right, everyone, let's prioritize these requests," he said. "Let's start with the most urgent cases and work our way down. I'll handle as many of the face-to-face meetings as I can."

Donna, who had come by to help, stepped in to manage the crowd. She had a natural talent for organizing chaos and quickly set up a system to streamline the process.

"Let's have everyone sign in with their name and the nature of their issue," she suggested. "This way, we can group similar cases and handle them more efficiently."

As the team implemented Donna's system, the office began to run more smoothly. Popi moved from one meeting to the next, listening intently to each person's concerns and offering practical solutions or promises to follow up.

Throughout the day, Donna remained steady, providing support where needed and ensuring that everything ran smoothly. Her efficiency and dedication did not go unnoticed by Popi.

"Donna, thank you for stepping in today," Popi said during a brief lull. "I couldn't have managed without your help."

"Of course, Popi," she replied with a smile. "I'm always here to help. Besides, these people need us."

As the day drew to a close, the office finally quieted down. Popi and his team had addressed most of the issues brought to them, and they had a follow-up plan.

Popi took a moment to reflect on the day's events. Despite the chaos and the sheer volume of requests, he felt a deep sense of fulfillment. This was why he had entered politics – to make a difference in people's lives, no matter how small.

Popi felt a renewed sense of purpose while driving back to Parliament Hill that evening. He knew the upcoming general election would be challenging, but he was ready to face it head-on. With the support of his team, the dedication of people like Donna, and the drive of individuals like Kyle, he felt confident that they could overcome any obstacle.

In the back of his mind, Popi knew that he still had personal matters to resolve, particularly with Donna. But for now, he focused on serving his constituents and preparing for the battles ahead. The road to the next election would be challenging, but Popi was determined to make every moment count.

Popi appreciated Donna's commitment and the value she brought to his office, even as a volunteer. Her presence helped maintain the efficiency and effectiveness of their work, especially given the increased demand from constituents.

One day, during another busy afternoon, Donna noticed a pattern in the issues being raised. She approached Popi with her observations, suggesting they could streamline their efforts by categorizing and prioritizing the problems based on urgency and impact. Popi agreed, recognizing the potential to improve their workflow and better serve the community.

Together, they set up a system where constituents' concerns were logged, categorized, and assigned to team members based on their expertise. This made the office more efficient and ensured that urgent matters received the attention they deserved promptly. Donna's organizational skills and Popi's leadership created a well-oiled machine that could handle the growing demands of the constituency.

The case that stood out was one of a woman whose child was hit by a police car. Now she had a bill to pay for the damage to the vehicle and a jaywalking ticket for her daughter, who was in the hospital. She couldn't afford a lawyer to fight for her and was concerned that the court system was too slow and needed help to help her daughter. Popi told her that he understood her case and would seriously consider it. The woman left all her documents with Popi and thanked him dearly before walking out with hope.

Popi sat at his desk, the weight of the woman's case pressing on him. He knew he had to act quickly to help her, but the situation's complexity required a careful approach. He decided to start by reviewing the documents she had left.

The second case weighed heavily on Popi as he listened to the woman's emotional plea. He understood the complexities and the difficult choices involved. Domestic violence was a serious issue, but he also recognized the dire consequences for the family if the husband were deported. The woman, while broken by domestic violence, was anxious about her kids growing up without their father. The woman's husband's deportation was imminent as an offender still waiting for his Canadian citizenship.

"I understand your concerns," Popi said gently. "This is a very complicated situation; we must handle it carefully. I'll look into what options we might have."

The woman thanked him tearfully and left Popi with another challenging case to tackle. He knew he needed to balance compassion with justice, and the stakes were high.

Popi intently listened as Donna introduced the third challenging case of the day, a young woman, her voice filled with compassion and concern. The girl, visibly anxious, clutched her hands together and glanced around nervously.

"Hi, I'm Paul Peters, but you can call me Popi. It's okay, you're safe here," Popi said gently, trying to put her at ease. "Donna told me a bit about your situation. We're here to help."

The girl, whose name was Maria, nodded hesitantly. "I just don't know what to do. I'm so scared. I can't return home and have nowhere else to go."

Popi's heart ached for her. At just 15, she faced challenges that would be overwhelming for anyone. She was pregnant and torn about what to do. Scared to get an abortion, she wanted help to find housing and financial resources to help her raise her baby. However, Popi and Donna didn't think it was good for her to go down that path. Popi promised to figure something out for her before time ran out, and Donna eased the woman's mind by reassuring her that Popi always kept his word.

Popi: A Rising Tide

As the month stretched, Popi knew that to genuinely support Mr. Church's quest to secure the next general election, he needed to tackle the staffing issue head-on. His recent experience with Kyle had reinforced his belief that competent, dedicated staff were crucial for navigating the complexities of federal politics.

Popi began by reviewing the current staff members working with Mr. Church. He identified who was performing well and who was merely fulfilling their primary duties. Understanding the team's strengths and weaknesses would help him make informed decisions about any necessary changes.

Popi directed Kyle to start recruiting new staff who were not only skilled but also genuinely motivated. He instructed Kyle to focus on candidates with proven track records in political work and those passionate about Mr. Church's vision. Kyle's keen eye for talent and understanding of what made a good team member was invaluable in this process.

Popi and Kyle planned a series of training sessions for the new and existing staff to ensure they were aligned with Mr. Church's goals and expectations. The focus was on improving efficiency, fostering a strong work ethic, and building a cohesive team that could work seamlessly together.

To ensure accountability, Popi introduced performance metrics and regular evaluations. Staff members were expected to meet specific benchmarks and demonstrate their contributions to the team's objectives. This approach helped identify issues early and ensured everyone was pulling their weight.

Kyle was tasked with organizing and streamlining Mr. Church's office operations. This included improving communication channels, setting up efficient workflows, and clearly defining all tasks and responsibilities. A well-organized office enabled Mr. Church to focus on strategic matters rather than getting bogged down by administrative issues.

Popi also established a routine for regular check-ins with Kyle and Mr. Church to monitor progress and address any concerns. These meetings provided a platform for discussing challenges and adjusting strategies as needed.

Understanding that a motivated team is a productive team, Popi also emphasized the importance of maintaining high morale. He encouraged open communication, recognition of hard work, and opportunities for team-building activities to foster a positive work environment.

By taking these steps, Popi aimed to create a robust support system for Mr. Church to help with his immediate needs and position them for long-term success in the upcoming general election.

Popi's approach of working and developing ideas independently was both a strength and a challenge. His preference for solitude allowed him to intensely focus on his ideas and plans without the distractions or compromises that might come from constant collaboration. However, this method also meant that he had to bear the full weight of his ideas and decisions, both their successes and failures.

Working alone allowed Popi to maintain a clear, undiluted vision of his goals and strategies. He could think through complex problems and devise innovative solutions without the

Popi: A Rising Tide
influence of competing opinions or constraints.

By developing ideas independently, Popi took full ownership of his successes and failures. This personal accountability drove him to work harder and be more meticulous, knowing that the outcome would reflect his efforts.

Solitary work often fosters originality. Popi's independent thinking allowed him to explore creative solutions and approaches that might not have emerged in a more collaborative setting.

Handling everything on his own placed a significant burden on Popi. If an idea failed or faced difficulties, he had to address these issues alone, which was sometimes stressful and overwhelming.

While Popi valued his independence, he recognized the importance of political collaboration. To balance his solitary work style with the need for teamwork, Popi delegated specific tasks or aspects of projects to trusted aides, allowing him to focus on the core elements while benefiting from the expertise of others.

Popi also engaged with crucial individuals for feedback at critical stages of a project to help refine his ideas without compromising his overall vision.

Establishing a network of reliable and competent colleagues who understood and supported his approach provided the necessary support and ensured his ideas were well-executed. Periodic reviews with his team offered fresh perspectives and identified any adjustments needed to improve outcomes.

By finding ways to integrate these elements into his workstyle, Popi continued to benefit from his independent thinking while also leveraging the strengths of collaboration to achieve his goals.

Popi's decision to present a plan to Mr. Church while stepping back from directly overseeing the campaign's details reflected his strategic thinking and understanding of the party's dynamics.

He crafted a comprehensive plan for Mr. Church, showcasing his dedication and strategic vision. By presenting the plan, Popi demonstrated his commitment to the party's success and willingness to contribute valuable ideas.

Popi's choice to decline to take direct charge of the campaign details was a strategic move. Given the existing resentment from other MPs, Popi recognized that assuming a prominent role in the campaign could exacerbate tensions.

Popi's decisions helped avoid alienating other MPs who might view him as a competitor or threat. By stepping back, he aimed to maintain a collaborative atmosphere and focus on winning the election.

This might also have been seen as a tactical retreat to manage internal politics, as the move could help him navigate the complex party dynamics and position himself strategically for future roles.

By asking Mr. Church to present the plan as his own, Popi aimed to mitigate potential conflicts and maintain a harmonious working environment. This approach also allowed Mr. Church to take credit for the strategic direction, which could bolster his position and support within the party.

Supporting Mr. Church in presenting the plan as his own could strengthen their working relationship. It demonstrated Popi's loyalty and willingness to work behind the scenes, which might earn Mr. Church's respect and gratitude.

Popi's approach allowed him to concentrate on refining and perfecting the plan without the distractions of managing campaign details. He thought that this focus would likely enhance the quality of the plan and its execution.

The biggest upside of Popi's plan was that stepping back could prevent immediate conflicts. Still, it also meant that he would have had less influence over the campaign's execution. Ensuring that the plan's details were implemented effectively would depend on the capabilities of those managing the campaign.

Popi planned to maintain open lines of communication with Mr. Church and the campaign team to ensure that his strategic vision was understood and integrated into the campaign.

Popi would also monitor the campaign's progress strategically, offering advice or adjustments as needed without being directly involved in daily operations.

By managing his role strategically, Popi balanced his contributions with navigating complex party dynamics, ultimately supporting the campaign's success while maintaining a harmonious working environment.

Popi's comprehensive and ambitious plan reflected his

commitment to addressing core issues and improving the lives of Canadians. He was always the one to shoot for the stars and hoped to hit the moon in the worst-case scenario.

One of his core ideas was to rewrite the Canadian tax code to benefit the average Canadian. He advised planning to make the tax code simple and the tax system more equitable. He suggested evaluating current tax codes and identifying areas for improvement. He hoped this change would reduce complexity and improve compliance, making the system more accessible and fairer for Canadians.

Ever the one to despise inefficiencies, Popi advised Mr. Church to identify and address overspending and inefficiencies in government contracts. He suggested implementing a rigorous review process for contracts as crucial. Mr. Church could sell the idea to Canadians as something that would lead to cost savings and more transparent government spending. He also emphasized the importance of selling the idea by comparing the expenditures and inefficiencies of the Liberal Government of Canada, particularly over the ten years they had been in power.

Generating additional revenue that could be used to lower taxes for average Canadians was also part of the plan. While he didn't offer specifics, he pointed to things like tax on streaming platforms and online purchases and boosting entrepreneurship to improve employment and employment standards, which would likely lead to more revenue in tax in the long term as well as enhance the Canadian GDP per capita, that is the amount of wealth generated by Canada as a share of each Canadian citizen. Basically, the more each resident contributes to the economy, the more wealth the country generates. Popi was aware of the resistance that the idea might face from tech companies and some consumers. However, he argued that the concept could still generate a public debate that could improve their polling numbers.

Another idea presented to Mr. Church came from Donna, and he only mentioned a few details about the plan while recommending that Mr. Church listen to the concept in its entirety from Donna herself. Her parents were immigrants, and her friends were first- or second-generation immigrants. If Mr. Church wanted to win the young vote, it would have been in his best interest to listen to some of the young Canadians themselves. Popi explained that immigration was no longer an issue of adding numbers to the population but had become a social issue that needed a multi-faceted approach that considered those already in Canada and those wishing to emigrate to Canada.

While he might have seemed callous in some of his radical ideas, Popi also believed in rewarding hard work for everyday Canadians. He suggested providing practical rewards and support for those contributing to the economy through things like substantial tax breaks for hardworking individuals. Acknowledging and rewarding dedication is something he believed would boost morale and productivity.

While Mr. Church liked the plan, he had a few concerns. He worried that the plan's more radical elements, such as the immigration reform, might not align with the party's current stance, which could lead to potential conflicts. He advised Popi to work on a few things to broaden the scope of his ideas beyond his core principles and show adaptability and a willingness to compromise, which could enhance his standing within the party.

Mr. Church was on the fence about simplifying the tax code and introducing new taxes on online services. He feared they might only be well-received if they led to tangible benefits, like lower Canadian taxes. However, that could've been another challenge, so it was part of a plan that still needed more work.

Additionally, some elements of the plan, particularly the overhaul of the tax code and immigration reforms, would require significant legislative and administrative effort. Therefore, Mr. Church was understandably worried that there could be pushback from various stakeholders, including businesses affected by new taxes or those opposed to immigration reforms.

Popi's focus on rewarding hardworking Canadians and improving government efficiency aligned with broader conservative principles and highlighted a practical governance approach. Balancing radical ideas with more pragmatic solutions allowed Popi to present himself as a forward-thinking yet grounded leader. All in all, Mr. Church admitted he had found a needle in the haystack.

Popi promised to continue refining his plan, addressing potential areas of contention, and advocating for its benefits to the public and party members. He also wanted to consider engaging with stakeholders, including business leaders, community representatives, and constituents, who would be crucial in gaining support and addressing concerns. Effectively communicating the plan's benefits and alignment with conservative values would help overcome resistance and garner broader support.

Popi's strategic approach, balancing radical ideas with practical solutions, positioned him as a proactive and innovative thinker capable of navigating complex political dynamics and working toward meaningful reforms.

Mr. Church's unexpected move to publicly acknowledge Popi's contributions was a strategic and tactical manoeuvre to address and manage the swirling rumours and growing tensions within the party. By framing Popi's ideas as crucial for the party's success, he defended Popi from the gossip and created a unified front to combat internal discord and external criticism.

Mr. Church's statement was designed to rally party members around a common goal. By highlighting Popi's ideas as key to the party's future success, he aimed to shift focus from internal conflicts to the shared objective of winning the election.

This move was meant to reduce internal animosity and encourage members to collaborate more effectively, potentially leading to a more cohesive and productive campaign.

Addressing the rumours head-on and positioning Popi as a valuable asset helped prevent speculation from becoming damaging headlines. By publicly endorsing Popi's contributions, Mr. Church sought to contain and neutralize potential fallout from negative rumours. He hoped this approach improved Popi's standing within the party and reassured both members and the public of the party's direction and strategy.

Emphasizing the importance of Popi's ideas and the necessity of party unity was likely intended to boost morale among party members. Knowing their collective effort could be crucial in securing electoral success may inspire more outstanding commitment and enthusiasm.

Additionally, by framing the situation as a critical juncture for the party's future, Mr. Church implicitly encouraged members to put personal grievances aside and focus on the broader goal of electoral success.

Popi would continue engaging with party members to build stronger relationships and gain support. Open communication and collaboration were crucial in maintaining a positive working environment.

Demonstrating his commitment to the party's success and addressing any lingering concerns from colleagues helped solidify his position and foster trust.

Popi gathered feedback from party members and adapted his strategies based on their input to enhance the effectiveness of his ideas and ensure they resonated with the broader party agenda. For this, he worked closely with his team and Mr. Church to implement the proposed strategies effectively and ensure they aligned with the party's goals and values.

Maintaining a positive public image and clearly communicating his role and contributions helped reinforce Popi's value to the party and mitigated potential negative narratives. Being transparent about his work and progress helped build credibility and trust with both party members and the public.

Popi and Mr. Church knew they needed to manage expectations carefully, ensuring that the party's goals were realistic and achievable within the given timeframe. They planned to continuously address any concerns or criticisms from party members with clarity and respect to help maintain a cooperative atmosphere and ensure the party remained united.

Popi: A Rising Tide

By strategically addressing internal tensions and publicly endorsing Popi's contributions, Mr. Church aimed to strengthen the party's position and set the stage for a more effective and unified approach to the upcoming general election.

Over the next few days, Popi made it a point to reconnect with each conservative party member at Parliament Hill. It was as if he were a sailor returning to familiar shores after a long voyage, hoping to mend old fences and forge new alliances. Each interaction was a delicate dance as he navigated the murky waters of political sentiment and personal disappointment.

Some members were forthright in their sentiments. They expressed their initial dissatisfaction with Popi's sudden ascent within the party, likening it to a newcomer arriving at a grand banquet and being seated at the head table without the customary courtesies. Yet, beneath their discontent lay a shared determination to rise above their grievances. "Grudges are like old shoes," one veteran member remarked with a rueful smile, "they can be worn out and discarded if one chooses to walk a new path."

In the spirit of unity, they agreed to set aside their reservations and work collectively toward a common goal: the defeat of the governing Liberal Party of Canada in the upcoming general election. Their resolve was a testament to the proverb, "United we stand, divided we fall." It was clear that despite their initial reservations, the stakes were high enough to encourage a cooperative spirit.

As Popi moved from office to office, some members presented belated congratulations on winning the by-election and becoming the newest member of the Conservative caucus. It was as if they were extending an olive branch, hoping to soften any lingering tensions and signal their support for his newfound role. "Better late than never," Popi thought as he accepted their gestures with gratitude, understanding that healing old wounds often required patience and perseverance.

Mr. Church had given Popi a significant responsibility: to serve as the bridge between his office and the rest of the party MPs. In this role, Popi was expected to facilitate communication and coordination, ensuring that the party's diverse voices were heard and harmonized. Mr. Church, recognizing Popi's boundless energy and confidence, believed that Popi's ability to manage these interactions would allow him to focus on the broader challenges facing the party.

Popi accepted the challenge with the resolve of a general preparing for battle. "The road to success is dotted with many tempting parking spaces," he mused, recalling an old saying that suggested perseverance was vital to progress. He knew that his role as the bridge would require skill, diplomacy, and a keen sense of responsibility. By handling these tasks effectively, Popi aimed to ensure that his focus remained on the party's critical issues rather than getting bogged down by individual concerns.

Popi felt the weight of his new responsibilities with each handshake and conversation. Yet, he also sensed a growing sense of camaraderie and a shared purpose. The road ahead was fraught with challenges, but the solidarity of the party members was a beacon of hope. As he walked through the halls of Parliament Hill, he was reminded of another old saying: "The best way to predict the future is to create it." Popi was determined to shape a future where the party could unite, overcome its differences, and emerge victorious in the battle ahead.

One notable incident occurred when a fellow conservative MP representing a lone riding surrounded by a sea of Liberal MPs sought Popi's counsel. Ms. Fox, as she was known, was feeling the weight of the world on her shoulders. Though traditionally Conservative, her constituency was increasingly inundated with Liberal supporters and business interests. The pressure was relentless, and she feared that if she didn't adapt, she might be forced to abandon her Conservative principles to retain her seat.

Popi listened intently as Ms. Fox expressed her concerns, the frustration and desperation in her voice palpable. It was a moment that brought to mind the adage, "When the going gets tough, the tough get going." Popi understood the gravity of her situation and knew that navigating such treacherous waters required both strategic insight and a steady hand.

After a moment's reflection, Popi assured her he would consider her dilemma carefully. As Ms. Fox turned to leave his office, Popi called her back, the heavy weight of her predicament evident in her posture. He had been mulling over her situation and felt a sudden surge of clarity.

"Ms. Fox," he said, "Here's a plan you might consider while we work on gaining momentum across the country."

He continued, "For now, I would advise you to adopt a neutral stance on contentious issues. Neutrality, while often considered a cautious approach, can be a strategic retreat when facing overwhelming pressure. It's like walking on a tightrope— sometimes, the safest way forward is to maintain your balance and avoid sudden moves."

Ms. Fox looked at him, puzzled yet hopeful. Popi went on, "Neutrality isn't where real change happens, but it can provide the breathing space you need. When you're under intense pressure, it's not the time to push for radical changes or take bold stands. Think of it as cooling things off. Maintaining a neutral position will give you time to develop a solid strategy tailored to your constituency's needs. It's a way to stabilize the situation and buy yourself some time to regroup and prepare."

He offered her a reassuring smile. "Remember, even the tallest oak tree starts as a sapling. Sometimes, the best way to weather a storm is to bend with it rather than break."

Ms. Fox nodded, visibly relieved. The plan wasn't a cure-all, but it offered a glimmer of hope and a practical way to navigate her challenging circumstances. She felt a renewed sense of purpose as she left Popi's office. The road ahead was still fraught with challenges, but Popi's advice had provided her with a strategic lifeline.

Popi, too, felt a sense of satisfaction. He knew that helping others navigate their trials was integral to leadership. His advice to Ms. Fox was a reminder that even in the complex world of politics, sometimes the most effective strategy was to buy time, stabilize the situation, and build a foundation for future success.

In a country where the Conservative Party of Canada held 98 out of 338 seats, and the Liberals commanded a formidable majority with 199 seats, the political landscape was starkly imbalanced. The Liberals had the numbers to push through nearly any legislation or policy they desired, and their

Popi: A Rising Tide

dominance left the Conservatives grappling for influence.

The power dynamics had led to a curious predicament: constituents who had once voted Liberal were represented by Conservative MPs. This shift sparked a cacophony of demands for their representatives to advocate for Liberal policies, aiming to benefit their respective ridings. Among the Conservative MPs caught in this crossfire was Ms. Fox, a moral and ideological leader who had run a successful campaign on a platform aligned with traditional Conservative values.

Ms. Fox, just a few years older than Popi, was a staunch advocate for conservative ideals, particularly those concerning women's issues. Her positions were notably anti-abortion, anti-LGBTQ, and fiercely supportive of traditional family structures. In a constituency that was nearly evenly divided between Liberal and Conservative supporters, her rhetoric began to stir trouble.

The situation was a powder keg, with Ms. Fox's uncompromising stance alienating a significant portion of her constituency who felt increasingly pressured by the prevailing Liberal agenda. After understanding the delicate balance required in such a politically charged environment, Popi offered Ms. Fox some guidance.

"Ms. Fox," he began, his tone measured and empathetic, "I've been reflecting on your current position and challenges. It's clear that you've held steadfast to your principles, which is commendable. However, in a riding as divided as yours, a more nuanced approach might be necessary."

He continued, "Think of it like this: when navigating through a stormy sea, sometimes you need to adjust your sails to reach your destination. I'm not asking you to abandon your beliefs but rather to find a way to temper your message. This isn't about compromising your values but finding common ground to serve as a bridge until the party can regain strength and influence."

Ms. Fox listened intently, her expression a mix of contemplation and reluctance. Popi added, "Consider offering a gesture that acknowledges the concerns of your Liberal constituents. Perhaps you could support or advocate for a policy that aligns with their interests, even if it's not within your usual stance. It's about buying time and demonstrating that you're attentive to their needs while remaining true to your core principles."

Popi offered her a reassuring smile. "It's a bit like planting seeds in rocky soil. By showing that you're willing to engage with the concerns of your diverse constituency, you're nurturing the ground for future growth. It's a strategic compromise that could yield positive results for both you and the party."

Ms. Fox nodded slowly, absorbing Popi's advice. She understood the necessity of balancing her ideals with the practicalities of her political environment. The suggestion to tone down her more controversial positions and find a way to connect with her Liberal constituents was a strategic move she hadn't fully considered.

She felt a renewed sense of purpose as she left Popi's office. While her commitment to conservative values remained unwavering, she now had a more straightforward path forward that allowed her to navigate the political storm with a blend of idealism and pragmatism.

Popi: A Rising Tide

Popi, for his part, felt a sense of accomplishment. He had successfully guided Ms. Fox toward a more pragmatic approach without compromising her core beliefs. It was a reminder that balancing personal convictions with the broader demands of a diverse electorate was crucial for sustaining one's role and influence in politics.

In his office at Parliament Hill, Popi adopted a distinct and deliberate approach to leadership. He was acutely aware of the delicate balance required to lead effectively without falling into the traps of complacency or ineffectiveness. Popi was determined to ensure that aides did not merely run his office, as he feared that could lead to perceptions of incompetence and loss of respect. Instead, he envisioned an office where every staff member actively participated in shaping the direction and success of his work.

Popi had inherited a diverse team—a mix of sharp minds and seasoned individuals who had long been entrenched in the Conservative Party's ranks. Some had risen through the ranks due to their sheer dedication and years of door-knocking for various Conservative candidates. Others were newcomers, bringing fresh perspectives and innovative ideas. Recognizing this mix, Popi sought to create an environment where everyone had an equal voice and contributed to the office's collective goals.

"I want this office to be a place where ideas clash and evolve," Popi often said. "If we're all just nodding along, we're not challenging ourselves or each other. I need a team that will question, debate, and refine ideas. That's how we'll ensure our work isn't just good but exceptional."

To foster this collaborative and dynamic atmosphere, Popi instituted a daily routine that became the cornerstone of his leadership style. Every day he was at Parliament Hill, the team would gather for at least an hour to delve into current affairs and news. This wasn't just a casual discussion but a focused session to understand how various issues might impact the party and where potential opportunities lay.

Popi would initiate these discussions with questions like, "What's the latest news on economic policies, and how might they affect our constituency?" or "How can we turn this current event into a strategic advantage for the party?"

The goal was to keep everyone informed and engaged with ongoing events and brainstorm actionable strategies to benefit the party. Popi believed that by involving his staff in these discussions, he was educating them and empowering them to take ownership of their roles and responsibilities.

"The world doesn't stand still, and neither should we," Popi would say with a determined gleam in his eyes. "If we're not staying ahead of the curve, we're falling behind. This team needs to be as agile and responsive as the issues we face."

Popi's approach was met with mixed reactions. Some staff members thrived in open discussion and critical thinking. In contrast, others struggled with the demand for constant engagement and debate. However, Popi was resolute in his belief that this method was crucial for cultivating a high-performing team.

Popi made it a point to provide constructive feedback and support to address the varied reactions. He encouraged staff members to voice their concerns and offer suggestions for improvement. He understood that leadership wasn't just about directing but about nurturing and developing his team.

In time, the team adapted to Popi's leadership style. They began to appreciate the value of being well-informed and the thrill of contributing to a strategic discussion. The office became a hub of activity and innovation, where ideas were tested, refined, and implemented purposefully and precisely.

Popi's insistence on keeping the team actively engaged in current affairs and strategic planning paid off. His office became a centre of political acumen and a model of effective leadership, transforming a diverse group into a cohesive and motivated team.

Popi's strategic manoeuvres extended beyond internal party dynamics and ventured into the complex world of cross-party negotiations and strategic realignments. With a keen eye for opportunities and a relentless drive to reshape the political landscape, Popi began to target independent MPs and members from other parties, aiming to bolster the Conservative Party's strength and influence.

In his quest, Popi was guided by a vision of "true freedom," a concept he passionately believed could resonate across the political spectrum. His approach was to identify MPs who, for various reasons, might be disillusioned with their current affiliations or who harboured misgivings about their party's direction.

His efforts were calculated and persistent. Popi reached out to several independent MPs, presenting them with a vision of a more unified and purpose-driven Conservative Party. He highlighted the potential benefits of joining a party that promised a seat at the table and a chance to influence significant change in Canadian politics. His pitch was not merely about party allegiance; it was about a shared commitment to values he believed were crucial for the nation's future.

Popi managed to win over two independent MPs through persuasive dialogue and by addressing their specific concerns and aspirations. Their transition into the Conservative Party was marked by a mixture of cautious optimism and strategic calculation. For these MPs, the move was both a new opportunity and a step towards aligning with a more structured and potentially influential party.

Additionally, Popi set his sights on the Liberal Party, recognizing that shifting key figures could significantly alter the political balance. He approached an MP from the Liberal ranks who had shown signs of dissatisfaction with the party's recent policies and internal conflicts. Popi's strategy was to emphasize the broader impact this MP could have by crossing the floor and aligning with a party that promised a different direction—one that valued her input and offered a platform for her ideals.

The persuasion was not without its challenges. The MP faced considerable pressure and potential backlash from her former party. However, Popi's argument—that her defection could be a bold move towards realigning Canadian politics and advocating for true freedom—resonated deeply. After several intense discussions and weighing options, the MP decided to cross the floor, joining the Conservative Party with a promise to bring her unique perspective and experience to the new role.

Popi: A Rising Tide

Popi's efforts did not go unnoticed. His ability to attract MPs from diverse backgrounds demonstrated his political acumen and strategic vision. While the process was fraught with risks and negotiations, successfully incorporating these MPs into the Conservative Party marked a significant milestone.

The arrival of the two independent MPs and the former Liberal MP brought fresh perspectives and bolstered the party's position. It was a testament to Popi's belief that change often requires bold actions and unconventional strategies. These additions increased the party's numbers, enhanced diversity, and enriched debates and policy discussions.

Popi knew that such moves would stir reactions within the political sphere. His actions would likely be scrutinized and debated, but he remained focused on his long-term goals. The new MPs added strength and complexity to the Conservative Party. Popi was prepared to navigate the ensuing challenges with the same determination that had
brought him this far.

His strategy of attracting MPs from different political backgrounds was a clear signal that Popi was not just a rising star in the Conservative Party but a key player capable of reshaping the broader political landscape of Canada.

Popi's accomplishments were undeniable. He had made significant strides for himself, the party, and his constituency. Yet, behind the façade of success, the toll on his mental health was becoming increasingly evident. The job demands were relentless, and the weight of expectations seemed almost unbearable.

Ever perceptive to Popi's struggles, Donna tried to reason with him about the need to slow down. However, her words seemed to bounce off him, falling on ears that were too tired to listen. Instead of insisting, she chose a different path: she stayed by his side, offering a calming presence in the chaos. Their relationship had now shifted again from one of mere colleagues to a bond of deep friendship.

Donna's gestures of care were subtle yet profound. She ensured that Popi ate nutritious meals and kept his apartment in order, creating a semblance of normalcy amidst the whirlwind of his life. Her actions went beyond the professional realm, reflecting a part of her nature that found joy in supporting those she cared about. Whether managing her drunk friends on nights out or maintaining a tidy environment for Popi, she was driven by a genuine desire to help.

Her commitment to her friends and Popi was a testament to her character. While she enjoyed socializing, she preferred to stay sober, always being the one to drive and look after others. Those fortunate enough to be close to her cherished her selflessness and dedication.

In this tumultuous period, Donna's steadfast presence was a beacon of stability for Popi. She embodied the spirit of friendship and support, quietly making a difference in ways that often went unrecognized but were deeply appreciated by those around her.

An Unprecedented Canadian Moment

Popi had rapidly ascended to a key figure within the Conservative Party of Canada, achieving this remarkable status within just a few years of leaving university and less than two years after officially entering politics. The accomplishments were significant and impressive, but for Popi, the sense of achievement was tempered by an understanding that there was still much work to be done.

His rise was not just a personal victory but a testament to his relentless drive and the strategic insight he had brought to the political arena. Despite the accolades and the role he had carved out for himself, Popi was acutely aware of the challenges ahead. The landscape of Canadian politics was ever-shifting, and he knew that maintaining and building upon his success required continuous effort, foresight, and adaptability.

Amid his accomplishments, Popi remained focused on the bigger picture. He was determined to consolidate his position, drive meaningful change, and ensure that his contributions would have a lasting impact. The journey was far from over, and he was prepared to navigate the complexities of politics with the same dedication and resolve that had brought him this far.

After a few intense months of dedicated campaigning, the general election day had arrived, and Popi's victory seemed almost inevitable. His relentless energy and unwavering commitment kept his momentum strong throughout, never wavering even after his previous by-election win. He had maintained an impressive lead in his constituency, consistently engaging with voters and addressing their concerns with an enthusiasm that had only grown since his initial success.

Popi's campaign had become a powerful force that resonated deeply with the electorate. His strategic prowess, combined with his genuine dedication to the issues, had solidified his position as a frontrunner. The excitement surrounding his candidacy was palpable, and as the results began to trickle in, it was clear that Popi was poised for a significant triumph.

Before the official announcement of his win, Popi's victory had already set the tone for the election, marking the first of 338 races in Canada. His success was not just a personal achievement but a symbol of the broader shift within the political landscape, demonstrating the effectiveness of his approach and the strength of his campaign.

As the evening unfolded, Popi was surrounded by a whirlwind of celebration and jubilation at the campaign headquarters. Supporters cheered, and the atmosphere was electric with the thrill of his victory. His constituency's enthusiasm was infectious, and Popi smiled and basked in the collective joy of his supporters. It was a moment of triumph for him, marking the culmination of months of relentless effort and dedication.

Yet, beneath the surface of this celebratory facade, a profound sense of unease lingered in Popi's mind. The real test was his win and the general election's outcome. The future of the Conservative Party of Canada, and with it, the potential to form a government, was still uncertain. Despite his strong performance and the support he had garnered, Popi couldn't shake the nagging worry about how the conservatives would fare on a larger scale.

Even though Donna had provided him with all the time and resources needed to support the Party and Mr. Church, Popi grappled with a sense of inadequacy. The weight of the responsibility was heavy, and he couldn't escape the feeling that the failure would somehow rest on his shoulders if the party didn't secure enough seats to form a government. The trust placed in him by the party and Mr. Church was a mantle he carried with both pride and pressure. In the quiet moments of reflection amidst the celebration, Popi couldn't help but feel that he had to do more and that his efforts still might not have been enough to steer the party toward the ultimate victory they all hoped for.

As the night wore on and the hours ticked toward morning, the air was thick with anticipation. Speculation swirled like a restless breeze through the campaign headquarters as the polling stations reported their results. Each update was a new thread in the intricate tapestry of the election, weaving together hopes and fears, victories and disappointments.

By the dawn of the next day, the long-awaited announcement finally came. The Conservative Party of Canada had secured 145 seats, surpassing the Liberal Party of Canada, who won 133 seats. The remaining seats were distributed among the independents and other smaller parties, reflecting a diverse political landscape. The news was met with a wave of jubilation and relief.

The conservative supporters, who had weathered countless

storms and endured relentless scrutiny, erupted in celebration. The air was filled with a mixture of joy and disbelief. After so many grievances with the outgoing Liberal government and its policies, the sense of a new beginning was palpable. There was an overwhelming feeling that change was on the horizon—a change hoped to correct what many perceived as past errors and steer Canada towards a better future.

Popi, while still in the midst of the celebration, could feel the collective sigh of relief that rippled through his supporters. The victory was a testament to his hard work, but he remained grounded, acutely aware of the challenges ahead. The Conservative Party's win meant they would now be responsible for delivering on their promises and leading the country through the next chapter.

As the morning light began to break, casting its gentle rays over the country, the air of celebration in Conservative Party headquarters was suddenly pierced by a surprising announcement from the Liberal Party. Despite losing the popular vote and the seat count, they were unprepared to relinquish their grip on power without a fight.

In Canadian politics, it is customary for the party with the most seats to form the government. However, the situation was anything but ordinary. The Liberals, determined to maintain their hold on governance, declared they would not bow out gracefully. They argued that, given the fragmented election results with a significant number of seats held by smaller parties and independents, they could still negotiate and form a coalition government.

This unexpected turn of events cast a shadow over the

Popi: A Rising Tide

Conservative Party celebration. The prospect of extended debates and potential legal challenges loomed large. The country watched with bated breath as the political landscape shifted again, with many people voicing their opinions, each coloured by their party allegiance.

Critics decried the move as a threat to democratic norms, questioning the fairness of the process. Supporters of the Conservative Party, who the initial results had buoyed, now faced the harsh reality that their victory was far from secure. The Liberals' strategy to cling to power through complex negotiations and potential coalitions ignited a fierce debate about the integrity of the democratic process and the nature of political power.

Amidst the chaos, Popi could feel the weight of uncertainty settling over him. The victory that had seemed so inevitable was now tangled in a web of political manoeuvring and legal uncertainty. The path forward was murky, with the potential for further political battles and shifting alliances. The country was on the brink of what could be a dramatic and contentious transition of power, and Popi's role in the unfolding drama was just beginning to take shape.

As the political turmoil raged on and Parliament Hill in Ottawa buzzed with heated debates and passionate exchanges, a single video captured the moment's essence. Amidst the clamour of competing voices and the uncertainty of the political landscape, a curious journalist managed to corner Popi for a brief interview.

In the video, Popi spoke calmly yet firmly, his voice cutting through the chaos with a clarity that resonated across the nation. "I respect the Canadian Constitution deeply," he began, his tone measured and thoughtful. "It's clear that according to our Constitution, the Liberals are within their rights to claim they can still lead despite losing the election. However, the question is whether they can indeed form a government."

Popi's words struck a chord. He continued, "There's no need for unnecessary bickering and grandstanding. If the Liberals are confident they can garner enough support to form a government, then let's put it to the test. The Constitution provides for such a process, and it's only fair that both parties have the opportunity to make their case to the Parliament."

His challenge to the Liberals was direct and pragmatic: "If the Liberals truly believe they have the backing to govern, they should prove it within the framework of our democratic system. This is a chance for both sides to demonstrate their capability to lead and gain the necessary support from the House."

The video quickly went viral, capturing the attention of a nation grappling with the uncertainty of its political future. Popi's call for a fair and transparent process became the focal point of the debate, providing a clear path forward amidst the confusion.

Within hours, both parties were given a 72-hour deadline to mobilize their support and present their case to Parliament. The clock was ticking, and every political strategist and campaigner was in overdrive.

Mr. Church, recognizing the significance of Popi's statement and the opportunity it presented, wasted no time rallying his team. He turned to Popi with a determined look. "We need a comprehensive plan to showcase our strengths and secure as much support as possible. This is our chance to prove ourselves, not just to the party, but to the entire nation."

Driven by the situation's urgency and his unwavering commitment to fairness and transparency, Popi set to work immediately. He began devising strategies to rally Conservative support, ensuring that every argument and every plan was robust enough to withstand the scrutiny of the coming hours. The challenge ahead was monumental, but Popi's resolve was more vital than ever.

Popi found himself in uncharted territory amid the unfolding political drama. The responsibility of navigating this turbulent situation was overwhelming. Despite his previous achievements and the significant strides he had made, this was a different kind of challenge that transcended the realm of idealism and delved deep into the pragmatic world of political manoeuvring.

Popi understood that what lay ahead wasn't about the best ideas or the most innovative policies. It was about the hard-nosed reality of politics: securing the necessary support to form a government. The challenge was no longer just about presenting compelling arguments or visionary plans. It was about rallying enough support to tip the scales in their favour.

Realizing the gravity of the situation, Popi and Mr. Church called an urgent meeting with all the recently elected Conservative MPs. The atmosphere was charged with anticipation as the MPs gathered in a conference room, a palpable sense of urgency hanging in the air.

Mr. Church addressed the assembly with a mixture of gravitas and resolve. "We're standing at a crossroads," he began, his voice steady. "The next few days will determine our party's future and our country's direction. We have a unique opportunity to demonstrate our ability to lead and bring about the change many Canadians yearn for."

Popi took over from there, his expression reflecting the seriousness of the task. "We must put our heads together and develop a strategy to maximize our chances of forming a government. This isn't just about our constituencies anymore. It's about uniting our efforts to build a coalition strong enough to support our cause."

He continued, "Over the next 24 hours, I want you to think critically about how you can contribute to this effort. We need fresh ideas, strategies to appeal to undecided MPs, and ways to strengthen our position. We must demonstrate that we have the vision and the capability to lead effectively."

As the MPs dispersed to deliberate and strategize, the weight of the upcoming task settled heavily on Popi's shoulders. He knew that the next 24 hours would be crucial. This wasn't merely a test of political skill but a challenge of uniting disparate voices and strategies into a cohesive plan.

In the quiet moments before the whirlwind of activity began, Popi took a deep breath. The path ahead was uncertain, but he was determined to navigate it with the same dedication and resolve that had guided him through previous challenges. The stakes were high, and the pressure was immense. Still, Popi was ready to give his all to ensure the Conservative Party could rise to the occasion and seize this pivotal moment.

Amid the political maelstrom, Popi found himself thrust into

Popi: A Rising Tide

an unofficial yet crucial role: that of the party whip. With the Conservative Party holding 145 seats, they needed to secure at least 25 additional seats from smaller parties or independent MPs to form a majority government. The task before him was daunting—convincing a sufficient number of these MPs to support the Conservative agenda and help them reach the critical threshold.

Popi knew the importance of this endeavour. The following 48 hours would be pivotal, not just for his political career but for the future of the Conservative Party and Mr. Church's aspirations. The gravity of the situation weighed heavily on him, yet he was determined to rise to the occasion.

He began by seeking counsel from seasoned politicians within the party. Their wisdom and experience were invaluable, and Popi was keen to absorb every piece of advice they had to offer. The seasoned MPs shared their insights on negotiating with smaller parties and independents, offering strategies and tactics that could make a difference.

One experienced MP, with a wry smile, advised Popi, "In politics, it's often said that you catch more flies with honey than with vinegar. Approach each conversation with a spirit of cooperation and mutual benefit. Make sure to listen more than you speak. Understand their needs and concerns, and show them how supporting our side can help address those."

Another veteran suggested, "Remember, the art of persuasion lies in framing your pitch in a way that aligns with their values and goals. Find common ground and emphasize how our proposed policies or compromises can be mutually advantageous. And don't forget—sometimes, a bit of flexibility and creativity can go a long way."

Armed with this advice, Popi set about crafting a compelling pitch. He knew he had to tailor his approach to each party or independent MP. His strategy involved highlighting how the Conservative platform could address specific issues that were important to them, offering concessions or partnerships where feasible, and demonstrating a willingness to work together for the greater good.

Popi was candid about his limitations and inexperience. "I may be new to this," he admitted during meetings with the MPs, "but I'm committed to working hard and doing everything possible to achieve our goals. I promise that if you give me your best ideas, I'll act on them and fight for the support we need."

Popi immersed himself in a whirlwind of meetings, negotiations, and strategic discussions as the hours ticked by. Each conversation was a balancing act—presenting the Conservative Party's case while addressing the concerns and priorities of potential supporters.

The pressure was intense. Every moment counted, and the stakes couldn't have been higher. Popi was acutely aware that the outcome of this critical period would determine not only the fate of Mr. Church's leadership but also the future direction of the Conservative Party.

Despite the whirlwind of activity and the looming uncertainty, Popi remained resolute. He was driven by a sense of duty and a commitment to seeing this through. The following 48 hours would test his resolve, political insight, and ability to unite and persuade.

Popi: A Rising Tide

In the heart of the storm, Popi's determination was unwavering. He was ready to navigate the turbulent waters of politics, hoping that his efforts would lead to a successful outcome and secure a new chapter for the Conservative Party and Mr. Church's leadership.

Popi's challenge was multifaceted, with ideological divides and competing interests creating a complex landscape of negotiations. The goal was to secure the support needed to form a government, and each party and independent MPs brought their own set of expectations and principles to the table.

For some smaller parties, the gulf between their core beliefs and the Conservative platform was vast. They championed ideals that clashed with the Conservatives' stances, making it difficult to incorporate their demands into a Conservative government agenda. For instance, parties with a strong focus on progressive social policies or aggressive climate action found aligning with the Conservative stance on these issues challenging.

One senior MP, reflecting on the situation, offered Popi a piece of wisdom: "We don't have to give them everything they want, Popi. Sometimes, it's more about finding a few commonalities and demonstrating a willingness to compromise. We need to show that we're reasonable and open to adjustments where feasible."

Popi took this to heart. He understood that negotiating with these parties would require careful calibration. It wasn't about adopting their entire platform but finding areas where compromise could be achieved without undermining

Conservative principles. The focus was on identifying policy areas where concessions could be made, particularly those that would not significantly impact the core Conservative agenda.

The independents were somewhat easier to sway. They were often less ideologically committed and more focused on pragmatic solutions. The key was addressing their concerns and demonstrating how supporting the Conservative Party could align with their interests or principles.

Popi engaged in numerous discussions with the independents, emphasizing practical benefits and showing a readiness to accommodate some of their key concerns. The negotiators clarified that while their demands could not be fully met, their input was valued and would be considered in the broader policy framework.

Popi, guided by the insights from seasoned MPs, proposed a strategic approach. The idea was to offer targeted concessions while holding firm on core Conservative policies. For example, while climate change was a contentious issue, Popi suggested adopting some measures that addressed climate concerns without drastically altering the Conservative stance. This could involve supporting incremental steps toward environmental sustainability without embracing radical policies.

Another area of negotiation involved welfare policies. While the Conservative platform traditionally advocated for reducing welfare expenditures, Popi proposed a nuanced approach. Instead of abrupt cuts, he suggested reforming welfare programs to improve efficiency and effectiveness, aligning with broader goals of fiscal responsibility while mitigating concerns from other parties.

Popi: A Rising Tide

Popi crafted his pitch carefully, emphasizing that the Conservative Party would listen and adapt where possible. He highlighted the pragmatic approach of negotiating with smaller parties and independents, showing that the Conservatives were committed to working collaboratively to form a stable and effective government.

In his discussions, Popi conveyed a sense of urgency and determination. "We're here to build a government that serves all Canadians," he told one group. "We're open to compromise on specific issues but also committed to upholding our core values. Our goal is to find common ground and work together for the betterment of the country."

Popi's efforts were relentless as the 72-hour deadline approached. He navigated the intricate web of negotiations with diplomacy, flexibility, and strategic insight. The pressure was immense, but Popi's resolve remained steadfast. He knew that every conversation, concession, and promise would play a crucial role in shaping the outcome of this critical political moment.

The stakes were incredibly high. Popi found himself at the centre of a political maelstrom, where every decision carried profound implications for the future of Canadian politics and the Conservative Party. The scenario was tense, and the path forward was anything but straightforward.

The three smaller parties—each holding the balance of power—had become crucial players in this unfolding drama. Their newfound leverage meant they could demand significant concessions, and their choices would shape the country's direction for years to come. Despite losing the election, the

Liberal Party of Canada was poised to remain in power if it could secure enough support from these smaller parties. This situation presented a critical juncture: either the Conservatives would form a government, or the Liberals would cling to power, potentially extending their tenure by accommodating the demands of smaller factions.

For Mr. Church, the situation was particularly dire. His political career was on the line, and the potential end of his leadership loomed large. Popi, who had grown close to Mr. Church and saw him as a mentor, was deeply concerned. He didn't want to see Mr. Church's career cut short by a failure to form a government. If the Conservatives lost this battle, Popi hoped the party would retain him as their leader for the next election. He believed this would allow them to capitalize on the momentum they had built and mount a more robust challenge in the future.

Popi recognized that the power dynamics at play were not just about policy but also about political survival. The Liberals and smaller parties were negotiating from a position of strength, knowing that any compromise could lead to a four-year extension of their governance. For the Conservatives, making the right moves was crucial for forming a government and preserving their prospects.

One seasoned MP advised Popi, "Sometimes, the best we can do is to accept that a temporary setback is just a step in a longer journey. If we can't form the government now, we must ensure we're prepared to return stronger."

Popi's approach to negotiations involved balancing immediate needs with long-term strategy. He understood that securing the

Popi: A Rising Tide

support of smaller parties was essential but also recognized that overly generous concessions could set a dangerous precedent. The Liberals, on the other hand, were aware that accommodating these parties would come with its own set of challenges. The potential for internal discord and policy disagreements meant that any coalition formed under duress might be unstable and short-lived.

Popi and his team worked tirelessly to craft a pitch that would appeal to the smaller parties without compromising the Conservative platform. He proposed various policies and compromises, emphasizing that while the Conservatives were willing to negotiate, they were also committed to maintaining a coherent and principled agenda.

In his discussions with party members, Popi emphasized the importance of focusing on the bigger picture. "We're at a crossroads," he said. "If we can't form a government now, we must use this as a learning experience and an opportunity to strengthen our position. We must show resilience and preparedness for the challenges ahead."

Popi's vision was clear: even if the Conservatives failed to form a government this time, they needed to emerge from the crisis with their integrity and leadership intact. He argued for a strategic retreat with plans to regroup and prepare for the next election if necessary. He hoped the Conservative Party would use the experience as a springboard for future success.

Each hour was crucial. The political landscape was shifting rapidly, and every action taken by Popi and his team would have a lasting impact. As the negotiations unfolded, Popi remained resolute, driven by a commitment to his party, his mentor, and his vision for Canada's future.

With the clock ticking and the weight of the situation growing heavier by the minute, Mr. Church made a pivotal decision that would shape the outcome of the election negotiations. After days of intense deliberation and the pressure mounting from every direction, he chose to go all in.

Mr. Church's decision was driven by the urgent need to secure enough support to form a government. He realized that if the Conservatives didn't act decisively, the Liberals might seize the opportunity to create a coalition government with one of the smaller parties, which held precisely the number of seats they needed to make a government. In this scenario, the power dynamics could shift dramatically. The smaller party would have significant leverage in a coalition government, potentially rendering the Conservative Party's 145 seats less influential.

Understanding the gravity of the situation, Mr. Church decided to pitch a compromise that included concessions on some key policy areas. This strategic move was designed to appeal to the smaller parties and secure their support. He knew that this was a high-risk, high-reward situation. If the Conservatives could demonstrate flexibility and a willingness to accommodate specific policies, they could persuade enough members to back their government bid.

Mr. Church's proposal included a range of policy concessions to address the smaller parties' concerns. He offered to implement several progressive policies:
- Enhancing environmental regulations and investing in green technologies.

Popi: A Rising Tide

- Adjusting welfare policies to address concerns from smaller parties about social safety nets.
- Committing additional funds to improve healthcare services was a primary concern for several smaller parties.
- Giving the smaller parties more power in some committees and allowing them to review and discuss budgetary concerns.

Mr. Church's pitch was carefully crafted to balance Conservative values and the demands of the smaller parties. He emphasized that while the Conservatives were prepared to make concessions, they would not abandon their core principles. Instead, they aimed to forge a pragmatic coalition that could govern effectively while respecting the diverse viewpoints within Parliament.

From experience, Mr. Church knew that while the Liberals might concede to some demands by the smaller parties, there was no way they would let anyone see how they were spending the taxpayers' money. Adding the climate and welfare policies was offered as a huge concession for the Conservative Party. He hoped this would send a message that they were willing to give up something core to their value to reach a mature compromise.

In his address to the smaller parties, Mr. Church stated, "We are at a crossroads in Canadian politics. The Conservative Party is committed to leading this nation with integrity and vision. However, we also understand the importance of collaboration and compromise in a diverse and democratic society. We are prepared to make reasonable adjustments to our policies to form a government that represents all Canadians. We believe this is the best path forward for our country, and we ask for your support in this crucial moment."

With only a few hours remaining before the critical vote, the urgency was palpable. Popi worked tirelessly to support Mr. Church's proposal despite his fatigue and the strain of the past few days. He reached out to key members of the smaller parties, making personal appeals and presenting the Conservative Party's offer as a genuine effort to build a more inclusive and effective government.

Popi's efforts were a testament to his dedication and resilience. He understood that while the negotiations were complex and fraught with challenges, the goal was to ensure the Conservative Party could form a stable government and move forward with its agenda.

As the final vote approached, the tension was almost unbearable. The fate of the Conservative Party, Mr. Church's leadership, and the future of Canadian politics hung in the balance. The smaller parties and independents would need to decide whether to support the Conservatives' bid for government or align with the Liberals in a potential coalition.

Popi and Mr. Church's efforts represented a crucial moment of political strategy and negotiation. Their ability to navigate the situation's complexities and secure the necessary support would determine whether they could form a government or face the consequences of a Liberal-led coalition. The next few hours would be decisive in shaping the future of Canadian politics.

In a decisive move, Mr. Church opted for a divide-and-conquer strategy, utilizing a meticulous approach to sway the smaller parties and independents. He leveraged detailed research on each candidate's campaign promises to craft a persuasive pitch.

The research revealed various promises made by the smaller parties to their constituents, primarily focused on provincial issues. These included:

- Commitments to streamline work for new immigrants and improve employment standards by raising wages.
- Promises for scholarships and improved opportunities for post-secondary education graduates or other students that forego post-secondary education.

Mr. Church's approach was to turn these promises into leverage. By aligning Conservative proposals with these commitments, he aimed to create an even more appealing offer for the smaller parties.

Mr. Church decided to send Popi on a critical mission. Popi was tasked with meeting a key MP from one of the smaller parties to discuss a practical and appealing proposal. The goal was to offer something tangible that the MP could present to his constituents, thereby increasing his chances of re-election.

Popi's strategy emphasized that party loyalty was secondary to securing meaningful outcomes for their constituents in this high-stakes situation. He argued, "In a potential coalition government, small parties could easily become mere pawns in a larger Liberal agenda. By negotiating for practical benefits now, you ensure you have something substantial to offer your supporters. If you align with the Conservatives, you will retain control over your political ideas while securing real, actionable outcomes for your constituents."

During the meeting, Popi laid out a compelling case to the MP. He focused on several key points. Popi highlighted how the proposed Conservative policies aligned with the MP's campaign promises, ensuring that the MP could deliver on their commitments to their voters. He pointed out that aligning with the Conservatives would give the MP more significant influence and the ability to impact policy decisions directly rather than being sidelined in a Liberal-dominated government. Popi assured the MP that by working with the Conservatives, he would not be bound by the Liberal Party's broader agenda. Instead, he could negotiate terms that were beneficial for his constituents.

Popi also made a personal promise, "I will ensure that any agreements we make are honoured and the promises made during your campaign are delivered. Your constituents deserve the commitments you've made, and I'm here to help you fulfill them."

Popi's arguments resonated with the MP, who saw the potential benefits of aligning with the Conservative Party. Popi successfully swayed the MP towards supporting the Conservative bid by offering a practical solution that aligned with the MP's campaign promises.

With time running short, Popi continued to work tirelessly, coordinating with other MPs and making final appeals to ensure that the Conservative Party could secure the necessary support. The next few hours would be crucial in determining whether the Conservative Party could form a government or if the Liberals would retain power through a coalition.

Popi's efforts were a testament to his strategic insight and dedication. The outcome of the negotiations would not only influence the immediate political landscape but also shape the future direction of Canadian governance.

Popi grappled with a pervasive sense of uncertainty as the minutes and hours ticked away in the race to secure enough support to form a government. The strategy to convince the MPs from smaller parties and independents had yielded numerous "maybes," leaving him in a precarious position. With each passing moment, the stakes grew higher, and the possibility of a setback became increasingly real.

Popi's previous few days had been filled with tense negotiations and a whirlwind of political manoeuvring. Despite his best efforts, many MPs remained non-committal, expressing cautious interest but withholding definitive support. This unpredictability was disheartening, as the outcome of these negotiations would determine not only the fate of the Conservative Party but also the future of Mr. Church's leadership.

Throughout this tumultuous period, Popi reflected on his respect for Mr. Church. He had come to admire Mr. Church not only as a seasoned politician but also as a leader who embodied qualities he deeply valued. Mr. Church's leadership temperament and motivational skills were exceptional; he had a unique ability to inspire confidence and foster a sense of unity within the party.

Popi recognized that Mr. Church's leadership was instrumental in navigating the Conservative Party through these challenging times. His strategic vision and steady hand had been crucial in formulating the plans and strategies that Popi had been implementing. Losing Mr. Church as the party leader would be a significant blow, not just to the party but also to Popi, who had grown to value his guidance and mentorship.

As the clock wound down and the final votes were being cast, Popi found solace in hoping things would turn out favourably. He could only pray that the efforts of the past few days would bear fruit and that the Conservative Party would secure the necessary support to form a government.

He hoped against hope that the negotiations would result in a victorious coalition and that Mr. Church's leadership position would be preserved. The thought of Mr. Church losing his job was troubling, and Popi felt a deep sense of responsibility to support him in any way possible.

Amidst the high-stakes negotiations and political calculations, Popi's admiration for Mr. Church and his commitment to the Conservative Party shone through. His dedication was not merely about political success but also about honouring the values and principles that Mr. Church had championed.

In the end, Popi's resolve was driven by a blend of respect, hope, and a deep-seated belief in the importance of solid leadership. The outcome of the negotiations would soon be revealed. Still, Popi's unwavering support for Mr. Church and his commitment to the party would remain constant in his journey.

As the moment of truth approached, the atmosphere in the parliamentary chambers was thick with anticipation and trepidation. The vote, a pivotal event in Canadian political history, promised to resolve one of the most uncertain and

Popi: A Rising Tide

unprecedented situations in recent memory.

Popi's heart raced as he awaited the final count. The weight of the past few days bore heavily on him. His attempts to sway undecided MPs and negotiate terms had reached a critical juncture. Now, it was time to see if all their efforts would culminate in success or disappointment.

Just as the tension seemed almost unbearable, Popi began receiving a flurry of messages from the MPs he had met with. The initial uncertainty and hesitation were giving way to something more promising. Many of the MPs expressed their doubts about the Liberals' promises, finding them less credible and practical than the concrete benefits the Conservatives offered.

These messages were a beacon of hope for Popi. They revealed that his persistent efforts and strategic pitches had made a significant impact. The idea of real, practical change for their constituents resonated more strongly than the grand yet unconvincing promises from the Liberals. The MPs were beginning to see the value in aligning with the Conservative Party, which had offered actionable solutions rather than lofty, uncertain assurances.

Popi meticulously tracked the incoming messages, each a potential step closer to the magical number of 170 seats needed to take power from the Liberal Party of Canada. His anticipation grew with each message, his focus unwavering despite the chaos around him. The number 170 loomed large in his mind, representing not just a numerical goal but the threshold between political defeat and a transformative victory for the Conservative Party.

As the MPs cast their votes, the initial signs were promising. The responses from the MPs, now aligned with the Conservative Party, provided a sense of cautious optimism. Popi's strategic negotiations and compelling arguments about practical benefits had struck a chord. The atmosphere in the chambers was electric, with each vote representing a crucial decision in the unfolding drama.

The final tally was more than just numbers; it was a testament to Popi's relentless efforts and the Conservative Party's resilience. As the results were announced, realizing that the Conservative Party had secured enough votes to form a government brought relief and joy. Popi's hard work had paid off, and the Conservative Party was on the verge of reclaiming control.

The sense of accomplishment was bittersweet, knowing the journey had been fraught with challenges and uncertainty. Popi's role in this monumental shift was undeniable, and his dedication to Mr. Church and the party had made a significant difference.

With the outcome secured, Popi took a moment to reflect on the tumultuous path that led to this victory. The experience had been gruelling and enlightening, revealing the intricacies of political manoeuvring and the importance of steadfast leadership. Popi's role in shaping this new chapter was evident as the Conservative Party prepared to take the reins of government. The road ahead would be demanding, but the victory was a testament to the resilience and determination of all who had fought for it.

As the hours ticked by, the atmosphere in the parliamentary

Popi: A Rising Tide

chambers grew increasingly charged. The votes were counted, and a palpable sense of anticipation filled the room. In a dramatic turn of events, the Conservative Party had exceeded the magic number of 170 seats—an extraordinary achievement that allowed them to form a government.

The announcement to supporters was met with a roar of triumph. Cheers and jubilation erupted at every conservative campaign headquarters and resonated nationwide. The Conservative Party's victory, after a decade of opposition, marked a monumental shift in Canadian politics. The celebrations were a testament to their political resilience and the hope that this victory heralded a new era for the country.

Amid the celebrations, Mr. Church, now the Prime Minister-elect, quickly made his way to Popi. With tears of joy and pride, Mr. Church enveloped Popi in a heartfelt hug. The embrace was more than just a gesture of gratitude; it symbolized the trust and partnership that had defined their journey. Soon, other Conservative members joined in, creating a sea of congratulations and cheers. Popi, surrounded by a chorus of grateful voices, was lauded for his instrumental role in the victory.

This moment was a turning point for the Conservative Party, which had been out of power for a decade. It was also seen as a significant moment for Canada, as the Conservative Party's new vision promised to reshape the political landscape. The victory was a political success and a beacon of hope for many who believed in the party's promises for a better future.

Despite the overwhelming focus on Mr. Church's new role as Prime Minister, much of the spotlight was on Popi. The young political strategist, who had risen to prominence remarkably quickly, was celebrated as the hero behind this unexpected triumph. His tireless efforts, strategic insight, and dedication had been crucial in securing the Conservative Party's success.

During the celebrations, Popi met with a few MPs from other parties who had voted for the Conservatives to form the government. Their gratitude was apparent, but so was their concern. They conveyed a straightforward message to Popi: they hoped he would keep his word. Their trust was contingent on the promises made during the tumultuous negotiations. Popi assured them their concerns would be addressed, and their hopes for meaningful change would not be in vain.

The victory began a new chapter for the Conservative Party, Mr. Church, and Popi. For Popi, it was an incredible realization of his influence on the fate of the Canadian government. From a recent university graduate to a pivotal figure in Canadian politics, his journey had been nothing short of extraordinary.

As the celebrations continued, Popi took a moment to reflect on how far he had come. The responsibility ahead was immense but also a testament to his hard work and determination. The future was filled with promise, and Popi was poised to play a crucial role in shaping it.

The story of this victory would be remembered as a testament to the power of perseverance and the impact one individual could make in the grand tapestry of politics. For Popi, it was a reminder that even in the most uncertain times, dedication and belief in one's vision could lead to transformative success.

In the aftermath of the celebration, Donna sought out Popi

Popi: A Rising Tide

with genuine warmth and admiration. "Congratulations, Popi," she said, her eyes reflecting pride. "The Conservative Party wouldn't have achieved this without you. I'm always proud to work alongside you because your heart is always in the right place. I hope you stay true to yourself no matter what happens in politics."

Popi's expression softened. "My father used to say, 'It's better to be hated for who you are than to be loved for who you are not.' I'm glad you see the qualities in me that others might not like. It means a lot to me."

They shared a heartfelt hug, each drawing strength from the other. Popi then suggested they go out for dinner to celebrate, but Donna had a different idea.

"It's late, and I'm not in the mood to cook something nice for you," Donna said. "I've had a long day, and it might be better if we just order in and eat in the comfort of your home. What do you say?"

Popi, appreciating her thoughtful gesture, agreed. They left together, ready to unwind and share a quiet, comforting meal amidst the whirlwind of their recent victory.

Popi and Donna enjoyed a serene and reflective evening together as the night unfolded. The conversation flowed naturally, touching on Popi's future and the shifting landscape of Canadian politics. They speculated about the roles he might take now that Mr. Church, his mentor, had become the Prime Minister of Canada. They both felt the excitement and the weight of the new political reality.

With a hint of teasing curiosity, Donna mentioned, "I wonder if Mr. Church has something special planned for you. After all, you're a big reason behind this victory."

Popi chuckled and shook his head. "Oh, come on, Donna. There are many more experienced people in the party who deserve key positions. If he gives me something significant immediately, it would stir up quite a bit of discontent."

Donna laughed softly and said, "Inexperienced politician? After what you've just accomplished for the party, that title no longer fits you. You've proven yourself."

They continued their conversation into the early morning, discussing everything from political strategy to personal dreams. Exhaustion eventually overtook them, and they both drifted into a deep sleep, content and fulfilled by the night's revelations.

In their shared quiet moments, Popi expressed his gratitude to Donna. "You know, if I'm the reason the Conservative Party could form a government, it's because you were the reason I could do all of this. Your support and care have been invaluable."

Donna's eyes softened, and she replied, "I'm glad I could help, Popi. It's a shame we couldn't make something more out of this, but knowing that I played a part in your success means a lot."

Their appreciation for each other was palpable, marked by an understanding and respect that transcended professional boundaries. Their bond was more than just a partnership; it was a genuine connection built on mutual support and shared values. As they rested side by side, it was clear that their relationship was a cornerstone of their successes and would continue to be a source of strength and encouragement in the future.

An Unexpected Visit

The cozy atmosphere in Popi's apartment was quickly overtaken by an unexpected mix of warmth and awkwardness when Donna unexpectedly encountered Popi's parents. She had planned to leave quietly without waking him, only to find herself face-to-face with Mr. and Mrs. Peters at the door. The surprise on both sides was palpable, and as Donna stood there, it was as if she had unintentionally opened the door to more than just a casual visit — she had unknowingly stepped into a new chapter of their relationship.

Sensing the tension, Popi broke the silence with a light-hearted comment, teasing Donna about her attempted escape. His humour successfully defused the awkwardness, bringing a smile to both his parents and Donna. Yet, the real bombshell dropped moments later when Popi introduced Donna as his girlfriend. Donna's heart skipped a beat, her shock mirrored by the sudden stillness in her body. However, she quickly gathered herself, extending a warm and gracious greeting to his parents.

The lightness returned when Popi's father, Mr. Peters, broke into a playful grin, teasingly suggesting that Donna must be the reason behind Popi's recent string of successes. Donna couldn't help but smile, but her mind was still reeling from Popi's unexpected label of "girlfriend." However, Mrs. Peters seemed genuinely relieved, her gaze softening as she acknowledged Donna's role in caring for her son. There was no mistaking the gratitude in her voice as she mentioned how glad she was to know that someone was looking after Popi, given how busy and demanding his life had become.

Despite her growing embarrassment, Donna instinctively tried to downplay her role in Popi's achievements. In her mind, all the credit belonged to him — after all, it was Popi's drive, intelligence, and hard work that had propelled him forward. She nervously brushed off the compliment with a humble smile, shifting the focus back to Popi's efforts, but the Peters weren't easily swayed. Their genuine warmth and affection only deepened the interaction.

As the conversation drifted on, Donna found herself gravitating toward Popi. The unexpectedness of the situation left her reeling. With a murmur, she leaned in and whispered to Popi, "Are you serious about this?" There was no denying the weight of her words — she needed to know if this was real or just a spur-of-the-moment declaration. Popi's response was neither dramatic nor verbal, but it carried a profound message. He reached for her hand, holding it firmly, and without a word, he intertwined their fingers.

The simplicity of the gesture caught Donna off guard, but it also carried an undeniable sense of sincerity. At that moment, Popi's touch conveyed everything words couldn't. His actions clearly affirmed that he meant what he said — she was not just part of his present but a pivotal part of his future. That small gesture, so intimate and so natural, solidified their connection. It was a bond that extended far beyond words, transcending the formalities of introductions or titles.

Donna's mind raced as the realization of what this meant sank in. While the day had started with her trying to slip out of Popi's apartment quietly, it was now clear there was no escaping the depth of her involvement in his life. With his parents' approval warmly enveloping her and Popi's unwavering hand in hers, Donna couldn't help but feel a sense of belonging despite the whirlwind of emotions swirling within her.

As she nestled into the moment, Donna knew their relationship had evolved. Popi's small but significant act had marked a new chapter for them both — one in which Donna was no longer just a part of his work or daily life but someone he was proud to present as his partner. The moment's weight lingered, a silent promise of what was to come.

The mood in the apartment suddenly turned as Mrs. Peters lightened the atmosphere with her humorous remark about future visits needing security screening from the federal government. Popi's parents had come with a surprise, revealing Sarah as Popi's biological mother. The room's atmosphere shifted as Mr. Peters shared Sarah's story, leading everyone to expect a joyful reunion.

Popi's reaction, however, was far from what anyone anticipated. Instead of the expected joy and warmth, he appeared visibly disappointed and irritated. The revelation had struck a nerve with him, and his discomfort was palpable.

Sensing the tension, Donna gently guided Popi into the bedroom, hoping to diffuse the situation and offer him some privacy. She provided him with a supportive presence, allowing him to process the unexpected turn of events away from the prying eyes of his parents and Sarah.

When they emerged, Popi approached Sarah with a reluctant hug, acknowledging her presence but clearly struggling with the emotional complexity of the moment. His demeanour made it evident that the situation was more challenging for him than anyone had anticipated. Despite his attempt to welcome Sarah into his life, the underlying tension and disappointment were apparent to those around him.

The room remained charged with unspoken emotions as everyone grappled with the unexpected and awkward reality of the moment.

Donna, aiming to shift the mood and offer a more pleasant experience for everyone, suggested they all go out for tea and possibly do some sightseeing. She recognized that Mr. and Mrs. Peters were well-rested and excited to explore the city, and she hoped this outing would distract from the apartment's tension.

Despite Popi's evident disappointment and annoyance with Sarah's unexpected revelation, Donna maintained a positive demeanour and encouraged a cheerful atmosphere. She understood that Popi's situation with Sarah was deeply personal, and she tried to keep things light for everyone's benefit.

Seeing that Popi's discomfort was primarily related to Sarah, Donna suggested that she take Sarah and Mrs. Peters out on her own, giving Popi some space to process his feelings. She encouraged Popi to use this time to show his father around, hoping this might help him find solace and distraction.

Popi agreed, and with a sense of reluctance mixed with obligation, he prepared to take his father on a tour. Donna, Sarah, and Mrs. Peters set off together while Popi and Mr. Peters ventured out to explore the city. The separation allowed both groups some time apart, giving Popi a moment of respite and a chance for Donna to manage the situation with Sarah and Mrs. Peters.

As Popi walked alongside his father through the bustling streets of Ottawa, discussing life's twists and turns, he couldn't help but feel the weight of their conversation settle deeply within him. The crisp autumn air echoed the gravity of their talk.

Mr. Peters, with a glint of paternal pride in his eyes, turned to Popi and said, "You know, son, when you find a good woman, she's like the sun that makes everything bloom. Life becomes much easier, and every challenge seems more bearable."

Popi, nodding in agreement, couldn't help but reflect on those words. "Donna is, without a doubt, the most amazing woman I've ever met. Her strength and kindness have been my guiding light through this chaotic journey."

Mr. Peters placed a reassuring hand on Popi's shoulder, his voice carrying the weight of experience. "I can see that. And if you truly care about her, don't let this chance slip away. If you make something of this, you'll have my deepest wishes for your happiness. I've seen what she can bring to your life, and it's nothing short of extraordinary."

Popi absorbed his father's words with a thoughtful silence, the compliment hanging in the air like a delicate aroma. The official status of his relationship with Donna had been framed as a close friendship, one that had a hint of romance in the past. But his father's endorsement and heartfelt wish forced Popi to reconsider the true nature of his bond with Donna.

Popi: A Rising Tide

Popi's mind wandered as they continued their walk, contemplating the depth of his feelings for Donna. The revelation of his father's sincere hope for their future together made him pause and reflect on the possibilities ahead.

As the conversation about Donna's role in Popi's life waned, Mr. Peters took a deep breath, a sombre shadow crossing his face. He seemed to wrestle with the weight of a burden he had been carrying for some time.

"Popi, there's something I need to share with you," Mr. Peters began, his voice laced with concern. "I have a feeling your mother is contemplating a divorce."

Popi, taken aback, asked, "Why do you think that?"

Mr. Peters looked down, his expression pained. "Things have been rough since you left. We've been fighting more often, and she's starting most of the arguments. It's like we've lost our way."

He continued, his voice trembling slightly, "I've also been struggling with my Parkinson's. The latest visit to the doctor didn't bring good news. The medication isn't working as well as we'd hoped. The prognosis isn't promising. The doctor mentioned that within a few years, I might need a wheelchair."

Popi's heart sank. "How do you feel about that?"

Mr. Peters shrugged, a resigned expression on his face. "It's part of life, son. Sometimes, you have to accept that certain things are beyond your control. There's no point in dwelling on what can't be changed."

Grappling with the gravity of his father's situation, Popi asked, "Have you talked to Mom about all this?"

"I haven't," Mr. Peters replied quietly. "We've been drifting apart, and I didn't see the point in sharing my struggles with someone who seems to be on the verge of leaving. It felt like adding to the weight of what was already there."

Popi was at a loss for words. He reached out, placing a comforting hand on his father's shoulder. "Whatever happens, Dad, I'll be by your side. I'm here for you, no matter what."

A faint smile flickered across Mr. Peters' face. "You know, Popi, I've heard that when you talk to your colleagues, you often bring up the lessons you learned from me as a child. It warms my heart to know that those stories of the old days still resonate with you."

Popi's eyes softened with nostalgia. "Those lessons have been a guiding light for me, Dad. I couldn't have become who I am without the wisdom you shared. The lessons on integrity, hard work, and kindness are values I carry with me every day."

Mr. Peters nodded, his eyes reflecting a mixture of pride and sadness. "It's good to hear that. I'm glad those stories made a difference. Knowing you've carried those lessons forward, even as I face these challenges, gives me solace."

They stood together in the crisp Ottawa air, the weight of the conversation hanging between them, but with a shared understanding that, despite the difficulties ahead, the bond of family and the lessons of the past would remain a guiding force.

Popi: A Rising Tide

As the ladies returned to the apartment, their faces were radiant with the joy of their day. They had spent the afternoon exploring street food vendors, marvelling at vibrant street art, and indulging in a soothing spa session. Their laughter and excitement were palpable as they recounted their adventures.

Mr. Peters, his face glowing with satisfaction, turned to Popi. "I must say, Popi, you've chosen a remarkable woman. Don't mess this up—she's a keeper." His tone was light-hearted, but his eyes conveyed genuine approval.

Popi chuckled, his eyes twinkling with affection for Donna. "I'll do my best, Dad. And while we're at it, you might want to remind Donna not to mess things up, either. She's been telling me for years that I'm the keeper, after all."

Donna laughed, a playful glint in her eye. "I'll do my best, but no promises. I've heard that the keeper might need a little guidance every now and then."

After a few more hours of drinks and conversation, filled with shared stories and heartfelt laughter, Mr. Peters, Mrs. Peters, and Sarah prepared to leave for the night. There was an air of reluctant farewell mixed with the anticipation of future gatherings.

"We'll be here for a few more days," Mr. Peters said. "If you both have time, we'd love to spend more moments together. It's been wonderful getting to know Donna and reconnecting with you."

Donna smiled warmly. "That sounds like a great idea. We'd love to spend more time with you."

Popi, though appreciative of the gesture, remained somewhat reserved. "We'll see how things go. I've got a lot on my plate right now."

With that, the visitors left the apartment, leaving Popi and Donna alone. The quiet that followed starkly contrasted the lively conversations and laughter that had filled the space.

Popi and Donna shared a moment of reflection, their connection deepened by the day's events.

Donna turned to Popi, her voice gentle. "It's been quite a day, hasn't it?"

Popi nodded, his expression contemplative. "Yes, it has. I'm grateful for your support and for everything you've done. It means a lot to me."

Donna took his hand, squeezing it reassuringly. "We'll get through this together. Whatever comes next, we'll face it as a team."

Popi smiled, his heart warmed by her presence. "I couldn't ask for a better partner."

As they settled into the quiet of the evening, their bond felt stronger than ever, a testament to the resilience of their relationship and the promise of a future built on mutual support and understanding.

Popi and Donna sat side by side as the apartment fell into a quiet hush, their earlier conversations replaced by a reflective silence. The weight of the day's events lingered, and Donna, her gaze soft and earnest, broke the stillness.

"Popi," she began gently, "what's happening between us? Where do we stand now?"

Popi hesitated, searching for the right words. The complexities of the recent days had clouded his thoughts. "I'm not entirely sure where we are," he admitted. "I just know that I want things to return to how they were before the by-election—if you're willing."

Donna's eyes brightened with relief and affection. "I couldn't be happier with that. I'm here for you, Popi, and I will do everything I can to honour and respect our relationship. You're someone very special to me."

Popi's gaze softened, a mixture of gratitude and concern in his eyes. "I don't want to dwell on the past or any mistakes I might have made. I just want us to move forward, together. I promise I'll do my best not to disappoint you."

The sincerity in his voice touched Donna deeply. She reached out, taking his hand in hers with a reassuring squeeze. "We're in this together, Popi. We've faced challenges and will face whatever comes next with the same strength and understanding."

As the night deepened around them, the warmth between them grew stronger. They shared a quiet moment of understanding, their bond reaffirmed by their trials and the love that had guided them through. Both Popi and Donna felt an immense sense of happiness and contentment, knowing that, despite the uncertainties of the future, they were finally back together and ready to face it as a united front.

Keeping Up with Life

When Mr. Church assumed the role of Prime Minister, he made a pivotal decision that would significantly shape his administration. He appointed Popi as the Minister of Interprovincial Affairs, a role crucial for maintaining harmony and effective communication between the federal and provincial governments. This position was designed to ensure that the rules of law were balanced and that the interests of the citizens were served with integrity.

Given the sensitive nature of the role, Mr. Church had anticipated potential infighting or resistance to the appointment. However, to his relief and surprise, the reaction was overwhelmingly positive. Much of the Conservative caucus recognized the merit of Popi's appointment and the unique qualifications he brought to the table.

Popi's role as Minister of Interprovincial Affairs was not just about bridging gaps; it was about fostering collaboration and ensuring that every policy and regulation worked in the best interest of Canadians. He was tasked with the delicate job of navigating the often complex and sometimes contentious relationship between the different levels of government.

The support for Popi's appointment came from various quarters. His track record of dedication and effectiveness in his previous roles had earned him respect across party lines. His ability to handle sensitive matters with diplomacy and fairness was widely acknowledged. The provinces appreciated having someone in the federal government who understood their unique challenges and needs and could advocate for their concerns while upholding the national interest.

Popi approached his new role with a sense of purpose and responsibility. He met with provincial leaders and federal officials to establish clear communication lines and outline his approach to the job. He aimed to ensure that provincial needs were heard and addressed while maintaining a unified national policy that benefited all Canadians.

The collaborative spirit fostered by Popi's appointment led to smoother interactions between the federal and provincial governments. Initiatives that required joint efforts progressed more efficiently, and the communication channels remained open and constructive.

In the end, Mr. Church's decision proved to be a wise one. Popi's appointment strengthened the government's ability to address complex issues. It exemplified the commitment to effective governance and the well-being of Canadian citizens. The success of this appointment was a testament to Popi's capability and the trust placed in him by both the Prime Minister and the broader political landscape.

As the evening approached, Popi was brimming with excitement and wanted to mark the occasion of his new appointment in a special way. He turned to Donna and proposed a celebration with a unique twist—he wished to host the gathering at her parents' house.

Donna raised an eyebrow, her surprise evident. "At my parents' place? Why not at your place?" she asked, her curiosity piqued.

Popi: A Rising Tide

It struck her as unusual but also fitting. Her parents had always been fond of Popi, and it made sense that he would want to celebrate this milestone with those who had supported him from the beginning.

Popi's eyes twinkled with anticipation and gratitude. "Well, your parents have been like family to me, and this moment feels too big not to share with them. Besides, your mom's cooking is legendary. I thought it would be nice to bring everyone together where they feel most at home."

Donna smiled, her heart warmed by his thoughtfulness. She appreciated how much Popi valued her family and understood his desire to include them in this significant chapter of his life. "That's sweet of you, Popi. I'm sure my parents will be thrilled. What do you have in mind for dinner? I want to make sure it's perfect for such a special occasion."

Popi's face lit up with a grin. "Anything you think would make the evening memorable. After all, we're celebrating my new role and everything that's led us here."

Donna nodded, already brainstorming ideas. "Alright, then. I'll make sure to prepare a feast worthy of the occasion. Is there anything specific you're craving?"

Popi shook his head with a chuckle. "Surprise me. I trust you to make it perfect."

With dinner plans set and both of them eager for the event, Donna felt a sense of excitement bubbling within her. She knew her parents would be delighted and looked forward to sharing this joyful moment with Popi and her family.

As they made their way to her parents' house, Donna couldn't help but reflect on the significance of the evening. It was a celebration of achievement, connection, and the cherished bonds that had supported Popi's journey. They were about to gather in a place that felt like home, surrounded by those who had always believed in him.

After a delightful dinner, which was a true culinary masterpiece thanks to the combined efforts of Donna and her mother, the evening took a turn that Donna had never reasonably anticipated. Having savoured every bite of the lovingly prepared meal, Popi suddenly found himself overcome with a new surge of emotion.

As the evening's laughter and joy filled the room, Popi glanced around at the warmth and happiness surrounding them. With a deep breath, he gathered his courage and moved to the centre of the room. With a mixture of nervous excitement and heartfelt resolve, he got down on one knee in front of Donna.

Donna's heart skipped a beat as Popi's gesture drew the attention of everyone in the room. His eyes, filled with sincerity, met hers as he spoke, his voice steady despite the tremor of anticipation. "Donna," he began, his tone rich with emotion, "I know I've never been one for grand gestures, but tonight, I wanted to make sure you knew just how deeply I feel for you. You've been my rock, my confidant, and my greatest support. I can't imagine spending the rest of my life without you by my side."

He reached into his pocket and pulled out a ring, its sparkling simplicity reflecting his love and commitment. "Will you marry me?"

Popi: A Rising Tide

Donna's breath caught in her throat. The enormity of the moment left her momentarily speechless. She looked around at her parents' beaming faces, their smiles radiating approval and joy. The warmth of their support enveloped her, and she knew instantly that her answer was a resounding yes.

Tears of happiness welled up in her eyes as she nodded, her voice trembling with emotion. "Yes, Popi. Yes, I will marry you."

The room erupted in cheers and applause, the celebration now taking on an even more joyous tone. Popi's face lit up with a radiant smile, and he gently slipped the ring onto Donna's finger. It symbolized their enduring love and the future they were about to embark upon together.

For Popi, this was more than just a proposal; it was the culmination of a journey filled with challenges and triumphs. He knew, with unwavering certainty, that Donna was the one he wanted to spend the rest of his life with. His parents' approval had only solidified his decision, and he couldn't bear the thought of facing a single day without her.

As they embraced, the room seemed to shimmer with the magic of their commitment, and the night became a beautiful tapestry of love, promise, and the beginning of a new chapter in their lives.

After Popi proposed to Donna, the joy in the room was palpable. The evening had already been memorable, filled with warmth and celebration, but the excitement wasn't over yet.

Popi, wanting to share this incredible moment with his parents, excused himself from the joyous crowd and stepped outside to make a phone call. His heart was still racing with the exhilaration of the proposal, and he was eager to share the news with his family. Meanwhile, ever thoughtful, Donna had already taken the initiative to video call Mrs. Peters, keen to share the beautiful news.

Mrs. Peters' voice was brimming with excitement as she saw the beaming smile on Donna's face. "I couldn't be happier for you both. Congratulations! I wish I could be there with you to celebrate in person."

Mrs. Peters' words were filled with heartfelt emotion, her happiness transcending the thousands of miles that separated them. Her genuine warmth and affection were evident, even through the screen. "You've always been such a wonderful person, Popi," she continued, "and I am overjoyed that you and Donna have found each other. I'm so proud of you."

Popi's father joined the video call briefly, his expression quiet with pride. "Congratulations, Son," he said with a warm smile. I'm proud of you, not just for the proposal but for everything you've accomplished. You've made an excellent choice, and I'm thrilled for you both."

Back in Donna's home, her parents were equally delighted. They had always held Popi in high regard, and this new development was their dream come true. Donna's father raised a toast in Popi's honour while her mother beamed with pride. "From the moment we met you, Popi," her mother said, "we knew you were someone special. Seeing you and Donna together and so happy—well, it just makes our hearts swell with joy."

Popi: A Rising Tide

As Popi and Donna hung up the call, they felt a deep sense of gratitude and happiness. The support and love from their families made the evening even more special, adding layers of joy to their engagement. The feeling of having both families' blessings made their commitment to each other feel even more profound.

With hearts full and spirits high, they returned to their celebration, knowing their journey ahead would be supported by the love and encouragement of those who mattered most. The night was now a blend of laughter, joy, and the promise of a future filled with shared dreams and cherished moments.

After finishing their dessert, Donna took it upon herself to clear the table and clean the dishes. As she was scrubbing away, her mother gently touched her shoulder and said, "Donna, why don't you go and enjoy the evening with Popi? You've both had such a special night. Let me handle the clean-up."

Donna looked up, her heart warmed by her mother's kindness. She hesitated for a moment, then nodded and smiled. "Thanks, Mom. I appreciate it. I'll be sure to make the most of the evening."

With that, Donna and Popi stepped out into the cool night air, their hearts still racing from the excitement of the proposal. They walked together, hand in hand, under the starlit sky, savouring the quiet serenity of the night. The city lights twinkled around them, mirroring the joy that sparkled in their eyes.

Popi looked over at Donna, his voice filled with tenderness. "I can't believe how perfect tonight has been. I never imagined it would turn out like this, but I'm so grateful it did."

Donna's eyes met his, her smile radiant. "I know, it's like a dream come true. I want to spend this evening with you and show you how much I appreciate everything you've done for me. You've believed in, motivated, and supported me every step of the way. I don't know where I'd be without you."

As they walked, the conversation turned to their future. Donna couldn't help but reflect on their past, including the difficult period that once strained their relationship. She brought it up hesitantly, her voice soft. "You know, Popi, I've been thinking a lot about everything that happened. I want you to know how much it meant to me that we could work through it."

Popi looked at her with a reassuring smile. "Donna, it's all in the past now. What's important is that we're here together, starting anew. We've come so far and can build something beautiful from here. The past is just that—the past. We have a clean slate now, and I'm excited to see where our future takes us."

Donna nodded, feeling a profound sense of relief and hope. The night was a fresh beginning for them, a chance to embark on a new chapter filled with promise and love. As they strolled through the streets, lost in their conversation and laughter, they knew they were stepping into a future where their shared dreams and mutual respect would guide them.

The city around them seemed to embrace their happiness. With every step, they felt more connected and ready to face whatever came next together. The evening was theirs, a beautiful start to a lifetime of new adventures, and they cherished every moment.

In the weeks and days that followed, Donna was swept up in

Popi: A Rising Tide

the whirlwind of wedding preparations, a dream she had cherished for over a decade finally coming to fruition. She eagerly began sharing the joyful news with friends and extended family, her excitement palpable as she spoke of the upcoming celebration. Each announcement was met with enthusiasm, and Donna was thrilled by the outpouring of love and support from those around her.

Popi, ever supportive and attentive, was determined to ensure that Donna's wedding day was everything she had envisioned. He expressed willingness to do whatever it took to make her dreams come true. "You know, Donna," he said with a smile, "whatever you want for this wedding, just let me know. I want it to be perfect for you, and I'm ready to do whatever it takes to make that happen."

Donna appreciated Popi's commitment and tried to involve him in every aspect of the planning. She wanted his presence felt in the details, ensuring his voice was heard, and his preferences were considered. "I want this to be our day, Popi," she said as they discussed seating arrangements and flower choices. "Your input matters just as much as mine. I want us to create this day together."

Despite the flurry of activity, Popi remained calm and focused on Donna's happiness. His responses to the wedding plans were always thoughtful and considerate. "Donna, I trust your judgment completely," he said one evening as they reviewed the guest list. "All I care about is that you're happy. If there's anything I can do to make sure you're smiling on our wedding day, just let me know."

Popi's unwavering support touched Donna. He was clearly

invested in making their wedding a beautiful reflection of their love and commitment. Their collaborative spirit made the planning process joyful rather than stressful.

As they navigated through the preparations together, their bond grew stronger, each decision reinforcing their shared vision for their future. Donna marvelled at how seamlessly they worked together, finding joy in the small details and delight in each other's company. The wedding was shaping up to be a celebration of their love and a testament to their partnership and mutual respect.

The wedding planning unfolded briskly as Donna and Popi were mindful of their professional commitments. Both were keenly aware that spending too much time on the wedding preparations could jeopardize the event and their essential roles and responsibilities. They understood that striking a balance was crucial; thus, they made a concerted effort to keep the planning process efficient and focused.

Donna's parents played a significant role in supporting the financial aspects of the wedding, alleviating any potential concerns about budgeting. Their generous contribution ensured that money was not a constraint, allowing Donna and Popi to focus on creating a memorable day without financial stress. With the groundwork laid and resources secured, the couple turned their attention to the finer details of their celebration.

Popi's recent successes and extensive Ottawa network proved invaluable assets. His connections, cultivated through years of dedicated service and charitable work, facilitated access to various luxurious options and bespoke services.

Popi: A Rising Tide

"Donna," Popi said with a grin, "I've been able to pull some strings with the folks I've met over the years. We've got access to one of the most exquisite venues in the city, and I can arrange for some of the best local businesses to cater to our needs."

The venue, chosen for its grandeur and elegance, was a testament to Popi's influence and connections. It offered an opulent setting that perfectly complemented the couple's vision for their special day. Personal service from top local vendors—from floral arrangements to gourmet catering—ensured that every detail would be handled carefully and precisely.

Donna was delighted with the arrangements. "Popi, I'm so grateful for everything you're doing to make this day so special," she said as they reviewed the final plans. "I can't believe how everything is coming together so beautifully."

Popi, ever the pragmatist, responded with a reassuring smile. "I want this day to be as perfect as possible, Donna. But let's remember, it's the love and commitment we share that truly matters. The wedding is just the beginning."

Their approach to the planning process was both pragmatic and passionate. They integrated their professional lives seamlessly with their personal celebration, ensuring neither was compromised. Though a grand affair, the wedding was handled with the efficiency and professionalism that characterized their lives.

The week leading up to the wedding was a whirlwind of activity, not just for Donna and Popi. At the constituency office, chaos reigned supreme. The office, typically a bustling hub of political activity, had become a pressure cooker of urgent issues that demanded immediate attention.

Donna and her team, already stretched thin with the wedding preparations, found themselves at the epicentre of this storm. Despite their best efforts to maintain order, the issues that had been put on the back burner months ago were now resurfacing with alarming urgency. Each problem required an immediate solution, from pressing constituents' concerns to unresolved case files that had piled up during the federal elections campaign and Popi's transition into his new role as Minister of interprovincial Affairs.

While Popi had been laser-focused on the general election campaign and settling into his role as a new minister, personal and constituency matters had taken a back seat. The new responsibilities demanded much of his attention, leaving little room to address these pressing concerns.

Donna knew Popi was deeply committed to his work and would want to handle these issues. Still, the wedding was imminent, and their time was limited. She took a deep breath and gathered her team.

"Alright, everyone, let's tackle this systematically. We need to prioritize the issues and delegate tasks effectively. I'll make sure Popi is briefed on the most critical matters. Let's remember that while this is a busy time, it's also a special one for Popi and me. We must get through this week without compromising our commitment to our roles and personal lives."

As the team set to work, Donna called Popi. "Hey, Love of my life. I know this is a hectic time, but the office is chaotic right now. We have a few urgent issues that need your attention. I'll brief you on the details when you have a moment, but I need your help sorting through them."

Popi, ever the problem-solver, responded with concern and resolve. "Donna, I'm aware of the crunch time. Let's prioritize these issues. I'll review everything you send over and ensure we have a plan. We can't let these problems overshadow our upcoming wedding."

The two exchanged a few more details and strategies before hanging up. Donna took a moment to gather her thoughts. Amidst the chaos, there was a silver lining—a reminder of why they were both so dedicated to their work and each other. They were facing this tumultuous period together, proving that their partnership was a source of strength even amid challenges.

In the middle of a hectic wedding week, Popi tackled the complex issues plaguing his constituency office with his characteristic resolve and strategic thinking. He and Donna had decided to postpone other personal matters to focus on the most pressing three, aiming to find solutions that would address immediate concerns and minimize long-term damage.

One of the critical matters was the controversial case involving a police officer who had struck a pedestrian, leading to a slew of legal complications and public outcry. The situation had reached a boiling point. Popi knew he had to act decisively to ensure a resolution that balanced fairness and practicality.

He contacted the Ottawa Police Chief to discuss the matter. The Chief, though aware of the situation, expressed a clear stance: no action could be taken unless the victim's mother agreed to drop the complaint filed against the officer involved.

Popi, ever the tactician, listened carefully before responding. "I understand the position you're in," he began, "but let me ask you this: What if the victim's mother decides to press charges of attempted murder? How would that impact the situation?"

The Chief dismissed the notion with a shake of his head. "That's unlikely to be accepted. There's no basis for such a charge."

Maintaining a steady tone, Popi responded, "Well, it's clear this could become a significant obstacle for you. If it escalates, it could complicate your work and put additional strain on the Mayor who appointed you."

The Chief listened intently as Popi continued, "Instead of allowing this to become a protracted and public battle, which would be detrimental to everyone involved, how about we find a middle ground? Let's avoid a full-scale confrontation with the police union. Instead, we can send a constructive message by recommending that the officer's superior be placed on administrative leave with pay. Additionally, we should look into ways to cover the victim's medical bills outside of what the Ontario government will cover, as this will demonstrate your office's commitment to addressing the situation responsibly."

Popi stressed, "I'm not here to dictate how you run your department, but an incident like this must be addressed adequately. If left unchecked, it undermines the trust between the community and the police force. We must resolve this to prevent further pain and suffering for the victim."

Popi: A Rising Tide

"I can find at least ten lawyers in the next 5 minutes willing to take this case, and they will drag you and your department through the mud until someone gives up," Popi added.

The Chief pondered Popi's proposal, clearly weighing the implications. "I'll need to consult with our legal team and see what we can do," he finally conceded.

Popi knew that this was a small but significant victory. By framing the situation as a cooperative effort rather than a contentious battle, he pushed for a resolution that respected both the victim's needs and the police department's constraints. As the victim's mother left the office with a glimmer of hope, Popi felt a sense of accomplishment, knowing they had taken a step towards addressing the issue without further exacerbating the tension.

During a whirlwind week filled with wedding preparations and political responsibilities, Popi addressed another pressing issue that demanded his delicate yet firm approach. The case involved a woman desperate to prevent her husband from being deported following his conviction for domestic violence. Popi knew navigating this situation required legal insight and a deep understanding of the personal and ethical complexities involved.

Popi met with the woman, who was visibly distressed and eager to find a way to keep her family together. She pleaded for his help, explaining that her husband's deportation would sever their family and potentially leave their children without a father. Popi listened intently, his expression serious as he considered the gravity of the situation.

"Listen," Popi began, his tone compassionate yet firm. "I understand your concern for your family, but you need to be aware of the implications of what you're asking. If you're advocating for your husband to avoid deportation, the legal process will demand some serious considerations."

He continued, "Given that your husband was convicted of physically assaulting you, pursuing a course of action to prevent his deportation raises significant red flags. If we proceed with this, it might be impossible to undo the damage later on. Your husband's conviction is serious, and any attempt to mitigate the consequences might have unintended repercussions."

The woman's eyes widened with worry as Popi laid out the stark reality. "Without a drastic intervention, it's likely your husband will be deported. The only way to potentially prevent this is for you to confess that you instigated the fight and pushed him until he hit you. I must warn you that this will not only land you in a difficult situation with the police but could also lead to a criminal record for yourself."

Popi paused, allowing the weight of his words to settle. "There's also a chance that if the police are unsympathetic, you could face jail time or other legal consequences. Understand that this path could jeopardize your future, especially if you need to report future domestic abuses. Admitting to being part of the problem might complicate your ability to seek help when needed."

Seeing the distress in her eyes, Popi added gently, "I advise you to go home and reflect deeply on this. Talk to your husband about the situation, and consider how it will affect you and your family. If this issue is not handled carefully, it could have lasting consequences that might leave your family fragmented."

He leaned forward, his voice steady but compassionate. "If you're truly committed to keeping your family together, you must weigh all options. Think about the long-term impact on your lives and the potential repercussions of any decision you make. This is a heavy burden, but making an informed choice is crucial."

Now visibly shaken, the woman nodded slowly, realizing the gravity of the decision before her. Popi's advice, though harsh, was meant to guide her through a complex legal and emotional minefield. As she left his office, Popi hoped she would take the time to reflect on her situation and discuss it thoroughly with her husband.

Popi knew dealing with such cases required legal solutions, empathy, and foresight. He hoped that his counsel would help her make a decision that considered the well-being of her family in the long run, even as he balanced his demanding professional and personal life.

While managing pressing political matters, Popi encountered another poignant situation that required his unique blend of empathy and pragmatic wisdom. A 15-year-old mother-to-be, visibly pregnant and in her second trimester, sought his assistance with finding accommodation so she could raise her child as a single mother. Her desperation was palpable, and Popi understood the weight of her predicament.

He listened attentively as she explained her situation, her eyes filled with determination and concern. Popi knew that the current economic climate made it increasingly difficult for single parents to secure stable housing and support. With compassion, he began to share a story from his own life that, though personal, might offer her a different perspective.

"Listen," Popi started gently, "I want to share something with you that might help you make a more informed decision." He paused, collecting his thoughts before continuing. "Years ago, a woman about your age was in a similar situation to yours. She faced the challenge of raising a child alone, and the circumstances were harsh. She chose to carry the baby until birth and then give up her baby for adoption, trusting that there were people out there who could provide a better environment for her child."

The young woman's eyes widened in surprise, and Popi continued. "The parents who adopted her child did an incredible job. They raised him with love and care, and he grew up to build a wonderful life for himself. Ironically, that child is now in a position where he advises others in similar situations, and I'm the one sharing his story with you."

Popi noticed the amazement on her face as she absorbed his words. "I've recently reconnected with my birth mother," he added with a smile, "and I couldn't be happier to have a relationship with both my adoptive parents and my biological mother. It's a full circle, and it has brought so much joy into my life."

He chuckled lightly, "Maybe someday my child will tell their story to someone else in a similar situation, and they'll find it inspiring too. Sometimes, the best way to navigate a tough situation is by looking at the bigger picture and making decisions that will lead to the best possible outcome for everyone involved."

Popi's tone turned more serious as he continued, "I know it's not an easy choice, but you might want to consider finishing your high school education and working towards building a stable life for yourself. Life is full of opportunities, and you don't have to wait as long as my mother did to rejoin your child's life if you take proactive steps now."

The young woman listened intently, her expression shifting from one of uncertainty to one of contemplation. Popi's story had touched her deeply, and she found a glimmer of hope and inspiration in his words.

"Thank you for sharing your story," she said, her voice filled with gratitude. "It's not just comforting but motivating to hear how things can turn out positively even after difficult choices. I will take your advice seriously and work on building a future for myself. Maybe one day I'll be able to tell my story and help others, just as you've helped me today."

Popi nodded, feeling a sense of fulfillment. "I'm glad to hear that. Life's challenges can be daunting but often lead to the most meaningful growth and change. Take care of yourself, and remember there are always paths to a brighter future."

As the young woman left his office, Popi hoped his personal experience had provided her comfort and practical guidance. He understood the weight of her decision and wished her the best as she navigated her journey, confident that her resilience and determination would help her forge a positive path forward.

With the complex situations now under review and everyone

given time to consider Popi's proposed solutions, he felt a cautious optimism. He knew the likelihood of objections or new complications arising from these solutions was minimal, but he remained vigilant.

Popi resolved to follow up with each party after a week to gauge progress and ensure that the proposed solutions were implemented smoothly. He was keenly aware of the delicate nature of these issues and understood that maintaining a proactive stance was essential to their resolution.

He planned to check in with the police department to ensure they adhered to the agreed-upon measures, including suspending the police officer's superior and reviewing the victim's medical bills. It was vital for Popi that the department handled the situation with sensitivity and transparency, maintaining the community's trust while upholding justice.

Simultaneously, Popi intended to liaise with the mayor's office to ensure that the case's broader implications were managed effectively and that the victim received any necessary support. He understood that the Mayor's office played a crucial role in addressing public concerns and reinforcing the integrity of local governance.

In addition, Popi planned to monitor the immigration office closely regarding the case of the woman's husband. It was important that the office handle the matter with fairness and consideration, especially in light of the proposed compromise. Popi wanted to ensure that the resolution did not create undue hardship for the family while respecting legal and ethical standards.

Popi: A Rising Tide

Finally, Popi intended to reach out to the young mother-to-be who had been contemplating her future and the adoption of her child. He wanted to ensure that she was comfortable with the plan and not unduly stressed by the decisions she faced. Popi recognized the importance of providing emotional support and practical guidance during such a pivotal time.

As Popi prepared to address these follow-ups, he felt responsible and committed to seeing each case through to a satisfactory resolution. He aimed to resolve these issues effectively and ensure that all parties involved felt heard, respected, and supported. As Minister of Interprovincial Affairs, he was dedicated to balancing compassion with practicality, always striving to uphold the values of fairness and justice in every decision he made.

After a whirlwind week of wedding preparations, Popi was finally set to marry the love of his life on a beautiful Saturday evening. The day was filled with excitement and elegance, and Popi's meticulous planning ensured that every detail was executed flawlessly.

Popi had put his heart and soul into making the wedding day truly special for Donna. He went above and beyond to add personal touches that made the day unforgettable. For instance, knowing how much Donna adored a particular Canadian iconic musician, Popi made sure she was the one to perform at the wedding. It wasn't just any band—it was Donna's favourite, creating an intimate and electrifying atmosphere.

The wedding ceremony occurred by a serene lake, chosen because it echoed Donna's cherished childhood playground. The setting was picturesque, with the lake's shimmering waters serving as a perfect backdrop. As Donna walked down the aisle, she was awestruck by her surroundings' beauty and the love surrounding her. It was as if every element of the day had been crafted to make her feel like the most special person in the world.

Emotion overwhelmed Donna as she approached Popi, and she struggled to find the words to express her profound happiness. Her heart was full of joy and gratitude, knowing she was about to start a new chapter of her life with Popi. The moment was more than just a formal union; it was the culmination of dreams, effort, and deep affection.

Popi, too, was deeply moved. As he spoke, he reflected on his upbringing and the loneliness he sometimes felt. But meeting Donna had been a turning point, filling his life with warmth and love he had never known. He shared his gratitude not only for Donna but also for his birth mother and the parents who had raised him. Popi's heartfelt words resonated with everyone present, revealing the depth of his emotions and the significance of this union.

The ceremony was graced by the presence of the Prime Minister of Canada, who officiated the wedding. Mr. Church's participation was a testament to the day's importance and added an official touch to the heartfelt celebration. Members of Parliament from various parties, including opposition Liberals, were also in attendance, setting aside political differences to join in the joyous occasion. Their presence symbolized a collective embrace of love and unity, transcending political divides for a moment of shared happiness.

As Donna and Popi exchanged vows, the air was thick with

emotion. It was a day of celebration, not just of their love but of the new life they were beginning together. With every detail meticulously planned and every heartfelt word spoken, the wedding was a beautiful testament to their journey and the bright future they were embarking upon together. The night was filled with laughter, music, and a profound sense of fulfillment as they danced into their new life, surrounded by those who supported and loved them.

As the evening unfolded and the celebration continued, the atmosphere was brimming with joy and camaraderie. With a warm smile, Mr. Church invited the newlyweds, Mr. and Mrs. Peters, to the dance floor. However, with a playful glint in her eye, a Member of Parliament corrected the Prime Minister, reminding everyone that it was actually Mr. and Mrs. Popi now, given that there was already a Mr. and Mrs. Peters.

While a bit cheeky, the joke lightened the mood and elicited a hearty round of laughter from the guests. The room was filled with the sound of merriment as everyone embraced the humour of the moment. Popi and Donna, now officially the newlyweds, were beaming as they took to the dance floor.

The scene was almost surreal as they danced under the lake's backdrop, with the shimmering lights reflecting off the water and casting a magical glow. The lighting created an enchanting ambiance, enhancing the beauty of the night and the depth of their emotions. It was a moment of pure magic, and the sight of the couple lost in their dance brought a collective tear to the eyes of many.

Popi, in particular, was overwhelmed by the moment. He had never imagined his life could reach such a pinnacle of happiness.

Finding Donna, someone who loved him so sincerely and wholeheartedly, was the most outstanding achievement of his life. In his heart, he knew that everything else—his successes in politics and accomplishments—paled compared to the joy he felt in making Donna fall in love with him.

As the couple danced, their love was palpable. The world around them seemed to fade, leaving only the two in their private bubble of bliss. For Popi, this was the culmination of dreams and the beginning of a new chapter filled with promise. The evening was a testament to their journey together, a celebration of their love, and a vivid reminder of how life had aligned perfectly for them.

Ultimately, it wasn't just a wedding but a heartfelt declaration of love and commitment shared with those who mattered most. The night celebrated what was to come and was a tribute to the remarkable bond that Popi and Donna had forged, which would carry them through the rest of their lives.

The Pressure of Politics on Love

After being married for almost two years, Popi and Donna settled into a cozy home, their sanctuary from the often hectic world of politics and responsibilities. One evening, as Popi entered their home, he was greeted by his wife's cheerful laughter, a sound that never failed to lift his spirits.

"Hey there, sweetheart," Popi said, scooping his wife into his arms. Her giggles were infectious, and for a moment, the weight of his day began to lift.

Donna composed herself, her eyes sparkling with excitement. "You won't believe the amazing news I have for you," she said, unable to contain her joy.

Popi smiled, though it was tinged with the weariness of a long day. "What is it, darling?" he asked, curious but tired.

Sensing his exhaustion, Donna gently led him to the living room and sat beside him. "I know you've had a tough day, but I promise this will cheer you up," she said, her voice soothing. "I just found out... I'm pregnant!"

For a moment, Popi was stunned into silence. The news was like a burst of sunlight breaking through storm clouds. He looked at Donna, her radiant smile and the glow in her eyes, and felt an overwhelming surge of joy.

"Are you serious?" Popi asked, his voice a mix of disbelief and joy.

Donna nodded, tears of happiness welling up in her eyes. "Yes, it's true. We're going to have a baby."

Popi pulled her into a tight embrace, his heart swelling with love and gratitude. "This is incredible news," he said, his voice choked with emotion. "I can't believe it. I'm so happy."

He then took a deep breath and looked at Donna, his expression growing serious. "I didn't want to worry you, but things have been hectic the last few days. I've been trying to keep the stress off you, but it's been tough."

Donna squeezed his hand reassuringly. "We're in this together, Popi. We'll handle whatever comes our way, just like we always have."

Popi nodded, feeling a renewed sense of strength and determination. "You're right. We've faced challenges before, and we've come out stronger. This news is just what I needed."

As they sat there, the weight of the world seemed to lift just a little. They knew that life would continue to throw challenges their way, but together, they could handle anything.

Popi kissed Donna gently on the forehead. "I love you so much," he whispered. "And I can't wait to meet our little one."

Donna smiled, her heart full. "I love you too, Popi. Our family is growing, and I couldn't be happier."

Popi: A Rising Tide

At that moment, amidst the chaos of their busy lives, they found solace in each other and the promise of their expanding family. It was a reminder that no matter how turbulent life could get, they had each other, and that was all they needed.

Popi received a frantic phone call while trying to relax with his wife. The news was shattering. Two years into the Conservatives' tenure as the government, tragedy struck both the party and the country. Mr. Church, a pivotal figure and mentor to Popi, had suffered a heart attack and passed away unexpectedly. The loss sent shockwaves through the hearts of many Conservatives nationwide.

Popi felt as if a dagger had been thrust into his heart. The man who had guided him, believed in him, and helped shape his political journey was gone. The effect of this news on Popi was profound, but he tried to remain composed.

Popi didn't want to dampen the joyful atmosphere at home. Donna had just shared the fantastic news of her pregnancy, and her happiness was palpable. He didn't want to cast a shadow over such a significant and joyous moment for their family. So, he swallowed the grief, forced a calm expression, and ended the call.

"Who was that?" Donna asked, noticing the change in his demeanour.

Popi took a deep breath, forcing a smile. "Just some work stuff," he said, trying to sound casual. "Nothing to worry about right now."

Donna looked at him with concern, but she knew better than

to press him. She trusted him to share when he was ready. Instead, she placed her hand on his, giving it a gentle squeeze. "Remember, whatever it is, we can handle it together," she said softly.

Popi nodded, feeling the weight of his grief and the responsibility to protect his family from it. He needed to find a way to process the loss of Mr. Church without letting it overshadow their joy.

However, Donna sensed that something was off. Popi's mood had shifted dramatically after that phone call, and she knew something was wrong. Popi was never one to stay down for long, and his prolonged silence was telling. With concern etched on her face, Donna finally asked, "Popi, what's wrong? What happened on that call?"

Popi hesitated, struggling to find the words. He looked into Donna's eyes, knowing he couldn't hide the truth from her. "It was about Mr. Church," he said quietly. "He had a heart attack. He... he didn't make it."

Donna's eyes widened in shock, and she immediately felt a wave of sorrow wash over her. "Oh, Popi," she whispered, her voice breaking. Tears welled in her eyes as she moved closer, wrapping her arms around him. "I'm so sorry."

The floodgates opened, and Popi let himself be vulnerable in her embrace. He held her tightly, his body trembling with grief. "He meant so much to me, Donna," he said through choked sobs. "I can't believe he's gone."

Donna's heart ached not just for Mr. Church but for Popi. She knew how profoundly Mr. Church had influenced him, shaping his career and providing guidance when he needed it most. The loss was monumental, and she felt helpless, knowing there was little she could do to ease his pain.

"Popi, we'll get through this," she said softly, her voice full of compassion. "He believed in you; his legacy will live on through your work. He would want you to keep going. Stay strong."

Popi nodded, but the grief was still raw. "I know, but it's just so hard," he admitted. "He was more than a mentor—he was like a second father to me."

Donna held him tighter, her tears falling freely. "I know, love. I know."

Popi mustered the courage to set aside his grief, at least for the evening, and focus on the joyous news of Donna's pregnancy. They sat together on the couch, holding each other close as the weight of the day's events slowly began to lift.

"Donna," Popi began, his voice gentle yet firm, "let's take tonight to celebrate our future. We'll deal with Mr. Church's passing tomorrow, but I want to be here with you and our baby right now."

Donna smiled, her eyes still glistening with tears. "You're right. Tonight is about us and our little one," she agreed, placing a hand on her stomach.

For a few precious hours, they managed to forget the tragedy. Instead, they immersed themselves in the excitement of becoming parents. They talked about names, nursery colours, and all the little things that come with preparing for a new addition to the family. In these moments, Popi felt overwhelming gratitude for having Donna in his life. She was his rock, understanding the depth of his sorrow and sharing in the heights of his joy.

"Donna," Popi said, his voice filled with emotion, "I can't thank you enough for being here with me. Losing Mr. Church is devastating, but knowing we're starting a family... it's giving me hope."

Donna reached out, squeezing his hand. "We'll get through this together, Popi. And I know Mr. Church would be so proud of you and the father you're going to be."

Popi nodded, feeling the truth of her words. "I know he would. And I promise I'll honour his memory by being the best father and husband I can be."

As the night wore on, they found solace in each other's arms, sharing quiet moments of reflection and anticipation. Popi felt a sense of peace, knowing that despite the heartache, there was a future filled with love and promise. He cherished Donna more than ever, realizing how much she meant to him and how integral she was to his life.

The next day would bring its own challenges, but for now, they held onto the happiness of their growing family. Popi's heart was whole, and he knew he could face anything the future held with Donna by his side. Together, they would navigate the storm, finding strength in their love and the new life they were about to bring into the world.

Popi: A Rising Tide

While some people in the party discussed funeral arrangements for Mr. Church, others were already embroiled in a power struggle over who would lead the party and, by extension, the country. For many, this was a golden opportunity that could catapult them into a position of power they might not have otherwise achieved on fair terms. Hijacking the leadership of a ruling party was, after all, the quickest path to becoming the Prime Minister of Canada.

Popi, however, had no interest in joining that frenzy. He knew the ensuing battle for leadership would only create chaos and division within the party. His sole concern was to ensure that everything from now until Mr. Church's burial went as smoothly as possible, honouring the memory of his mentor and providing stability during this turbulent time.

Popi couldn't believe the audacity of some of the MPs. While mourning Mr. Church, they had already started lobbying for his support in their bids for party leadership. Approaching him at such a sensitive time felt like the height of opportunism, and he wasn't shy about expressing his disdain.

"Have you no shame?" he asked one particularly eager MP, his voice laced with frustration. "We're supposed to be honouring Mr. Church's memory, not jockeying for power."

Despite the chaos, Popi remained steadfast in his decision not to run for party leadership. He focused on stabilizing the party and the government during this turbulent period. It was a relief for many within the party who viewed him as a formidable threat. Still, those vying for leadership were desperate for his endorsement. They saw his influence and popularity as key to securing their positions.

Meanwhile, with the Prime Minister position vacant, the Minister of Finance was appointed interim Prime Minister until the party could elect a new leader. Unsurprisingly, the interim Prime Minister sought Popi's assistance in maintaining order.

"Popi," the interim Prime Minister said during a private meeting, "we need your help to keep things stable. Your influence and organizational skills are crucial right now. Can I count on you?"

Popi nodded, understanding the gravity of the situation. "Of course. I'll do everything I can to support you and ensure a smooth transition."

Popi's role became one of mediation and stabilization. He worked tirelessly to manage the various factions within the party, ensuring that the leadership contest remained as civil as possible. He met with candidates, listened to their pitches, and provided guidance while clarifying that his endorsement would not come easily—or perhaps at all.

"Look," he told one ambitious MP, "my priority is the stability of our party and our country. I'll support whoever can prove they have the best interests of both at heart, not just their ambitions."

The state funeral for Mr. Church was a solemn and grand affair, befitting a leader of his stature. Thousands gathered to pay their respects, from high-ranking officials to ordinary citizens who admired his work. The ceremony was filled with heartfelt eulogies, a military honour guard, and tributes from world leaders.

Popi: A Rising Tide

However, the tranquillity of the public mourning contrasted sharply with the turmoil behind closed doors. The infighting among the Conservative Party members persisted, driven by ambition and a lack of clarity about the future leadership. This unprecedented situation in Canadian history left many uncertain about what would happen next.

As the days passed, the Conservatives finally elected a new leader. Popi's response was notably restrained when asked about his feelings regarding the new leader. He didn't hide his disappointment at how the leadership contenders had handled themselves during such a sensitive time. To him, it felt like Mr. Church's death had been used as a political stepping stone rather than a moment to honour a dedicated public servant.

"I'm not thrilled about the process," Popi admitted to a reporter. "Mr. Church deserved more respect than what was shown during this period. But we have a new leader now, and my focus remains on the work Mr. Church and I started for our party and our country."

Popi's grief was still palpable, but he threw himself into his work with renewed determination. He was resolved to see through the initiatives he and Mr. Church had begun, from environmental policies to social programs aimed at improving the lives of Canadians.

Donna was his steadfast supporter. She understood the complexity of his emotions and the heavy burden he carried. She encouraged him to stay focused on their shared vision for the future, reminding him of the importance of their work not just for themselves but for the country.

"You're doing the right thing, Popi," Donna reassured him one evening. "Mr. Church believed in you, and so do I. Together, we can ensure his legacy continues to thrive."

Popi nodded, feeling a mix of sorrow and determination. "You're right, Donna. We must keep pushing forward—for Mr. Church, Canada, and our future family."

As the new leader settled into his role, Popi continued to guide the party, advocating for policies and initiatives that aligned with Mr. Church's vision. His integrity and commitment earned him respect from colleagues and constituents alike, even after he chose to stay out of the leadership fray.

The weeks following the funeral were a blur of meetings, policy discussions, and constituency work. Popi made it a point to check in with the individuals he had helped before the wedding, ensuring that their issues were being addressed and they had the support they needed.

Life gradually began to find a new rhythm for Popi and Donna. They navigated their professional responsibilities while also preparing for the arrival of their first child. Despite the challenges, they found strength in each other, their love deepening through the shared experiences of joy and sorrow.

One evening, as they sat together in their living room, Donna looked at Popi with a gentle smile. "You know, I think Mr. Church would be proud of how you're handling everything. You're carrying on his legacy with such grace and determination."

Popi took her hand, feeling grateful for her unwavering support.

Popi: A Rising Tide

"I couldn't do it without you, Donna. You're my rock. And together, we're going to make a real difference."

Popi and Donna knew there would be more challenges ahead with the political landscape still in flux. But they also knew they had each other and a shared commitment to making their country a better place. And with that, they faced the future with hope and resolve, ready to honour Mr. Church's memory by continuing the work he had started.

With the opposition Liberal Party seizing the opportunity, they moved forward with a vote of no confidence against the Conservative government. The internal disarray within the Conservative Party had become so pronounced that even some of their own MPs sided with the motion, prioritizing the nation's stability over party allegiance.

Though not involved in the leadership contest, Popi watched with a heavy heart as the party he had worked so hard for crumbled under the weight of internal conflict and external pressure. The vote of no confidence passed, triggering another federal election just two years after the last one.

The atmosphere was tense. The Conservatives scrambled to present a united front, but the recent upheaval left them vulnerable. Meanwhile, the Liberals, capitalizing on the disarray, quickly rallied their base and prepared their campaign strategies.

Although deeply affected by Mr. Church's death and the subsequent political chaos, Popi remained committed to his work. He focused on his constituents and continued pushing forward the policies he and Mr. Church had championed. Donna constantly supported him, helping him balance their personal and professional challenges.

As the election campaign ramped up, Popi was approached by various factions within the Conservative Party, each seeking his endorsement and support. However, he remained steadfast in his decision not to run for the party leadership, instead concentrating on his responsibilities as an MP and Minister of Interprovincial Affairs.

The new Conservative leader and Prime Minister of Canada, Mr. Paulson, was a figure who commanded attention and instilled both fear and respect. Known for his authoritative style, Paulson's leadership was marked by a strict, uncompromising approach. He did not ask for cooperation; he demanded it. His campaign to become leader was driven by grand promises that many within the party found unrealistic. Still, these promises had nonetheless secured his election.

As Paulson took the helm, anxiety spread throughout the Conservative Party. Many members were apprehensive about his leadership style and the potential consequences for the party's unity and public perception. The internal turmoil was palpable, and the Conservatives were widely believed to be headed for significant losses in the upcoming election. The only question was how severe those losses would be.

Popi observed the unfolding situation with a mixture of concern and determination. He understood the gravity of the party's predicament and the need for robust and cohesive leadership. However, he also recognized the dangers of Paulson's approach. Despite his reservations, Popi chose to focus on what he could control—continuing his work and supporting his constituents.

Popi: A Rising Tide

One evening, Popi and Donna were discussing the party's state and the upcoming election. Donna asked, "How do you think things will play out with Paulson in charge?"

Popi sighed, "It's hard to say. Paulson's leadership style is divisive, and his promises during the campaign have set high expectations that may not be feasible. There's a lot of anxiety within the party, which doesn't bode well for us in the election." Donna nodded, "But you've always focused on solutions and helping people. That's what sets you apart. Even if the party struggles, you can still make a difference."

Popi smiled, appreciating her support. "You're right, Donna. I can't control everything, but I can continue doing my job and serving people. We'll face whatever comes together."

As the election campaign progressed, Popi remained committed to his principles. He campaigned for candidates he believed in, met with constituents, and continued to advocate for the policies he and Mr. Church had championed. He avoided getting drawn into the internal conflicts and power struggles that plagued the party under Paulson's leadership.

Despite the challenges, Popi's dedication and integrity earned him respect from many within the party and his constituency. He was seen as a stabilizing force in a time of uncertainty.

The Conservative Party's predicament was severe: only six weeks to turn around their fortunes with an unreasonable leader at the helm and a fragmented party struggling to find unity. The Liberals, by contrast, were capitalizing on their united front and the continued popularity of their leader from the previous election. The Liberal campaign was well-oiled and efficiently managed, contrasting sharply with the turmoil within the Conservative ranks.

The media and public discourse were increasingly skeptical about the Conservative Party's chances. Jokes about smaller parties potentially outperforming the Conservatives in seat counts were becoming more common, reflecting the serious concerns about the party's viability. The situation was dire, with many predicting that the Conservatives would face significant losses in the upcoming election.

Despite the odds, Popi remained focused and determined. He engaged directly with his constituents, emphasizing the most critical issues. He held town hall meetings, addressed concerns personally, and worked to reinforce the connections he had built over the years. He leveraged his relationships within the community to organize grassroots support. This included volunteers and local leaders who could mobilize voters despite the party's broader struggles.

Popi worked on framing his record and achievements in a positive light. He focused on his tangible benefits to his constituency, making a case for why he should be re-elected despite the party's overall challenges. He was transparent about the party's difficulties but focused on constructive solutions. This approach aimed to differentiate himself from the broader party turmoil and present a hopeful vision for his role.

Popi avoided getting involved in the internal conflicts and power struggles within the Conservative Party. He knew that aligning himself with the ongoing disputes would only further alienate voters and distract from his core message. He advocated for party unity and collaboration whenever possible,

Popi: A Rising Tide

even if it meant taking a backseat in broader party discussions. He aimed to show that, despite the party's issues, dedicated individuals were still working for the country's best interests.

Popi made strategic appearances in the media to advocate for his policies and highlight his commitment to his role. He used these opportunities to counterbalance the negative press surrounding the party. He and his team worked on providing a positive narrative about his campaign efforts and the impact of his work, hoping to influence public perception and rally support.

Popi explored potential alliances with smaller parties where feasible. These alliances aimed to secure additional support and create a more robust position in critical areas. He reached out to influential figures within his constituency who could help amplify his message and provide additional support.

During the chaos, Popi became a beacon of sanity. He listened to the concerns of frantic MPs and offered pragmatic advice, even as the party crumbled around them. The weight of Mr. Church's death and the disastrous leadership vacuum had created a perfect storm. Still, Popi focused on the glimmer of hope that remained.

"Look," Popi said to one particularly worried MP, "we're facing a mess of epic proportions, but let's be real. The leader we've got now is about as popular as a snowstorm in July. The public sees him as a figurehead with no vision, and that's the harsh reality."

He continued, "Mr. Church was a giant, and his absence left a gaping hole. The party didn't just lose a leader; it lost direction.

But don't mistake this for the end. The Conservatives still have some solid candidates who can be the backbone of a strong opposition. It's not about waiting for a miracle; it's about rallying what we have left and proving we can still be a formidable force."

The MP, though anxious, took solace in Popi's calm and measured approach. He acknowledged the challenges but emphasized the need for strategic action rather than despair. "Our task now," Popi said, "is to find a way to present a unified front and show the electorate that we have credible alternatives. We may be facing an uphill battle, but a strong opposition can make a difference."

His leadership, though informal, offered a roadmap through the turmoil. Popi's focus shifted to mobilizing the remaining strong candidates and leveraging any available resources to craft a coherent message for the upcoming election. He knew that while the party was deeply fractured, it still had the potential to play a significant role in shaping the future of Canadian politics.

Truthfully, amidst the Conservative Party's turmoil, Popi found himself lost, as though he were a ship adrift in a stormy sea. The party's disarray was palpable, each day bringing new waves of uncertainty threatening to capsize their already fragile hopes. Popi wrestled with the mounting chaos, feeling the weight of responsibility more acutely than ever. It was as if the world had spun off its axis, and he struggled to keep his footing on a slippery slope.

After much deliberation, Popi reached what he would later recognize as the most self-preserving decision of his life. With a heavy heart, he decided to confront the truth head-on despite knowing it would be harsh. He spoke candidly before his colleagues, cutting through the fog of denial and despair.

"Let us face the facts," Popi said, his voice steady but laden with the gravity of his message. "The party is in disarray, and the path ahead is difficult. I believe it is clear that we are not poised to win this election. We are likely to come in third, if not worse. If you care about retaining your seats, I urge you to focus on your own campaigns. The party, as it stands, cannot offer you the support you need."

The room fell silent, the weight of his words settling over them like a heavy fog. Some faces were etched with despair, while others appeared to have just been handed a bitter pill to swallow. Popi knew this truth was not what they wanted to hear, but he believed that honesty was the only compass in these treacherous waters.

"Hard though it may be," he continued, "I must prioritize my own re-election efforts. I encourage you to take the momentum from past campaigns and use it to fuel your successes. The winds of change may be unfavourable, but with determination and focus, you can still find a way to navigate these rough seas."

His colleagues nodded slowly, absorbing the gravity of his words. The proverb, "You can lead a horse to water, but you can't make it drink," echoed in Popi's mind. He had done his part in guiding them to the truth; the rest was now up to each individual's resolve and effort.

As the meeting concluded, Popi felt a pang of sorrow for the state of the party he had once hoped to lead to greatness. Yet, amidst the uncertainty, he found solace in the clarity of his path forward. The road ahead was steep and fraught with obstacles. Still, Popi was determined to navigate it with the same grit that had carried him through countless challenges.

The election results were as predictable as they were disheartening for many within the Conservative Party. Popi, buoyed by a substantial surge of support from his constituents, secured his re-election with a resounding landslide victory. It was a testament to his appeal and relentless efforts during his tenure. Yet, the same could not be said for his colleagues. The party's overall performance was a far cry from his personal triumph.

The fallout was severe. Over half of Popi's fellow MPs lost their seats, a casualty of the Conservative Party's widespread defeat. The new Prime Minister, Mr. Paulson, who had stepped into the role following Mr. Church's untimely demise, also faced the brunt of this electoral upheaval. With the Conservative Party losing its grip, the political landscape of Canada had shifted dramatically.

The Liberals emerged victorious with a sweeping mandate, securing over 200 of the 338 available seats. This landslide victory granted them a commanding majority, a stronghold that would enable them to govern with relative ease. Popi watched as the Liberals prepared to assume control with a mix of apprehension and grim resolve. The prospect of a single party holding such unchecked power was a source of deep concern for him.

In a sombre reflection, Popi mused, "It seems we're not just losing an election but witnessing the onset of a new era. The Liberals are poised to rule unchallenged for the next four years.

Popi: A Rising Tide

With their majority, they will pass laws and policies with little to no opposition. The thought of it sends a shiver down my spine."

The Liberals' dominance meant they would have the leeway to implement their policies without significant hindrance. For Popi, this was a daunting reality. His distaste for the Liberals' management of taxpayer money was well-known. He feared their spending habits would lead Canada into an era of excessive debt that could burden future generations.

Popi joked with a wry smile, "It looks like my generation won't be the ones paying for this election loss. It's going to be my kids' and grandkids' problem. Let's hope those future generations will be prepared for the bill."

Despite his biting humour, Popi's concern was palpable. The prospect of a future shaped by unchecked Liberal policies weighed heavily on him. Yet, amidst the uncertainty, he resolved to continue his work with the same dedication that had defined his political career. His focus now was to navigate the shifting tides of Canadian politics, advocate for his principles, and prepare for the challenges ahead.

Back home, Donna eagerly awaited Popi's return, her heart heavy with concern. She knew that while his victory was a bright spot, the party's defeat was a significant blow to him. The weight of the election results hung over Popi like a storm cloud, and Donna was determined to offer him solace and cheer as he grappled with the aftermath.

As Popi walked through the door, Donna greeted him with a warm embrace, her smile a beacon of comfort in the dimly lit room. "I know today was tough," she began softly, her voice gentle and reassuring. "But I want you to know how proud I am of everything you've accomplished. You've given your all, and that's something to be proud of, no matter the outcome."

Popi managed a faint smile, though his eyes betrayed his fatigue and frustration. "There's nothing I can do about the results," he said, his tone reflecting resignation. "I did my best, but now it's just a matter of waiting and continuing to bring value to my constituents. The rest is beyond my control."

Donna took his hand and led him to the dinner table, where she had prepared a comforting meal. The aroma of home-cooked food filled the air, a small but meaningful gesture of support. "We can't change what happened, but we can make the most of tonight," she said, trying to lift his spirits. "Let's focus on celebrating your win for a while."

They sat together, sharing a quiet, intimate dinner. The conversation was light, deliberately steering away from politics. Donna spoke of simple joys and everyday moments, her presence a balm for Popi's troubled mind. With each bite and with each laugh, the tension eased, if only a little.

As the evening wore on, they moved to the living room, where soft music played. Popi took Donna in his arms, and their shared embrace was a silent testament to their love and solidarity. In the warmth of their home, away from the chaos of the political world, they found solace in each other's company.

Donna looked up at Popi, her eyes filled with affection. "We'll face whatever comes next together," she said softly. "Tonight is for us. Let's enjoy it and be grateful for what we have."

Popi: A Rising Tide

Popi nodded, his heart swelling with gratitude for Donna's unwavering support. "You're right," he said, his voice filled with sincerity. "Tonight is about us. Thank you for being my rock."

They spent the rest of the evening wrapped in each other's arms, their love providing a much-needed respite from the storm outside. In those quiet, tender moments, Popi found a glimmer of hope amidst the uncertainty bolstered by the unwavering strength of his partner by his side.

As the new parliamentary session commenced under the Liberal government, Popi found himself again at the epicentre of political intrigue. With the party in disarray and the Conservative leadership in question, the spotlight shifted to him as speculation grew about his potential run for leadership.

At home, Donna was deeply concerned. She and Popi had made a promise when they got married: that significant decisions would be made together, with her feelings and their shared future always in mind. Now, more than ever, Donna pleaded with Popi to step back from the relentless political grind.

"Popi," she said one evening, her voice tinged with love and worry, "we need to focus on building our family. We've talked about this. If we don't have a strong foundation, we risk starting our life together on shaky ground. I'm not asking you to abandon your ambitions—I just want you to slow down and think about what's best for us, for our future."

Popi listened, his heart heavy with the weight of her words. He knew Donna wasn't opposed to his ambitions; she wanted him to balance them with their shared dream of building a stable family life. Her concern was a reminder of their promises to each other, which now felt more critical than ever.

When a few party members approached him, eager for his endorsement for leadership, Popi made a firm decision. He told them, "I'm not going to support any one person. I believe in letting the party members across Canada have their say. It's crucial that we elect a leader who not only aims to win elections but also focuses on repairing our party's core values. I will support whoever emerges with a true commitment to those values."

Popi's stance reflected his commitment to both his personal and professional life. He wanted to honour Donna's wishes while staying true to his principles. It was a delicate balance but one he was determined to maintain.

Popi remained in the background as the leadership race continued, allowing the party to find its way without his direct involvement. He concentrated on his role as an MP, using his influence to advocate for meaningful reforms and to support his constituents. Meanwhile, Donna and Popi worked together at home to build the strong foundation they both desired.

Their evenings were filled with quiet moments of togetherness away from the clamour of politics. They talked about their dreams, fears, and plans for the future. Donna's support was unwavering in these moments, and Popi's resolve to balance his political and personal life grew more robust.

Popi knew the road ahead would be challenging, but with Donna by his side, he felt more equipped to face whatever came next. Their promise to each other to build a life together, grounded in love and mutual respect, remained at the heart of their decisions, guiding him through the complexities of his personal and political worlds.

Electing a new Conservative leader came and went. Still, the struggle to unite the party continued unabated throughout the Liberal government's tenure. The party remained fractured, and its internal battles seemed to deepen daily.

Watching Popi grapple with his diminishing enthusiasm for the Conservative Party he once held dear, Donna grew concerned. She worried that perhaps her desire for him to focus on their family might have inadvertently diminished his passion for politics. It was a troubling thought, and she needed to address it directly.

One evening, as they sat together in their cozy living room, Donna broached the subject with gentle concern. "Popi, I see how disappointed you are with the current state of the Conservative Party. You've always been so dedicated to it. I'm worried that maybe my wish for us to focus on our family has somehow taken away your love for politics. I want you to know that whatever you decide to do, I'll support you fully—even if it means you need to repair the party you've always cared about."

Popi listened intently, touched by Donna's words but feeling the weight of his disillusionment. "Donna," he began, his voice tinged with frustration and weariness, "it's not that you've taken anything from me. My love for politics hasn't waned because of you. The internal strife and the degradation of principles within the party have troubled me. I've watched people use political positions to further their agendas rather than working for the common good. It's disheartening."

Donna reached out, taking his hand in hers. "I understand that, but you've always been the man who stood up for what was right. You fought for change and faced challenges head-on. I'm afraid you've lost sight of that. I want you to remember the man I fell in love with—the fearless leader who could take on any challenge, no matter how daunting."

Popi sighed, a mixture of sadness and resolve in his eyes. "I've thought about running for the party leadership myself, but I'm concerned that my political experience, or lack of it, will be scrutinized and used against me if I do. The infighting within the party would only get worse. My biggest fear is that I've become someone who has lost the drive to make the kind of change I once fought for. I feel like I've become someone I no longer recognize."

Donna squeezed his hand reassuringly. "Popi, you're still the same man I fell in love with. I still believe in you and your ability to make a difference. If you're passionate about this, I'm here to support you, no matter what. What matters most is that you stay true to yourself. When you're at your best, it brings out the best in all of us. You're a rising tide that raises all boats."

Popi looked at Donna with gratitude, his heart softened by her unwavering support. "Thank you, Donna. Your belief in me means more than you can know. I'll think about what you've said and find a way to balance my passion for politics with the life we're building together. I don't want to lose sight of who I am or what I stand for."

Popi: A Rising Tide

Donna smiled, her eyes filled with warmth and love. "We'll face this together. Whatever happens, we'll navigate it side by side. I'm here for you, just as you've always been here for me."

At that moment, Popi felt a renewed sense of hope. With Donna's support, he began to see a path forward, one where he could honour his commitment to his principles while nurturing the life they were building together. It was a delicate balance, but he was determined to achieve it.

After four years of Liberal rule with a majority government, the electorate's disillusionment was palpable. Many who had once supported the Liberal Party became increasingly alienated, leading to a markedly low voter turnout in the next election. The result was a deeply fragmented political landscape.

The Liberals, despite their diminished support, still secured 166 seats—just shy of a majority. The Conservative Party, though it managed to chip away at the Liberals' previous dominance by reducing their seats from over 200 to 166, faced a harsh reality. The low voter turnout wasn't something to celebrate; it was a stark reminder of the apathy that had set in among the electorate.

Popi saw through the veneer of what some might have viewed as a victory. The diminished Liberal seat count was not a testament to the Conservative Party's success but a reflection of the voters' disengagement. It was a troubling indicator that the electorate was disenchanted and that, in Popi's eyes, was more disheartening than the prospect of another term under the Liberal government.

In his reflective moments, Popi reflected on the root of the problem. The core issue wasn't merely the Liberal Party's shortcomings but a broader disillusionment with the political process. The lack of enthusiasm was a glaring sign that people felt disconnected from the political system. This sentiment translated into a lack of motivation to vote.

Popi knew that a fundamental shift was needed to turn this around. The path to winning elections wasn't just about capitalizing on the opposition's failures but about reigniting public interest and involvement in the political process. He understood that for people to come out to vote, they needed more than just a choice between parties; they needed to feel that their vote mattered and could make a difference.

One evening, he shared his thoughts with Donna as they sat together, contemplating the future. "Donna, it's clear that people are tired and disillusioned. The voter turnout was abysmally low. It's not enough to criticize the Liberals or highlight their failures. We must give people a reason to believe in the political process again. We must show them that their voices matter and that change is possible."

Donna nodded, her expression thoughtful. "I understand, Popi. The challenge now is to inspire that belief. People need to feel that there's something to vote for, not just against. They need to see a vision that resonates with them and addresses their concerns. It's about reigniting hope and trust in the system."

Popi's resolve strengthened as he considered their conversation. "Exactly. It's not just about winning an election; it's about rebuilding faith in the process itself. Suppose we can connect with people on a deeper level and demonstrate that their participation is crucial to shaping the future. In that case, we might be able to turn this tide around."

The road ahead was fraught with challenges, but Popi was determined to face them head-on. With Donna's support and unwavering commitment to meaningful change, he set out to address the fundamental issues that led to voter apathy. His goal was not just to win the next election but to restore confidence in the political system and make every vote count.

The Conservative Party was in disarray, desperately scrambling for a leader who could restore their waning influence. The urgency was palpable as the party sought a replacement for their second ousted leader since Mr. Church's passing. The race was crowded with candidates, but none resonated with the average party member or the broader electorate. Many hopefuls lacked recognition or possessed resumes that did little to inspire confidence.

One sweltering summer afternoon, as the deadline for announcing candidacies loomed just a week away, Donna broached a suggestion that caught Popi off guard. "Why don't you consider running for the party leadership?" she proposed, her tone a mix of encouragement and earnest concern.

Popi laughed softly, brushing it off with a hint of disbelief. "Maybe Canada isn't ready for a young prime minister," he said, trying to mask his uncertainty with humour.

Donna's eyes were steady, her voice unwavering as she pressed on. "Popi, you're exactly what this party needs right now. You have a rare ability to bring people together, even when they're divided. You've done it before—getting compensation for those wronged by the city, resolving the tensions between the police officer and the pedestrian's family. You've faced challenges head-on and found solutions where others saw only obstacles."

Popi looked at her, contemplating her words. Donna continued, her voice filled with conviction. "You've always had an extraordinary talent for uniting people, for finding common ground. The Conservative Party is at a crossroads and needs someone who can offer more than just traditional solutions. You have the vision and the experience to bring hope and revitalization. This is your chance to show the country there's still a way forward."

She spoke with the kind of clarity that comes from deep belief, and Popi felt a stirring of hope within himself. "But Donna, the stakes are so high," he replied, his tone a mix of awe and apprehension. "What if I can't live up to the expectations? What if I'm not enough?"

Donna took his hand, her touch reassuring. "Popi, every great leader has faced doubt and uncertainty. What sets them apart is their willingness to step up despite the fear. You've already shown you can tackle difficult situations and make a difference. Imagine what you could do with the leadership of an entire party."

Popi took a deep breath, letting her words sink in. Donna's faith in him was both humbling and motivating. He knew that if he chose to run, it wouldn't be just about his ambitions but about offering a new direction for the party and, potentially, the country.

Donna smiled, her eyes sparkling with encouragement. "Just

think about it. You have the chance to be a beacon of hope and renewal. And no matter what you decide, I'll be by your side, supporting you every step of the way."

Popi acknowledged Donna's point with a thoughtful nod, yet he couldn't help but raise a concern. "Donna, this will be a massive undertaking for both of us. Maybe it's wiser to wait a few years once we've settled into our family life. It's a lot to juggle right now. Our daughter is almost starting preschool, and I want to spend more time with her. Of course, I also want to be with our second little one on the way."

Donna, however, was steadfast. She knew that when Popi's adrenaline was pumping, he was unstoppable. "Popi, I understand your concerns, but I also see the spark in you. When you're energized and passionate, there's nothing you can't achieve. I want to see that version of you again, the one who feels alive and driven. Even if you don't win, the campaign itself will reinvigorate you. It's the fight and the challenge that will make you thrive."

Popi considered her words carefully. Donna's faith in his potential was both reassuring and motivating. "You're right. I'll think about it," he said, drawing her close and kissing her forehead tenderly. "Thanks for always being my rock."

Donna smiled, her heart warmed by his trust. "Good night, Popi. I believe in you. No matter what you decide, we'll face it together."

As Popi settled into bed, the weight of the decision ahead felt a little lighter. Donna's unwavering support had rekindled his determination, and he knew that whatever path he chose, he would face it with the strength of her encouragement.

When Donna awoke the following day, the room was quiet and still, except for a single note on her pillow. As she read the simple but heartfelt message, her heart skipped a beat:

Donna,

I've decided to take the plunge. I'm throwing my hat into the ring. Thank you for believing in me and pushing me to find this spark again. I'll do this for us, our future, and Mr. Church.

Love you always,

Popi

XOXO

Donna's heart swelled with a mix of pride and apprehension. She could feel the weight of his decision, the hope and determination in his words. She knew Popi had always been driven by his principles and respect for Mr. Church's legacy. This was more than just a political move; it was a heartfelt tribute to someone who had shaped his career.

As news about Popi's candidacy broke out, it was as if a wildfire had been set ablaze. The announcement became the talk of the nation, eclipsing even the recent political upheavals. Social media exploded with a frenzy of activity, with memes circulating at lightning speed. Some celebrated Popi's audacious return to the fray with humour and admiration, while others skeptically questioned his age and experience. Yet, despite the mixed reactions, the buzz was undeniable.

Popi's track record was formidable, and his political reputation was solid. The criticisms would inevitably centre around his youth and the relative inexperience compared to some seasoned contenders. But Popi was ready for that. He knew the criticisms would come, but he was determined to leverage his solid accomplishments and unwavering commitment to his principles.

In a remarkably short span, donations poured in from supporters and well-wishers, securing his candidacy with the kind of momentum that was impossible to ignore. This was no small feat; it was a clear sign that his appeal was substantial and his support was genuine. Popi understood that this was likely his singular chance to make a significant impact, and he was ready to seize it.

As he prepared to embark on this new chapter, Popi reflected on his motivations. The image of Mr. Church, the man who had once been his mentor and inspiration, loomed large in his mind. This campaign was not merely a political endeavour—it was a tribute to a mentor who had guided him and a commitment to his principles.

With determination fuelling his every step, Popi resolved to honour Mr. Church's legacy by fighting for the values he believed in. This was his chance to make a difference, to rally the party and the nation, and to show that even in the face of adversity, the spirit of dedicated leadership and integrity could shine through.

As Donna approached her third trimester, the weight of the growing family and the demands of Popi's campaign created a complex tapestry of emotions. Popi was concerned about the stress this would bring to Donna. Still, her response was a beacon of positivity and support.

When Popi broached the subject with her, he asked if she was okay with the intense demands of his campaign and the toll it might take on their lives. Donna's eyes sparkled with excitement as she replied, "Honestly, I'm not thrilled about you diving into the Conservative leadership. But I'm overjoyed that you're aiming for the highest office in the land. That's something worth fighting for."

She continued, her tone light and playful, "Our kids are incredibly fortunate to have you as a father. Although, let's face it—if they ever want to outshine you, they'll have some pretty big shoes to fill!"

Popi's heart swelled with gratitude. He looked at Donna with profound appreciation and said, "Thank you for everything. There's no way I could have come this far without you. Your support means more to me than you can imagine."

Donna's smile was warm and reassuring. "If you're truly grateful," she teased, "then you better go out there and secure that leadership. Because being the First Lady of Canada is the only thing I'm dreaming of right now."

They shared a heartfelt laugh, their connection more potent than ever. Popi pulled Donna into a tender embrace and kissed her softly. As he prepared to leave for the campaign trail, his heart was lighter and his resolve firmer. Donna's unwavering

Popi: A Rising Tide

support was the bedrock upon which he would build his campaign, and he knew that with her by his side, he could face any challenge that came his way.

With one last look of affection, Popi walked out the door, ready to take on the challenges of his campaign with renewed vigour. He knew that he carried with him the strength and love of his wife and the dreams they shared for their future.

The Leadership Race

Three weeks into the campaign for the Conservative Party leadership, Popi found himself navigating a whirlwind of challenges and triumphs. He had managed to mobilize a remarkable level of support from across the country, tapping into his constituency and reaching out to his affiliations from the university. A deep-seated belief in a fair distribution of influence across the nation drove his efforts. He recognized that winning the leadership wasn't just about garnering the most votes but about representing Canadians from coast to coast.

However, this broad approach also came with significant disadvantages. Established and mature politicians, with their entrenched bases in their hometowns or home provinces, had a leg up in local support. Popi knew this race would be an uphill battle, but each passing day seemed to bring new complications.

One evening, after a particularly gruelling day on the campaign trail, Popi sat down with Donna. She was glowing with her second pregnancy, her presence a calming balm to his weary soul.

"Popi," she began, her voice soft yet firm, "you've done an amazing job so far. You've rallied support from places some of these seasoned politicians wouldn't even think to reach. That's your strength."

Popi sighed, running a hand through his hair. "I know, honey.

Popi: A Rising Tide

But the attacks... they're relentless. It's not just my lack of experience they're targeting. They're digging into my family and my university days. They're painting a picture of me that isn't true."

Donna reached out, taking his hand in hers. "A wise old saying goes, 'You can't make a silk purse out of a sow's ear.' These attacks are desperate attempts to undermine you because they fear your potential. Remember, 'Smooth seas do not make skillful sailors.' Every obstacle you face now is forging you into a stronger leader."

Popi looked into her eyes, finding solace in her unwavering support. "You're right, as always. But it's hard not to let it get to me. I've worked hard to get here, and sometimes it feels like I'm fighting an uphill battle with a heavy load on my back."

Donna smiled gently. "Popi, 'The darkest hour is just before the dawn.' You've faced tougher challenges before. Think of all the people who believe in you, who see the integrity and passion you bring to this race. 'When the going gets tough, the tough get going.'"

Her words were a balm to his spirit, a reminder of why he had embarked on this journey in the first place. Popi nodded, a determined glint returning to his eyes. "I'll keep fighting, Donna. Not just for me, but for you, our kids, and everyone who believes in a better future."

The days that followed were gruelling. Popi travelled across the vast Canadian landscape, shaking hands, attending town hall meetings, and speaking passionately about his vision for the party and the country. His opponents' attacks didn't cease; if anything, they intensified. They scrutinized his family, dug into old university pranks, and tried to paint him as inexperienced and unprepared.

But Popi stood firm. He countered each attack with grace, never stooping to their level. Instead, he focused on his message of unity and progress, reaching out to voters with sincerity and conviction.

One evening, as he addressed a crowd in a small town in Nova Scotia, Popi spoke from the heart. "I know some say I lack the experience of my opponents. But let me tell you, experience is about more than just years served. It's about the heart you bring to the service and the integrity of your duties. 'A clear conscience is the sure sign of a bad memory,' but I remember every promise I've made to you, and I intend to keep them."

The crowd applauded, their support a powerful reminder that he wasn't alone in this fight. Popi knew that with each passing day, he was becoming more resilient and more determined to see this race through to the end.

Back at home, Donna continued to be his rock. She encouraged, uplifted, and reminded him of the bigger picture. "Popi, 'Rome wasn't built in a day,' and neither will your campaign be. Keep at it, one step at a time. 'Good things come to those who wait.'"

With renewed vigour, Popi pushed forward, determined to show Canada he had what it took to lead the party and the country into a brighter future.

With all the mounting stress of the campaign, Popi received a call from Donna. She told him that Kyle would be calling him soon and gently asked him to be friendly, even though she knew he was under pressure. Donna understood that Popi, when stressed, could sometimes say things out of frustration and struggle to convey his thoughts or feelings without seeming insensitive. Popi chuckled and reassured her, "I'll be on my best behaviour, love."

When Kyle called, Popi could sense his nervousness. After exchanging some small talk, Kyle got to the point. "Popi," he began, taking a deep breath, "I need to ask you the biggest favour I've ever asked. But please know, if you're not comfortable, it's okay. No matter your answer, I hope this won't complicate our relationship."

Intrigued, Popi leaned in. "Kyle, what's going on? You know you can ask me anything."

Kyle took another deep breath and said, "My relationship has gotten serious, and I'm planning to get married. I wanted to ask if you would do the honour of performing the ceremony."

Popi laughed, a warm and hearty sound, shaking his head. "Donna thinks I'm going to overreact to something so beautiful? Kyle, you're like a younger brother to me. When I describe you to others, I always say you're my brother-in-law. You mean so much to Donna, which means you matter to me, too. You're family, and I'd be more than happy to officiate your wedding. It's an honour."

Kyle's face broke into a relieved smile, his eyes shining with gratitude. "Thank you, Popi. That means the world to me."

Popi added, "Listen, Kyle, you're family. We stand by each

other through thick and thin. I'm here for you, always."

The two men shared a moment of understanding, their bond strengthened by this heartfelt exchange. Popi felt a sense of peace wash over him, a reminder of what truly mattered in life beyond the stress and chaos of the political arena.

While most of their previous conversations revolved around Donna, this was the first time Popi and Kyle had a heart-to-heart discussion involving just the two of them. They had always respected each other, but Kyle had been unsure of Popi's thoughts about his personal life and sexual orientation, so he often kept his distance. It was a great relief for Kyle to hear that someone he deeply respected and admired looked at him as family.

Popi called out to him as Kyle was about to hang up the phone. "Kyle, how would you feel about the Prime Minister of Canada performing the ceremony instead?"

Kyle was silent for a moment, a bit puzzled. "I don't know the Prime Minister of Canada personally," he replied.

Popi smiled. "You will, in a year or so after the next federal election."

Kyle chuckled, shaking his head. "I don't think I can wait for a year. Besides, politics is always unpredictable. For something so uncertain, I can't put off an important part of my life."

Popi's eyes twinkled with determination. "Kyle, it's a question of faith. When it comes to faith, you either have it or you don't. There's nothing in between. Take some time to think about it."

Popi: A Rising Tide

Kyle paused, considering Popi's words. Then he replied, a stubborn look on his face. "I don't need any time to think about it. I know right now that I want to wait until you become Prime Minister. I have that much faith in you."

Popi felt a surge of gratitude and pride. "Thank you, Kyle. That means more to me than you know. But remember, this conversation stays between us."

Kyle nodded, his eyes filled with conviction. "Of course, Popi. My faith in you is unshakeable."

Popi felt a renewed sense of purpose as he hung up the phone. The road ahead would be arduous, but moments like this, filled with trust and belief, were the fuel that kept him going. He knew he had to fight for himself and everyone who placed their faith in him. And with Donna's unwavering support and Kyle's newfound confidence, Popi felt more ready than ever to take on the challenge.

The leadership election was only six weeks away, and while Popi was in the lead; it was not a commanding one. The race was still open, and anything could have happened to tip the scales against him. Due to his actions since his university days, including his defence of Ahmed, the international student, Popi often walked a fine line between being seen as a strong advocate and being labelled an extremist. His opponents found it easy to paint him as a sympathizer to extremist causes because of his willingness to defend those on the fringes.

Trying to shake off these labels took Popi time and effort. He spent days strategizing and searching for ways to redirect the conversation, but no clear solutions emerged. The constant pressure and stress of the campaign weighed heavily on him.

One evening, feeling particularly overwhelmed, Popi did what he always did in such moments—he turned to Donna. Since moving to Ottawa, she had become his pillar of support, his confidante. He didn't expect her to solve his problems; instead, he needed her sympathetic ear and comforting presence.

He found Donna in their living room, curled up with a book. Seeing him, she set the book aside and opened her arms, inviting him to sit beside her.

"Long day?" she asked softly.

Popi sighed deeply as he sank into the sofa. "You could say that. The labels, the accusations... It's like a cloud that follows me everywhere."

Donna stroked his hair gently, her touch soothing. "I know, Popi. It's unfair and frustrating. But you've always stood for your beliefs, which makes you who you are."

He looked at her, his eyes filled with worry. "What if it's not enough this time? What if people only see the labels and not the real me?"

Donna took his hand, squeezing it reassuringly. "People will see the real you, Popi. You have a way of connecting with them, of showing them your heart. Remember when you defended Ahmed? You stood by him because it was the right thing to do. That's the Popi people need to see—the one who fights for justice, who cares deeply for others."

Popi: A Rising Tide

He leaned his head on her shoulder, feeling the weight of the world slightly lift. "You always know what to say," he murmured.

"It's because I know you, Popi," she replied. "And I believe in you. So many people do. You have to keep showing them who you are."

Popi felt a renewed sense of determination. With Donna by his side, he knew he could face whatever challenges lay ahead. Her unwavering belief in him gave him the strength to continue fighting for himself and everyone who counted on him.

"Thank you, Donna," he whispered. "For everything."

She smiled, kissing his forehead. "Always, my love. Now, let's figure out how to show the world the real Popi."

With Donna's support, Popi felt ready to tackle the next six weeks with a renewed sense of purpose. The path ahead was uncertain, but he knew he could face anything as long as he stayed true to himself and had Donna by his side.

Since Popi dedicated himself to full-time politics, Donna had taken over all the community services and charity events they had organized since before he entered federal politics. With Donna's motivation and focus on his leadership, she successfully expanded their "Project for Hope" across the greater Ottawa area. Her vision extended beyond the local sphere; she had grand intentions to spread the initiative throughout Ontario and beyond.

Donna's days were filled with tireless efforts, coordinating events, rallying volunteers, and reaching out to those in need. Her dedication was unwavering, and she thrived on the challenges of expanding the project. The balance she shared with Popi was a cornerstone of her strength. She knew she could always turn to Popi for inspiration whenever she hit a roadblock or felt her ideas needed to be fixed.

One evening, after a particularly long day, Donna sat at the kitchen table, surrounded by notes and plans. She felt the weight of her ambitions pressing down on her. Expanding provincewide was daunting, and she wondered if she was biting off more than she could chew.

As if on cue, Popi walked in, tired but with a warm smile on his face. He saw the familiar furrow in Donna's brow and immediately knew she was wrestling with something.

"Hey, darling," he said, pulling a chair beside her. "What's got you looking so serious?"

Donna sighed, leaning back in her chair. "It's the expansion of Project for Hope. I want to take it provincewide, but the logistics are overwhelming. I'm hitting roadblocks, and I'm not sure how to move forward."

Popi reached out, taking her hand in his. "You've done amazing things with this project, Donna. You've touched so many lives. What's the biggest hurdle right now?"

Donna rubbed her forehead. "It's mainly the funding and getting enough volunteers. We've done well locally, but scaling up requires more resources and people. I'm just not sure where to start."

Popi: A Rising Tide

Popi thought momentarily, and then his face lit up with an idea: "What if we organize a fundraising gala? We could invite some of my connections in politics and business. It would not only raise money but also awareness for the project. And for volunteers, we could partner with local universities and community groups—they're always looking for service opportunities."

Donna's eyes sparkled with renewed energy. "That's brilliant, Popi. A gala could bring in the needed resources and create a buzz around the project."

Popi squeezed her hand, his eyes full of encouragement. "And you know I'll be there every step of the way. We can do this together, just like always."

Donna smiled, feeling the familiar warmth of hope and determination. "You always know how to lift my spirits, Popi. Thank you."

"Anything for you, Donna," he replied softly. "Your passion for this project is inspiring. And remember, even when it seems tough, you've got me in your corner. We'll figure it out together."

With Popi's support, Donna felt reinvigorated. She knew that no matter how ambitious her goals were, she could count on Popi to help her navigate the challenges. Their partnership was a perfect blend of passion and practicality. This balance allowed them to dream big and achieve even more significant results.

The following days were filled with planning and organizing. Donna reached out to potential donors and partners, while

Popi used his political connections to garner support. The fundraising gala was set in motion, and it quickly became the talk of the town.

A few days after Popi confided in Donna about his campaign stress, she suggested he take a break from the campaign. Popi initially resisted, arguing that he was running against time and every moment was precious if he wanted to win the leadership race. However, Donna insisted, reminding him she knew him better than he knew himself.

"Trust me, Popi," she said gently. "You need a break; staying home will help clear your mind. Remember our understanding: when one of us is stuck, we listen to the other."

Popi sighed, recognizing the truth in her words. They had always relied on each other during difficult times, and he knew he had to listen. Reluctantly, he agreed.

"Alright, Donna," he said. "I'll stay home for a few days. But only because I trust you."

Donna smiled, relieved. "Thank you, Popi. It'll be good for you, I promise."

Popi didn't explain the real reason for his sudden absence to anyone on his campaign team. Instead, he told them it was a family emergency.

"I need to step away for a few days," he said. "But I trust all of you to keep the campaign moving forward. Keep working hard, and I'll be back soon."

Popi: A Rising Tide

His team didn't question him, understanding the gravity of his request. They assured him they would continue their efforts in his absence.

As Popi started his break from the campaign, he felt a mix of anxiety and relief. He knew Donna's suggestion was for his own good, but the pressure of the campaign lingered in his mind. When he arrived home, Donna greeted him with a warm hug, her presence immediately soothing his frazzled nerves.

Over the next few days, Popi allowed himself to relax. He spent time with Donna, sharing meals, taking walks, and simply enjoying each other's company. They talked about everything and nothing, allowing the familiarity and comfort of home to restore his spirit.

One evening, as they sat on the porch watching the sunset, Popi turned to Donna. "You were right," he admitted. "I needed this. I feel clearer, more focused."

Donna smiled, taking his hand in hers. "I'm glad, Popi. You're always so driven, and sometimes you need to step back to see the bigger picture."

Popi nodded, appreciating her wisdom. "Thank you for always being my rock, Donna. I couldn't do this without you."

"And I couldn't do what I do without you," she replied. "We're a team, remember?"

Popi smiled, feeling a renewed sense of determination. "Yes, we are. A dream team. And with you by my side, I know we can achieve anything."

Rumours, misconceptions, and misconstrued statements swirled incessantly around Popi. Many well-established politicians, who had long harboured dreams of leading the party themselves, resented the idea of someone significantly younger than them taking the reins. This resentment fuelled a relentless wave of negativity aimed at Popi, serving as a stark reminder that politics, particularly at the national level, was indeed a blood sport.

Popi had been adept at controlling the narrative in his battles since his university days. He understood the systems he was working within and had developed strategies to either attack their weaknesses or navigate their complexities. However, national politics was an entirely different beast, especially in terms of the race to become a country's leader. Pressure mounted from all directions, and Popi felt the crushing weight of negative scrutiny from voters and other politicians for the first time.

The whispers of doubt and the barrage of criticism started to take a toll on Popi. He agreed with Donna that if things ever became too overwhelming, he would have the option to step back from the leadership race. But there was more at stake than just his political career. His father had always been one of his biggest supporters, and quitting the race would feel like letting him down. Moreover, the strength and foundation of his relationship with Donna were rooted in his leadership skills and his ability to get things done. He feared that giving up on the leadership race might strain his marriage.

After spending a few rejuvenating days at home, Popi returned to the campaign trail with a newfound vigour and a contagious enthusiasm. His transformation was palpable, and everyone on

Popi: A Rising Tide

his team noticed the change. The weariness that had shadowed his steps was gone, replaced by a confident stride and a bright, determined gaze.

"What happened to you while you were away?" one of his staffers asked, half-jokingly, as they gathered for a strategy meeting.

Popi grinned. "Sometimes, all you need is a little time with the people who know you best to remind you of who you are and why you're fighting."

With renewed energy, Popi unveiled a series of innovative ideas to change the campaign's narrative. He addressed the team with a clear plan, though it was unorthodox and fraught with risks.

"We need to change the perception," Popi began. "But considering some of the allegations levelled against me, it won't be easy. We need to create a different narrative or, in some cases, an illusion of an alternative narrative."

The room fell silent as his team absorbed the complexity of his approach. The idea involved layers of social psychology, something many on the campaign were not well-versed in. Doubts began to surface.

One of the senior advisors voiced the concern of many, "Isn't this a bit manipulative, Popi? This isn't the kind of politics you're known for."

Popi nodded, understanding their hesitation. "I know it sounds manipulative. And to some extent, it is. But it's all about perception and interpretation. We'll still deal with the facts on the ground; we'll just present them differently. Right now, this is the only realistic way to neutralize the attacks and stay in the race."

His honesty struck a chord. Popi admitted that he hated having to resort to such tactics, but he explained the necessity of the approach. "Politics is often about perception. It's not about lying or creating falsehoods but about framing the truth in a way that resonates with people. If we don't adapt, we might as well pack up and go home."

The team pondered his words. They knew the stakes were high and that this was no ordinary campaign. Popi's determination and willingness to adapt to the brutal realities of politics were inspiring and sobering.

One of his campaign managers spoke up, "Alright, let's do this. But let's ensure we stay true to our core values as much as possible."

Popi smiled, a hint of relief in his eyes. "Absolutely. We'll walk this fine line carefully, ensuring we don't lose ourselves in the process. Remember, our goal is to give people hope and a reason to believe again."

Popi's campaign implemented the new strategy over the next few days. They focused on highlighting his achievements and strengths, reframing past controversies more positively. The goal was to shift public perception and present Popi not as a young, inexperienced candidate but as a passionate, driven leader ready to take on the mantle of leadership.

Despite the initial skepticism, the strategy started to pay off.

Popi: A Rising Tide

Public opinion began to sway, and the narrative around Popi slowly changed. He was no longer just the young politician with a controversial past; he was now seen as a dynamic leader capable of bringing fresh perspectives and real change.

Popi and his team faced numerous challenges as the campaign progressed, but their resolve never wavered. They continued to push forward, adapting to the ever-changing political landscape with resilience and creativity. And through it all, Donna remained Popi's unwavering pillar of support, her belief in him never faltering.

Popi's chances of winning the leadership race grew stronger with each passing day. It was a tough, uphill battle, but he was determined to see it through for himself, Donna, and the future they envisioned together.

As Popi travelled across the country, his campaign took him back to his hometown, where he was greeted with a hero's welcome. The pride and affection of his fellow townspeople were palpable. The streets were lined with supporters, their cheers echoing with a genuine warmth that transcended politics. For many, Popi wasn't just a politician; he symbolized their shared dreams and aspirations. His success was their success, a testament to their hometown's ability to produce someone who had risen to high places.

Popi was struck by how little had changed as he walked through familiar streets. The faces were the same, and so were the small details he remembered about them. He greeted old friends and neighbours with the same ease he had always shown, asking after their families and recalling little anecdotes from their past conversations. His ability to connect on such a personal level only deepened the affection and support he received.

Eventually, Popi made his way to his parents' house. The mood was sombre as he entered. The once lively and warm home now felt heavy with tension. His father, Mr. Peters, had been grappling with the progression of Parkinson's disease, and it had taken a visible toll. The wheelchair now accompanied Mr. Peters everywhere, symbolizing his increased need for support. Although he could still move short distances with a cane, the wheelchair provided relief and ease.

Popi had thoughtfully modified the house to accommodate his father's condition—wider doorways, accessible features, and a wheelchair-friendly layout. His heart ached to see the physical changes, a poignant reminder of the impact of illness on his family. Yet, the actual strain was the palpable discord between his parents.

The warmth and camaraderie that once characterized their home had shifted to a cold, distant silence. Popi could feel the weight of the unspoken tension between them. The sight of his parents, once so full of shared joy, now reduced to barely managing civil exchanges, struck a deep chord in him.

He approached them with a mix of determination and apprehension. "Mom, Dad, it's so good to see you. I wanted to invite you to Ottawa for the election results, no matter how things turn out. It would mean a lot to me to have you there."

His mother looked up, her face etched with the strains of worry and weariness. "That's very kind of you, Popi. We'd love to be there, but we'll need to see how things go with your father's condition."

Popi: A Rising Tide

Mr. Peters nodded in agreement, his voice a shadow of its former strength. "I'd like that, son. But, as your mother said, we must take things one step at a time."

Popi sensed the heaviness in their voices and the underlying issues that neither of them was ready to address directly. He chose his words carefully. "I understand, Dad. I just wanted you to know how much your support means to me. No matter what happens, I'm grateful for everything you've both done for me."

There was a moment of silence, a rare pause where the weight of unspoken emotions hung. His parents exchanged a look—a brief, tender glimpse of the connection they once shared.

His mother reached out to touch Popi's hand and said softly, "We're proud of you, Popi. Just remember to take care of yourself, too."

Popi nodded, a mix of relief and sadness washing over him. He could see how much the years had changed their relationship and challenges. But he also saw a glimmer of the family bonds that had once defined them.

Popi sat beside his father, a deep concern etched on his face. Once vibrant with laughter and shared joy, the room now felt heavy with an unspoken tension. Popi tried to lighten the mood with a hint of humour, though his eyes revealed the seriousness behind his words.

"Dad," he began, his tone a mix of warmth and worry, "I must admit, I'm a bit concerned. It seems like things are getting worse between you and Mom. At this point, I'm afraid one of you might be charged with 'homicide secondary to domestic violence'—you know, just kidding, but this's tough to see."

Mr. Peters managed a faint smile, his eyes clouded with the pain of his condition and the strain of his relationship. "I suppose there's some truth to that, Popi. Your mother and I… we've been struggling. I think she feels trapped. She thinks I don't understand, but she's probably convinced that if she leaves now, she'll be abandoning me at a time when I need her most."

Popi's heart ached at the sight of his father's vulnerability. "But it sounds like she's torn. She's angry, and that anger is turning into something more. It must be incredibly hard for both of you."

Mr. Peters nodded slowly, his gaze fixed on the floor. "It's complicated. I think she feels guilty about leaving me like this, and that guilt is morphing into resentment. I've tried to accept it, thinking that if she needs to go, then she should. But I also understand why it's hard for her. Taking care of someone who's so ill is a heavy burden. She's caught in a cycle she can't break."

Popi sighed, feeling the weight of his father's words. "I really don't think Mom wants to leave you. I will talk to her and see what's going on from her side. Maybe there's a way to help you both find some understanding or at least ease the burden."

His father's eyes met his, filled with gratitude and a hint of resignation. "I'd appreciate that, Popi. I know your mother means well, and she's been doing her best. It's just… sometimes, the pressure becomes too much."

Popi patted his father on the shoulder. "I'll do what I can.

Popi: A Rising Tide

You've always been there for me, and I want to make sure that you're both supported. I'll talk to Mom and see if there's a way to help ease the tension."

As Popi stood up to leave, he took one last look at his father. There was a profound sadness in the air but also a glimmer of hope that things might improve with a bit of understanding and communication. He knew that his campaign was important, but family came first. He felt a renewed determination to bridge the gap between his parents, to offer them the support and understanding they needed in these trying times.

With a final nod to his father, Popi set off to find his mother, ready to delve into the complexities of their family dynamics and hopefully find a way to heal the fractures that had formed.

After a few minutes of exchanging pleasantries and small talk, Popi decided it was time to address the underlying tension he had sensed. He gently broached the subject with his mother, his voice tinged with concern.

"Mom, I've talked with Dad, and he's shared some things with me. I'm worried about what's going on between you two. He thinks you want to leave him maybe because of his illness, but I don't believe that's the case. Can you help me understand what's happening?"

At first, Mrs. Peters dismissed the question, insisting everything was fine. "Oh, Popi, it's just the usual ups and downs of being married for so long. We're just like any other couple. There's nothing to worry about."

But when Popi gently pressed, revealing his father's feelings,

Mrs. Peters' façade of calm crumbled. She sank into a chair, her shoulders slumping with the weight of her emotions. Her voice trembled as she spoke, her guilt and regret spilling out.

"It's not what your father thinks, Popi. I don't hate him. I hate myself," she said, her eyes brimming with tears.

Popi, taken aback, urged her to explain. "What do you mean? Please, tell me more."

Mrs. Peters took a deep breath, her hands clasped tightly in her lap. "When we tried to have children and couldn't, it shattered me. We went through so many tests, and it was initially blamed on your father's health. But then we learned it was me. I had serious health issues that made it nearly impossible to conceive."

Popi listened intently, his heart aching as he absorbed the new information. He had never known the details of their struggles with fertility. "I didn't know any of this. What happened next?"

Mrs. Peters continued, her voice softening with a mix of sorrow and admiration. "Your father was incredibly supportive. He never made me feel like I was less of a woman. He even told me he was okay with not having children if that's how it had to be. His love never wavered, and I was always grateful for that."

She paused, her gaze distant as she remembered. "But when he was diagnosed with Parkinson's disease, I felt lost. I didn't know how to help him the way he helped me. For our fertility issues, we found solace in adoption. We were blessed with you, Popi, and I always joke that we hit the lottery."

Her eyes filled with tears again. "But with his illness, there's no solution. I feel helpless. I'm not angry at him; I still love him dearly. I'm angry at myself because there's nothing I can do to ease his suffering. It's a different kind of pain."

Popi's heart ached for his mother, and he reached out to her, placing a comforting hand on her shoulder. "Mom, there's something you can do. It's not about fixing everything but about being there for Dad. He's not asking for much. He's feeling incredibly lonely, and losing the love of his life on top of his illness is more painful than his physical suffering. What he needs is to feel that he's not alone, to know that you still see him as the man he is, not just his disease."

Mrs. Peters looked up, her eyes reflecting a mix of hope and uncertainty. "What should I do?"

Popi spoke with conviction. "Have a serious conversation with Dad. Tell him how you feel about him as a husband, not just as someone with Parkinson's. Remind him of your love for him, and let him know that he still matters deeply to you despite everything."

Mrs. Peters nodded slowly, the weight of her guilt beginning to lift. "I'll do that, Popi. I want to help him. I don't want him to feel like he's lost everything, including me."

Popi gave her a reassuring smile. "That's all he needs right now, Mom. Your presence, your love. It's the greatest support you can offer."

After a few hours at home, Popi had engaged in a heartfelt conversation with his parents, hoping to mend the rift between them. Rejuvenated by the familial support and newfound clarity, he rejoined his campaign, determined to regain his commanding lead in the dwindling weeks of the election race.

Popi threw himself back into the campaign trail with renewed vigour. He made a series of videos and speeches that integrated the profound insights he had gained during his brief respite. His messages resonated with an authenticity that captivated many. The contrast between his fresh energy and his opponents' entrenched, weary politics became starkly evident.

He effectively leveraged his ability to spotlight long-standing issues in the political landscape that the old guard had ignored or inadequately addressed. Popi's critiques were sharp and unyielding; he exposed the empty promises and ineffective communication that had plagued Canadian politics for decades. By calling out seasoned politicians as power-hungry figures who had failed to deliver meaningful solutions, Popi drew a clear line between their failed approaches and his vision for change.

In his campaign, Popi juxtaposed his efforts to drive societal change—long before he entered federal politics—with the ineffectiveness of those who had held power but failed to enact substantive reforms. This comparison highlighted his proactive stance and genuine commitment to improvement.

Popi's unapologetic, no-nonsense approach became the centrepiece of his campaign. His candidness and frustration with the status quo struck a chord with younger voters, who saw in him a reflection of their own disillusionment with past leadership and a beacon of hope for a more effective and responsive government.

For others, Popi's relentless drive for change redefined him

Popi: A Rising Tide

from a so-called extremist to a passionate advocate for the future of Canada. His focus on tangible solutions and his willingness to challenge established norms gained him respect and admiration from those who yearned for a departure from the old ways of politics.

Through his candid and vigorous campaign, Popi not only revitalized his image but also managed to transform voter perception. He emerged as a figure, not of radical extremism but of intense dedication to improving the lives of Canadians. His ability to connect with the electorate on a personal level, addressing their frustrations and hopes, reinvigorated his campaign and positioned him as a serious contender for the leadership position.

From the moment Popi seized control of the narrative, he harnessed that momentum to propel himself forward, effectively solidifying and extending his commanding lead in the race. The shift in his campaign strategy proved transformative. While his opponents could only cling to critiques of Popi's perceived inexperience and youth, their attacks lacked substance and failed to resonate with voters. Instead of presenting concrete evidence of his inadequacies, they resorted to perpetuating extremist rhetoric that increasingly appeared desperate and unfounded.

On the other hand, Popi adeptly countered these attacks with well-documented evidence. For each criticism thrown at him, he provided receipts—tangible proof of the failures and shortcomings of his rivals. He meticulously cataloged instances where his opponents had demonstrated incompetence or made questionable decisions in their political careers. By presenting this evidence, Popi exposed their vulnerabilities and effectively challenged their credibility.

Whenever his opponents struggled to defend their records or rebut Popi's claims, he would magnify their failings with hyperbole and analytical critique. He framed their past actions as emblematic of why they were unfit to lead Canada, drawing a stark contrast between their flawed track records and his vision for the country.

In his campaign speeches and debates, Popi highlighted his rivals' inconsistencies and errors, making it clear that their inability to address their own shortcomings made them unreliable leaders. He did not merely criticize for the sake of criticism; instead, he used his opponents' histories to illustrate a broader point: that their past failures were indicative of a broader pattern of ineffectiveness and untrustworthiness.

Popi's strategic approach not only solidified his lead but also resonated with a public that was increasingly disillusioned with the old guard. His campaign demonstrated a rigorous commitment to transparency and accountability, endearing him to voters seeking genuine change and competent leadership.

As the election drew nearer, Popi's ability to turn his opponents' criticisms into a showcase of their inadequacies helped to fortify his position. His campaign continued to gain traction, capitalizing on the growing recognition that he represented a fresh and credible alternative to the entrenched politicians of the past.

The day of the vote counting arrived with a palpable sense of anticipation and excitement. The convention hall, a grand space filled with the buzz of eager chatter, became a vibrant tapestry

Popi: A Rising Tide

of conservative party members and supporters. As Popi entered, it was immediately apparent that his presence was far more than symbolic. The air was charged with the energy of celebration, and it was evident that his victory was not just a question of "if" but of "by how much."

The event was transformed into a de facto celebration of Popi's ascent to the leadership of the Conservative Party of Canada. The crowd, a sea of enthusiastic faces, seemed to be there to witness the crowning of a new leader rather than just the announcement of election results. His parents, a central part of the day's proceedings, were positioned near the stage, with his father seated in his wheelchair—a testament to the long journey they had all endured together. Sarah, Mrs. Peters, radiating pride and hope, stood beside him and Donna with her pregnancy glow, expecting any minute, reflecting a picture of support and love.

Popi's heart swelled with pride as he looked around at the faces of those who mattered most to him. It was a momentous occasion, and he was surrounded by the people who had supported him through thick and thin. The magnitude of the event was not lost on him. As the results were finally announced, the room erupted into jubilation. Hands were raised high, glitter rained down from above, and the "Popi! Popi! Popi!" chant filled the hall.

In that electric moment, Popi felt as though his entire life was flashing before his eyes. He reflected on his journey—from his early days of struggle and determination through the trials and triumphs that had led him to this pivotal point. The realization of what he had achieved and the distance he had travelled was overwhelming. The echoes of his past challenges seemed to merge with the present triumph, making the victory all the more poignant.

Surrounded by cheers and the sight of his loved ones beaming with pride, Popi understood the gravity of this achievement. He was on the cusp of becoming the next Prime Minister of Canada. This dream had once seemed distant but was now tantalizingly close. It was a milestone that would forever be etched in his memory, a testament to the hard work, perseverance, and unwavering support from those around him.

As the crowd embraced this joyous celebration, their clapping, cheering, and singing filling the convention hall with a wave of euphoria, a sudden and jarring shift occurred. Popi's father, Mr. Peters, who had been seated in his wheelchair, was determined to join the festivities. With remarkable determination, he rose from his chair; his efforts met with a roar of encouragement from the crowd.

Amid the jubilation, Mr. Peters' right knee buckled unexpectedly. In an agonizingly slow moment, he lost his balance and fell forward. The festive atmosphere was abruptly shattered as Mr. Peters' face hit the edge of the stage with a sickening thud. The impact was immediate and severe, causing him to collapse unconscious.

The hall, once alive with exuberance, fell into stunned silence. The cheers and songs gave way to gasps of horror and concern as the reality of the situation sank in. Popi's heart sank as he turned away from the triumphant scene, his focus shifting entirely to his father.

Rushing to his father's side, Popi's eyes widened with alarm.

Popi: A Rising Tide

The sight of Mr. Peters lying motionless on the ground, with a pool of blood forming around his head, was both terrifying and heart-wrenching. The severity of the situation was apparent—Mr. Peters had hit his head hard, and the unconsciousness was a grave sign of serious injury.

The paramedics, responding with swift efficiency, arrived on the scene. They carefully attended to Mr. Peters, assessing his condition with practiced precision. Popi, overwhelmed with a sense of helplessness and dread, accompanied his father as the paramedics lifted him onto a stretcher. A heavy silence now overshadowed the once jubilant atmosphere as Popi followed the paramedics, clinging to the hope that his father would be okay.

As the ambulance doors closed, Popi was left grappling with a whirlwind of emotions—celebration abruptly transformed into fear and concern. His father's well-being took precedence over everything else. With a heavy heart and a mind racing with worry, Popi sat beside his father, determined to be there for him through whatever came next.

As the ambulance pulled away from the driveway, Donna and Mrs. Peters held hands, praying for the best. At that moment, Donna whispered to her mother-in-law, "I think my water just broke."

It was an emotional roller coaster as Mrs. Peters was anxious about her husband and now excited about her second grandchild. They called another ambulance and took Donna to the hospital. The end of the event was nothing anyone had anticipated, but it was something to be etched into everyone's memory.

Popi found himself in an emotional maelstrom in the sterile, tense hospital environment. The initial wave of triumph, so vibrant and alive, had quickly been replaced by a profound sense of dread. Popi's world seemed to tilt on its axis as the surgeon's sombre words sank in. The celebration of his victory and potential future as Prime Minister felt distant and hollow in the face of his father's critical condition.

The surgeon's grave update left Popi grappling with the harsh reality of the situation. The possibility of severe internal bleeding and the likelihood of the worst outcome cast a dark shadow over everything. Popi's mind raced through a cascade of memories—his father's unwavering support, the early days of learning to ride a bike, and the countless moments of guidance and love that had shaped his life.

Each recollection poignantly reminded him of how central his father had been in his journey. The irony of celebrating a monumental personal achievement while facing the potential loss of his father was almost unbearable. The contrasting emotions were a heavy burden, making it difficult for Popi to focus on anything other than fearing the worst outcome.

The news of Donna being in labour at the same time he was anticipating the worst outcome for his father's condition was anticlimactic. He had wanted to share this moment with his father as a moment of passing the torch to a different generation. The words of appreciation he had for his father and the promises he wanted to make to his father about how he would raise his son were now only a memory that never was.

Popi was enveloped in a profound sense of helplessness as he waited for news. The emotional roller coaster of celebrating a career milestone while confronting the possibility of losing a loved one was overwhelming. The hospital's sterile walls and the distant hum of activity seemed a world apart from the vibrant celebration that had been just moments before.

In that space between hope and despair, Popi clung to the fragments of his father's legacy and the hope that he could still be part of a happy ending. The moments he had shared with his father and the lessons learned were a testament to their bond, and Popi prayed that those memories would not be the only things left to hold onto. Sadly, the birth of his son had been overshadowed by this rollercoaster of emotions.

The news of Mr. Peters' passing was a crushing blow to Popi. In the immediate aftermath, he felt an overwhelming sense of numbness and disbelief. As tears flowed freely around him from family and friends, Popi's grief manifested in a quiet, introspective solitude. He was withdrawn, grappling with the enormity of his loss and the weight of the moment.

When he finally embraced his mother, the raw emotion of the situation came flooding through. His promise to keep going, to ensure that life would move forward despite the profound loss, was a heartfelt declaration of his commitment to honour his father's memory. The pain was palpable in his voice, a mix of sorrow and determination as he sought to reassure his mother.

Mrs. Peters' concern for Popi's well-being was evident as she tried to offer comfort. Her words of hope and encouragement were meant to be a balm for Popi's wounded heart. She shared fond memories of Mr. Peters' pride in Popi, bringing a bittersweet smile to his face amidst the tears. Her reminder that Mr. Peters would have wanted him to continue living his life to the fullest was a poignant reflection of the love and expectations his father had always had for him.

Popi was not enthused even as the conversation turned to the new addition to their family. The news of a healthy son coming into the world was a much-needed deflection of the current state of affairs in an already tumultuous day. His mother's gentle nudge added a complex layer to his emotions. It was a bittersweet moment, a small glimmer of joy amid the profound sorrow.

The simultaneous arrival of this new chapter in his life, coupled with the loss of his father, created a unique blend of emotions for Popi. It was a reminder that life, with all its highs and lows, continued to move forward and that there were still reasons to find hope and carry on even in moments of profound grief.

As Popi processed the dual realities of his father's death and the addition to his family, he found himself standing at a crossroads. The future seemed both uncertain and filled with potential. In his heart, he resolved to honour his father's legacy by embracing the new beginnings and challenges ahead.

Popi's reflections on the coincidences of significant political events being shadowed by personal losses were both haunting and revealing. It was a heavy realization that his political career seemed intertwined with significant personal hardships. The thought that every milestone in his political journey came with a personal cost weighed heavily on him. Yet, his mother's gentle reassurance helped him see these moments from a different perspective.

Her reminder that not all significant events were negative—

Popi: A Rising Tide

highlighting the day he got his biggest promotion in politics and Donna accepted his proposal to be his wife—offered a glimmer of hope amidst the darkness. It was a perspective that helped Popi reconcile the duality of his experiences, seeing both the highs and lows as part of a larger narrative of his life.

Popi's gratitude for Donna's unwavering support was deeply heartfelt. Her role in his life had been a source of strength and stability, especially when he felt most vulnerable. His promise to honour his father's memory by giving his all in politics was a powerful testament to his father's impact on his life and ambitions. The assurance that Donna would be by his side, regardless of the outcome of the general election, gave him the resolve to face the future with renewed determination.

As Popi vowed to give everything he had to make his father proud, it was clear that his commitment went beyond political ambition. It was a personal mission fuelled by the legacy of his father's faith in him and the unwavering support of the one person who had always been his constant.

This moment of clarity and resolve marked a turning point for Popi. The journey ahead, though fraught with challenges, was now framed by a renewed sense of purpose and an unwavering commitment to honour his father's legacy. Whether he succeeded or faced setbacks, Popi's dedication to his cause and the people who mattered most in his life remained his guiding force. His mission to become the next Prime Minister of Canada had just taken a fourth turn and launched him into the final stretch. He vowed to give it all and hoped for the best, as he promised to be the rising tide that would raise every Canadian.

THE END